Praise for Lynette Eason

"[A] suspenseful mystery and a great love story of personal discovery."

—*RT Book Reviews* on *A Silent Fury*

"Eason's third Santino sibling [story] has a wonderful mystery and plenty of suspense."

—*RT Book Reviews* on *A Silent Pursuit*

"Fast-paced scenes and a twist...keep the reader engaged."

—*RT Book Reviews* on *Her Stolen Past*

Praise for *USA TODAY* bestselling author Laura Scott

"[A] page turning combination of suspense and second chances."

—*Harlequin Junkie* on *Primary Suspect*

"*Primary Suspect* by Laura Scott is truly enjoyable from start to finish... An excellent choice for fans of law enforcement heroes, medical drama, and run-for-your-life romantic suspense!"

—*Reading Is My Superpower*

PROTECTING HER DAUGHTER

LYNETTE EASON

HARLEQUIN® SELECTS™

Recycling programs
for this product may
not exist in your area.

ISBN-13: 978-1-335-40667-5

Protecting Her Daughter
First published in 2016. This edition published in 2022.
Copyright © 2016 by Lynette Eason

Under the Lawman's Protection
First published in 2015. This edition published in 2022.
Copyright © 2015 by Laura Iding

For questions and comments about the quality of this book,
please contact us at CustomerService@Harlequin.com.

Harlequin Enterprises ULC
22 Adelaide St. West, 41st Floor
Toronto, Ontario M5H 4E3, Canada
www.Harlequin.com

Printed in U.S.A.

CONTENTS

Lynette Eason is a bestselling, award-winning author who makes her home in South Carolina with her husband and two teenage children. She enjoys traveling, spending time with her family and teaching at various writing conferences around the country. She is a member of Romance Writers of America and American Christian Fiction Writers. Lynette can often be found online interacting with her readers. You can find her at Facebook.com/lynette.eason and on Twitter, @lynetteeason.

Books by Lynette Eason

Love Inspired Suspense

Holiday Homecoming Secrets

True Blue K-9 Unit

Justice Mission

Wrangler's Corner

The Lawman Returns
Rodeo Rescuer
Protecting Her Daughter
Classified Christmas Mission
Christmas Ranch Rescue
Vanished in the Night
Holiday Amnesia

Visit the Author Profile page at Harlequin.com for more titles.

PROTECTING HER DAUGHTER

Lynette Eason

God is our refuge and strength,
a very present help in trouble.

—*Psalms* 46:1

This book is dedicated to those in law enforcement. Thank you to the men and women who put their lives on the line every day to make the world a safer place for me and my loved ones. "May the Lord bless you and keep you, may He make His face to shine upon you. Amen."

Chapter 1

Zoe Collier gripped the pitchfork and stabbed it into the bale of hay. "I'm going to grab some water bottles from the fridge, okay?"

"Okay, Mom." Nine-year-old Sophia turned the water off and started wrapping the hose.

"Remind me to put some in the fridge out here for later."

"Put some out here for later," Sophia dutifully said.

"Haha. Come on in after you finish that, and we'll make some cookies."

Zoe relished her daughter's grin. One that used to flash all the time before the kidnapping attempt a month ago. She'd been walking home from school when a car pulled up beside her. The vehicle door had flown open, and hands had reached for Sophia. Zoe had been standing on the porch watching it, horrified at the possibility that the man would manage to get her daughter into the vehicle. She'd raced toward them screaming for Sophia to run. Sophia had, and the car had squealed away.

Zoe shuddered.

Then the attempt to run Zoe off the road and leave her in the ditch—or worse, have her go over the side of the cliff...

She shook her head.

At least now they were safe until she could figure out whom to trust and ask for help. Running two hundred miles away from Knoxville, Tennessee, to this little town in the middle of nowhere had seemed like a good idea a few weeks ago. Now she wasn't sure.

Oh, the people in town were friendly enough, but she and Sophia were so isolated out here. More isolated than she'd intended or understood it to be when she'd taken the job. She drew in a deep breath. But it served its purpose. "Stop it. Get the water and put your worries behind you. You have a painting to finish," Zoe told herself. She was extremely grateful she could work from anywhere. Her paintings sold well in a variety of shops all over the country, providing a good living for her and Sophia. She looked over the area. If she could live anywhere on a permanent basis, it would be somewhere like this. A rich land with horses to ride and plenty of fresh air to breathe.

"Hey, Mom?"

She turned back to Sophia. "Yes?"

"When is Lily going to have her baby?"

Lily, the pregnant heifer. "Any day now."

"Is Doctor Aaron going to come check on her today?"

At the mention of the hunky veterinarian, Zoe's heart turned a flip. "Yes, he'll be here soon, I imagine."

"I like him." Sophia skipped back to the hose to finish wrapping it.

Yeah, I do, too. She'd run into him at the local diner when he'd walked in with a service animal he had been training. Sophia had been instantly captivated by both man and beast. Zoe hadn't been far behind. When she realized he was the vet who would be checking on Lily on a daily basis, she'd ordered her heart to chill. To no avail. It still did a little happy dance every time he showed up.

She walked up the porch steps and reached for the knob of the door. Only to stop and snatch her hand away.

The door wasn't shut all the way. The black crack from top to bottom mocked her. She stepped back, her pulse ratcheting up several notches.

She knew she'd shut the door. With the indoor cat, who liked to make her escape whenever the opportunity presented itself, Zoe was extra careful with the doors. So why was it open? Had Sophia—

"Mom!"

Sophia's harsh scream spun Zoe around. Her fear spiking, she froze and stumbled a full turn. A large man held Sophia by her ponytail, a gun pointed to her head. Her daughter cried out again and tried to pull away, but he held her easily.

"Let her go!" Zoe moved toward them, her only thought to get her child away from the man.

He moved the weapon so it pointed at Zoe, his finger tightening on the trigger. A cruel smile tilted his thin lips upward. "Bye-bye."

Zoe shook, somehow made her legs work and ducked behind the wheelbarrow just as a loud crack splintered the air. Sophia screamed, a high-pitched, ear-piercing wail full of terror. Zoe's legs gave out and she hit the ground hard. She tried to think, but the horror sweeping over her wouldn't let her. She had to get to Sophia. She had to get her child back.

"Stop, you moron! Don't shoot her!"

Zoe's breath came in pants, her terror lessening a fraction as relief filled her. Someone had come. She nearly sobbed. She forced her legs to stand, to take a step toward the man who still held a crying Sophia. He kept the gun held on Zoe, but glanced at the other man who'd stepped from inside the house, cell phone pressed to his ear. "Don't shoot her!"

Relief fled and fear gripped her again. What was this second man doing in her house? She headed to Sophia who continued to struggle in spite of the pain inflicted by the man's hold on her hair. With his other hand, he aimed the weapon at Zoe, but didn't pull the trigger, his gaze still darting between her and the man behind her. When she was two steps from Sophia, her daughter's eyes widened and her attention focused behind her. Zoe turned to look over her shoulder, saw a flash of movement. Before she had time to think, something crashed into the side of her forehead, pain exploded through her skull and she fell to the ground.

Aaron Starke stepped up to the counter and took the two prescription bags from Lucille Andrews, the pharmacist for the Wrangler's Corner Pharmacy. "Thanks."

"No problem. Hope your mom feels better fast."

"It's just an ear infection. She should be fine in a day or so."

"And thanks for taking that out to Zoe. I know she'll appreciate it."

"Happy to do it. See you later." He headed back to his truck and tossed the bags onto the passenger seat. One for his mother and one for the pretty single mom he couldn't seem to get out of his head. Although he really needed to.

Well, he was going out to the farm anyway to check on the pregnant heifer. Taking the prescription was only being neighborly, nothing else. Right? Right.

Ten minutes later, he turned into the Updikes' drive and followed it up to the main house. A large four-bed-room home, it looked lived-in and loved, with Thanks-giving decorations hung on the door and a small flag with the words "Thankful for Blessings" stuck in the ground. He figured that was Zoe's doing. He didn't re-member Martha Updike bothering with that kind of thing.

Aaron coasted to a stop at the top of the drive. An old pickup truck sat in front of him. He'd never seen it before and knew Zoe didn't drive it. She had a Jeep Wrangler. Maybe she had family visiting? Then he no-ticed the open barn door and frowned. Why would Zoe have the door open when the temperatures were already dropping and were supposed to hit record colds tonight?

He climbed out of the truck and pulled his heavy down coat tighter against his throat. He shoved his hands into his gloves and settled his hat more firmly on his head. Snowflakes drifted down littering the ground that was already starting to turn white. Aaron tromped across the few remaining dried twigs that would be green grass come springtime and knocked on the door. "Zoe? You in there? Sophia? It's Aaron Starke."

He peered inside and all the animals looked well taken care of with fresh water in their buckets and clean stalls. Aaron walked down to the office and unlocked it. He placed Sophia's medication on the desk, left the office and locked it behind him.

His next stop was to check on Lily the pregnant cow. She'd been brought in out of the cold and now stood in one of the horse stalls looking fat and ready to get the whole thing over with. He checked her and found the calf had turned. "Well, that's good news," he told her and gave her bulging belly a light pat.

He cleaned up in the large barn sink then decided to check on Zoe. He thought it strange she hadn't come out to at least say hi and ask about the cow. She had all the other times he'd been by. And every time he'd seen her and talked to her, he'd wound up leaving with her on his mind. Where she stayed. Constantly. He'd learned a few things about her. She loved her daughter, she was a very private person—and she was worried about something.

Satisfied that all was well in the barn, he left and shut the door behind him. A frigid wind blasted across his face, and he shivered. He headed to the house, his heavy boots crunching the brown grass that would soon be covered in the snow still coming down.

A glint from the ground caught his eye, and he stopped. He stooped down to poke into the dirt and snow with a gloved finger and uncovered a silver necklace with a pretty blue charm. He picked it up, and a red liquid substance slid onto his tan glove. He frowned.

Lifted his hand and sniffed. The coppery smell of blood reached him. He spied a large footprint in the area next to the where he'd found the necklace. A boot print too large to be Zoe's.

He looked up, truly concerned for Zoe and Sophia now. He glanced back at the earth and realized the blood wasn't just limited to that one spot. It trailed drop by drop to the front porch. He followed it, saw more blood on the steps. It could be a simple thing. Maybe she cut her hand on one of the tools in the barn or Sophia fell and scraped her knee or…something.

But the necklace in the dirt bothered him. It hadn't been there long. There was no rust or embedded dirt. And the blood was still fresh.

If it had been just one thing, he might not have been overly concerned, but the open barn door, the necklace, the trail of blood that had only just begun to dry, her car parked in the covered area but no sign of Zoe or Sophia…the boot print.

She was here. Somewhere. The blood suggested close by and in trouble. He moved up onto the wraparound porch and saw more drops of red at the base of the door. He tried to see in the window, but the gauzy curtain blocked his view. Aaron walked around the perimeter of the house and saw nothing else amiss.

He knocked on the door. A scuffling sound came from inside but no one answered. He knocked again. "Zoe? You in there? You okay?"

Zoe stared up at the man who pointed the weapon at the end of her nose. Her head throbbed, but at least the blood had begun to dry. Fear pounded through her and she couldn't stop shaking. Sophia clung to her and buried her face in Zoe's neck. "Get rid of him," her captor growled. "Now. Or I'll have to shoot him."

"We don't need any more trouble, Pete," the other one muttered from his position by the window. He held the gun loosely in his left hand. Comfortably. As though he used it on a regular basis.

"Like I don't know that," Pete said. The angry scowl twisted his face into something from a horror movie. Zoe wanted to close her eyes and shut them all out, but she couldn't. She kept her arms around Sophia's slight frame. Her daughter was so little, so vulnerable.

"Now, I said." He jabbed the gun at her, and Zoe flinched. She glanced at the door and back at the man who'd intervened and saved her only to hold her and Sophia captive. She rose on shaky legs, stumbled then caught herself. Sophia rose with her, refusing to let go. Zoe's head swam and bile climbed into her throat. She breathed deep and the dizziness settled.

The man called Pete grabbed Sophia by the arm and jerked her away from Zoe. Sophia cried out. Pete slapped a hand across her mouth. "Make another sound and I'll shoot your mother, you understand?"

Zoe stood frozen, wanting to smash the man's face in, but knew one wrong move could cause him to hurt her daughter. "It's okay, honey, just sit still for a minute, all right?" she said.

Sophia's gaze clung to hers, but she gave a small nod. Pete relaxed his grip a fraction, and Sophia didn't move even as silent tears tracked a path down her ashen cheeks.

"Hey, Zoe? You okay? It's Aaron Starke. I came to

check on Lily and wanted to say hi." The pounding on the front door resumed, and she walked over to it.

The man near the window lifted his weapon, an unneeded reminder that he was watching. Zoe closed her eyes and drew in a desperately needed calming breath, praying for strength—and some way to convey the fact that she needed help without putting the person at the door in harm's way.

With one last glance at Sophia, she pulled on every ounce of inner strength, ignored the throbbing in her head and opened the door. Aaron stood on the front porch. His large frame filled the doorway, blocking the icy wind and the sunlight. He had to be half a foot taller than her own five foot eight. She forced a trembling smile to her lips. "Hi."

He offered a frown in response. "I came by to check on that pregnant heifer and saw some blood on the ground and a necklace. This yours?" He held it out to her as his gaze landed on her right temple.

"Um. Yes. Thanks." She took it and stuffed it in her front pocket.

He leaned in to take a closer look. "What happened? That looks like a pretty bad gash."

She raised a shaky hand to lightly touch the wound. "Oh, that." A laugh slipped out, but it sounded nervous to her ears. Scared. She shifted her weight from one foot to the other and her eyes darted away from his only to return a fraction of a second later. "I was…ah…clumsy, tripped over the water hose in the barn and hit the side of the stall. I was just getting ready to clean the wound when you knocked."

"Why don't I give you a hand? I'm pretty good at

that kind of thing. Granted, most of my patients are of the four-legged variety, but the concept is the same." He moved as though to enter and panic filled her.

She shifted and blocked his entrance. "Really, I'm fine. I can do it."

He paused, his eyes probing the area behind her. She knew he couldn't see anything but the stairs that led up to the second floor. "Well. Okay. If you're sure." He backed up, his boots clunking on the wooden porch.

No! she wanted to scream. She widened her eyes and cut them to the side window. *Don't leave!*

But he simply tapped his hat in a gentlemanly gesture and turned to go. Then spun back. Her breath caught. Had he figured out she needed help? Did he know someone stood behind her with a gun? "Oh, by the way," he said, "I was in the pharmacy a little bit ago getting a prescription for my mother and Mrs. Lucille gave me Sophia's medication. I left it on the desk in the office in the barn."

"Oh, th-thank you. We were getting low."

"I'll just go get it for you."

"No, no, that's okay, I can get it. I'm going to have to go out there and…ah…fill the water buckets anyway."

He tilted his head and gave a slow nod. "All right then. Holler if you need anything."

She nodded but couldn't force any more words out of her tight, tear-filled throat. This time when he turned around, he didn't look back. She shut the door with a soft snick and turned to find the two men staring at her.

Pete let go of Sophia and she rushed at Zoe, wrapping her arms around her waist and holding tight. Zoe met Pete's gaze since he seemed to be the one in charge. "Now what?" she whispered. "What do you want?"

His eyes dropped to Sophia. "Her."

Chapter 2

That niggling feeling wouldn't leave him alone. Aaron sat in his truck outside the house, but didn't crank it. Instead he dialed Lance Goode's personal cell number. Lance was a deputy with the Wrangler's Corner sheriff's department and a good friend of the Starke family. Aaron's brother, Clay, the sheriff, was out of town until later that evening so the safety of Wrangler's Corner fell on Lance's shoulders. The deputy answered on the second ring. "Hello?"

"How far are you from the Updike farm?"

"Not too far. Why?"

"Something weird's going on here."

"Aren't the Updikes out of town?"

"Yeah." The curtain on the window by the door fluttered. He cranked his truck and debated whether or not to drive off. "But Zoe Collier and her daughter, Sophia, are staying here while the Updikes are on their cruise. I just knocked on the door and she answered, but she had a gash on her head that she said she got from falling against the side of the barn."

"You have reason to doubt her?"

"No, not really, but she just looked...scared. And she said something about having to go out there and fill up the water buckets. I was just in the barn, Lance. The buckets are full of fresh water and the hose is neatly wrapped and hanging on the reel."

Lance made a noise low in his throat. "That does sound kind of odd. If she hit her head, she might have a concussion or something. Be a little confused."

"Maybe. She didn't seem confused, just scared."

"All right. I'm on my way. It's probably nothing but I'll come check it out."

"Thanks. I guess I'll head on back to the office." Aaron hung up and put his truck in gear. His secretary, Janice Maynard, was out on maternity leave and his partner was on vacation for the next three days.

Managing by himself was a huge headache, and he should have listened to his father's advice about hiring a temporary person to fill in, but then he'd have the headache of training the person. He grimaced. He still hadn't decided which choice was the lesser of the two evils. Regardless, he didn't like to stay gone too long. Then again, that was one of the advantages of living in a small town. Everyone had his cell number and if someone needed him, they'd call.

Aaron drove down the drive and out of sight of the house then stopped at the base of a sloping hill. He tapped his fingers on the wheel. He couldn't do it. He couldn't just leave. There'd been something in her eyes when she'd looked at him then cut her eyes toward the left. Had someone been there? Someone she'd been afraid off? What if an abusive ex had found her or something? Or what if she really did have a concussion? He didn't remember seeing any sign of one when he'd looked into her green eyes, but he hadn't been looking for one, either. Had her pupils been even?

He grunted. Nope. He couldn't leave. Aaron turned the vehicle around and drove back up to the house. He parked next to the strange truck and shut the engine off. He hesitated only a second before he opened the driver's door and stepped out. He stared at the other truck, walked over to it and looked inside. Fast food wrappers and cigarette butts littered the cab, but nothing that set off any alarms. He sighed and marched back up to the front door. Before he could knock, the door opened and he found himself staring down the barrel of a gun.

Aaron froze. Now his internal alarms were ringing. Okay, he'd thought she'd looked scared, but this wasn't what he'd pictured. The angry dark eyes behind the gun glittered. "Get in here, hero. You had your chance to leave, but guess you get to join the fun."

Zoe wanted to weep. Her only hope of rescue had just joined them as a hostage. Aaron lifted his hands in the surrender position and walked into the house. His eyes landed on her and Sophia, huddled together on the couch. She knew she probably looked terrified as she locked her gaze on his. Well, that was fine. She *was* terrified.

Aaron moved closer to them, putting his body between her and Sophia and the gun. The other man, whose name she hadn't learned yet, shut the door behind Aaron. "What's going on?"

"Just taking care of a little business is all. Now hand over your cell phone and your weapon."

"I'm a veterinarian. What makes you think I have a weapon?"

Pete laughed without a smidge of humor. "You don't live in this kind of town and *not* carry a weapon." His hard eyes turned to chips. "Hand it over."

Aaron didn't bother to protest, just pulled his .38 special from his shoulder holster and gave it to the man. When he did, his keys fell to the floor.

"I'll take those, too. No sense in giving you something that could poke an eye out." Aaron hesitated then snagged his cell phone from the clip on his belt and released that, as well. From her position behind him, she could see the tension in the set of his shoulders and prayed he didn't do anything that would cause one of the men to shoot him. Or her. "What kind of business?" Aaron asked.

"Shut up." Pete looked at his partner. "Now what?"

"Tie him up," the partner said. He eyed Aaron. "Anyone know you're here?"

"Several people know I'm coming out here on a regular basis to check on one of the heifers ready to deliver any day now." He stayed still while Pete used duct tape to secure his hands behind him.

The partner shoved the gun at him. "Let me rephrase the question. Anyone know you're here right now?"

"No, but when I don't show up for dinner, my family will be looking for me."

Zoe stayed still, listening, feeling Sophia's heart beat against her side. Her rapid heartbeat. Zoe looked closer and saw the sweat on her daughter's forehead. She lifted Sophia's chin and looked in her eyes. She stood. "My daughter needs some food."

"Shut up and sit down," the partner said without taking his eyes from Aaron.

Zoe stayed put. "My child needs sugar in her system. She has diabetes. Her sugar is dropping, and I need to give her something sweet. Now." She tried to keep her voice steady and firm. She failed miserably on the steady part. She lifted her chin and met Pete's eyes when he finally turned them on her. "She could die and while I don't think you care if I do, for some reason you want her alive."

The man's eyes narrowed, and he stared at her as though trying to figure out if she was telling the truth or not.

Zoe wanted to scream. Instead, she clamped down on her emotions and pointed at Sophia. "Look at her. Sweating, rapid pulse, lethargy. If we don't regulate her blood sugar, she could faint and go into a coma."

For a moment he simply studied her. "Fine. Get her something, but Cody's going to be watching you. You try to get a knife or something, and you'll pay, you understand?"

"I understand. I just want to get her some orange juice." Zoe turned to Sophia. "Stay right here. I'll be back in a second."

"No, Mom—"

"Shh. You need some sugar. Do as I say, sweetie."
She tried to comfort Sophia while watching the man
with the gun. His impatience escalated, and she backed
toward the kitchen. Sophia's lower lip trembled.

Aaron moved closer to Sophia. "It'll be a bit awkward, but you can hold my hand, honey. Your mom will
be right back."

Sophia's eyes darted back and forth between her
mother and Aaron, and she nodded. Zoe suspected
she was feeling a bit dizzy as she simply laid her head
against the back of the couch and shut her eyes.

Zoe moved toward the kitchen, not wanting to leave
Sophia, but knowing the man beside her baby was an
honorable one—at least according to everything she'd
heard about him during the short time she'd been in
town—and wouldn't let anyone hurt Sophia if at all
possible.

Zoe acted fast. She could feel Cody's eyes on her,
watching, waiting for her to make a wrong move. She
grabbed the orange juice from the refrigerator and a
glass from the cabinet. Her hands were shaking so hard
she was afraid she'd spill the liquid. She stopped for a
second and took a calming breath.

Then she picked up the carton and poured the juice
into the glass. Sophia didn't usually have a problem with
her diabetes when she ate right, got her exercise and did
what she was supposed to do, but it had been a stressful
few weeks and her body was reacting to it. This situation definitely wasn't helping.

Zoe hurried back into the den and over to Sophia.
"Here, honey, drink this."

Sophia wrapped her hand around the glass while Zoe

helped her. Her daughter drank the juice while Zoe's eyes met Aaron's. His shoulders gave a slight twitch, and she realized he was using her as a shield while he worked on getting his hands free. She stood over Sophia for as long as she dared then turned to find their two captors in conversation. Discussing how to kill them? Bitterness welled and she tamped it down. *God, get us out of this, please.*

"Sit down," Pete said and jabbed her with his weapon.

Aaron stilled, and Zoe sat beside Sophia who seemed to already be doing better with the juice. Zoe set the glass on the table then turned back to Sophia. She ran a hand over her daughter's face and pulled her close. Pete and his partner, the one he called Cody, moved to look out the window then went back to their discussion. Aaron leaned closer. "What do they want?" he whispered.

"I don't know." She wasn't going to tell him what the man had said about wanting Sophia. Not while her daughter was listening to every word.

"How many are there?" Aaron asked.

"I've only seen the two."

Pete turned a sharp eye in their direction, and she snapped her mouth shut then leaned over to kiss the top of Sophia's head. A ringing phone broke the tense stillness.

Pete turned away to answer, and Cody disappeared out the door. "Lance is on his way out here," Aaron said, his voice so low she had to strain to hear it. Pete bent his head and muttered something into the phone. "He may be here already."

"Who's Lance?"

"A deputy sheriff. I called him and told him something was wrong out here. He said he'd head over and check it out."

Hope blossomed and she prayed.

"I got my hands free," he whispered. "Sit tight. Better do this while there's only one. While I distract Pete, you grab Sophia and run."

"Don't—"

Pete hung up and walked back into the den. "Looks like we're stuck here a bit longer."

"What are you waiting for?" Aaron asked.

"Instructions."

He turned slightly, and Aaron sprang from the couch. He slammed into Pete, and they both went to the floor. Sophia screamed, and Zoe clutched her close. Aaron grunted as a fist caught him across the cheek. Zoe looked for a weapon she could use to help. Aaron rolled, avoiding another fist in the face. "Run, Zoe!"

Zoe pushed Sophia toward the front door. "Go. Run as fast as you can into the trees. Hide until you hear me calling. I'll find you." She wanted her child safe, but she wasn't going to leave Aaron to fight alone.

Sophia ran for the door and unlocked it. Zoe grabbed a vase from the end table next to the sofa.

The back door crashed in and a deputy stepped into the kitchen. She could see him assessing the situation in a lightning-fast second. He moved through the small hall into the den and aimed his weapon at the men on the floor. "Police! Freeze!"

Aaron rammed a punch into Pete's gut, and the man gasped, rolled to his knees and put his head on the floor.

Aaron stumbled back. Sophia froze near the front

door then ran back to Zoe who set the vase back onto the table and gathered her child close.

Lance moved quickly and cuffed the man on the floor while Aaron went to the window to peer out. "There's another one. He left just a minute ago."

The front door slammed open.

Zoe gasped and spun to find Cody and yet a third man standing there with weapons aimed at them. Lance lifted his gun and aimed it at the two men. "Drop your weapons."

The third man stepped closer. "I don't think so." He simply shifted his gun so that it was pointed at Sophia. "Now everyone is going to settle down." His gaze darted between Lance, Aaron and the man on the ground. He came back to Lance. "Lose your weapon and your phone and uncuff Pete." Lance glared but didn't argue, placing his gun and cell phone on the table with the others. Aaron sank back onto the couch, dabbing his bruised cheek. The newcomer waited until Pete was on his feet before he spoke. "Thought you said you had him tied up."

"He was," Pete grunted with a scowl.

"Tape him up again. Put his hands in front of him so we can see what he's doing with them." He flicked a glance at Lance. "Both of them."

Despair welled in Zoe as Aaron and Lance submitted to having their hands bound in front of them. She wanted to wail in frustration. They'd been so close. So very close. She huddled with Sophia and prayed—in spite of the fact that she was convinced that God didn't care what happened to those she loved.

Chapter 3

Pete got up from the floor and turned his dark eyes on Aaron. The venom there sent a cold shiver of fear through him. And certain knowledge that Pete wanted to kill him. Aaron figured if the man got his hands on a gun, it would all be over. Aaron had made an enemy for life. One he'd better not ever let have access to his back. He felt sure he could take the man in a one-on-one fight, but Aaron knew he was no match with bound hands. He kept his gaze steady, refusing to flinch. Finally Pete looked away, grabbed his weapon from the floor and aimed it at Aaron.

"Put it away, Pete," the newcomer ordered.

"But Jed—"

"Now. There'll be time for revenge later." Aaron didn't like the fact that the man could speak without raising his voice and the two men did as ordered. Jed turned his gaze to the blond man. "Cody, get on the phone and find out what the problem is. We can't stay here forever. Start the truck and once we're away from here we'll figure out what to do with them."

Cody tossed his shaggy blond hair out of his eyes and snagged his phone from the back pocket of his jeans. He punched in a number, shot them all a vicious look and backed out the door. Aaron glanced at Lance who'd also placed himself in a protective stance between the men and Zoe and Sophia. A cold feeling had settled in the pit of Aaron's stomach. These men didn't think anything about using each other's names. Because they didn't plan on anyone being able to tell who they were?

Pete stepped forward and taped Lance's hands together then gave him a shove onto the couch. Lance landed with a grunt beside Zoe.

When Pete moved his attention to him, Aaron looked at the new guy who'd displaced Cody with his authority. Jed. "Look, if I don't check in with my family, they're going to come looking for me."

"Shut up."

"My brother is the sheriff of this town," Aaron continued softly. "Unless you want him on the doorstep as well, you'll let me text him and let him know I'm going to be busy all night delivering that calf out in the barn. I also have some medication for my mother I picked up at the pharmacy. My dad's going to be calling and wondering why I haven't dropped it off yet."

Jed's eyes narrowed and he cut a glance at Pete. Aaron turned his attention to him. "And in case you're wondering, I don't want my family coming here and stumbling into this mess. I'm not trying to put some-thing over on you. I'm actually just trying to keep my family away from you. Less trouble for you, too, if no one else shows up." Might as well say it like it is. Even then, there wasn't any guarantee that Clay wouldn't come by to check on him or take it upon himself to come get their mother's medicine, but with Sabrina due to deliver their first child any day now, he figured Clay would stay pretty close to home once he got back from his trip. Which meant he might send someone. Either way it would involve putting someone else in danger if he didn't let them hear from him.

Jed eyed him. "Fine." He jutted his chin at Pete. "Text what he tells you."

Pete's eyes narrowed, but he found Aaron's phone. "You've got four new texts."

"Like I said, better let me answer them, or I'll have people looking for me." He met Pete's gaze. "And they know where to find me."

Pete looked to his boss for confirmation. The man nodded. "Who and what do I text?"

Aaron gave instructions, not even trying to insert a hidden message in his words. It would be too obvious anyway. He added. "One more. Text to my dad, 'Calf due to deliver any moment. Won't have time to drop off Mom's meds. See if Doc Whaley will give her two pills to tide her over till I can get there probably tomorrow.'"

When the messages had been sent, he allowed Pete to duct-tape his hands together once again. One less thing to worry about. His family wouldn't come out to the farm and find themselves in danger. He sat back on the sofa while the other two men paced and muttered and checked their phones. They were waiting on something. Orders from someone?

Cody stomped back into the house, flakes of snow melting in his hair, blistering curses on his lips. "I gotta go into town and get a part. The truck won't start."

"What? What happened?" Jed asked.

"I don't know. I think it's a spark plug."

"Take mine." Jed tossed Cody his keys. "Don't be long."

"Guess I'll be as long as it takes."

At Jed's cold stare, Cody ducked his head. "But it won't take long." He trudged back out, and Aaron heard the vehicle start up and drive away.

He turned his attention to the boss. "You mind if I check on the heifer out in the barn?"

A heavy sigh slipped from the man. "You mind if I put a bullet through your head?"

A whimper escaped Sophia, and Aaron's fingers flexed into fists. He forced himself to relax. "Come on, man, it's an animal." He gestured to Zoe and Sophia and Lance. "As long as you have them, I'm not going to do anything stupid."

Jed studied him then nodded to Pete. "Fine. Go with him."

"What?"

The two exchanged a silent look. "Go with him," Jed repeated.

Pete lifted a brow. "Right." He shot Aaron a grim smile. "Let's go."

Aaron figured that exchange between the partners was permission for Pete to kill him. His heart thudded a faster beat, and he sent up prayers for safety and wisdom. Truly all he'd wanted was to get in the barn and deliver the calf should the mama be ready. Now, it appeared he was going to have to fight for his life.

Zoe didn't miss the interaction between the three men. She jumped up. "I'll go with you. You might need some help." Then she stopped. She wasn't leaving Sophia behind, though. "Sophia's a great help in the barn, as well."

"This isn't some country club vacation!" Pete yelled. "Sit down and shut up!"

Zoe sat, and Sophia buried her face in her side with a low cry. Zoe pressed a hand against the little girl's head, trying to offer comfort. "Shh…"

"I'll be fine," Aaron said. "Just do what they say."

She bit her lip. "But—"

"Don't argue, Zoe," Lance said. She frowned. Sophia pulled on her hand, so she snapped her lips shut.

Pete followed Aaron out the door and Zoe couldn't help the prayers that slipped from her lips. She looked at Jed. "What do you want? Why are you doing this?" She glanced at his phone. "Who are you waiting for? Who's supposed to call?"

He waved the weapon at her. "You just need to be quiet. You've led us on a merry chase."

"Was it you who tried to kidnap Sophia from her school?" She regretted the question when his gaze slid from her to Sophia. He didn't answer. *"Why?"*

"Shut up!"

Lance reached over with his hands taped together at the wrist, and clasped her fingers in a light squeeze. Zoe clamped her lips closed. Lance sat so quiet she'd almost forgotten about him. She shot him a frantic glance. Jed's phone rang, and he stepped back still keeping an eye on them as he answered. As soon as he averted his gaze, she leaned toward Lance. "He's going to kill Aaron," she whispered. "We have to do something."

Sophia's arms tightened around her at her words, but she couldn't just sit there and let Aaron die.

"Aaron has a plan," Lance said. "I could see it in his eyes. Let's let him play it out."

"What if it backfires? What if he needs help?"

"I know Aaron, he'll be all right."

Zoe saw the worry in his eyes and wondered if he really believed it or was just trying to ease her mind. She feared the latter. "But—"

"Hey! Zip it!" Jed's shout made her flinch, and she blinked back a surge of tears. Lance's hand stayed clamped around hers and she sank back against the couch even as she looked for a way to secure a weapon— or something to release Lance's hands with.

Aaron went straight to his truck and pulled his vet bag from the passenger seat. It was awkward with his hands taped, but he managed. Pete didn't say anything, just watched him. Aaron ignored him and headed for the barn, his mind spinning. *God, help me, please. Don't let him kill me. Let me be ready to fight back when he strikes.*

Once inside he went to Lily's stall and saw the heifer pacing. The area had been extended so it was double the size of a normal stall. Lily lay down then got up. After repeating this for several minutes, she finally stayed down. She lowed, a painful groan that Aaron knew would grow in intensity in the next few minutes.

Aaron looked at Pete. "I need my hands. She's ready."

"Not a chance."

With his hands still taped in front of him, Aaron got the heater and turned it on. He placed it in the stall and watched the heifer get up then lie down again. This time she let out a loud bellow that shook the rafters of the barn.

Pete watched him, his dark eyes hard. Cold. His right hand held his weapon in an easy grip. His finger played with the trigger.

Aaron gave a shudder as fear swept through him. But he kept his cool. He had to. Zoe, Sophia and Lance were probably going to need him. The gun swung up. A Glock.

All it would take to end his life was the twitch of the man's finger. "If you kill me before she delivers, this cow is going to put up such a holler she'll bring the neighbors down on you." As if to confirm his words the heifer let out another moan. Louder this time than the last.

Pete frowned then scoffed. "What neighbors?"

"There's the Garrett farm to the left and the Hunt farm to the right." He lifted his chin to the north. "Up that way just behind the tree line, there's a pretty big general store. The owner is there every day and he'll hear the cow bawling if I don't deliver this calf. The owner of the store is Michael Richardson and a good friend of the Updikes. He'll be here within minutes to find out what's going on. You want that?"

Aaron's words seemed to sink in. Pete cursed and

spit on the ground, but at least he removed the gun from Aaron's face. "I saw that store. Stopped to get gas there. Dude asked twenty questions and wouldn't shut up about wondering who I was visiting and spending the holidays with." He scowled.

"Yep, that's Michael." He paused. "Or you can kill me, I guess, and deliver the calf yourself." The heifer chose that moment to make her presence known with a screeching groan that morphed into a low grunt. Pete flinched, his eyes darting to the barn door as though he expected someone to start pounding on them at any second. "At least if I'm here if someone shows up," Aaron said, "I'll be able to reassure them that everything's all right." He met Pete's gaze. "Trust me, I don't want anyone hurt. If someone shows up, I'll make sure they think everything is just fine."

The heifer bellowed again.

"Or I could just shoot her."

Aaron winced. "Yeah, you could. And again, bring attention to the fact you're here. True, this is the country and people carry guns. And use them. But we're mostly civilized and neighbors around here still respond to gunshots."

"No one came when I shot at that pretty little lady in there."

"You're fortunate. You want to push it?"

Still glaring, Pete pulled a large knife from his front pocket and flipped it open. "Guess I could just use this then."

Aaron winced. "Yes, I supposed you could." He sighed. "Come on, man, let me deliver the calf and be done with it."

Pete hesitated, and Aaron really didn't like the look in the man's eyes. The cow groaned, and Pete muttered a few choice words. He leaned toward Aaron, and Aaron braced himself, expecting to feel the knife sink into his flesh.

One swipe was all it took to split the tape holding Aaron's hands together. Aaron hissed as the blood rushed to his fingers and he flexed them even while his brain scrambled for an escape route. He needed to do something and fast before Cody came back—or Pete decided to throw caution to the wind and exact his revenge.

He looked at Lily. She hadn't gotten up again so she was definitely ready. At least the barn was warm. The heater was a heavy-duty propane deal that put out enough warmth to keep the stall nice and toasty. A plan began to form even as he shrugged out of his coat. He maneuvered his way around to the heifer and rubbed her head to reassure her. She knew him and didn't seem nervous around him. Aaron prayed for an easy birth. Her moaning and bellowing continued. He looked up to see Pete had moved closer, his hard eyes flat. Waiting. Every so often they would flick toward the door. Good. Aaron's words had him thinking someone would show up.

Aaron knew as soon as he delivered the calf he was dead. While he worked with the mama and baby, he thought, planned and prayed. He pulled the calving chains from the bag he'd dropped on the ground. Pete lifted the gun. "What are you doing?"

"They're to help pull the calf out if I need them. I might not, but I need to have them nearby."

Pete stayed silent, but watchful.

Aaron worked with the heifer, soothing her and rubbing her belly, feeling the baby move. Thankfully, it wasn't breech any longer. It had turned the right way and from here on out, the heifer would do most of the work. Aaron would assist while he went through the plan over and over in his head.

Finally, after a number of hard contractions and bellows from the soon-to-be mama, he saw the calf's legs poking out and slipped on a clean pair of gloves to help the baby out into the world. "Hand me those chains, would you?"

"I'm not here to help."

That's what he figured the man would say. Aaron gritted his teeth and left the chains on the bag. He didn't really need them anyway. He wrapped his hands around the baby's legs and heard the heifer give another moan, waited on the next contraction, then pulled. While the mother let out one last bellowing yell, the calf slipped onto the fresh hay and Aaron worked to clear its nose. He then teased a nostril with a piece of straw to make it sneeze. It obliged and Aaron went to work on the afterbirth. Once he had everything finished, he rolled his head and glanced at his captor from the corner of his eye.

Pete had moved closer, the gun now trained on Aaron. Aaron casually pulled the gloves from his hands and dumped them in the trash bag he'd brought out.

He stood as though to stretch, but instead, in one smooth move, spun, grabbed the heater and swung it around into Pete's head. The man didn't even cry out. He simply slumped to the ground, the weapon landing with a thump on the hay. Aaron grabbed the calving chains and tied the man up. Heart pounding, adrenaline surging, he stood back and looked at his handiwork. A long gash in the man's head bled freely, but Aaron didn't think he'd done too much damage. And Pete might manage to get out of the chains eventually, but it would take him a bit of time. Hopefully, he and the others would be long gone by then and law enforcement would have things under control.

Breathing heavily, Aaron pulled Pete from the stall then went back and grabbed his coat. He shoved his hands into the sleeves, grabbed Pete's gun, then slipped back out of the stall shutting the mama and baby in behind him. He stuck Pete's gun in his shoulder holster.

A phone, he needed a phone.

He patted the man down, searched his pockets and came up empty. Great. There was a phone in the office.

He raced to it and twisted the knob. Locked. And he didn't have his keys. Aaron stepped back, lifted a foot and kicked. The door shook, but held. Three more kicks and it swung open. He grabbed the handset from the base and turned it on. Listened.

To nothing.

He groaned. They'd cut the landline.

He stopped and pressed a hand against his forehead. *Think, think. Consider your options.*

And came up with one.

Overpower Jed, get the others out before Cody came back. Or Pete woke up. It wasn't a great plan—or even a plan at all—it was just what he knew he had to do.

Aaron slipped out of the barn and up to the house. He figured boss man would be in the den or at least near it to keep an eye on Lance, Zoe and Sophia. He'd go in the front door as he figured it was probably still unlocked.

His rushing adrenaline made him shaky and clumsy. He took a deep breath. He wasn't a cop, this wasn't his deal. He was perfectly happy to leave catching the bad guys and rescuing people to Clay and the deputies, but today it fell to him.

He wanted to hurry, but had to be careful. If he got caught this time, there wouldn't be a third chance for escape. They didn't need him as Pete had just proven while in the barn. He and Lance were collateral damage. He couldn't believe Pete had bought his story about neighbors coming to check on the cow. Most likely, they'd have heard her and figured she was giving birth and Aaron was there to help. Birth was a noisy affair, and the neighbors knew that. Aaron's hunch that Pete wouldn't know that had paid off.

At the front door, he paused, placed a hand on the knob and twisted slowly. Nothing happened, so he cracked it enough to see inside. The foyer, the living area to the left, dining to the right. The den was straight ahead. He slipped inside and shut the door behind him.

He listened, ear tuned to the slightest sound, muscles bunched and ready to act. Sounded like Jed was on the phone. He glanced out the window and thought he saw a vehicle down the drive. Cody coming back?

Heart racing, he moved until he could see Lance still on the couch with Zoe. Sophia sat between them. He caught Lance's eye. Lance blinked but made no other indication that he'd seen Aaron.

"Fine. I'll take care of it. I'll deliver them both tonight. And you'd better have the rest of my money."

Aaron raised the gun.

Lance shifted. "Hey, when are we going to get something to eat? Sophia needs some food even if you're not going to feed the rest of us."

Jed stepped into view, the back of his head toward Aaron. He pointed to Zoe. "Go fix something."

Zoe moved to stand when Aaron stepped up behind Jed and placed his gun against the man's head. "Move and you die." The man froze. "Put the weapon on the counter." Jed did. With his free hand, Aaron took the gun and held it. He nodded to Zoe. "Cut Lance loose."

She raced into the kitchen and came back with a knife. She cut the tape and Lance stood. Jed twitched like he wanted to try something. Aaron pressed the gun harder. "Don't." The man stilled.

"Hey, Jed, Pete? I got the part," Cody called as the back door slammed behind him.

Chapter 4

Zoe froze, but didn't have time to stand there for long. Jed started to call out, but Lance's fist shot out and caught him in the jaw. Aaron brought the gun down on the back of his head for good measure and the man crumpled to the floor. Lance took the gun from Aaron. "Get them out of here. I'll deal with Cody."

But Cody appeared in the small hallway between the kitchen and the den before Lance could get there. Cody stood for a brief moment, his jaw swinging as he took in the scene, but Zoe didn't stop in her rush to get Sophia out of the house. She reached the large bookcase next to the front door and pulled Sophia next to it praying it was out of the line of fire. She could feel her child's body trembling, but she never made a sound.

"Hey!" She saw Cody's hand lift, the gun aimed at

Lance. Lance dropped and rolled in front of the counter and out of sight. Aaron fired his weapon and she saw Cody spin into the wall then hit the floor. Zoe moved away from the bookcase and toward the door, pulling Sophia with her. She looked back to see Cody roll and bring his weapon up again, firing even as Lance aimed at him and pulled the trigger. She dropped to the floor covering Sophia's body with hers. The loud cracks made her ears ring.

"I'm going to kill you! All of you! I don't care about the money anymore, you're all dead!" Pete's bellow came from the kitchen somewhere behind Cody. She heard the door slam once again. Lance leveled his weapon toward the kitchen and fired back. She wanted to get Sophia out, but was afraid to move. Afraid it would be the wrong direction and one of them would catch a bullet. She heard a curse and saw Jed move, shake his head then sit up.

Then Aaron was beside her grabbing Sophia from her and pushing her toward the door. "Go, go, go."

Zoe, Aaron and Sophia raced through the front door. Aaron snagged Sophia's heavy coat as he passed it. Bullets pelted the doorframe, and Sophia screamed. Zoe just followed expecting to feel the slam of a bullet at any moment. Lance was backing out behind them, firing back, keeping the three men at bay.

"Head for the trees!" Aaron urged her. "Don't look back, just run. I've got Sophia."

"Go!" Lance hollered as he whipped around and fired his gun once again. She heard a harsh scream from one of their pursuers but didn't turn. Five more steps and they'd be in the shelter of the trees. The house had been built with a plan to utilize the wooded area for shade during the summer months. Even stripped of most of the leaves, the trees would offer them the most protection. The frigid wind made her flinch, but she couldn't stop now.

Zoe raced into the thicket and turned to find Aaron carrying Sophia in his arms. Lance brought up the rear. He continued to look over his shoulder as they ran. "They're still coming."

"At least they're not shooting," she panted.

"I got one of them, I think. The one they called Jed. Just winged him, though." Lance stayed close. "Keep going. We're going to follow the tree line all the way around and head up to the store on the hill. Hopefully Michael is there and will have a phone we can use."

"Won't they think of that?" Zoe asked.

"Yeah," Aaron grunted. "I basically told Pete about the place when I was trying to convince him to let my hands free. If we head up there, we'll just put Michael in danger."

Zoe kept casting glances at Sophia. "You okay honey?"

"Just scared," came her small voice.

They kept moving in the direction of the store. "I don't want to put Michael in danger," Zoe said. A shot cracked a tree in front of her.

"Run," Lance ordered.

"Run where?" Aaron grunted, but picked up the pace. "The caves." He answered his own question.

"Yeah, good idea. The caves," Lance said. "Go."

Aaron didn't hesitate, just made a forty-five degree turn and forged a trail for Zoe to follow. Lance brought up the rear. Aaron sloshed through a shallow creek, and Zoe followed, gasping when the cold water hit her legs, but she didn't stop. She could get warm later. Prayers winged heavenward. Weakness wanted to invade her, and she stumbled. Aaron snagged her elbow with one hand even as he kept a grip on Sophia with his other.

Aaron passed the first cave they came to, skirted around brush and trees then simply disappeared. Zoe skidded to a stop. Lance passed her, grasped her hand and pulled her behind him. When he stopped, she found herself in a cave. And cold. So very cold. She couldn't feel her feet anymore. Shivers racked her as Lance stayed at the entrance, his weapon ready. Aaron set Sophia on her feet then helped her into her coat. Sophia let him, but when he stepped back, she moved to Zoe and wrapped her arms around her waist. "I'm scared, Mom," she whispered.

"I am, too, honey, but God's taking care of us."

Sophia looked back and forth between Lance and Aaron. "Yes, I think you're right."

"Now we just have to find a way to call for help," Aaron muttered.

Sophia slipped a hand into the front pocket of her jeans and pulled out a cell phone. "Will this help?"

Aaron stepped up to them, took the phone from Sophia's small hand and looked at the screen. It had about a half battery life, but only one bar. Once out of the cave, he knew there would be a better signal. "Where did you get this?" he whispered.

"That really mean man you called Pete left it on the

end table after he tied up Deputy Lance," she said, keeping her voice as low as his and pointing to Lance.

"So you snagged it, huh?"

"Yes." She shrugged. "I was going to try and call 911, but I couldn't do it without someone seeing me so I was just waiting until I could either do it myself or give one of you guys the phone. But that never happened so I just held on to it."

Aaron blinked. "Nice job," he whispered. "Are you sure you're nine?"

"Pretty sure," she whispered back and shot him a weak grin.

Zoe lifted a hand to push Sophia's hair out of her eyes. He noticed the fine tremors racking her and figured she was just as cold as he was.

He punched in the number of the police department and held the phone to his ear on the off chance it would work. The call dropped. He looked at Zoe. "Need a signal."

She nodded and shivered. "Try a text. Sometimes a text will go through when a call won't."

Aaron did. He shrugged. "It says it went, but I don't know if it did or not. We need to make a call. Lance," he whispered.

"Yeah?" Lance turned to face him.

Aaron slipped up beside him and handed him the phone. Lance's eyes went wide. "Thank Sophia," Aaron said.

Lance blinked then gave a tight smile. "Good going, kid."

Sophia nodded. "You're welcome."

Lance went back to the entrance of the cave, and

Sophia snuggled next to her mom. Zoe shuddered and pulled her closer. Zoe hadn't had a coat on inside the house and she hadn't had time to grab it before their dash for safety. Now she just had on a sweatshirt over a black turtleneck, and her jeans were soaked to the knees. Aaron shrugged out of his heavy down coat and draped it around her shoulders. She frowned at him. "Thanks, but don't you need it?"

"I'm fine. I worked up a sweat running with Sophia in my arms."

She hesitated then nodded. "If you're sure, I'll just use it to warm up a bit then give it back."

"I'll let you know if I need it."

Their whispers barely sounded in the darkness. The chill of the cave hit him hard, but he wasn't going to let her know that. He hoped they wouldn't be staying put very long anyway. Lance walked back to them. "I think they've passed us. I'm going to slip out of the cave and see if I can get a signal."

Aaron nodded, and Lance again returned to the entrance then disappeared outside. Sophia snuggled in between him and Zoe, and Aaron wrapped his arms around them, pulling them close to share body heat. The cave wall was cold, and the chill seeped through his sweater.

Within seconds, Sophia's head rolled against his chest and her breathing became even. "She fell asleep," he whispered in Zoe's ear.

"Unbelievable. Well, it's been an ordeal between the attack and the diabetes. She's feeling the effects." She froze. "I don't have her medicine," she whispered. "I didn't have time to grab it."

"In the right-hand pocket of my jacket. I snagged it from the office after I knocked Pete out."

Zoe let out a low breath. "Thank you so much." She turned toward him, but shot a glance over her shoulder. "Do you think Lance is all right?"

"I hope so. I don't think he would have left the cave if he thought the men were still out there. It looks like all three of them managed to survive the shots. I think I winged the one called Cody, but it wasn't enough to stop him."

"So it's still three of them."

"Looks like it." He gently shifted Sophia until she rested against Zoe. "Hold her. I'm going to check on him."

"Be careful," she whispered. "Oh, you need your coat."

"I'll be fine. Stay put."

He moved before she could voice the protest he saw on her lips.

As he moved to the entrance of the cave, a shot rang out, and Lance dove inside.

Sophia woke with a jerk, and Zoe held her even as her own heartbeat picked up speed. "Why are they shooting again, Mama?"

"I don't know, honey, just be brave."

Lance knelt on the floor and looked back at her then Aaron. "I got a call out, but help's a good ten minutes away. Even then I'm not sure they'll be able to pinpoint our location."

"Even with the cell phone?" Zoe asked.

"Possibly, but the bad guys are heading this way."

"Were they shooting at you?" Aaron asked.

"They left Pete behind to cover the area where they lost us. Just in case we found a hiding place. Smart," he murmured then shook his head. "Just as I hung up with dispatch, Pete shot at me. He's not too far away. We're going to have to come up with a plan. If the others come back to join him, we're going to be sitting ducks."

Zoe sucked in a breath while Sophia tensed.

"Then we'll have to play a little game of hide-and-seek," Aaron said.

Lance lifted a brow. "What do you have in mind?"

"You and I are going to leave the cave and pin down where Pete is. Then I'm going to distract him while you sneak around and tackle him."

Lance grunted. "That sounds great in theory. I don't know that we should leave Zoe and Sophia in here alone."

"We'll be fine," Zoe said. "We have to do something. A plan of action is better than waiting for them to come shooting."

Lance slid his gaze to Aaron. "You have a plan to avoid getting shot while distracting him?"

Aaron nodded and removed his hat. "Oldest trick in the book. I just need a stick."

Zoe stood and stomped her feet trying to get some feeling back into them. Finally they started tingling and then hurting and she just prayed that none of them had permanent frostbite damage. But that was the least of her worries. She'd be happy with all of them getting out alive.

Aaron slipped out of the cave with Lance right behind him. Zoe positioned herself near the entrance so she could see—and help somehow if possible. Aaron wasn't a police officer, but that didn't seem to faze him as he prepared to face down a killer.

Ducking low, he searched the ground, and she saw him close his hands around a stick that suited him. Still keeping himself as small a target as possible, he placed the hat on the end of the stick then slowly raised it. Lance, hunched over and cautious, moved into the trees then stopped.

Zoe's nerves vibrated. Would it work? Would they be able to carry out such a dangerous and risky plan?

Another crack echoed through the trees and Aaron's hat flew from the stick.

Aaron hissed when his hat landed on the ground beside him. He picked up the hat in case he needed to use it again and hoped Lance was paying attention to the direction the bullet had come from. He moved a bit up the hill. As far as he could tell the bullet had come in at a downward angle. That meant the shooter was above him. He caught Lance looking at him. Aaron pointed upward.

Lance nodded and started moving. Slowly, quietly. Where were the other men? Why hadn't they shown yet?

Then he remembered. Sophia had taken Pete's phone. He didn't have a way to contact the other two who'd gone ahead of him.

But they'd no doubt heard the shots.

Which meant he and Lance had very little time to take Pete down. Aaron moved carefully, using the trees as shields, doing his best to stay invisible. Just up ahead, he thought he saw movement. But was it Lance or Pete? Or someone else?

He stayed still, feeling his heart pound in his chest. He wasn't a hunter, but he'd grown up with three brothers and knew his way around a game of hide-and-seek in the woods. Granted, his brothers hadn't been shooting at him, but still...

More movement. Aaron lifted the hat. Nothing. He moved it to the right, away from his body. A shot sounded. The bullet whizzed by but missed the hat. Then a thud and a yell. Aaron moved faster and found Lance on top of Pete wrestling for control of Lance's weapon. Pete rolled. Lance's gun flew from his fingers, and Pete dove back into Lance and landed a solid punch on his cheek. Lance howled and struck back. Pete took the hit on his jaw, but Aaron saw him reach back to his ankle. And pull a gun from his ankle holster.

Aaron moved, kicked out. But Pete moved unexpectedly and instead of getting the man's wrist, Aaron's boot landed on Pete's forearm. Pete yelled, but didn't drop the gun, instead he turned it toward Lance and fired. Only Lance was rolling and the bullet slammed into the ground beside him. Lance rocked to his feet and went head first into Pete's gut. They both went down, Lance's hands wrapped around Pete's wrist, holding the gun away from him. Aaron couldn't get in a good kick without possibly usurping Lance's tentative advantage in the fight.

Aaron dove for Lance's weapon, got it in his hands, pulled the slide to chamber the bullet and spun to find Lance losing his grip on Pete's wrist. Pete landed a punch to Lance's midsection, and the deputy lost his hold. Pete lowered the weapon to Lance's head.

Aaron fired. Once. Twice. Center mass. Pete jerked

but didn't go down. He turned the gun toward Aaron. Before he could pull the trigger, Lance knocked the gun out of his grasp. Aaron snagged it, held both guns on the bleeding, screaming man while Lance rolled him to his stomach and fastened the cuffs around his wrists.

Lance sat back on his heels and swiped at his bleeding face. He looked up at Aaron. "Thanks," he gasped.

"Yeah." He stuffed the weapon in the waistband of his jeans. "Yeah."

The sirens finally reached their ears. Aaron pulled his sweater off, leaving his long-sleeved T-shirt still on. He dropped beside Pete and pressed the material against the man's wounds. "We have to keep him alive," Aaron said.

"You work on him. I'm going to keep an eye out for the other two while I get back to the cave to check on Zoe and Sophia. I'll call Clay to tell him exactly where to come."

"Good." He glanced around. "Hopefully, these trees will be enough cover for the time being."

Aaron felt for a pulse and found it relatively strong. He must have missed anything vital. Relief flowed. As much as he hated what Pete was, he didn't want to be responsible for the man's death.

"I don't know where the other two went, but I'm guessing if they heard the sirens, they took off."

Aaron nodded. "They might be gone for now—" he looked up and caught Lance's eye "—but I don't doubt they'll be back."

Chapter 5

Zoe settled herself in front of the fire Aaron had finished building about thirty minutes ago. Once the authorities had arrived on the scene near the cave, things had gone quickly. They'd been ushered to the local hospital, they'd given their statements, answered a zillion questions, been examined and finally released. Sophia's sugar levels were slightly elevated, but not enough to admit her. Zoe would keep a close eye on her throughout the night.

Although it was only six o'clock in the evening, it was dark outside, the sun setting early this time of year. She stared at the dancing flames and considered the day. One day. Half a day, actually. Not even twelve hours and she felt as though she'd just lived a lifetime. She ran a hand down her cheek and decided it was probably better not to think about it. She knew things could have ended far differently, and the only thing she knew to do was be grateful it had ended the way it had—and try to figure out the *why* of it all.

Aaron came back into the den, two sodas in his hands. She looked away from the fire as he took the seat on the couch next to her. "It's over," he said.

She accepted the offered drink and popped the tab. "No, I don't think it is." She met his gaze, thinking how kind his eyes were. Deep blue and filled with an ocean of compassion, caring...and strength. To match the rest of his well-muscled physique. He really was a handsome man. She looked away and took a sip of the sugary drink. She didn't drink colas often, but tonight she wanted one while she wrestled with the fact that she was attracted to him. Which was the last thing she needed. "And neither do you." She wasn't staying in Wrangler's Corner. Being in the small town was merely a necessity right now. She would be going back to Knoxville and her life as soon as possible.

"No, I don't." He took her hand, and she let him in spite of her misgivings. "How's Sophia?"

"She's in her room cuddling with her favorite stuffed animal and watching TV, a comedy she's seen a dozen times, but never seems to tire of." She gave him a small smile. "She needs something to laugh about. Tickles, the cat, is sleeping at the foot of the bed, too."

"And she's all right staying in her room by herself?"

"For now. When it's time to go to sleep I have a feeling she'll be keeping me company." She looked back at the fire. "Have you heard from the hospital?"

"Lance called while I was in the barn with the horses. Pete survived surgery."

She squeezed his fingers. "I'm glad."

"You are?"

"Yes. It's true I'd feel safer if he was dead, but aside from living with the regret that I already see in your eyes, Pete is our only chance to find out why the men are after Sophia. But whatever happens, you shot him to save Lance, Aaron. To save us all. You're a hero as far as I'm concerned. I imagine Lance feels the same way."

He flushed and cleared his throat. "I'm no hero, Zoe."

"Maybe not in your eyes."

He took a swig of the soda then set the can on the coaster on the coffee table. Then his eyes lifted to the painting above the mantel. "That's beautiful. Who did that?"

"I did." She turned to look at the painting she'd done shortly after Sophia's seventh birthday. "It was a lovely day at the park that afternoon. So peaceful and serene. Sophia was on the swing, and I was pushing her. Trevor took the picture, and I turned it into an oil. It's one of my favorites. I couldn't leave it behind when we left Knoxville."

"Of course not."

"I was in such a hurry when we left Knoxville that I'm surprised I remembered to grab most of what I needed to continue to work."

"You're very talented. Have you been painting all your life?"

"No, just since high school. I started during a very tough time in my life. My parents were going through a pretty messy divorce and I needed an…escape. I found it

in painting…and some other not so productive things."
She twisted her fingers together. Now why say that?
Because she wanted to confide in him? Trust him? Did
her heart know something her mind didn't? He'd put
his life on the line to keep her physically safe, that was
true. She wasn't sure she was ready to trust him emotionally, though. And until she was, she'd better keep
comments like that to herself.

"What are you going to do now?" he asked. His question surprised her. She figured he'd push for more information, more details. Moments from her past better
forgotten for everyone.

She gave a slight shrug. "I don't know. I'm thankful
there are deputies outside that are willing to stand guard
tonight, but they can't do that every night. I guess I'll
have to run again."

"Run? Again?"

She blinked. They'd been through so much over the
past few hours she'd forgotten he didn't even know why
she was in Wrangler's Corner. "I'm originally from
Knoxville. About a month ago someone tried to kidnap Sophia while she was walking home from school."

"What?"

She nodded. "We just lived five houses down from
the school. It's a pretty busy street, but she liked to walk
so I let her because there was a crossing guard. The day
of the incident I was standing on the front porch watching for her. The crossing guard made sure she got across
the street, then when she was almost to our house, a gray
sedan pulled up beside her and the back door opened. I
immediately had a bad feeling and yelled at her to run.
Thankfully, Sophia didn't hesitate. I guess she heard

the terror in my scream. The person in the vehicle was already getting out when Sophia took off, but he managed to grab her backpack. She slid out of it and ran as fast as she could toward me. The person drove away. I was so scared I didn't even think to get a license plate."

"What did the police say?"

"There were a lot of witnesses and confirmed it was definitely an attempted kidnapping. The police took it very seriously and looked into it. They had officers patrolling the school before and after hours for about a week and it was all over the local news, of course. But when nothing else happened, they decided whoever it was had moved on. They alerted everyone in the area to be on the lookout for the gray sedan, but truly, there are a lot of gray sedans out there. They said it was probably just a random thing and it wouldn't happen again, but I couldn't stop looking over my shoulder. I didn't want to leave Sophia with anyone, didn't want to take my eyes off her."

"I can understand that," he said softly. "So you came here?"

She hesitated. "Yes, but only after someone tried to run me off the road."

He stilled. "Run you off the road?"

"It was late at night. I'd finally been able to leave Sophia with my sister-in-law, Nina, for a few hours to go to a Bible study. On my way home, I was on one of the back roads between my house and the church. I passed a side road and headlights came on. A car pulled behind me and rammed my back end. I managed to avoid a wreck and get my car under control. The person was coming back for a second hit when several vehicles came from the opposite direction. The car drove off and I drove to Nina's house. Sophia and I just stayed there for the night. I called the police, reported it and—" She shrugged. "That's it. I'd had enough. So I emailed Amber." She gave him a flicker of a smile. "My old college roommate."

"My sister?"

"Yes."

He narrowed his eyes. "College roommate? Why don't I remember you?"

She gave him a small grin. "There's no reason you should. I came to the ranch with Amber a couple of times on weekends, but you and your brothers…well, you guys were never there much."

"And we never really paid attention to who Amber brought home."

"No, from what I recall, everyone was kind of going in their own direction. Seth was doing the rodeo thing. I remember that clearly. Clay was into law enforcement in Nashville. You were always working with an animal or away at school or something." She shrugged. "I don't really remember."

He reached out and touched her hair, let a dark curl wrap around his finger like a baby's small hand. Then he captured her gaze. "I should have paid attention." Zoe let herself get snared in his eyes for a brief moment before she cleared her throat and looked away. Aaron's hand dropped. "So, you ran. And now this. You're being targeted."

She nodded. "It looks that way."

"But why?"

She shook her head and looked up at him again. "I

truly don't know. I make a decent living with my painting and I have some money from my husband's life insurance policy, but it's not enough to commit a crime for."

"You'd be surprised," he murmured. "What happened to your husband?"

"He was killed in a car wreck." She swallowed and looked away. "Just about a year ago."

"I'm sorry."

Tears threatened. "I am, too. He was a good man." And he'd deserved better than her. But she'd keep that to herself.

"I'm sure he was."

"Regardless," she said, "I don't know why anyone would be after Sophia. I mean I can think of what some people would do with a kidnapped child and it makes me sick to my stomach, but truly, for someone to go to this much trouble to get her…" She bit her lip and shook her head as she looked down at her hands. "I mean, sure, I can see someone spotting a child walking home alone and thinking it's a good opportunity to snatch her. But when that plan was thwarted, wouldn't you think he'd move on to someone else? Why keep coming back for her? Why go to all this trouble? Something else is going on, but I just don't know what it is—or how to go about finding out what it might be."

"You have a good point. And one other thing."

"What?"

"You said that the back door opened. That means there was more than one person involved in the attempted snatch."

"Yes. The police mentioned that, as well," she said.

"And, no, I can't think of anyone who would do something like that. Believe me, I've thought about it. At first, though, I figured it was just a random act. You know, someone who was cruising the school zone, watching for a child walking alone or something. They saw Sophia and didn't realize I was looking for her."

"But?"

"But then I realized after someone went after me that it wasn't random. Someone was targeting us. And that terrifies me not just because I'm afraid they're going to try again, but because I don't know how to prepare for it, defend against it—or from which direction the next attack will come."

"Hey." He placed a finger under her chin and lifted it until their eyes met. "You have help now. You're not alone in this. We'll figure it out."

She felt the heat rise in her cheeks. "We?"

"Yes. We. And Clay and Lance." He smiled. "What's the point in having cop friends and family if they can't help you out once in a while? Although, I will say Lance and the others might actually be more help than Clay right now. He's a bit distracted with his wife due to have their baby any day now."

Her lower lip trembled. She hadn't felt quite so... what? Cared for? Protected? Yes, to both. She hadn't felt either in over a year. Maybe even longer. It felt strange... and wonderful all at the same time. She sighed. "Well, I hope they can find the men who did this so they can't hurt anyone else." Or come back to try again.

"You and me both." He rubbed his chin and studied her. "So tell me more about yourself. Your background. I know you were married, but your husband died in a car wreck." He glanced at the oil painting again. "I know you're incredibly talented. And I also know you have a daughter who's smart as a whip. And I know you're both in danger."

She pulled in a deep breath and let it out slowly. "Yes, that about sums it up."

A low chuckle rumbled in his chest. "I don't believe it. There's got to be more."

There was more all right. She mentally flipped through the things she could tell him that wouldn't send him flying out the door. "I have a good church in Knoxville and some good friends that I've left behind. I love my job. Being able to work from home, painting portraits, that's my dream come true. It's a great job for a single mom." She gave a soft laugh. "Painting is also my therapy. I really enjoy the people, the clients, that I get to work with."

"What about Sophia?"

"Sophia has a few friends from school, but she's not the most social kid. She and I spend a lot of time together and I like that. Our next-door neighbor has a girl about Sophia's age and they run back and forth between the houses, but Sophia is happy on the farm with the animals and never wants to leave."

"What about you? Are you happy on the farm?"

"Yes. I grew up on one. Even though my father worked as an accountant, he inherited the land that we lived on. I think he was considering selling but then... everything kind of blew up and my parents divorced." She shrugged. "That's about it."

He reached out and ran a finger down her cheek. "All surface information. I want to know *you*."

Zoe stiffened. "What do you want to know?"

"Why did you turn to my sister for help? Why not go home to your parents? Are they still living?"

"They're alive."

"But?"

"We're not close." His eyes narrowed and she wanted to squirm, but refused. "I had a rather rocky upbringing. Like I said, my parents split up. They divorced when I was in high school. They each went their own way and aren't interested in pretending to be a family when the holidays roll around. So we just do our own thing. I send them a card with Sophia's picture each Christmas and call it good."

"That's really sad."

She shrugged. "Yes, it is, but it's okay, too. I've accepted it and moved on. I don't let it bother me." Much. Holidays were definitely worse than other times during the year, though.

He shook his head. "Do you have any brothers and sisters?"

"A brother. He's older than I am and was headed to college when my parents divorced."

"And you two don't talk?"

She hesitated then slowly shook her head. "I don't even know where he is."

She could tell she'd shocked him. A man who was so tight with his family wouldn't be able to comprehend her dysfunctional background.

"Why don't you know where he is?"

She shook her head. How could she explain the horrendous fight she and Toby had had before he'd left. That her last words to him had been *I hate you. Get out.*

I never want to see you again. How did she explain the year she'd spent in rehab, getting her life straightened out, getting her heart right with the God she'd thought had surely given up on her? How did she tell him that she was not only in physical danger, she was in the middle of a faith crisis, as well? "We had words. An argument about him going to college and leaving me to deal with the fallout of our parents' marriage. I know he didn't leave me because he wanted to. He had to go. He wasn't strong, either, and couldn't handle staying at home. He would often get in between my parents, trying to be a buffer and it wore on him. Emotionally, physically." She shook her head. "So, he left, and we lost touch for a while and by the time I was in a position to reach out to him, I didn't know where to reach out *to.*" She'd searched for him, though. She'd tried to find him at college only to learn he'd dropped out. She'd checked all of his friends she could think of and no one had seen him. She'd even reported him missing to the police and they'd turned up nothing. Her heart had broken and she'd just assumed he might have changed his name to get away from the reporters and their constant questions about their father's criminal activities. "I don't know why they went after him like they did. Maybe because no one ever expected it." She certainly hadn't believe it. She shrugged. "I really don't know."

Aaron wanted to ask more questions. She could see them in his eyes, rolling onto the tip of his tongue, and weariness swept over her. She didn't want to answer any more questions. Not now. She stood. "I'm just going to check on Sophia."

He nodded. "Sure."

She went to Sophia's room, her mind spinning, emotions scattered. She had to get herself together. Talking about her past had shaken her. She didn't need to reveal any more of herself to this man. She was leaving. She had to take Sophia and they had to run. There was no sense in pouring her heart out to Aaron in her den. No point in getting to know him or letting him get to know her. Being vulnerable didn't sit well with her. She wasn't comfortable with it.

She walked into Sophia's room and found her daughter asleep, arms wrapped around her favorite stuffed animal. She looked so peaceful Zoe didn't bother her. She just backed out and shut the door leaving it cracked so she could hear if Sophia called out to her.

For a moment she simply stood in the hallway and pressed her forehead to the doorjamb. *Lord, please show me how to protect my child, help me to be wise in the choices I make and the people I trust.*

Because she knew that if she didn't have some divine intervention, things were not going to end well for her or Sophia.

Aaron fielded the numerous texts from his family members while he waited for Zoe to return. With sadness in his heart, he realized she'd texted and called no one to tell about her ordeal. His family might drive him crazy sometimes, but at least they were there. It was a huge comfort to know he could count on them and that they loved him unconditionally. Just like they all loved his sister, Amber, and were glad to see her when she put in an appearance, but didn't expect her to be around much.

He couldn't imagine being so terribly alone in the world. And he wanted to help Zoe, he really did.

He'd meant it when he said that she had help, that he and Clay and Lance would work with her to figure out who was behind the attack here at the ranch, but he needed to put the brakes on his attraction for her. No, more than that, he needed to bury it. Deep. He'd picked up on her reticence to share about herself with him and he couldn't help but wonder why. She was hiding something, but what? He rubbed his eyes. It didn't matter. Falling for the single mom would be a huge mistake. Hadn't he already learned that lesson?

She stepped back into the den and took her seat on the couch. She'd changed into sweats and a long-sleeved T-shirt. Her sleeves hung midpalm, and she looked comfortable. And vulnerable. And incredibly attractive. "Sophia fell asleep," she murmured.

"She's had a long day."

"Mmm. Yes. A traumatic one. I pray she doesn't have nightmares."

"Or you, either. Are you going to be able to sleep?" he asked.

"I don't know. I might doze, but I'll probably sit in the recliner with Mr. Updike's .45 Winchester."

"You know how to use it?"

"I wouldn't touch it if I didn't." Her eyes flashed. "And I won't be caught without a weapon again."

He lifted a brow, and a deep respect started to build. She might need help, but she'd do her best to help herself, as well. Looking at her now, he couldn't imagine he'd thought her fragile or helpless. The vulnerability had disappeared with the lift of her chin and now he thought she looked strong and capable. As well as intensely determined. "Good," he said and stood. "I guess I'll head on home." He spotted a pad and pen by the recliner and snagged the items. He wrote on the top sheet of the pad. "Here's my cell number and my parents' landline number. And here's Clay's personal cell number." He set the pad back on the table. "If you need anything at all, just call and someone will be here before you can hang up, all right?"

He saw her blink back tears. She nodded. "Okay," she whispered. "Thanks."

"You're welcome, Zoe." He grabbed his coat. Once he had his gloves on, he looked back at her and swallowed. Her eyes beckoned. He could see the fear still lingering. "You'll be safe tonight."

"Yes, tonight."

He backed toward the door. He had to get out of there before he did something stupid like take her in his arms and hug her. Or kiss her. He nearly tripped, righted himself and closed his hand around the door knob. He cleared his throat. "I'm just going to check on the heifer and the calf, and then I'll be on my way."

"Of course. Thank you again for everything, Aaron. I know how much I owe you."

"You don't owe me a thing. Get some rest." He forced his gaze away from the shimmer of her dark eyes. With supreme effort, he opened the door and walked out.

The sharp wind hit him full in the face and he shivered. He might be used to the bitter cold, but that didn't mean he liked it. Picturing himself on a tropical beach, playing in the sand with Sophia or swimming in the surf with Zoe, he pulled his scarf from his pocket and wrapped it so that the cold didn't cut as bad. Then he blinked the images from his head. If he was going to bury his attraction for Zoe, he couldn't be imagining beach days with her. He looked around. But if they did wind up somewhere, it would definitely be a beach. No skiing. He was ready for warm weather. But not with Zoe. No way. That kind of thinking would only lead to heartache.

The snow had stopped for now, but the way the air smelled said there was more to come.

He spotted the Wrangler's Corner police cruisers. One was positioned strategically near the barn with a view of the back of the house and one right out front. He squinted and waved. Ronnie Hart, who had a good view of the back of the building, waved back. A new deputy who'd been hired about a month ago, Ginny Garrison, also lifted a hand in acknowledgement then typed something into the computer she had open on the tray attached to the dash.

Probably making note of his departure. He walked over to Ronnie, and the man lowered his window. "Thanks for watching out for her."

"No problem. Nice job out there on the mountain."

He still couldn't believe he'd shot the man. Pete. The man had a name. "I couldn't let him shoot Lance."

"For sure. Maybe you should hang up your stethoscope and go to the police academy."

Aaron laughed but it had little humor. "No way. I'm happy being a vet." He nodded in the direction of the barn. "I'm just going to check on Lily and then I'm heading home." He glanced back at the house and saw the flickering of the television through the curtains. So sleep wouldn't come any time soon for her. He wondered if she would actually be able to doze off.

"You think those guys will be back?"

Aaron looked back at Ronnie. "Yes. Unfortunately, I do."

Ronnie nodded and patted his weapon. "Then we'll be ready."

Aaron's jaw tightened and he felt for the weapon he'd retrieved from the kitchen table where it had been left when everyone scattered from the house earlier. The weight of it against his side brought comfort, reassurance. "Yes. Yes, we will."

Chapter 6

Zoe couldn't bring herself to sleep in her room. Instead she'd lain down beside Sophia and figured she'd spare the child waking in the middle of the night to come find her. Careful not to disturb the still-sleeping Sophia, she rolled over to check the clock.

Seven forty-five.

So she'd actually slept. She really hadn't thought she would, but having the two deputies outside had allowed her adrenaline to settle down. She slid out from underneath the covers. Goose bumps pebbled her skin, and she shivered. She needed to bump the heat up a notch.

On sock-covered feet, she padded to the window and pushed the curtain aside to peer out. She could see Lance sitting in the cruiser sipping coffee from a thermos cup. A light dusting of snow covered the car. Ronnie must have left and Lance had taken over sometime during the night. He glanced up, saw her looking and lifted a hand. She waved back, then released the curtain and let it fall back into place. She walked to the thermostat, knocked the heat up two degrees then hurried to her room at the opposite end of the hall.

After a quick shower, she went to her room and pulled on warm clothes, a hat and her boots. As she dressed, she thought about her situation. How had she gotten to this point? Whom had she made so mad that he or she wanted to kill her? It made no sense and only made her brain hurt to think about so she switched gears to breakfast. She mentally ran down the list of the items in her refrigerator and decided she had enough food for everyone. The least she could do was feed the two deputies who'd spent the majority of their night watching over her house. But the animals came first. When she stepped outside, Lance opened the door to his cruiser to join her. "Everything all right?"

She shot him a smile and let her gaze roam the area. "Yes, as of right now, everything is fine. I just have to take care of the animals."

As they were speaking, Aaron's SUV pulled into the drive. Her heart flipped and she had no choice but to acknowledge that she was glad to see him this morning. He parked next to Lance, climbed out and shut the door. When he turned, his blue eyes landed on her and flashed with pleasure. "Morning, y'all."

So. He was as glad to see her as she was him. Butterflies swarmed and she crossed her arms even as she nodded. "Morning." She couldn't fall for him. She couldn't. He was a good man. A good man who deserved a good woman. A woman who didn't bring danger and heart-break with her. She cleared her throat.

"I haven't heard otherwise so I'm guessing you had a quiet night?" he said.

He'd been worried. "It was quiet, thanks. I'm just headed to the barn to take care of the animals. If you'll give me about thirty minutes, I'll fix you all breakfast."

Lance's brow rose. "Sounds good to me. If Aaron and I help you, you'll finish faster."

She smiled. "Hungry?"

"Starved. I'll do just about anything legal for a home-cooked meal. Just ask Mrs. Starke."

Zoe laughed. "Come on then. We can knock this out in no time."

The three worked together in the barn caring for the animals. She let the horses out into the pasture, filled the barn cats' bowls with water and food and made sure most of the stalls were clean for the horses' return. There were two horses who needed a little extra attention, but she had hungry men on her hands so she'd do the other two later. They could wait an hour or so.

Aaron checked on the calf and the new mother. The little one nudged up against his mother looking for his breakfast. Zoe watched them and smiled. "I love animals. They have so few expectations, want so little. Food, water and a warm place to sleep."

He looked up. "We should all be that way, huh?"

She shrugged. "Maybe. Right now, all I want is my child to be safe and I want to stay alive so I can take care of her."

"We're going to make that happen."

She blinked against the sudden surge of tears and

drew in a deep breath. She needed a change of subject. "Sophia's excited to come out and see the calf. They seem to be doing well."

"They're doing great," he said. "When it warms up a bit, we'll let them out in the pasture with the others."

Aaron ran a gloved hand down the calf's back, his touch gentle and caring. She wondered what it would be like to be on the receiving end of that tenderness.

Actually, she already knew the answer to that question. Hadn't he held her in the cave when she'd been afraid? Hadn't he treated Sophia with the utmost gentleness and caring when she'd been so afraid?

Zoe rubbed her head where the beginning of a headache threatened. What was she thinking? She needed to focus on keeping Sophia safe and figuring out who was after her, not daydreaming about romance with a man. And this man in particular. She looked up and his gaze snagged hers. "Thank you, Aaron. For everything." She knew she sounded like a broken record with her thanks, but she wanted to make sure he understood how much she appreciated him and his efforts.

His eyes softened further. "You're welcome." His gloved hand ensnared hers, and he gave it a little squeeze. Her heart thudded a little faster, and she returned the squeeze even as her brain sent warning signals about getting too close to him. "Come on, I'm starving," he said.

"Me, too. Let's get cleaned up and we'll eat."

She stood at the kitchen sink, letting the water warm up as she tried to steer her thoughts from the fact that the good-looking vet had stolen his way into her heart in such a short period of time. She sighed and finished washing up then let the men do the same while she got started on breakfast. Twenty minutes later she had bacon, eggs and pancakes on platters. Pitchers of orange juice sat on the table and the coffee finished dripping into the carafe. She pulled the plates down and set the table. Then she hauled down enough glasses and placed them next to the plates.

Aaron entered the kitchen and lifted his nose, testing the air. "Something sure smells good."

"There's plenty, too. Could you get that bottle of syrup from the pantry for me?"

"Sure." He crossed to the room and opened the pantry door. She moved to grab the salt and pepper from beside the stove, and they both turned at the same time. Her nose bumped his hard bicep, and she lost her balance. His free arm came around her waist and kept her from bouncing back into the stove. "You okay?"

His musky scent wafted over her. The strength of his arms gave her security. His nearness made her yearn for things she'd been trying to put from her mind. And now it was all back and she had to ignore it all again. She swallowed. "I'm fine." He let her go. Reluctantly, she thought. "Let's dig in." She moved away from Aaron and stepped to the window to wave to Ginny who still sat in the cruiser watching the area.

Ginny came inside, and Zoe started moving the platters of food to the table. She was reaching for the pitcher of orange juice when Aaron's hand brushed hers. She froze for a slight second and let the sensation wash through her. When she looked up, he gave her a faint smile. "I'll get it."

She gave a little nod. He'd done that on purpose. He

knew he unsettled her and was having a little fun with it. She couldn't say she minded. "Okay. Thank you."

Sophia came into the kitchen rubbing her eyes and yawning. She stopped mid-yawn when she saw everyone at the table. Zoe walked over and smoothed her child's bed hair. "We've got company."

Sophia shrugged. "Hi."

Aaron slid out of the chair beside him. "Wanna sit with me?"

"Sure." Sophia climbed into the chair next to him and studied him. "How's the baby calf?"

"She's doing just fine. Her mama is taking good care of her."

Sophia scratched her nose and looked at Zoe. "Just like my mama takes care of me."

"Exactly."

"And you do, too."

"I do?"

"Yes. You protected us from the men shooting at us so I think that qualifies as taking care of us." Zoe choked on a laugh and turned away to hide her grin. Then she heard Sophia again. "Did you stay outside of my house all night?" She shifted her gaze slightly and saw that Sophia was talking to Ginny and Lance.

"All night," Ginny said as she dumped a helping of eggs onto her plate. She licked her lips. "And it was worth it. I'd take this in place of my regular paycheck any day."

"I'll be sure to pass that on to Clay," Lance said.

Ginny snickered. "I'll deny it."

Lance grinned. "Too late. I've got witnesses. Right, Sophia?"

Sophia's gaze darted back and forth between the two. "I'll take the fifth."

Lance, Ginny and Aaron cracked up and Aaron tweaked Sophia's nose. "Where did you hear that?"

"My daddy said it one time when mama asked him if he liked the new dish she'd fixed for dinner one night."

"Smart man," Lance murmured.

"He'd have been smarter if he'd just said he liked it if you ask me." More laughter, and Sophia beamed at being the center of attention.

Zoe heard their banter and even smiled at Sophia's precociousness. But she couldn't help the shudder that ripped through her at the memory of why the deputies were needed at her home. It was all well and good to be friends with them, but friendship wasn't why they were here.

Zoe sat at the table and stared at the people who surrounded her. Good people. People who didn't even really know her, but had fought to keep her and Sophia safe. A lump of gratitude wanted to form in her throat, but she forced it back and took a bite of the eggs.

"Mmm, this is amazing," Ginny said. "My sister would love this."

"Who's your sister?" Sophia asked.

"Her name is Tracy."

"Where is she?"

Sadness flickered in Ginny's eyes, making Zoe curious. Ginny finally said, "She's at a special home in Nashville."

"What kind of special home?" Sophia asked.

"It's for people who have special needs."

"Like what?" Sophia asked.

"Honey—" Zoe tried to stop the line of questioning, but Ginny shook her head.

"It's okay. I don't get a chance to talk about her much. Tracy is mentally disabled, which just means her brain works in different ways than yours and mine."

"I know what you mean." Sophia nodded. "There's a boy like that in my class. My teacher says he's special needs. His name is Todd and he's got Down Syndrome plus he stutters. But I like him cuz he's nice and he picked up my paper for me when Jordan pushed it off my desk." Sophia stabbed her eggs. "I like Todd a lot better than Jordan."

Ginny's eyes softened. "Then you understand. Tracy's a great girl. You'd like her."

"How old is she?"

"She's twenty. She'll be twenty-one next month."

"Maybe you can take me to meet her some day. We can take her some of my mom's cooking. She'd probably like that."

Ginny let out a small laugh. "You're right about that."

Sophia turned her attention back to her food, and Ginny continued to express her pleasure at the breakfast treat.

But Zoe couldn't seem to relax and enjoy the food. In fact, if she were eating sawdust she might not recognize the difference. Indecision and uncertainty swarmed within her. What should she do now? She looked up and found Aaron watching her.

He gave her a small frown. "You okay?"

She nodded but couldn't answer. She looked away then back up. Glanced between him and Lance and Ginny. "So what happens now? I mean you can't stay outside my house all night every night. What are my options?"

Lance put his fork down and wiped his mouth with the napkin. "Clay's asked me to head the investigation. His wife is due any day now so he's sticking close to home. We need to look at your background, any enemies you might have formed. Is there anyone who'd come looking for revenge for any reason?"

Zoe swallowed hard. Her background. How she didn't want to have to go there. "I had a few pretty wild teenage years," she said softly, "but nothing that would send someone after me after all this time. I haven't been in touch with anyone from high school in years."

"What about college?"

She shrugged and shook her head. "No, by the time I got to college, I'd cleaned up my act and had my head on straight. My parents' divorce was ugly. I was messed up and confused about a lot of things. And then I met Nan Livingston. She saw something in me that she decided was worth investing in. Because of her, I was able to dream, develop goals and plans and I knew that if I wanted to achieve those then I had to focus. So I did." That was the simple version, but all truth. Thinking about Nan brought a pang of grief, sharp and fast. It pained Zoe to think of what Nan would say about her current spiritual state.

"What about your husband?" Aaron asked. "He was killed in a wreck a year ago, right?"

"Yes."

"Was he involved in anything that he shouldn't have been a part of?"

She was shaking her head before he finished the question. "No way. Trevor was as straight as they come. A rule follower to the nth degree. There was only black and white for him, and he never deviated from doing the right thing." She knew now that was why she'd been so drawn to him. She'd craved the stability she saw in him. "I met him in college, and we hit it right off. We got married six months after we met and then had Sophia. He was a good man." She looked at Sophia who was listening with wide eyes. "And a great dad."

"I miss him," Sophia said with a sigh. "I miss going with him and Grandpop to see Thunderbolt race."

"I know, baby."

"Thunderbolt?" Aaron asked.

"Our horse," Zoe said. "Or rather, Trevor's. He enjoyed owning a racehorse. Trevor and Alexander, Trevor's father, would take Sophia to the racetrack to cheer on Thunderbolt. It was something they all did together." She smiled. "There was no gambling involved, Trevor didn't believe in it. But he loved to watch the horses race."

"Grandpop told Daddy he should sell Thunderbolt and get his money while he had a winner, but I'm glad he didn't."

"I am, too." Zoe ran a finger down her little girl's cheek. "Trevor took a lot of pleasure in that horse. The fact that he got to spend time with his father and Sophia doing something he loved just made it that much sweeter." She gave a little shrug. "So, no. This has nothing to do with Trevor. I don't know *what* it has to do with, but it's not him."

* * *

Aaron couldn't help but wonder if she was right. She sounded so positive, but could Trevor have been involved in something without Zoe knowing about it? Probably. Most spouses could manage to hide things from the other one if they truly wanted to. But had Trevor been one of those? That was the question.

Aaron downed the last of his coffee then set the cup in front of him. He looked at Lance. "So, until we figure out what all of this is about, what's the plan to keep Zoe and Sophia safe?"

Lance sipped his orange juice and shook his head. "I'll talk to Clay, and we'll come up with something. I definitely don't think they should be alone."

A knock on the door sounded, and Aaron saw Zoe jump. She settled a hand over her heart, took a deep breath and started to rise. Aaron placed a hand on her arm. "I'll get it."

He pulled his weapon, and Lance stood, too. "If it was one of the bad guys from yesterday, I don't think he'd be knocking," Lance said.

"I know, but I'm just being careful."

Lance and Ginny both pulled their guns and held them ready. "Good idea, but while there are cops in the house, let us handle it. Put your gun away."

Aaron did so and Lance walked to the door, staying to the side and not moving in front of the windows. He peered out and relaxed, shoving his weapon back in his holster. "It's Clay." He opened the door.

Clay stepped inside and nodded. "Morning."

"Morning," Aaron said. "What brings you out here this early?"

"I'd thought I'd drop in and check on Zoe and Sophia, but I'm glad you're here."

"You need something to do while waiting for that baby to be born?"

Clay scowled at him and Aaron couldn't help the small smile that lifted his lips. Clay was always the one in control. "You find me amusing right now, don't you?"

"A bit."

"Thanks."

"Anytime."

Clay's features morphed into concern. "I wanted to let you know that there won't be any charges brought against you on the shooting yesterday."

Aaron let out a slow breath. "Thanks. I wasn't really worried, but you never know."

"Yeah, well, with all the testimony from Lance and Zoe as to what happened, it's an open-and-shut deal."

"How is he?" Aaron asked. "The man I shot."

"He's still alive, but unconscious. I've got a deputy on him and orders to be notified as soon as he wakes up so I can question him."

"Do you know who he is?" Zoe asked.

"Peter Garrett. A guy with a rap sheet as long as your arm. Robbery, assault—"

"Murder?" Aaron asked.

"No, everything but that."

"Well, he was willing to add it to the list yesterday," Lance muttered.

"Yeah. Fortunately, he failed. We did manage to take into custody a man by the name of Cody Jansen."

"Blond hair, blue eyes and mean as a snake?" Aaron asked.

"Sounds like one and the same." Clay tapped the screen of his phone and brought up the mug shot. He turned it around so Aaron could see. Zoe moved closer to look over his shoulder. She gave a small gasp. "That's him."

"Yep," Aaron agreed.

"He's got a bullet in his shoulder. He showed up in a Knoxville hospital, and officers there nabbed him. He's under arrest, but so far is refusing to talk." Clay rubbed his eyes, and Aaron thought he looked tired.

"I might have shot him, too." He blinked as he remembered pulling the trigger as the man came through the small hallway. "There was so much chaos, bullets were flying and all I could think of was to make sure I got Zoe and Sophia out of there before one of *them* got shot."

Clay clapped him on the back. "Not to worry. We'll get it all figured out. You won't be held responsible for defending yourself and them, but when all this goes to court, you'll have to testify."

"I'm ready."

"I figured you would be. I've already got your gun from yesterday so we'll have ballistics run tests to see what bullets came from what gun. I hope to return the weapon to you before too long."

Aaron nodded. "It's fine. I have another one at home I can carry until then. How's Sabrina?" Aaron asked.

Clay swallowed. "She's fine. Just fine. Really good. Yeah. She's…fine."

"Okay," Aaron said with a raised brow, "maybe that was the wrong question. How are *you*?"

Clay scowled at him. "I'm fine, too. Or I will be as

soon as the baby gets here." He huffed out a breath and shook his head. "Can't stand all this waiting."

Aaron clapped him on the shoulder. "Well, that's no surprise, you've never been good at being patient. Hang in there, big brother."

"Yeah." Clay settled his Stetson back on his head. "All right, I'm out of here then. Ginny, you want to head on over to the hospital to relieve Ronnie? I'm sure he's ready to get home."

"Sure thing, Sheriff." She finished off her last bite of eggs, grabbed her coat and gloves. "Thanks for the breakfast," she said to Zoe. "It was delicious. Wish I could cook like that."

Zoe smiled. "You're welcome. And anytime you want to learn, I'm happy to give you a few lessons."

Ginny grinned. "I might just take you up on that. Tracy would flip." She slipped out the door and Aaron heard her cruiser engine come to life. He looked at Zoe. Cooking lessons? Did that mean she planned on sticking around for a while? The smile slipped from her lips, and her eyes shadowed. Was she wondering the same thing?

Clay started to leave then turned back to her. "Who did you tell that you were leaving Knoxville and coming to Wrangler's Corner?"

"No one. The day after someone tried to run me off the road, I went home from Nina's, packed my car with what I thought we'd need, and left."

"Did you notice anyone following you?"

"No. And I was looking. I drove around for hours before finding an out-of-the-way hotel. We stayed there for about a week before Amber got back to me with this ranch-sitting opportunity."

Clay blinked. "Amber got you this job?"

Aaron explained what she'd told him last night. Clay shook his head. "Glad to know she's talking to someone," he muttered.

Aaron understood. Their sister's job as a travel writer took her all over the world, and she rarely made it home—or answered her phone. Email was definitely the best way to reach her. "All right, well, stay put and—"

Zoe's gasp cut him off.

Aaron frowned. "What is it?"

"Smoke, I think." She moved closer to the window, and her eyes widened. "The barn. It's on fire!"

Zoe grabbed her coat and headed for the door then looked back at Sophia. The child's eyes were wide and filled with fear. She couldn't leave Sophia alone. Clay went to the window, peered out then came back. "I'll stay here. If this is some ploy to get us out of the house and leave you alone with her, we're not going to let that happen." He looked at Lance. "You and Aaron go. Zoe, you stay here with me and Sophia."

She shook her head. "I can't do that. This is my responsibility. My fault. You stay here with her," she beseeched him, torn between the desire to stay with her child and keep her promise to take care of the place. But Clay was a police officer. She had full confidence in his ability to protect Sophia. Much better than she could for sure. "Keep her safe, Clay, you hear me? Keep her safe."

Zoe raced out the door with Aaron on her heels, and Clay's frustrated shout ringing in her ears. Lance brought up the rear, but he didn't bother to argue with her. There was no time to consider how foolishly she might be behaving. As long as Sophia was safe, Zoe's only thought was to take care of the property she'd been entrusted with.

Smoke now poured from the open door. She covered her nose and mouth with her scarf and stepped inside. The two horses she'd left in their stalls whinnied their fear and paced restlessly in the confined space. The thick smoke nearly blinded her, and Zoe squinted against the haze. "Where's the fire?" she asked. Then coughed.

Aaron stepped in behind her and pulled the collar of his coat up over his mouth and nose. Through the haze, she could see him, but visibility was getting worse by the second. He pointed. "There!"

At the end of the barn, she could make out flashes of orange. "The hay," she said. "You let the animals out. I'll get the extinguishers. There are two in the office."

"Be careful!" Aaron hollered at her even as he moved to the stalls of the two horses. Aaron released them and they headed for the exit without hesitation. Zoe entered the office and grabbed the first extinguisher from its mount on the wall then snagged the one behind the desk. She raced back into the center of the barn to see Aaron leading the mama heifer and her baby out. When she came up behind him, he held out a hand and she slapped the larger extinguisher in it. Lance had already pulled the hose from the rack and cranked the water on full blast. He began to drag it toward the back of the barn wetting everything in his path.

Once the animals were safely out, she and Aaron moved through the smoke. The heat was intense, the flames already reaching for the nearest wooden stall.

She pulled the pin and held the held the nozzle of the extinguisher toward the flames.

Aaron came up beside her and did the same. At first the flames fought back and Zoe despaired that the extinguishers weren't doing any good. She struggled for breath and began to grow dizzy, but gritted her teeth and held the stream of foam steady. And slowly, they started to win the battle. The flames flickered then faded. But the smoke was fierce.

She dropped the extinguisher and went to her knees, her lungs straining and finally succumbing to the lack of oxygen.

A hand on her upper arm pulled her to her feet, and she stumbled after Aaron. Lance held on to her other arm and the three of them exited the barn into the fresh air. "Are you okay?" Aaron gasped then gave a hacking cough.

Zoe sank to the cold ground and gasped, sucked in the fresh air, coughed and finally felt the world settle. "Yes. I think so. Are you?"

He nodded. "Lance?"

"Yeah."

A sharp crack broke the air, and Zoe felt a burning sting along her left arm.

"Get behind the tractor," Lance yelled. "Someone's shooting!"

Chapter 7

Just as in the barn, Aaron grabbed her right arm and headed toward the tractor. Lance had his weapon out and was right beside him, his back toward Aaron, his gun aimed in the direction the shot had come from. Aaron pulled her around the front of the tractor and she slumped to the ground, her back against the heavy rubber tire. Lance rounded to the other tire and hovered there.

Aaron's heart thumped hard in his chest and he dropped to his knees in front of Zoe. "I'm getting really tired of being shot at."

"Tell me about it," Zoe muttered. She shifted and sucked in a deep breath. "Ow."

He looked down and saw blood seeping through her

heavy tan coat. Fear thrummed through him. "Oh, no, Zoe, you're hit." He scooted closer.

"Hit?" She frowned. "As in shot?" She didn't protest as he slid her wounded arm out of the sleeve. She gave a low hiss of pain but otherwise stayed silent.

"Yes, but the fact that you're talking and making sense is encouraging." He looked up at Lance. "You see the shooter?"

"Not yet."

"Lance? Aaron?" Clay shouted.

Aaron turned and peered around Zoe and the tire. "We're okay, Clay! Zoe's hit, though not bad."

"You're sure she's okay?"

Aaron examined the wound. No bullet hole, but a nice groove in her upper arm that would need a few stitches. "I'm sure."

"Backup's on the way. Stay put. I've got Sophia right here with me and she's fine."

Zoe seemed to deflate once she heard that Sophia was safe. Her eyes closed, and she leaned her head back against the tire. Another shot rang out. A puff of white snow lifted into the air just next to the tractor. Aaron flinched and tucked his head against his chest. Zoe drew in a deep breath, but didn't move. Prayers slipped from his lips.

This time the sound of gunfire came from the house. Zoe shot into a sitting position. "Sophia!" Aaron spun to see Clay at the window shooting back into the direction the original shot came from.

"It's okay, she's all right. It's just Clay. He must have seen something." And been absolutely sure of what he was shooting at or he wouldn't have fired back. Sirens wailed in the distance, and Aaron let out a slow breath, hoping the sound would scare the shooter off the property. And that someone would be able to chase him down and catch him.

Police cruisers pulled into the drive and parked in front of the house. The car doors opened, and officers stayed behind the protection they offered. "Who went to the woods? The shots came from the woods behind the barn." Clay's voice came from behind the cracked front door.

"Parker and Joy." Aaron thought he recognized Walter Haywood's voice in response to Clay's question. Parker Little and Joy West were two other deputies with the rapidly expanding Wrangler's Corner sheriff's department.

"Stay put until we hear from them," Clay ordered. "Aaron, Lance? You still okay?"

"We're all right," Lance called back. He caught Aaron's gaze. "How bad is it?"

"Not that bad." Zoe's pale features worried him. Her eyes were open and watching, though. He leaned in for a closer look. "A couple of stitches, and you'll be fine. Okay?"

"Yes, it stings, but I don't think I'm going to die from it."

If he thought there was any chance she was in danger of dying from the wound, they wouldn't still be behind the tire. Somehow they'd be on the way to the hospital. He shrugged out of his jacket and pulled his sweater and long-sleeved T-shirt over his head. He yanked the sweater back on then fished in his jeans for the pocket-knife he'd started carrying.

If he was ever duct-taped again, at least he'd have a fighting chance. Using the knife, he cut off one of the sleeves and wrapped it around her upper arm, pulling it tight to stop the bleeding and to hold the edges of the wound together. He looked at her. "Best I can do without my medical kit."

"It's fine," she whispered. "Thanks."

"It needs to be washed out and you probably need a round of antibiotics, but we'll have to worry about that a little later." She gave him a tight, grim smile and shifted with a grimace. "Pain pills might not be a bad idea, either."

"No," she bit out, her eyes hard, jaw tight. "No pills."

Aaron raised a brow. "Okay. No one's going to force them down your throat." He pulled her coat back around her, leaving her arm free of the sleeve, but under the warm material.

She sighed. "Sorry. Didn't mean to snap. I... I used to have a drug problem."

He froze for a slight second as her words registered. He saw her face flame red and knew she was already regretting her words. "It's all right," he said. "No pain pills then." He looked at Lance. "Haven't heard any shots for a few minutes."

"Yeah." He glanced toward the house. "Clay hasn't said to move yet."

Several tense minutes passed and Aaron thought his heart might beat out of his chest thanks to his rushing adrenaline. Movement near the tree line captured his attention. "Lance?"

"I see it."

"Hold your fire," Clay called out. "Joy's near the trees. The shooter's gone."

Lance stood. Aaron waited a few seconds then helped Zoe to her feet. She held her arm against her stomach and he kept a steadying hand at her back. "Let's get inside and get that cleaned up."

Aaron led her to the house while Clay and his deputies discussed strategy. Clay had already notified the proper authorities of the incident with a request to have neighboring law enforcement available should they be needed until the shooter was caught.

"Sophia?" Zoe called. "Where are you?"

"Mom!" Sophia rushed from the den to her mother.

Zoe wrapped her good arm around her child and held on tight. "It's okay, baby. It's okay."

"Sheriff Starke pulled the couch from the wall and told me to get behind it. He told me to stay right there between the couch and the wall and I did."

Zoe kissed the top of Sophia's head. "I'm very proud of you for obeying." Her eyes filled, and she looked at Clay. "Thank you for keeping her safe."

"Of course," Clay said.

Sophia pulled back and frowned at the blood on her mother's arm. "Why are you bleeding? Are you hurt? What's wrong?"

Sophia shrugged the rest of the way out of the jacket and Aaron took it form her. "I'm okay," she said. "It's just a scratch."

He watched them together and felt his heart clench. They were all each other had at this point. "What happens to Sophia if something happens to you?" he asked her quietly.

She stilled. "She goes to live with Trevor's sister, Nina, and her husband, Gregory."

"And does Sophia come with any money attached?"

Zoe swallowed and he saw her follow his line of thinking. "Um. Sophia," she said, "will you go get the first-aid kit out of the bathroom?"

Sophia pressed her lips into a tight line and didn't release her grip on her mother. She looked back and forth between the adults then nodded. "Sure, I'll get it, but I know you're just sending me out of the room so I won't hear what you're going to say next." She shot a look at Zoe's arm. "But since you're hurt I'll let you get away with it this time." She turned and headed for the bathroom. Aaron lifted a brow, and Zoe's lips curved slightly even though her eyes didn't smile.

"You have your hands full with her, don't you?" Clay asked from his position near the kitchen door. Every once in a while he'd look out.

"A bit."

More than a bit, but she wouldn't trade raising Sophia for anything. She shook her head. "And no," she said to Aaron. "Sophia doesn't come with money attached. The only money I have is from the life insurance policy Trevor had taken out a couple of years ago. I think it's for two hundred fifty thousand dollars or something like that. Not enough to kill someone for."

Aaron lifted a brow. "You'd be surprised. Who's the beneficiary for your life insurance?"

"Sophia."

"And who gets Sophia if something happens to you again?"

"Nina. Trevor's sister." She raked her good hand through her tangled hair. She felt the color drain from her cheeks. "They would get custody and therefore control of the money and any other assets that I have."

"Here, Mom." Sophia came back into the kitchen carrying the first-aid kit.

Aaron took it from her. "Thanks."

"Can I watch?"

"You *may*. As long as it's okay with your mom." He shot a glance at Zoe and she nodded, her mind not on her arm, but on the deduction Aaron's questions had led her to.

Nina? Really? "It's okay," she murmured. She focused in on Sophia, her eyes automatically monitoring the color in her cheeks. She seemed all right, but she would check her sugar levels again in a bit.

Clay spoke into his phone then turned back. "That was Lance. They've cleared the area. The shooter is gone, but they found the place he shot from. A crime scene unit's on the way from Nashville to process the area. Lance said he doesn't want to assume anything, but he thinks the shooter is the one who got away. The one they called Jed."

"I think that's probably a safe assumption." Aaron cut the sleeve of her sweatshirt away from her arm then cleaned it up before pulling out a needle and suture thread. Zoe's eyes widened. "You're going to sew it up?"

"I carry the stuff for humans, too." He rolled his shirt up and showed her the scar on his left forearm. "Ever since I got tangled up with that angry bull last year, I make sure I can patch myself up if I need to."

"A bull did that?" Sophia asked.

"Nah, I got away from him. It was the rusty nail on the fence that got me when I went over. Sliced a big ole gash in my arm."

Sophia winced. "Wow. How bad did that hurt?"

"Big-time bad."

"So you're going to sew up Mom's cut?"

"Sure. If she wants me to." He looked at her and Zoe saw a gentle compassion there. And a willingness to let her make the call about her medical treatment. He wouldn't be offended if she refused to let him work on her arm. "Or," he said, "we'll just take her to the hospital and let another doctor do it."

"Aren't you a real doctor?" Sophia asked.

Aaron smiled. "The animals think so."

"It's fine," Zoe whispered. "I trust you." And she did.

Aaron sobered. "I have some numbing medicine. You'll only feel the first prick of the first needle."

"That's fine."

"Are you allergic to anything?"

"No, nothing."

The other officers milled around writing notes and recording every detail so when it came time to do the paperwork, everything would be right there and they wouldn't have to rely on memory. She watched them from the corner of her eye so she didn't have to see what he was doing.

Aaron worked quickly and efficiently and soon Zoe had a neat little row of five stitches in her upper arm. He'd been true to his word. Other than the initial prick of the first shot and a few slight tugs, she hadn't felt a thing. Sophia had never taken her eyes from him and his work on Zoe's arm, fascinated by the whole procedure.

Zoe's attention had been distracted anyway. She kept remembering the look on Aaron's face when she'd said she used to have a drug problem. She felt heat flush her face. Why had she told him that? And at that moment of all times? What was she thinking to let that kind of information loose when they'd been dodging bullets and fighting for their lives?

But other than his initial hesitation, he didn't seem fazed by the knowledge. She did think he'd bring it up again when they were alone. So now that she'd let the cat out of the bag, what was she going to tell him? The whole sordid story?

Yes. He deserved it. He was putting his life on the line for her, and she owed him nothing less than the absolute truth. She blew out a breath and tried to focus on her arm. Which wasn't hard. It throbbed with a fierce ache, but she'd deal with it. Without drugs.

Clay finally came back in and sat at the table. "How's the arm?"

Zoe drew in a deep breath. "Fine. Or it will be thanks to Aaron."

Clay nodded. "As you know, the shooter got away. We found some cartridges that tell us he was using a .45. Probably a rifle with a high-powered scope."

"I'm glad he missed." She looked at her arm. "Mostly missed anyway."

"Me, too. But…"

"But?"

"I don't think you're safe staying here, and I don't

have the manpower to spare to protect you like you need it out here on the farm."

"So what are you saying, Clay?" Aaron asked as he repacked his supplies in the bag.

"I'm saying I think she needs to leave here. Go somewhere it will be easier to keep an eye on her. We can do this here at the ranch only on a short-term basis. If this situation is going to stretch out for any length of time then we need to come up with a better solution."

"Like what?" Aaron said.

"And where would I go?" she asked. "What about the animals?"

"I've already thought about the animals," Clay said. "We'll simply move the horses to our parents' ranch. There are plenty of hands to help take care of them. However, I don't think it's wise to take you and Sophia out there."

"No, of course not. We'd just bring trouble down on your family."

"It's not so much that as it is there's no place to put you. Mom and Dad have started renting out the cottages on the property again and they're all occupied right now—especially with Thanksgiving just around the corner."

"So what did you have in mind?" Aaron asked.

"Well, there are two options. One is Sabrina's grandmother's bed-and-breakfast. But that might be an issue if someone tried to get to Zoe there."

"No." Zoe lifted her chin and looked him in the eye. "I won't put any more innocent people in danger. You and Aaron and Lance are bad enough but at least you know how to defend yourselves."

He nodded. "I had a feeling you might feel that way. The other choice is also a place in town, right off the main street and across the street from the B and B. It's also near the sheriff's office. It's a small house, two bedrooms and one bathroom, but it's vacant. I recommend you and Sophia move there for now."

Zoe swallowed and looked at Aaron then back to Clay. "All right. If you think that's what we need to do, then we'll do it." And when she could think again, she'd see if she could figure out another place to run to. A place far away from Wrangler's Corner and the men who wanted her dead.

Chapter 8

It had only taken Clay a matter of hours to get everything set up, but it wasn't until the next morning that they'd made the move. Clay had been fairly certain all of the activity at the Updike ranch would keep any would-be intruders away from the place for the duration.

He'd been right. Zoe had packed while Aaron got his folks' agreement to take the horses. The other lower maintenance animals would be fine as long as the weather cooperated and someone could come out once a day to care for them. Aaron would do it himself if he had to.

Now Zoe and Sophia were as comfortable as they could possibly be after having been held hostage, chased through the woods, shot at and then uprooted from their home away from home.

Two days after the incident, Aaron sat next to Lance in the cruiser and watched the front door of the house. The yellow home with green shutters and the wrap-around porch was perfect according to Zoe. The only thing that made him slightly nervous was the door. It had a wood frame but was glass from top to bottom. And behind that door were two people he was coming to care for. Two people he had no business thinking about as much as he was. "It's been quiet," he said.

Lance nodded and took a bite of the sandwich Aaron had brought over to him. "I like it that way."

"I do, too, but it makes me nervous."

"I know what you mean." Lance glanced at him. "You're taking quite a bit of time away from your practice."

"Nah, I'm just making a few more house calls than usual. Nate's back from vacation and covering the office." Nathan Godfrey, his partner. "He and Jill had a fight so he's working extra hours to stay out of the line of fire."

Lance's jaw tightened. "Running away from your problems in a marriage won't do it much good."

Aaron nodded. Lance had been in a troubled marriage a couple of years ago. His wife had made a lot of rotten choices and had eventually died because of them. "I've never been married, but watching my parents and my siblings, I know that's the truth." He shrugged. "They'll work it out eventually."

"Whatever happened to that woman you were seeing a while back? I haven't noticed her around lately, but haven't had a chance to ask you about her."

Aaron winced. "Darla? She moved away about six months ago."

"Moved? As in permanently?"

"Yes."

"I'm sorry."

"Me, too." He glanced at the house again. "At least I was. I don't think about her much anymore." Of course if he consciously thought about it, he clearly remembered the sting of her betrayal. The heartache he'd felt when he realized she'd used him. And the anger. He never wanted to feel that kind of heartache again. Lance followed his line of sight. "She's a pretty special lady."

"You think?"

"I think *you* think so."

Aaron looked away. "Maybe." No maybe about it. Zoe was special. But he'd already decided he didn't want to get involved. Okay, correction. He did want to get involved, he wanted to take the time to explore the feelings she evoked in him every time he was around her, but he couldn't shake the fear of getting his heart broken again when she returned to her life in Knoxville. He simply wouldn't do it. And he wasn't sure he was open to a long-distance relationship. Maybe, though… if that was what Zoe wanted.

"What happened? Why'd she move away?"

"She didn't like living in a small town. She wanted to be in the city with the bright lights and," he said with a shrug, "I didn't." But he'd thought about it. Especially when she'd announced she was leaving town. In the end, she'd left and he'd stayed right where he'd always wanted to be. Home. With family and helping the good people of Wrangler's Corner. But Zoe was different. Could he put all that aside and follow Zoe to Knoxville? He wasn't sure. And she hadn't asked so he didn't know why he was even thinking along those lines anyway.

Ginny Garrison walked out the front door of the house and gave them a wave. Aaron climbed out of the cruiser and walked up the front steps to meet Ginny. "Is she ready?"

"Almost."

"Are you okay staying with Sophia?"

"Of course. She's a great kid."

"Thanks," Zoe said from behind Ginny. "She likes you, too."

Ginny smiled and backed up to let Aaron inside. He took in Zoe's appearance and felt his heart thud an extra beat. She looked beautiful if still a bit pale. "Are you sure you're up to this?"

"I'm sure. It's my left arm that was hurt. I'm right-handed."

Yesterday, she'd requested a trip to the shooting range to brush up on her skills. She had a concealed weapon permit for the state of Tennessee but it had been awhile since she'd gone shooting.

Aaron hadn't been so sure the trip was a good idea, but he couldn't discount her reasons for wanting to do it. He led her to the cruiser. While Aaron was occupied with teaching her to shoot, Lance would be their eyes and ears on the surrounding area.

She slid into the backseat and Aaron took the front next to Lance. Lance glanced in the rearview mirror. "You used to shoot a lot?"

Aaron turned to see her nod. "Trevor and I used to go on the weekends to the shooting range. We used to try a lot of different guns. I've always enjoyed going to the range and have missed it since Trevor's been gone." She shrugged. "I just haven't had the heart to go." Her jaw firmed. "But I need to do this for Sophia and myself. I appreciate everything you all are doing, but I really need to be able to protect us."

No wonder she'd been so comfortable with the Winchester rifle at the Updikes'.

Small talk filled the car for the next hour until Lance turned onto a gravel drive that led to the parking lot of the shooting range. When Lance parked, Aaron climbed from the car and opened the door for Zoe. She slid out and he hustled her inside. Lance followed at a more sedate pace and Aaron knew he was checking out the surrounding area, watching the passing cars to see if any of them slowed or looked suspicious.

"Aaron, long time no see, man."

Aaron looked up to find Keith Nance, the owner of the place, behind the counter. "Hey there." Aaron led Zoe over and shook Keith's hand. "Good to see you." Keith was in his midsixties and still worked out an hour every day at the gym he'd built behind the shop. His bulging muscles attested to his dedication. "Keith, this is Zoe, a friend. She has her concealed weapon permit."

"But I need a little practice before I'll feel comfortable carrying again."

"You have a gun?" Keith asked her.

"No, I'll need to purchase one."

"That's not a problem. Do you have one in mind?" He reached under the counter and pulled out a stack of paperwork and a pen.

"Something small and easy to carry in my purse or

pocket, but one with a safety like the Smith & Wesson M&P Shield 9 mm. I have a child so I need the safety."

Aaron blinked. She knew her weapons. Keith appeared to be impressed, as well. "You've shot one before?"

"Yes."

"They're hard to keep, but I actually have one of those in stock. Got a shipment in two days ago." He went to the vault behind him and opened it.

He disappeared inside and Zoe looked at Aaron. "I left Knoxville so fast, I didn't think to get mine." She shook her head. "You would think that would have been the first thing I'd have gone after, but all I could think of was getting Sophia away, getting somewhere safe. I hadn't looked at that gun since Trevor died. It's still in a safe in the bedroom."

"It's understandable. You were probably in a state of shock, scared, not thinking straight."

She gave him a tremulous smile. "Yes. To all of the above."

When Keith came back, he held the small gun. "Here you go."

She nodded. "Perfect. Now, I just need an ankle holster and I'll be all set."

Zoe knew she'd surprised the men with her weapons knowledge, but Trevor had been an enthusiast and she supposed it had rubbed off on her. Then again, growing up on a small farm in the middle of nowhere, she'd handled rifles and pistols on a regular basis. One never knew when a rattlesnake might decide to take up residence in an empty barn stall or a wild wolf come looking for some lunch in the chicken coop. She'd been around guns her entire life.

Once she filled out the paperwork, she paid for the gun with her credit card. No sense in worrying about being traced by it. The bad guys already knew where she was. And maybe if they saw she'd purchased a gun, they'd think twice about coming back.

She doubted it, but one could hope.

Aaron led her back to the range, and Zoe was relieved they were the only ones there. She drew in a calming breath as she realized what she was doing. Preparing herself to defend herself and Sophia. Planning to shoot at someone if she had to. Shooting at targets was easy but could she really shoot at another human being? She prayed she wouldn't have to find out.

Zoe held the gun while Aaron opened the box of ammunition. He watched as she expertly loaded it. "I don't think you're going to need much practice."

She gave him a slight smile. "Probably not, but it's been over a year since I've handled a weapon."

He pressed the button to bring the target holder in. He clipped the paper with the black silhouette onto the holder and set it out about fifty feet. She slipped on the protective eyewear and inserted the earplugs.

He did the same and nodded. She lifted the pistol with her right hand, her left hand coming up to add support. She felt the stitches tug, but the pain was tolerable. Zoe closed one eye and focused on the target in front of her. Then pulled the trigger. Then pulled it again and again and again.

When she finished the last shot, she lowered the

weapon. Aaron pressed the button to pull the target in close. Zoe's lips tightened as she studied it.

"You did great," Aaron said.

"A few wild shots, but a few center mass, too," she said. "Not too bad. Once I got the feel for the gun it all came back to me."

"Nice. Want to go again?"

"Sure."

Within a few minutes, she was back at it. With each round, her circle of holes in the paper got tighter and tighter.

"That's some good shooting, Zoe," Aaron said. "I'm impressed."

Zoe set the gun on the small bench in front of them and pulled her earplugs out. She could hear him okay, but he sounded muffled, like he was far away. She stared at the latest target with the holes. "I don't think I could shoot someone, Aaron."

"If it comes down to his life or yours, or his or Sophia's, I think you could."

Tears filled her eyes and she glanced up at him, not caring if he saw the wetness. "Yes, I could for Sophia." She sniffed, and a tear traced down her cheek. He lifted a hand and thumbed it away, but left his palm cupping her cheek. She drew in a sharp breath.

"Clay will figure out what's going on. The man in the hospital will wake up eventually, and Clay will get him to talk."

Zoe closed her eyes against the lovely sensation of his touch. She had no business feeling an attraction for him. Not when she was fighting for her and Sophia's lives. She opened her eyes and met his. "Aaron, I appreciate everything you and your family and friends have done for Sophia and me, but I think it's time for us to run again."

"How is that going to help?"

She sighed. "Well, for one, it'll give the authorities time to try and figure things out. But I can't run without help."

He frowned. "What do you mean?"

"I want you to help us disappear."

Aaron stared at her. At this beautiful woman he'd only known for a few weeks and yet felt incredibly drawn to. Drawn to against his better judgment for sure, but still he couldn't deny it. So once again he found himself falling for a woman who wasn't planning on sticking around but didn't mind using him to get what she needed. He was such a gullible idiot.

He withdrew his hand from her silky skin and drew in a deep breath even as he berated himself for feeling a depth of hurt that he had no business feeling. "Fine. You want to run? Run. Clay and Lance will help you get everything together." He grabbed her gun, made sure it was unloaded with the safety on and handed it to her. She stuffed the remaining bullets in her bag and shot him a troubled look.

The hurt in her eyes pierced him and Aaron immediately felt guilty. It wasn't her fault he had issues. "Ah, man. I'm sorry I snapped. Come on, let's get out of here."

"Aaron, what's wrong? What did I say?"

"Nothing." He couldn't get into it right here. The door opened and he tensed, but it was a young couple ready to take on the range. He and Zoe slipped around them and out into the store.

Lance looked over his shoulder from his position by the door. He took in Zoe's face then let his eyes connect with Aaron's. The question there made Aaron grimace. He shook his head and Lance frowned, but didn't say anything.

Aaron waited for Zoe to get in the car. She didn't look at him when he shut the door for her. Instead, she shoved the newly purchased weapon into her bag and clamped her lips tight. Aaron told himself not to let it get to him, but the hurt didn't go away.

"Is Sophia all right?" Zoe asked.

Lance nodded from his position behind the wheel. "I just talked to Ginny about five minutes before you came out of the range. Ronnie came by, and the three of them are together. Ginny said something about sugar-free s'mores in the fireplace."

Aaron glanced back at her and noticed her jaw loosen slightly. "Zoe wants to run, Lance, and she needs your help to do it." He forced the words out. If she wanted to leave, he'd help her. He wouldn't like it, but he'd help her. And then he might treat himself to a long vacation. Alone.

Lance raised a brow. "Is that right?"

"Yes," she said with a troubled look at Aaron. He avoided her gaze in the mirror. "It's the only thing I can think to do. I can't keep tying up the sheriff's department. Anyone who stays with us or is near us is in danger." Aaron's heart thawed slightly when her voice thickened. "I'm sorry, but I just don't know what else to do."

Lance nodded. "I understand. Let me run it by Clay and see what he thinks."

"Thanks," she whispered. Then closed her eyes and leaned her head against the window.

Aaron rubbed his chin and fell into silence while he wrestled with his thoughts. Lance drove with a quiet confidence and alertness that made Aaron feel glad the man had come with them. "So, why would you want to kidnap a kid and get rid of her mother?" he asked Lance in a low voice.

"Because there's some advantage. Something the kidnapper gets. Money? Highly likely." He grimaced. "There's the whole human trafficking thing, of course, but this feels like something more. Those men at the house were waiting on something. They were communicating with someone."

"Speaking of which, I wonder if Clay had any success tracing the numbers from Pete's phone."

"We'll be sure to ask him." He tapped his fingers on the wheel. "They didn't want Sophia hurt."

"It sure seemed that way. So it's someone who cares about Sophia, but not Zoe?"

"No, Zoe's obviously in the way."

"She said her sister-in-law offered to have them move in with her and her husband, but Zoe didn't want to. You think she could be forcing the issue?"

"It makes sense. Get rid of Zoe and get custody of Sophia—and get control of any money that might come with her."

"I don't think the motive is money," Zoe said.

Lance grunted. "I hate to tell you this, but it's almost

always about money." His phone rang. "It's Clay." He pressed the Bluetooth button on the radio. "Hello."

"Lance, where are you?" Clay's voice filled the car.

"Still with Aaron and Zoe. What's up?"

"Our guy Pete is still out cold. He roused a bit and then went back under so he's no help right now. But I've been doing some digging into Trevor Collier."

Zoe stirred. "Trevor?"

"You found something?" Lance asked.

"Maybe. Looks like he had a thing for the horses."

"Gambling?"

A gasp came from the backseat, and Aaron turned to see Zoe shaking her head.

"Yeah," Clay said. "But I can't find that he ever lost that much. I mean his bank accounts are closed now, of course, but I was able to access them and there's nothing there to indicate it was an addiction."

"Maybe he was using someone else's money."

"He wasn't gambling," Zoe said. "He hated gambling."

"Then what was he doing at the tracks?" Clay's voice came over the speaker. "His buddies at the office said he was there most weekends."

"Like I told you earlier, Trevor was there to watch Thunderbolt race. He hated gambling, but he loved horses." She glanced at Aaron. "Trevor's grandmother had left him a trust fund and when she died he bought a horse with the money. The prestige of owning a winning horse was something he enjoyed. It was just fun for him." She shrugged. "A hobby that paid well."

"Paid well how?"

"Trevor got a percentage of every race the horse won,

he allowed other people to pay him to use Thunderbolt in the hopes of producing winning offspring. There's a whole slew of ways a horse can generate income without gambling, you know this."

"Yes, but I wasn't sure that's what you meant."

"It was. Trevor went to the track on race days to support and encourage the jockey who was a good friend, almost like a son to Trevor. He just wanted to cheer him on. But Trevor didn't gamble. Ever."

"You hear that, Clay?" Lance asked.

"I heard it."

"But you don't believe me," Zoe said, her lips pressing into a flat line.

"It's not a matter of—"

Lance stiffened. "Hang on, Clay."

Aaron straightened. "What is it?"

"What is what?" Clay echoed.

Lance's fingers tightened around the wheel and he looked back. "There's a car coming up fast on our rear."

They'd taken the back roads to Nashville instead of the highway thinking it would be easier to spot a tail than on the busy interstate. They were about thirty minutes outside of Wrangler's Corner on a two-lane road that ran between sprawling acres of land with private homes. The area was sparsely populated, but not isolated at all. Would someone really try something out in the open like this? Of course they would. "Looks like you were right to be concerned about someone following us."

Lance stepped on the gas, and the car surged forward just as a bullet shattered the back window.

Chapter 9

Zoe screamed and ducked down into the seat, the seat belt sliding off her shoulder and allowing her to lie flat against the upholstery. All she could think was that she was grateful Sophia wasn't with her. She covered her head as the car swerved left then back right. "Stay down!" Lance hollered. Another pop, and the vehicle surged forward, limped a few paces then jerked to a stop. "Watch out, he shot out the tire and he's going to hit us!"

Zoe rose up and caught the flash of movement in the side window. When the slam came, she rocked to the side, hit the door with her shoulder. Ignoring the flash of pain, she gripped the door handle and held on.

Another crunch against the driver's side, then the teeth-grating screech of metal on metal. An engine revved, tires squealed.

Then silence.

Her heart pounded in her ears.

Then her seat belt flew off and hands clamped down on her upper arms and pulled. She let out a low scream. "It's me," Aaron said. "Come on. They shot out the tire, and we can't sit here."

Zoe scrambled out of the car, her arm throbbing when she pushed too hard with it. Aaron's grabbing it hadn't helped. She ignored it, knowing he hadn't meant to hurt her, and followed Aaron around to the side of the car. "How did he find us?"

"Who knows?"

Lance rounded the front of the car, his weapon drawn, face tight. "They drove off, but that doesn't mean they won't be back."

Aaron was already on the phone with Clay. Zoe listened, her mind spinning, blood still pounding through her veins with ferocious force. This was getting ridiculous. She was going to have to grab Sophia and disappear. She couldn't keep putting people in danger. Even if they were cops. But Aaron wasn't a cop. He'd just stumbled into this mess.

While Lance kept watch and Aaron held her against him, they waited, not wanting to leave the relative cover the vehicle provided. "What kind of car was it?" Aaron asked.

Lance glanced at him. "It was a dark blue sedan. A Ford, I think. I got a partial plate, it was a Tennessee one. G34 something."

Sirens sounded in the distance but were closing the gap fast. Zoe let Aaron's warmth wrap itself around her. She shouldn't let him comfort her. She should move away, but she was so tired, so worn out, so scared...

Three police cruisers pulled to a stop, and the sirens cut off abruptly. Zoe slipped out of Aaron's arms. She heard Clay send two of the deputies to search the area but as she hugged her coat around her, she met Aaron's gaze and knew he was thinking the same thing she was. The shooter had escaped once again.

When Clay had finished taking all of the information the three of them could give him, he motioned for Joy to join them. She approached and Clay said, "Do you mind taking Zoe home? We've got to get a tow truck out here and get this scene cleaned up."

"Of course I don't mind." She smiled at Zoe. "Come on."

"I'll go with her," Aaron said.

"And I'm going to have Ronnie follow you to watch your back," Clay said. "We don't need a repeat of this." He lifted his notebook. "Now I'm going to go put this partial plate into the system and see if I can get a hit."

Zoe walked with Joy to the woman's cruiser and slid into the backseat. She shut the door. Tremors shook her, and she knew it was from the adrenaline crash. She took a deep breath closed her eyes. Then opened them. She looked up to see Aaron standing there. "Want some company?"

"Are you still mad at me for wanting to leave?"

"No."

She scooted over, and he slid in beside her then wrapped an arm around her shoulder. She laid her head against him. "Why did you get so upset when I asked you for help?"

He glanced out the window, and she followed his gaze. Joy and Clay stood talking next to the driver's door.

"I had a bad experience, and your statement sort of brought it all back."

She shifted and looked up at him, into those eyes that she never grew tired of looking at. Probably why she dreamed about them sometimes at night. She blinked, pushing the thoughts away. "What happened?"

"I recently dated a woman named Darla. She and I knew each other from high school. We'd been good friends, hung out with the same crowd, that kind of thing. She eventually married a guy named Barry Foster. About four years into their marriage things turned ugly and she and Barry divorced. Anyway, about a year ago, she found a hurt puppy on the side of the road and brought him into my practice. She was sweet and we hit it off while catching up. I took her to dinner and we wound up in a relationship that I thought had the potential to lead to something permanent. Her son was a great kid." He looked away and swallowed. "But she had other plans. Apparently she knew as soon as Barry heard she was interested in someone else, he'd come crawling back. She kept pushing him away, toying with him, telling him she was going to marry me when she actually had no intention of doing so."

"Oh, my, how awful of her. I'm so sorry."

"Apparently she was just using me to teach Barry a lesson."

"Did it work?"

"I guess. She went back to him and the three of them moved out of town shortly after that."

"I'm sorry."

"It's okay. Now." He shot another glance out the window. Joy was writing something down. Zoe waited to see if Aaron had more to say. "When I first met you in town, I wanted to get to know you better, but you didn't seem interested." She looked away. She wasn't blind. She'd seen the spark of interest in his eyes and had felt a tug on her heart in response. She'd been interested, but also wary. He cleared his throat and placed a hand under her chin. "I'm just saying you're the first person I've looked at twice since Darla. The first person to capture my attention and I'm curious to see if…ah… that could grow into something. To put it awkwardly, but there you go."

She let out a low shaky laugh. "Wow. You just kind of lay it out there, don't you?"

He gave a derisive chuckle. "Not usually, but I want you to understand so I'm trying to make sure I'm pretty clear. I'm saying that my feelings have a lot to do with why I reacted so strongly. I don't want you to leave." He sighed. "But I'm not a completely selfish moron. I do want you to be safe."

She frowned. "I want that, too. I've grown to love Wrangler's Corner and the people who live here, but someone is out to kill me and take my daughter away. I just don't know what else to do." She felt like a broken record.

"We'll figure it out." He leaned over and kissed the top of her head, and her pulse shifted into overdrive. "I'll help you do whatever you need to do."

"Thank you," she whispered just as Joy opened the driver's-side door and climbed in.

"Did you find anything out?" Aaron asked.

"Not much. We matched the plate with the car and it came back as stolen. But the home it was taken from has security cameras around the perimeter so we might get a hit from one of those."

"I'm not holding my breath."

"Yeah, I wouldn't, either."

The ride back to town was silent and calm, but Zoe's tension didn't ease until the small house came into view. It looked like a haven, an oasis in her world gone mad. It was exactly the kind of house she would have chosen to buy had she been looking. But she wasn't. She was hiding out, praying whoever was after her and Sophia would either give up and go away or be caught.

However, for now, she was thankful to be alive, grateful for the friends who'd taken it upon themselves to protect her and Sophia. Especially the man beside her. Her mind lingered on Aaron's story—and from the pensive look on his face, he was thinking about hers.

When he'd told her his experience, he hadn't tried to hide the pain he'd suffered, hadn't tried to brush it off as no big deal. He'd let her see him, who he was deep inside. And that made her want to get to know him even more. One reason she'd been able to open up about her past and her struggle with the addiction. Even now, some days the desire to use something to escape reality prodded her, but thanks to coping strategies and thoughts of her daughter, she was able to resist. Getting to know Aaron on a deeper level would just make leaving harder.

But if running meant keeping Sophia safe then she'd do what she had to do. And that might just break her heart.

The next two days passed without incident, which just made Zoe's nerves stretch tighter and tighter until she thought they'd surely snap if she even moved wrong.

Sophia had an escort to and from school and someone with her at all times while on campus. Letting Sophia out of her sight kept Zoe on pins and needles until her child was back safe, but Sophia enjoyed the interaction with the other children and needed it. She needed for her life to feel normal. So while it was her desire to smother her child and keep her close, she'd decided to trust the people helping her. To a point.

Zoe couldn't help but stay tense, constantly wondering when the other shoe was going to drop. Now that she didn't have the animals to take care of, she spent her days alternating between racking her brain, searching for a reason someone would want to kill her, and painting. She still took online orders and didn't want to get too far behind. Customers were counting on her to get the paintings done in a timely manner for gifts.

Zoe walked into the small sunroom and stared at her half-finished painting. She studied the photograph then picked up her brush. Swift strokes finished the newborn's rosy cheeks and long lashes. Zoe glanced at the clock then moved into the kitchen to sit on the bar stool in front of the open laptop.

The gun felt heavy in her ankle holster, but after the latest incident, she wouldn't be caught without the weapon.

She finished the last bite of her club sandwich and clicked on the link that would take her to the email detailing the transaction of the horse she and Trevor had purchased together. This morning, she'd been getting

Sophia ready for school when Ginny had picked up the newspaper and said something about the local winter bazaar that was to be next weekend with vendors and every kind of food available. And pony rides.

The mention of the pony rides had made Zoe think of the conversation in the car about Trevor and the horses. They thought he'd been gambling, but he hadn't been. She would have known because she kept up with the money and their bank accounts. He could have used money from his business, she supposed, but there'd never been any hint that anything had been amiss there. She thought she'd been clear about that fact when they'd all been at the house for breakfast, but figured they had to do their own investigation, their own digging for facts. And while she appreciated the thoroughness, she hated that they'd wasted time that could have been spent going in another direction.

She scanned the email that contained all of the documents that pertained to the purchase of Thunderbolt. She read it again, but nothing looked any different than the first time she and Trevor had gone over it together.

A knock on the door brought her head up, and she stood but allowed Joy to answer it. Joy kept a hand on her weapon while she looked out the window. Then her tense posture relaxed. "It's Aaron."

Two little words that sent Zoe's heart beating a little faster. Anticipation leaped inside her, and she curled her fingers into fists. She really had to put this whole attraction thing aside. Unfortunately her heart had other ideas. She wanted to bolt to the foyer mirror and check her hair and what little makeup she'd applied this morning, but resisted.

Aaron stepped inside and gave her a small smile. "Hi."

"Hi."

"I had a break at the clinic so thought I'd come by and see how you were doing."

She shrugged. "I'm hanging in there."

"I'll be in the study," Joy said. She disappeared through the open door to the left, and Zoe appreciated the deputy's discretion.

She led Aaron into the kitchen and gestured to the computer. "I'm just trying to figure out who's behind all this and if our purchase of Thunderbolt had anything to do with it."

"Any success?"

"Not really. Although for some reason I keep coming back to the conversation in the car about Trevor and the racetrack." She shook her head. "I know Trevor wasn't gambling, though, so it's not that he owed people money. Clay and Lance have already determined that. I thought maybe there was some detail in the purchase agreement that I'd missed, but I can't see anything out of the ordinary."

Aaron sat on the stool next to her. "Where's the horse?"

She ran her palms down her jeans. Being around him always seemed to make her hands sweat and her pulse kick it up a notch. "He's boarded at a barn in Knoxville where the monthly fee is drafted from an account set up especially for that. The jockey, Brian Cartee, goes by the stable and rides the horse on a regular basis and then races him during the season. Any money generated is automatically deposited back into the same account.

Brian's crazy about that horse and spends as much time as possible with him. It's a wonderful arrangement." She shook her head. "Trevor was like a father to Brian. Brian was devastated when Trevor was killed in the accident."

"What happens to the horse if something happens to you?"

She frowned. "You think this is about the horse, too?"

"I don't know. How much is he worth?"

She stared at him, her brain whirring. "A lot," she whispered. "The last time Trevor checked he said Thunderbolt was valued at a quarter of a million."

Aaron's eyes widened. "That is a lot."

She pressed her thumb and forefinger against her eyes as she thought. Then she looked up. "Yes, it is a pretty good chunk of change, isn't it? So it could be someone after the money that Thunderbolt would bring. Why not just steal the horse?"

"Have you ever tried to sell a black market horse?"

She wrinkled her nose and frowned. "Of course not."

"Thunderbolt's a well-known horse in the racing arena. He'd be recognized as soon as he got to the tracks."

She pondered that. "True."

"So who gets control of the horse if something happens to you?" he asked again.

"He goes to Sophia."

"And Sophia goes to…"

"…Nina and Gregory," she said. "It keeps coming back to them, doesn't it?"

"I'm afraid so."

She shook her head. "I don't believe it. They don't need the money. Gregory makes a very comfortable living as an attorney, and Nina can't keep up with all of the interior design requests she gets. And besides, Nina is crazy about Sophia. She'd never take a chance on her being hurt."

"Well, the plan was to hurt you, not Sophia, right?"

"That's what it looks like, yes, but still…" Her frown deepened. "You know, something else just occurred to me."

"What?"

"When the men first showed up at the ranch, one of them, Pete, had Sophia by her hair and was pointing his gun at her. When I started to go toward him, he lifted the gun and aimed it at me." She shuddered. "I could see it in his eyes. He was going to shoot me right there in front of my child. I dove and he pulled the trigger. Then the other man came out of the house, the one they called Cody. He yelled at Pete to stop shooting. At first I thought he was there to rescue us, but he wasn't, of course. But he said they couldn't kill me. Not yet."

"So they need you for something."

"I guess."

"So shooting at us and running us off the road weren't attempts to kill you, but to *get* you?"

She shrugged. "It's the only thing I can really come up with."

"Now I'm confused. If they simply manage to kill you, everything goes to Sophia and Sophia goes to your sister-in-law and her husband."

"Along with control of any assets that I have."

"You didn't leave anything for your parents or your brother?"

"No," she snapped. "Why would I?"

"There's a lot of bitterness in those words," he noted quietly.

She drew in a deep breath and stood. Paced into the living area that connected to the kitchen. The open floor plan would allow Aaron to keep his gaze on her. She could feel it boring into her back. She stopped at the mantel that held two pictures. One of her and Sophia, and one of her and Trevor and Sophia as a newborn.

She got a grip on her emotions. "I'm sorry, I didn't mean to sound bitter. I had a very trying childhood. I've made peace with it. Mostly. But I don't want to talk about that right now." She waved a hand in dismissal of the subject. "Trevor and I talked and he set everything up that way anyway. I didn't argue with him." She paused. "Although I will say that if I knew where my brother was, I'd include him in my will."

"Well, maybe Clay or Lance needs to pay a visit to Nina and Gregory."

She rubbed her eyes. "I don't know. Maybe."

His phone rang, and he snagged it from the clip on the side of his jeans. "Excuse me. It's Clay."

"Sure."

"Hello?" She watched him while he listened. He had faint lines at the corners of his eyes, probably from squinting into the sun. His skin was tanned even in November and his firm jaw spoke of strength, not just physical, but an indication of his character. Something she'd already seen in action. And then his full lips flattened and his cheeks whitened beneath the tan. "Okay. Thanks for letting me know. I'll see you when you get here." He hung up and stared at the wall without blinking.

"Aaron?"

"He's dead."

She blinked. "Who?"

"Pete. The guy I shot."

Chapter 10

Zoe let out a low gasp. Aaron slid off the stool and made his way over to the couch where he dropped onto the cushion and let his hands dangle between his knees. His chin rested on his chest and he stared at the floor. Zoe came to sit beside him. "I thought he was going to be okay."

"So did I." He rubbed his eyes. "There'll be an autopsy, of course."

"Did he ever wake up?" she asked.

"No." Her shoulders slumped, and he wrapped an arm around her and drew her to him. At first she resisted then she let him. He ignored the warning his brain sent his heart. He'd known her a very short time, but already he was finding ways to weave her and her child into his life, keenly aware of the possibility that he might be setting himself up for a hard and painful fall. He swallowed as another fact hit him. "I killed a man."

She looked up. "Oh, Aaron, I'm so sorry."

He shook his head. "It's sad. I'm sad, but I couldn't let him hurt Lance."

"Of course you couldn't. If you hadn't shot Pete, Lance would be dead."

"I know. I realize that of course, but it's still…" He rubbed a hand down his cheek and knew she was right. It wasn't that. He just didn't have the words to explain the feeling. And he knew that if he could go back in time to the very moment he pulled the trigger, he'd have to do it again. Pete hadn't given him a choice.

Her arms slid around his neck, and she laid her head on his chest. His breath caught and he closed his eyes, wishing things were very different. He placed a finger under her chin and lifted it until her lips were a fraction of an inch from his. And then he kissed her. A slow tender exploration that didn't last nearly as long as he wanted. She didn't resist, but he could feel her hesitation. When he lifted his head, she opened her eyes and looked into his. "Is this wise?" she whispered.

"Probably not." Actually, it was definitely not. "But I won't apologize. The more time we spend together, the more I feel…"

"I know, I feel the same, but—" she looked away then back "—I'm not staying in Wrangler's Corner forever, Aaron," she whispered. "Just until this is over." She shook her head. "And maybe not even until then. I have a life to get back to. A business. A family. Of sorts. They're my in-laws, but they've been good to me." She gave a soft grunt. "Better than my blood family."

"Yeah. I know." He'd managed to convince her to stay this long, but every time he knocked on her door, he half expected to find her gone. The uncertainty was playing havoc with his emotions, and he knew he'd have to make a decision soon about keeping his heart out of the equation. He ignored the little voice that mocked him, insisting it was too late. He cleared his throat. "Clay's on his way over. He said he wanted to talk to you about the phone calls traced back to Pete's phone. He should be here any minute."

She sniffed and nodded. "All right."

"How's Sophia handling everything?"

"She's still doing okay. She sleeps in my bed these days, and I let her. If I thought it would be best for her, I'd keep her shackled to my side, but I don't want her living in fear. I have to admit, though, letting her go to school is one of the hardest things I do."

"She likes school."

"Yes. She's made some sweet friends. And she really likes it here in Wrangler's Corner—minus the people shooting at us and chasing us."

The knock on the door brought Joy from the study, her hand on her weapon. Again, she relaxed after looking out the window. "It's Clay." She opened the door and let him in. He stepped into the foyer and pulled his gloves off. A light dusting of snow fluttered to the floor.

"It's snowing again," Clay said.

"You're kidding," Aaron deadpanned.

Clay rolled his eyes and then frowned. "How are you holding up?"

Aaron sobered. "I'm processing."

Clay's attention turned to Zoe. "I can't stay long. I

need to get back to Sabrina, but wanted to stop by and check on you as well as let you know that I got some information."

"You could have called."

Clay shrugged. "Yeah, I could have."

"You're restless and it feels good to have something to do other than pace?"

Clay grimaced. "You always could see beneath the surface."

Aaron slapped his brother on the shoulder. "What have you got?" Aaron asked.

"First, as you know, the car we got the partial plate on came back stolen from just outside of Knoxville and hasn't been recovered yet. We've got a BOLO on it so hopefully one of our deputies will spot it."

"You said 'first.'"

"We also got some information from the phone Pete used."

Zoe leaned forward. "What kind of information?"

"The phone itself was a burner, not traceable as to who purchased it, et cetera, however, we checked all the numbers, incoming and outgoing. He'd erased almost all of the numbers, but one was interesting."

"Who?" Zoe whispered. Aaron clasped her cold fingers in his warm ones.

Clay pursed his lips then blew out a low breath. "There was one call that came in about the time you were being held hostage by the three men on the Updike farm."

"From who?" Aaron demanded.

"The Bishop residence in Knoxville, Tennessee."

* * *

The room spun for a moment before Zoe drew in a deep breath and commanded herself not to pass out. "It can't be," she whispered. "I don't believe it. Nina's always been a little overbearing and selfish, but there's no way she or Gregory would send killers after me. They have no reason to."

"Knoxville is a good two-hour drive from here," Clay said. "I'm going to send Lance and Parker to question them."

"We can't just call them?"

He shook his head and Zoe heard his phone buzz. "I want the element of surprise, and I want their reactions carefully noted." He glanced at his phone and his eyes widened. "That was a text from Mom. I've got to get to the hospital. Sabrina's in labor."

Zoe gasped. "Then get out of here. You have to go."

"I am. My mother and Sabrina's grandmother are with her. I think Seth and Tonya are arriving in a couple of hours so it's going to be a bit crazy." His eyes narrowed and he looked at Zoe. "But don't think I'm lowering my guard when it comes to your and Sophia's safety. Joy checked in just a few minutes ago and said all was well."

"Good." Zoe nodded. "But you need to go. Give Sabrina my best. You're going to be a great dad."

Clay swallowed and paled slightly, but the joy in his eyes was unmistakable. "Well, I do have three children already," he mumbled. "It's not like I don't know what being a dad means." He looked at Zoe. "Sabrina and I adopted three."

Aaron cleared his throat. "This is his first birth,

though," he said to Zoe. He turned his gaze back to Clay. "I've never seen you this spooked."

Clay snorted. "I'm not spooked." He blinked against a suspicious moisture Zoe thought she saw in his eyes, but decided she must have been mistaken when he shot his brother a hard look. "I just don't want anything to happen to them."

Aaron softened and pushed all kidding aside. "They'll be fine. You've been waiting for this for a long time."

"Yeah. Lance is in charge while I'm with Sabrina. If you need anything get in touch with him. He knows how to get a hold of me if he needs me." The two brothers hugged, and then Clay slipped out the door.

Aaron shut it behind him.

"He's terrified," Zoe mused.

"Yes, he is. Not of being a dad or taking care of a baby, but more that something could go wrong with the birth. I don't know how he would survive that." Aaron drew in a deep breath and shoved his hands into his pockets.

"Are you all right?"

"Like I told Clay, I'm still processing the fact that Pete died, but in the end, I'll be okay. He made his choices and I had to make mine."

She moved back into the living area, and he followed. "Aren't you going to the hospital?" she asked.

"Babies take a while to get here. I'm not in a huge hurry." She nodded and he sat on the couch and leaned his head back. Staring at the ceiling for a moment, he said nothing. She let him have his quiet moment. Finally he looked at her and asked, "Are you okay? That was some pretty shocking news Clay just delivered."

She rubbed her temple. "Am I okay? No, not really. I don't understand why Nina or Gregory would have anything to do with this." She pursed her lips. "So what's the next step? What do we do?"

"Like Clay said, Lance and Parker will pay them a visit along with someone from the local police force. He may subpoena phone records, financial statements..." He shrugged. "That sort of thing."

"You sure know a lot about investigations. Did you get that from listening to Clay?"

"Clay and Stephen."

"Where is Stephen now? I haven't heard anything about him recently."

He realized she didn't know about his brother Stephen's death. "Amber didn't tell you?"

"Tell me what?"

"Before Clay took over, Stephen was the sheriff here in Wrangler's Corner. He was killed when he got too close to a drug ring."

She paled. "No, she didn't tell me. We haven't really spoken much. Just an email exchange here and there. I'm so sorry to hear that."

He nodded. "His death hit us all hard. Clay came home from Nashville where he'd been working as a detective. He solved Stephen's murder, and while we're glad for the closure, we still miss him."

"I'm sure." She lifted her chin. "I want to go with them."

"What?"

"To Knoxville. If Lance goes to confront my sister-in-law and brother-in-law, I want to go."

He frowned. "I don't think that's a very good idea."

"Maybe not, but I want to see their faces and hear their words for myself."

He gave a slow nod then checked his phone and rose. "I'll tell Clay. I guess I need to get going. I don't want to miss the birth of my nephew or niece."

"Let me know how it goes."

"Of course." He paused. "Do you want to come?"

"I'd better not. I don't want to take a chance that whoever is after me will follow us to the hospital or something. You go. Celebrate this time with your family."

He lifted a hand to cup her cheek. When she didn't pull away he leaned over to place a light kiss on her lips. She blinked up at him. "At some point we're going to talk about what's going on between us, right?" he asked.

She gave a little sigh. "There's definitely something there, isn't there?"

"Definitely."

"When this is all over, we'll talk." She frowned. "Assuming I'm still alive."

He scowled. "You'll still be alive. If I have anything to say about it, you'll still be alive." He kissed her again. This time a little longer, and now she felt the hint of desperation he couldn't quite hide.

When he lifted his head, her eyes glittered with unshed tears. "I hope you're right, Aaron. I really hope you're right."

She shut the door behind him and pressed cold fingers to her warm lips. "What are you doing, Zoe?" she whispered. "Don't put your heart on the line, it'll just get broken. Not only that, you'll break his, too."

"What?"

Zoe spun to find Joy in the doorway between the

kitchen and the foyer. Zoe gave a low laugh. "Nothing. Just talking to myself."

"Anything you want to share?"

"No. It's all right." Or it would be if she could follow her own advice and keep Aaron at arm's length. She had to.

She glanced at the clock. She had a couple of hours before Ginny would bring Sophia home. "I'm going to make a few phone calls."

"Sure thing. I'm just going to walk the perimeter of the house, take a look around."

"All right."

Joy slipped out the front door, and Zoe returned to the computer. Her cell phone lay on the table next to the mouse. She picked it up and scrolled through her list of contacts. When she came to Nina Bishop, she stopped. And pressed the button. It rang once. Twice.

Zoe hung up.

Clay had said he wanted the element of surprise, and she couldn't interfere. She rubbed her eyes. That had been dumb. She shouldn't have pressed the button.

Thankfully, Nina wouldn't recognize the number. Zoe had bought a disposable phone at the first stop on her way out of town. But still…

She set the phone back on the table. She and her sister-in-law had never been best friends, but they'd always gotten along and chatted amicably when they'd been together for holidays or birthdays. Did Nina have it in her to be a part of a plan to kill her? Zoe couldn't fathom it but couldn't deny it sure looked like it.

Restless, she stood and paced to the window. She stood to the side as she'd been taught and looked out.

From her angle, she could see Sabrina's grandmother's bed-and-breakfast. A large white house that had been built in the late eighteen hundreds. It looked quiet. Deserted. The whole street was almost eerily vacant. She shuddered and tried to put a lid on her overly active imagination. Then again, who could blame her for seeing the possibility of danger at every turn?

With a low growl of frustration, she grabbed her phone and powered up her e-reader application. She scrolled through the novels. "No mysteries, thank you. I need a comedy."

She settled on one, curled up on the couch and began to read until her eyes grew heavy. The slamming door jerked her from the light doze she'd slipped into.

"Mom?"

"In here, Sophia."

Sophia ran into the den and dropped her backpack on the floor near the recliner then climbed in Zoe's lap. Zoe buried her nose in her child's hair then kissed her cheek. "How was your day?"

"It was good. Very exciting."

"Really?" Zoe shot a look at Joy who hovered in the doorway. Joy raised her brows and gave a slight smile. Zoe's pulse slowed slightly.

"Yes," Sophia enthused. "Gordon brought a frog to school. It was part of his science project, but then Leon opened the cage and the frog jumped out. All the other girls screamed, but I helped catch it." She shot Zoe a brilliant smile. "And then Gordon hugged me and said I was awesome for a girl."

Zoe released a slow breath and sent up a silent prayer of thanks. Finally, her child was acting like a child, not the solemn miniature adult she'd become ever since the *first* kidnapping attempt. "You are awesome. Period." Her phone buzzed, and she snagged it. Aaron. To Sophia, she said, "Why don't you go get your snack out of the refrigerator? It's time for you to eat a little something." Sophia nodded and skipped into the kitchen. Zoe raised the phone to her ear. "Hello?"

"Hi, Zoe." Aaron's voice rumbled sweetly in her ear. "Just thought I'd let you know that baby girl Starke is here. When she decided it was time to enter the world, she did it fast, kicking and screaming. Nothing wrong with that kid's lungs, that's for sure."

"Oh, that's so great! And everyone is doing well?"

"Just perfect."

She smiled at the excitement in his voice. He'd be a great uncle. "What's baby girl's first name?"

"They haven't decided yet. Apparently that's been up for discussion for a few weeks." He cleared his throat. "Lance came by, and he and Parker are going to Knoxville to talk to your sister-in-law tomorrow."

"Tell them I want to go."

"I really think you need to stay here under protection with Sophia and Ginny and Joy."

She considered his words. She was touched that he was so concerned. The deep caring in his voice made her heart flutter and anxiety bit her. She was going to break his heart if she wasn't careful. Or vice versa.

But he might be right. If her sister-in-law and her husband were behind the attempts on her life, did she really want to face them? But what if they weren't responsible? What if she left Sophia and something happened? "All right, I'll stay here."

"Good. I think that's a wise decision."

She heard him gasp.

"What is it?" she asked.

"My sister, Amber, just walked in."

"Oh! Tell her I said hello."

"Okay, I'll talk to you later." She hung up and leaned her head against the wall and tried to calm her racing heart. She was thrilled for Clay and Sabrina and the Starke family. A baby was a beautiful thing. Sophia came back into the den with her peanut-butter sandwich and settled herself on the couch beside Zoe. Zoe ran a hand over her child's hair and Sophia snuggled into her side. Yes, a baby was a beautiful thing. And so was her nine-year-old daughter that someone wanted to kidnap. Her throat tightened. And the prayer slipped out. *Please, God, keep us safe.*

Chapter 11

Aaron clapped Clay on the back. "Congratulations, big brother."

"Thanks. I have to say that was the most amazing thing ever. Well, second to Sabrina agreeing to marry me. Actually, they're neck and neck."

Aaron grinned then moved aside to let his sister take her turn at hugging Clay and admiring their new niece. When she stepped back, he caught her hand. "You've missed too many family milestones. Glad you could make it for this one."

Her mouth smiled, but her eyes remained shuttered. "I am, too, Aaron. I don't miss them because I want to."

He narrowed his eyes. "What's going on with your job?"

She blinked. "What do you mean?"

He shook his head. "Are you really a travel writer?"

"Of course."

The lack of expression made him wonder, but he didn't have time to get into it with her.

Lance waved Aaron over, and he gave his sister one last hug just in case she took off without saying good-bye as she'd been known to do.

He joined Lance who led him outside of the room. "What is it?"

"Just wanted to let you know we did a little digging into Zoe's in-laws and biological family."

"What did you find?"

Lance referred to his phone. "When we dug into the Bishops, Zoe's in-laws, red flags started waving."

"What'd you find?"

"You know how Zoe said they weren't hurting for money? That they had no reason to harm her or try to get Sophia?"

"Yes."

"Turns out that's not quite true."

Aaron stiffened. "What do you mean?"

"Seems they've fallen on rough times financially."

"Meaning what exactly?"

"They're not in bankruptcy or anything, but they're in debt and obviously struggling. The creditors are going to start lining up pretty soon."

Aaron blew out a low breath. "So that gives them some motive for wanting to get their hands on the horse."

"That's the way I see it. They know Zoe isn't worth much. The only real money she has is tied up in that horse."

"So if they get rid of her, they get Sophia and the

horse. They sell the horse for a quarter million and keep the money. That would pay quite a few bills."

Lance rubbed the back of his head. "That's what I'm thinking. We're still investigating, but it's not looking good for the Bishops."

"What about her biological family? Were you able to track them down?" Aaron glanced through the open door at his parents. There were completely enamored with the baby girl as were Clay and a beaming Sabrina. He wanted to be in the midst of them, but he just couldn't let this go. He needed to help Zoe figure this out.

Lance nodded. "There could be some motive there, but their contact with each other has been so sporadic over the years, it's hard to tell. Here's what I do know. Her dad is a real winner. He was an accountant for a large firm in Nashville. He was caught embezzling from the company funds and was arrested when Zoe was thirteen years old. He spent three years in prison. When he got out, he came home to divorce papers, but didn't actually move out until about a year after that."

"Nowhere to go?"

"Or didn't want to go and refused to."

"What about Zoe's mother? She let him stay there?"

"Not sure he gave her a choice. The divorce wasn't final for a long time so he may have just refused to sign the papers. I could track down the lawyer and find out if we need to. It's weird. Zoe disappeared without a trace for about a year shortly after he got out and went home, then resurfaced to get her GED. She went on to college and excelled. She got her degree in zoology and worked in a local zoo for a while before she married her husband. After that, she was a stay-at-home mom and now a widow."

Aaron sucked in a deep breath then let it out slowly. "A widow on the run from a killer."

"Yes."

"And you don't know where she was for that year?"

"Nothing came up on the original search, but there are other ways to find out stuff like that. It may take me a while, but I can do it."

"What about her brother?"

"His name is Tobias Potter," Clay said. "He fell off the grid around the age of twenty-one, and there's nothing I can find on him."

"Does he have a record?"

"Nope."

Aaron rubbed a hand across his chin as he processed the information. "Weird that both of them disappeared."

Clay nodded. "Are you going to ask her about it?"

"Yes."

"Want me to look into it?" Amber asked.

Aaron jumped. "Still sneaky, aren't you, sis?"

She lifted a brow, innocence radiating from her. "What do you mean?"

"You know what I mean. But what do *you* mean that you could look into it?"

She shrugged. "I do a lot of travel articles, you know that. I also do some investigative pieces every once in a while. As a result I've got contacts in…um…some influential places. I can make a few calls."

"You were roommates. Why would you have to make some calls?"

Amber flushed. "Yes, we were roommates, but we weren't superclose friends." She held up a hand. "And before you start casting blame on me, Zoe was very tightfisted with her past." She shrugged. "And I didn't push it. We talked mostly about things in the present, and she didn't share much about her past at all. Now. Do you want me to make the calls or not?"

Aaron cocked his head, fighting to keep his skepticism from showing. "What kind of calls?"

"Productive ones. Yes or no?"

"Yes," Aaron said, still watching her eyes. They gave nothing away.

She nodded and walked away.

Aaron looked back at Lance. "Do you ever get the feeling there's more to her than meets the eye?"

"What do you mean?"

Aaron shook his head "Some things just don't add up with her." He grimaced. He didn't have time to dwell on his quirky sister right now. "Whatever. Maybe she can come up with something. I'm going to head back to the office then I hope to swing by Zoe's before going home."

"Ginny and Joy are there. Ginny has to leave, but Joy will be there all night."

"Good." Aaron waved at his mother who had the baby snuggled up against her. "And let me know if they come up with a name, will you?"

"Of course."

Aaron sent a text to Zoe letting her know his plans and checking with her. She responded: Everything is quiet here. Plan to stay for dinner with us if you like. See you soon.

* * *

While Sophia watched a video in the den, Zoe put the finishing touches on the dinner. Aaron would arrive at any moment and her heart wouldn't stop fluttering like a butterfly trapped in her chest. On the one hand, she'd almost forgotten how wonderful it felt to anticipate the attention of a man, an admirer. On the other hand, she really had to quit thinking about him as a potential boyfriend. He'd made his interest clear, but her life was too crazy to commit to anything right now, even dating. And Aaron deserved more than a "maybe."

Still…he was coming to her house, and she was excited to see him. Every minute they spent together drew them closer, and she was selfish enough to admit she didn't want to give that up.

She checked in on Sophia who looked up from the television. "Is Doctor Aaron going to be here soon?"

"Soon."

Sophia smiled, and her eyes twinkled their eagerness to see her friend. Zoe went back to the kitchen. Aaron had completely captured her child's heart, and she wasn't far behind. She gulped and stirred the mashed potatoes, checked the rolls and opened the oven to poke the chicken. Almost ready. And nothing left to do with her hands. She clasped them in front of her and tried to imagine a life without fear, without danger—without Aaron. The last part hurt, and she knew she was in trouble. Not just the physical kind, but the emotional kind. So what was she going to do?

"Something smells good in here."

She turned to find Ginny in the doorway. "Thanks. I made enough for you and Joy, too."

Ginny's eyes widened. "Really?"

"Really."

"Wow, that's so nice of you, but Joy is going to stay the night and I'm going to be back first thing in the morning. Do you think I could get a to-go plate?"

Zoe laughed. "Of course."

"Could I ask you a question?"

Zoe tilted her head. "Of course."

"You've shared a little about your family with me and I understand that you're estranged, but is there no one that you could have turned to during this time? To help protect you, I mean? No other friends?"

Zoe sighed and stirred the beans—that didn't need stirring—while she tried to decide how she wanted to answer that. "No, not really. Like I've explained, my family isn't close. And quite frankly, I haven't wanted to take a chance on putting anyone else in danger."

"What about your in-laws? Nina and Gregory or your father-in-law?"

Zoe stared at the deputy. Ginny gave a little laugh. "Sorry, but Sophia's quite a talker. I feel like I know each member of the Collier and Bishop families very well."

Zoe blew out a little breath and laughed as she pulled a paper plate and some tin foil from the pantry. "Sophia is definitely a talker." She rubbed her nose and considered her words. "I suppose I could have asked my father-in-law," she finally said. "He's a hard man to get to know, but I like him. He's always been very generous to me. Even after Trevor died." She shrugged and spooned the food onto the plate then covered it with the foil. "And

I know he loves Sophia but like I said, I didn't feel like I could put him and the others in danger, you know?"

"So he offered to help?"

"Yes. And truthfully, maybe I should have accepted it, but I just didn't want anyone to know where we were until I could figure out what to do. If we'd stayed with him or even my sister-in-law and her husband, whoever was after Sophia would still know where she was. I didn't want that."

"Why don't you call him and ask him to help you now?"

Zoe frowned. "For the same reasons. I don't want to bring this trouble, this danger, into their lives. I've thought about it many times, but am trying to be patient and let Clay and Lance and all of you do your job." She rubbed her forehead. "Or maybe I should just go to him. It sure would make things easier on you guys, wouldn't it?"

"Maybe. It sounds like he would do anything to protect you."

"He would."

Ginny shrugged. "So why not call him?"

Zoe stared out the window. "No. Not yet. I'm not ready to do that yet."

"I understand." Ginny smiled. "Thanks for letting me be nosey."

"Any time." Zoe handed Ginny the plate, and the deputy grinned.

"Thanks," Ginny said. "I'll see you in the morning."

"I'll be here."

Joy stuck her head in the kitchen. "I think there's

someone snooping around outside. I'm going to take a look. Ginny, you stay with her, all right?"

And there it was. The reminder that not all was well in her world. Zoe stiffened and watched Ginny instantly go from wide-eyed hungry woman to a trained professional. Ginny practically threw the plate onto the counter then went after her coworker.

"Wait!" Zoe called and made it into the foyer in time to find Joy halfway out the door and Ginny standing with her hand on her weapon. "Aaron's on his way over. He should be here any minute." She pulled her phone from her pocket. "I'll try to reach him and let him know what's going on, but just watch for him."

"I'll be careful. Lock the door behind me," Joy said. And then she was gone, shutting the door behind her. Zoe dialed Aaron's number with one hand and locked the door with her other. She felt her nerves rise to the surface of her skin. His phone rang four times then went to voice mail. "Aaron, if you get this, be careful around my house. Someone was outside, and Joy is looking for him." She hung up and dialed again.

"Mom?"

She turned, phone pressed to her ear, to see Sophia watching them, a frown on her face and worry drawing her brows together. "Yes?"

"What's wrong?"

"Nothing I hope." Again the call went to voice mail.

Sophia scampered over to her, and Zoe drew the child to her side. Ginny stood near the edge of the window and peered out, careful to stay out of the line of fire. Zoe hit the lights and sent the room into darkness. Light from the kitchen filtered through the foyer and into the den.

She moved and kept Sophia right beside her. A thud sounded behind her coming from the kitchen. She whirled and Sophia gasped, but stayed right with her. Ginny stood there, the moonlight filtering through the blinds with enough light for Zoe to see her finger to her lips. In her other hand, she held her weapon.

Zoe pressed her lips together.

A knock on the door startled them all. "Aaron," she breathed. Where was Joy? The tension curling in her belly formed into a hard ball. Ginny moved to the door.

"Zoe?" Aaron called. "What's going on? Are you all right?"

Ginny opened the door and pulled him inside and shut and relocked the door. "Someone's outside. Did you see Joy?"

His frown deepened. "No."

Her lips tightened and Zoe's fear level doubled. "She could be hurt," Zoe said. "I tried to call you but you didn't answer."

He checked his phone and grimaced. "It's on silent." He flipped the button. "Want me to check on Joy?"

Ginny paced from the window to the door. "She could have caught the guy," Ginny said. She checked her radio then looked at Aaron. "Joy, come in, are you there?" Zoe noted that she didn't use the police lingo. The two women were friends, coworkers. And Ginny was worried. Zoe's fear surged and she sent up a silent prayer. She had to.

"Joy didn't call for backup," Ginny said, hesitating. She was clearly torn between staying with Zoe and Sophia and going outside to find her fellow officer. "I'm calling for backup," she said, dialing her phone. Zoe thought she heard Lance's voice saying he was on the way.

"Go find her," Zoe said.

"Go," Aaron echoed. "I'll stay here with Zoe and Sophia."

"I can't," Ginny whispered. "I can't leave you." She paced to the door then the window. "The floodlights are on. Someone tripped them."

"I'll check the back of the house," Aaron said. He disappeared through the foyer into the main area, bypassed the kitchen and went to the back door off the living room. Zoe's gaze darted between Aaron and Ginny.

She moved a few steps into the den and waited while he peered out. She heard his gasp. "What is it?"

"Joy. She's on the ground and she's not moving." He glanced back. "Stay here."

"Aaron, no!" Ginny and Zoe said in unison.

But they were speaking to his back.

Aaron stepped onto the porch. He back itched like someone had painted a big target on it, but he assured himself that the person was after Zoe and Sophia, not him. The pep talk didn't help, but it didn't stop him, either. It *did* help to hear the sirens approaching. He knelt beside the still deputy and felt for a pulse. It pounded beneath his fingers and he drew in a breath of relief.

"Is she all right?" Zoe called from the porch.

"She's alive. Get back inside." His fingers ran over the back of her head and encountered a large lump. He didn't want to take a chance on moving her in case she had a neck injury.

He heard a rustle to his left and spun to see a shadow

move into the few trees at the edge of the property. "Hey! Tell Ginny he's out here!"

Aaron bolted after the now fleeing figure. No way was he letting this guy get away. He had a chance to end this now. He heard Ginny and Zoe call his name, but the adrenaline rushing through him lent speed to his feet and heightened his senses. His blood pounded in his veins. He heard the moment the person moved from the lawn onto the pavement. With Zoe's house right in the center of town, there were only a few sporadic trees and he was now past them, his eyes on the figure he refused to lose. The figure was smaller than Aaron, but quick as lightning. He noted the stares of the people he passed, but ignored them. He just prayed the guy didn't pull his weapon and start shooting.

He heard running feet behind him and figured it was Ginny. Either backup had arrived or she felt like she could leave Zoe and Sophia alone long enough to help in the chase. Or the person he was after had brought help. No time to rethink his decision to go after the man.

The fleeing man whipped around into the open and then disappeared around the side of the small café. People on the street turned to stare, but Aaron sped past them. He figured the man was heading for the road that ran behind the next strip of stores. He gritted his teeth, put on a burst of speed and closed the gap.

His fingers grazed the man's collar, then he hooked a finger on the inside. Joy's attacker went down, and Aaron tumbled after him. They both hit hard and the air left Aaron's lungs with a whoosh. Slamming into the asphalt at full speed *hurt*.

Stunned, Aaron lay there for a brief second that he

couldn't afford. Finally, with a pained grunt, he heaved himself to his feet and moved toward the man who'd caused them all so much trouble. The attacker saw him coming and pushed himself to his knees. Aaron moved faster and shoved him back to the cement then reached over to grab his mask.

The man rolled to his back, and his fist shot out to catch Aaron in the stomach. Aaron lost the rest of his breath when he went down to his knees, but the mask came off. Their eyes met.

"Freeze! Police!" Ginny's voice rang out.

A gun appeared in the man's hand, pulled from somewhere behind his back. He shoved it at Aaron who threw himself to the side. A shot rang out. The gawkers on the street screamed and dove for cover. The man backed away then turned and ran. Ginny didn't return fire, and Aaron saw why. An elderly couple stood frozen with fear right in the line of fire watching the fleeing criminal. Aaron rolled to his feet, ignoring his aches and pains and stumbled after the man. Just in time to see him jump into a black sedan and roar away.

Zoe's nerves had stretched to the breaking point by the time Aaron came limping up the back porch. Ginny walked behind him throwing glances over her shoulder every few seconds. Paramedics were lifting Joy onto the stretcher. Sophia hovered at Zoe's side. "Stay here, honey," Zoe told her.

"But Mom—"

"Stay here. You'll be able to see me. Don't move."

Zoe ran down to him and met him halfway across the back lawn. "Are you all right?"

"Yes. I'm fine. You shouldn't have come out of the house. It's possible he could circle back."

She grabbed his arm and he winced. "He's gone for now. And you're not fine, you're hurt."

"Just bruised. I landed pretty hard when I tried to recreate my days of Friday night football."

Zoe trotted along beside him. "I heard a gunshot."

"Yes, but he missed."

She led him up the steps and into the house. Sophia stood just inside the door where Zoe left her. Her tight face of concern met them. "Are you okay, Doctor Aaron?"

"I'll be just fine, sweetie."

Sophia didn't look convinced. "Did you get shot?"

"No, sweetheart, I fell."

Zoe led him to the kitchen table and he sank into the nearest chair. She pulled another chair around for him to prop his leg on. "He got away, didn't he?" she asked.

"Unfortunately," Aaron said. "Is Joy going to be okay?"

"Yes, Ginny waited for the paramedics to check her then took off after you. He must have caught her by surprise and hit her pretty hard with something."

"Probably the gun he had with him," Aaron murmured.

Zoe shuddered. "I'm so sorry about all of this."

"It's what they do, Zoe," Aaron murmured. "No apology necessary."

"But it's not what you do. You shouldn't be chasing intruders across my backyard."

He reached out and cupped her cheek. "It's okay, Zoe. I want to be here for you. We all do."

She knew that, but she still didn't want them to be in danger because of her. Sophia hovered. "Will you get Doctor Aaron a glass of water, hon?"

Sophia jumped into action. She poured him a glass of water and handed it to him. He chugged it. "Thanks, Sophia."

"You want another one?"

"Sure."

Once he had it refilled, Zoe drew Sophia next to her side. "Tell me everything." She hated for Sophia to have to hear it, but the child needed to understand the danger involved.

"Actually," Lance said, coming into the kitchen from the living area, "tell *us* everything." Deputy Walter Haywood followed, his notebook out, pen ready. Once Aaron finished relaying the events to Walter and Lance's satisfaction, he rubbed his eyes. Zoe could see his weariness wearing on him. Lance looked tired, as well. "You got a pretty good look at this guy?" Lance asked.

"Yeah, I managed to get his mask off and could describe him or pick him out of a lineup. Ginny may have seen him, too."

Lance nodded. "Come down to the station and work with Edie as soon as you can."

"Edie?" Zoe asked.

"Edie Travers," Walter said. "She's a local artist who's trained as a sketch artist. She mostly works with the Nashville Police Department, but offers her services to Wrangler's Corner when it's needed. Which, thankfully, isn't often."

"I can do that," Aaron said. "Tell her to call me with a time."

"Good. I'll see if she can meet with you first thing in the morning," Walter said.

Aaron nodded. "Fine."

"And while you're doing that," Lance said, "Parker and I are going to head to Knoxville to see if we can talk to the Bishop family." He looked at Zoe. "Walter will be watching you while Ginny stays with Sophia."

"Okay," Zoe said. "Let us know what you find out?"

"Of course."

"How is Joy? Have you heard anything? Is she going to be all right?" Zoe asked.

"Ginny's with her." He glanced at his phone. "She said she would text me when she knew something, but before they took off to the hospital, the paramedic said he thought she'd just had a hard knock to the head. A possible concussion, but he seemed to think she should be just fine."

Relief swept over her. "I hope so."

"All right, you guys get to your dinner, and I'll be in touch. Parker's going to be here for a while then I'll take over around one in the morning. That way we can both get some rest before we have to leave for Knoxville."

Lance left, and Zoe walked into the kitchen to pull the chicken from the oven. She grimaced and glanced up at Aaron who'd followed her. "It's a little over done, but it's edible."

"I'm sure it's amazing."

"If you'll tell Parker and Sophia it's ready, I'll get it on the table."

Aaron let his eyes linger on hers. She looked away to focus on the food. He sighed and walked to the den where Sophia played a game on the laptop and Parker rotated between the windows, pushing the curtains aside to peer out. "You guys ready to eat?"

Sophia popped up from the chair. "I am. I'm starving."

Aaron held out a hand and she grasped his fingers. The walls around his heart cracked even further and he knew he was in trouble. He'd always loved children and animals, took joy in and wanted to protect their innocence, unconditional love and loyalty. Probably why he'd fallen so hard for the single mother who'd run off with her ex-husband. And now he was doing it again. He grunted at his foolishness. He could fight it. Probably should. Over the past few days, this duo had done serious damage to the walls he'd erected around his heart.

They walked into the kitchen, and Sophia pulled him over to the chair next to hers. He smiled and settled himself at the table. Parker looked uneasy. "I'll just nibble while I keep tabs on the windows. I don't want to let my guard down."

Zoe nodded. "Of course. Feel free to fix a plate and take it into the den."

Parker did and when he vanished into the next room, Aaron looked at Zoe on one side of him and Sophia on the other. He swallowed hard. They could be a family. A small unit doing life together. He found he wasn't opposed to the idea and that set his self-protective alarm bells clanging. Hadn't he just been thinking he needed to repair the damage to the walls he'd put up?

She wasn't going to be here long. She was leaving and she was taking Sophia with her. Not necessarily because of another man, but the end result would be the same. He'd be alone with his shattered heart once again.

"Aaron?"

He blinked. "Oh, sorry, just thinking."

"About?"

He cleared his throat. "Ah…" His phone rang, rescuing him from having to come up with an answer. He pulled the phone from the clip. "Excuse me, it's Lance. I need to take it."

"Of course," Zoe said.

"Hello?"

"Aaron, Edie's in Knoxville for the day, but said she could fit you in after we talk to the Bishops. How do you feel about riding with us in the morning?"

He mentally ran through the list of things he needed to do in the morning. "That's fine. I'll let Nate know what's going on. If he's not planning to be there, I can shut the office for the day." He never closed except for the weekends and emergencies. He figured this qualified.

"Good. Be ready around eight. I'll pick you up."

"I'll be ready."

"Oh, and interestingly enough, Amber had some success in finding out where Zoe spent that year she went off grid."

"Really? Where?" He didn't look at her, afraid she'd pick up on the fact that she was the topic of conversation.

"She wouldn't say. Just said it wasn't anything illegal and if Zoe wanted us to know, she'd tell us."

Aaron rubbed his chin. "Huh. Okay then. Good to know."

"She said she ran into a dead end on Zoe's brother, though."

"Okay. Thanks." He hung up and saw Zoe and Sophia watching him. "I'll be riding to Knoxville in the morning with Lance and Parker." He explained the reason why.

She nodded. "I hope it helps catch this person."

"I do, too." He cleared his throat. "Would you like for me to say the blessing?" She frowned and he paused in the act of bowing his head. "What is it?"

Her frown slipped into a forced smile. "Nothing. Of course you can say the blessing."

"My mom's mad at God," Sophia whispered.

Zoe flinched. "Soph…"

Sophia shrugged. "Well, aren't you?"

Zoe's face reddened. "I'm not mad at God," she said. "I might be a bit frustrated with Him, but I'm not mad."

"You're not speaking to Him. I think that means mad."

At Zoe's ferocious frown, Sophia poked her lip out. Her gaze flicked to her mother, to Aaron then back to her mom. "Sorry," she muttered. "Was that 'crossing the line'?"

"By several feet."

Sophia ducked her head. "I'm sorry."

Aaron reached under the table and snagged the girl's fingers and squeezed. She looked up at him. At Zoe's sigh, Aaron said, "I think she'll forgive you."

Zoe gave a humorless chuckle. "All is forgiven. Now pray so we can eat." Her lips softened. "Maybe it's time I started saying grace again anyway. Even in the midst of all this craziness, there's quite a bit to be thankful for." Her eyes lingered on his and then slid to Sophia.

Aaron bowed his head and Sophia left her small hand in his. "Lord, we ask that you bless this food. We pray that you touch Joy with healing. Please protect Zoe and Sophia and those who are trying to catch the person after them. Thank you so much for the protection you've already placed around them. Amen."

"Amen," Sophia echoed.

Aaron thought he heard a whispered "Amen" from Zoe, as well.

He looked at the two females sitting on either side of him. He realized he wouldn't be building any walls around his heart. It was too late. He had fallen fast and hard. Now he added a silent prayer just between him and God. *Please don't let anything happen to them, and I'd really appreciate it if you'd convince Zoe to stay in Wrangler's Corner. But if for some reason this isn't to be, show me how to pick up the pieces and move on after they're gone.*

Chapter 12

Within the cover of the enclosed garage, Zoe zipped Sophia's coat then watched her get into the backseat of the police cruiser. Ginny sat at the wheel speaking into the phone. "Yes, that's fine. It's not a problem, I've got it covered. Bye." She hung up with a frown.

"Problem?" Zoe asked.

"No, not really. Just something concerning my sister. I'll deal with it later."

"Anything I can do to help?"

"No." She offered Zoe a confident smile. "Have a good day."

"I will. You, too."

Zoe shut the door, thought two seconds then opened it before Ginny could back the car out. Sophia looked up. "Did you forget something?"

"Come on back inside, hon. You're not going to school today." She just couldn't send her. She looked at Ginny. "I'm sorry. It's not safe. Especially not after last night. I just don't want to let her out of my sight."

"But I want to go," Sophia protested. "And I'm with Deputy Ginny. I'll be fine."

Still Zoe stood frozen with indecision raging.

"I understand your fear," Ginny said. "But really it might be more safe for her to be at school than here, though."

"What do you mean?"

"At the school, there's the school resource officer as well as a plainclothes officer at each entrance of the building. After what happened last night, Clay called in a few of his buddies from when he was with the Nashville Police Department. There are some plainclothes watching your house, as well."

"Oh." She drew in a deep breath. "Well, in that case…"

"She'll be fine, I promise."

Still Zoe hesitated. "Come on, Mom, I'm going to be late. Please?"

"All right," she said. "With all that security, I guess you're right."

"Yes!" Sophia pumped her fist in the air, and Zoe stepped back. Ginny gave a small salute and Zoe pressed the button to lift the garage door.

She watched them leave then pressed the button once more to lower the door. Back inside, she paced from window to window, peering out and wondering where those plainclothes officers were. Then again, if they were good at their job, she wouldn't be able to see them, right?

A knock on the door stiffened her spine. Deputy Haywood pulled his weapon and moved from the kitchen barstool to the door to look out. He relaxed a fraction and holstered his gun. "It's Sabrina's grandmother, Yvonne Mayfield, from across the street. She runs the bed-and-breakfast."

"Of course. Please, let her in."

Walter opened the door and the woman stepped inside. In her hands she held a basket covered with a red-and-white checkered cloth. "Hello."

"Hi there. I know we haven't been properly introduced, but Clay mentioned your troubles and I wanted to stop by and see if you needed anything. I'm Yvonne Mayfield, but you can just call me Granny May."

"Well, thank you, Granny May. I'm Zoe. Won't you come in and have a seat?"

"No, I've got to get back." She handed Zoe the basket. "Just enjoy those and get the basket back to me anytime."

Zoe lifted the edge of the cloth and cinnamon wafted up to her. "These smell yummy."

"Oh, they're good all right." The wizened woman smiled revealing a full set of white dentures. She had to be in her eighties, but she stood ramrod straight, shoulders thrown back and head held high. "Well, you stay safe, young lady. And I'll be watching out for you, too."

Zoe felt a knot form in her throat. Small-town life. She could grow to love it. "Thank you. And congratulations on the birth of your great-grandchild."

Her face glowed. "It's definitely exciting." She

glanced over her shoulder. "Gotta run now. You take care."

Zoe thanked her again and the deputy opened the door for her. When he turned back, his eyes were on the basket.

Zoe held it out to him and he grinned, reached in and promptly wolfed down two of the cookies.

"I take it you're familiar with Granny May's cooking?"

"Yes, ma'am. Can't beat it."

Zoe took one of the cookies and let him carry the basket into the kitchen. She wondered if there would be any left if she wanted another.

Wrangler's Corner. A small town with a sweet woman who didn't let a little trouble keep her away from welcoming a stranger. A deputy's office that was going all out to keep her and her daughter safe. And a man named Aaron Starke who obviously wanted her and Sophia to stay in town for the duration, but was willing to put his own wants on the back burner if it meant keeping her safe.

She walked into the kitchen to find Walter finishing off one more cookie. He reddened. "You caught me."

She laughed. "It's fine. My daughter has diabetes so I have to monitor her sugar intake very carefully. Go ahead and eat them, just save her one."

He smiled. "I won't argue with you."

"I figured." Yes, she could get used to a place like Wrangler's Corner. She might be tempted to make the town her permanent home if she could just figure out— and stop—who wanted to bury her in the local cemetery.

Chapter 13

The drive to Knoxville passed in a blur and soon Aaron found himself staring up at a large house in one of the best neighborhoods in the city. "Nice," he said.

"Yeah." Lance put the car in Park. A local police cruiser sat at the curb across the street and Lance nodded. "Good. They're here. I called before we left Wrangler's Corner and asked that someone monitor the house and let me know if anyone left. So far, everyone must still be here."

Walter reported in, and Aaron thought about Zoe sitting at home waiting for news. He hoped they'd have some to give her soon enough. Lance stepped out of the vehicle, and Aaron shivered when the cold air blasted him. "I'm going to just hang here, is that all right?"

Lance nodded. "That's fine." He paused. "Actually, why don't you go with us?"

"Why?"

"You got a look at the intruder last night. Let's see if you recognize Gregory Bishop."

Good point. "All right." Aaron got out of the car and Lance nodded Parker to go first. Parker led the way followed by Lance and Aaron.

"Stand off to the side," Lance said. "If it's him and he recognizes you then there could be trouble. I don't want him to see you until the last minute."

"Right." Aaron stood where directed. Parker knocked and then stepped back and to the other side. Just in case someone decided to shoot through the door? Possibly.

But no bullets came through the door. Instead, it swung open and a woman in her late twenties with blue eyes and auburn hair stood in the entryway. "Yes?"

Lance flashed his badge as did Parker. "We're deputies working a case. We're also friends of your sister-in-law, Zoe Collier."

"Zoe?" Surprise lit the woman's eyes. "Is she all right? And Sophia?"

"Yes, they're both fine for now."

"Oh, good." She placed a hand over her chest. "You scared me."

"Do you mind if we come in and ask you a few questions?"

The request seemed to fluster her for a moment but she stepped back and let them in. She didn't question Aaron's presence, and he didn't offer her an ID or explanation.

She led them into the family room and gestured for

them to take a seat on the large leather sofa. "You said Zoe and Sophia are all right."

"Yes, ma'am. Is your husband home?"

"Yes, he's in the garage. We just got back from vacation last night and he's cleaning out the car."

"Vacation? Where did you go?"

"Just to Radnor Lake. We have a house there."

"I see." Aaron figured Lance was making notes to check that out. "Do you mind asking your husband to come in here? It'll save me the trouble of having to ask the same questions twice."

A small frown drew her brows together, but she simply shrugged. "Of course." She stood and Parker followed her. Aaron figured he wasn't taking a chance she'd go after a weapon. Lance's phone beeped while the two were gone. He looked at it then muttered something under his breath.

"What was that?" Aaron asked.

"Sorry. Clay texted. He just got the autopsy result for Pete, the guy you shot."

"Yeah." *The guy you shot.* Aaron didn't think he'd ever get used to hearing those words.

"Looks like he didn't die from your gunshot wounds."

Aaron blinked. "He didn't?"

"No. He was suffocated."

Zoe checked the clock and frowned. Sophia should have been home by now. She thought about giving Ginny a few more minutes, but then decided she might as well check in now. She dialed the number and waited. When it went to voice mail, she hung up and tried again. Anxiety kicked in. She dialed Clay's number. "Hello?"

She could hear the baby crying in the background. "I'm so sorry to bother you."

"Zoe? It's no bother. What can I do for you?"

"Sophia was supposed to be home about fifteen minutes ago. I tried Ginny's number, but she didn't answer. I know it's silly to panic because of a fifteen-minute delay, but I was wondering if you could get in touch with Ginny and just see where they are."

"Of course. Stay by your phone and I'll call you right back."

"Thank you." She hung up and fought the urge to crumple to the floor and wail. Somehow, she knew something was dreadfully wrong. *Please, God, let Sophia and Ginny be all right.*

Her phone buzzed. "Clay?"

"Actually, this is your father-in-law, Zoe. How are you doing?"

"Alexander? I-I'm fine. How are you? How did you get this number?"

"Well, I wasn't exactly sure it was you, just hopeful. Nina said she'd had someone call and hang up from a number she didn't recognize. The more I thought about it, the more I thought it might be you. It's good to hear your voice, sweetheart."

She used a shaky hand to shove a lock of hair behind her ear. "Yours, too, Alexander."

"How's Sophia?"

"She's fine."

"Well, I…ah…was wondering if you'd be willing to meet me and have coffee somewhere. I have some things I'd like to talk to you about."

"Like what?" She glanced at the clock. Why hadn't Clay called her back yet?

"Like the fact that you just disappeared with Sophia. I miss her, Zoe. I want her home."

Zoe let out a little sigh. "I know, Alexander. That's what I want, too, but someone tried to kidnap her. And then someone tried to run me off the road. The police said they couldn't do anything so I had to run. And since we've been here, you wouldn't believe what's happened."

"Then come home where I can protect you. Go pack your bags and I can come get you and Sophia."

She closed her eyes and searched her mind for the right words. He just didn't get it. "I've got help and I've got protection right now. Coming back to Knoxville wouldn't be the safest thing for us to do right now."

"Zoe—"

Her phone buzzed. She looked at the screen then pressed the phone back to her ear. "I've got to take this call, Alexander. I'll talk to you later."

"Zoe—"

Another beep from Clay. The last one before the call would go to voice mail. She switched lines. "Clay?"

"Zoe, I can't reach Ginny, either." His grim tone made her stiffen. "Sophia never showed up to school," he said.

She gasped. "What? Why didn't the school call me?"

"They said a woman called claiming to be you and said Sophia was sick and would be staying home today."

"No I didn't! Who? Who called?"

"I don't know. I've requested phone records from the school, but it's going to take a little bit to get them.

I'm also cross-checking the records against Nina's and Gregory's numbers."

"How long is a little bit? What about Sophia?" Tears threatened, but she had to hold it together.

"I've got every available deputy searching for her and Ginny. I've tried pinging her phone, but it's not registered as being on. But I'm also checking her phone records and texts as we speak."

"What do I do? How can I help? Where is she, Clay?"

"I don't know, Zoe, but don't panic. We'll find her. Stay by the phone, I'll be in touch."

He hung up and Zoe sank onto the couch, her legs no longer having the strength to support her. She buried her face in her hands and tried to gather her thoughts. Sophia, her child, her baby, was missing and she didn't know who had her. Zoe dropped to her knees. "Please, God, take care of her and bring her and Ginny back safely."

Chapter 14

Aaron sat back, his breath leaving his lungs with a whoosh. "Suffocated? Is he sure?"

"He's sure."

"But how? Why? Who?"

"All good questions." Footsteps interrupted the conversation. Aaron looked up to see Nina enter the living area followed by a man in his early thirties. He looked tanned in spite of the time of year. He also looked unfamiliar. This wasn't the man he'd tackled. He looked at Lance and gave a subtle shake of his head. Gregory wasn't the man he'd chased last night.

Lance pursed his lips and took a seat. The Bishops did, as well. "What's this all about?" Gregory asked.

"It's about your sister-in-law, Zoe Collier."

Gregory frowned. "What about her?"

Lance launched into the explanation of the attempts on her life and the results of his investigation. "It appears that one of the men hired to kidnap or kill— we haven't determined exactly which one they were attempting—received a phone call from this number." He read the number.

Gregory rocked back, and Nina gasped. "What?"

"That's your home number, right?" Lance asked.

"Well, yes, but—"

Their surprise was real. Aaron grimaced. Would they never get to the bottom of this?

He let his gaze wander the room once again. He noticed the collage of horse pictures on the far wall and figured they portrayed the horse Trevor and Zoe had owned. He stood and began looking at each picture, wondering if Zoe or Sophia were in any of them. He found them in several. They looked happy enough. Trevor was a handsome man. Sophia looked a bit like him. In the last picture, Aaron stopped and looked closer. The man petting the neck of the horse looked familiar.

"I don't believe it," Nina said. "Gregory?"

Gregory spread his hands. "When was the call made?"

Lance told him, and Gregory shook his head. "That's impossible. There's been no one here."

"Did you have a house sitter? A pet sitter? Anyone that might have come in to put your mail on the counter?"

"No. We don't have any pets, and we stopped the mail service until tomorrow. I'm telling you, there's no way someone managed to get in our house without setting off the security alarm, much less use our phone."

Lance rubbed his head. "All right, then is there anyone else who has a key to your house, the code to your alarm, who might have decided to come in for any reason without your knowledge?"

"No, no keys out there, but…" Nina bit her lip.

"But what?" Parker asked.

She sighed. "We have a garage code. There are several people who have it and can get in the house that way."

Lance ripped a sheet of paper from his notebook. "Write down their names, will you?"

She took the paper and pen from him and began her list. While she wrote, Lance cleared his throat. "I know that this is a rather delicate subject, but we've done some investigating into your backgrounds. We've noticed you're having some financial issues."

Nina's head snapped up. "Investigating *us*?"

"Yes. Everything points to you or your husband being behind everything that's happened to Zoe and Sophia over the past few weeks. We had to run down every lead."

Her face turned a bright red and she stood, dropping the paper on the floor. "That's ridiculous. What leads? How would we benefit from anything happening to Zoe?"

"You get Sophia if she dies," Lance said without raising his voice or changing his expression.

Nina sank back into her seat and looked at her husband. "Yes. That's true, but she doesn't come with any money."

"Thunderbolt," Gregory said.

Lance nodded. "And with Sophia, you get Thunderbolt whose worth is estimated at around two hundred fifty thousand dollars. That would go a long way toward paying off some of those creditors you're going to have knocking on your door soon."

"Why do you think we've been up at the lake house this time of year?" Nina demanded. "We're getting it ready to put on the market to sell."

Lance leaned back and Gregory stood to pace while Aaron watched him. There was something in his expression, something he wasn't saying. "What is it?" Lance asked him.

Gregory stopped midpace. "I don't know. Nothing. I'm just trying to think."

"About?"

"Nothing."

"Something. What is it?"

Gregory spread his hands in a beseeching gesture. "Look, I made some bad investments. My father-in-law talked me into investing in several companies owned by a friend of his. A little over two years ago, the bottom dropped out. I managed to get out before I lost everything. My father-in-law hasn't been so fortunate. I warned him. I told him I thought he needed to sell, that something was wrong with the way the stock was dropping, but he insisted on hanging in there. We've been helping him as much as we can, but we're about at the end of our resources."

"This is all his fault," Nina said. "And yours," she directed to Gregory. "If you hadn't listened to him, we would be fine."

"We're still fine," Gregory snapped. "As soon as the lake house sells, everything will be okay again. It's just going to take some time."

"Time that we don't really have."

"Yes, we do. We'll get through this." He moved to sit beside his wife and took her hand. She sniffed and looked away, but left her hand in her husband's. He looked at Lance, then Aaron. "And we don't need to kill my sister-in-law to do it. You're looking at the wrong people."

Lance nodded and rubbed his head. "One last question. Why would you call the men at the ranch?"

"What men?"

"The men who were after Sophia and Zoe. The men who held a law enforcement officer and three innocent people hostage," Lance said.

Gregory's eyes widened, then he frowned. "I don't know what you're talking about. I just told you that we weren't here. There was no one *in this house* to make any calls *from this house*. You must be mistaken."

Lance stayed silent for a moment. When he didn't seem to have anything else to say, Aaron tapped the picture that held the familiar figure. "Who's this guy with the horse?"

With a perturbed look at Lance, Gregory turned his attention to Aaron and walked over to squint at the picture. "Oh, that's Brian Cartee. He's Thunderbolt's jockey. Why?"

Before Aaron had a chance to answer, Lance's phone buzzed. He glanced at the screen. "Excuse me, I need to take this. It's Clay calling, hopefully with an update." He stood and walked into the foyer. Aaron followed him with every intention of eavesdropping. Plus, he'd just placed the man in the picture.

"Missing?" He heard Lance suck in a deep breath. "All right. Ginny, too? Yeah. Yeah. I'll tell him."

When he turned around, Aaron didn't like the expression in Lance's eyes. "Tell me."

"Someone attacked Ginny's car. There are bullet holes in the side of the car and blood on the ground. She and Sophia are missing."

Aaron felt light-headed for a moment. "Missing? Blood?"

"I'm asking for help from the FBI. We don't have the resources they do and I don't want to take any chances on this not ending well."

"We need to get back now."

"Yes."

"But first. That man in the picture on the Bishops' mantel? Brian Cartee? He's the jockey for Sophia's horse. I've seen him before."

"Where?"

"When I tackled him outside of Zoe's house. He's the one who attacked Joy and the one who ran from me."

Lance sucked in a deep breath. "This just keeps getting more and more interesting. We need to let Zoe know."

"I'll be in the car. I'm calling her to fill her in and let her know we're on the way." He pulled his phone from his pocket and hit her speed-dial number.

Zoe was still in a state of numbed shock when the three men walked into the house five hours later. She stood when they stepped into the den. "Brian? Brian

Cartee is the man who attacked Joy? Who managed to overpower Ginny and grab Sophia? And where is all the protection she said was in place?"

Lance and Clay exchanged glances. "Protection? What are you talking about? You mean about Parker and Walter?"

"No, she said Clay had called some friends from Nashville and they were watching the school and the house and—" At Clay's blank look, she snapped her lips together. "She lied. Why would she lie?" She shuddered and bit back a sob. "She's a part of it."

Clay pulled his phone. "I've got some calls to make." He looked at Zoe. "I'm sorry. Ginny's new, but she came with good references, and I've never had any reason to believe she'd do something like this. I'm going to figure out what's going on right now." He paused. "But before I do, why would Brian be in Nina and Gregory's house?"

She rubbed her head. "I don't know. I don't know anything. None of this makes any sense."

"Let's think about this. Why would Brian come after you or Sophia now? What does he gain if you're dead and Sophia in his possession?"

"Nothing! That's what I'm saying. If I die, everything goes to Nina and Gregory. Including Sophia."

"What if they've worked a deal with him?" Aaron said. "You said he wanted the horse. How bad do Nina and Gregory want Sophia? You said Nina wanted the two of you to come live with her?"

"Well, yes, but she wouldn't do this." She shook her head. "No, something's not adding up. We're missing something else."

"Does Brian have access to Nina and Gregory's house?"

She rubbed her forehead. "No, not that I know of. He and Trevor were really close, but Gregory is a bit of a snob. He doesn't associate with people he considers not on his level. So to speak." She grimaced. "In other words, no. There's no reason Brian would have been in their house."

"Unless he broke in," Aaron said.

Zoe shook her head. "He would have set the alarm off."

"Not if someone gave him the code," Lance said.

"Which Gregory would do if Brian was doing his dirty work."

"Maybe," Aaron said and shrugged. "It's all speculation."

Clay pursed his lips. "All right. You think some more on it. I've got a BOLO out on Brian. He wasn't home when officers went by his house earlier. They stopped by the barn and there was no sign of him there, either." He exchanged a look with Lance. "Which could mean he's somewhere close by. Be sure to keep your eyes open."

"Of course."

"Now about—"

Zoe tuned them out as her thoughts went to Sophia. She knew Brian. Trusted him. Would feel safe with him. Would he hurt her? Scare her? Know to give her her medicine? Sophia kept an emergency insulin kit in her backpack. She stopped and spun toward the men. "Did Sophia have her backpack with her?"

Clay pulled the phone from his ear. "If she had it

when she left the house, she—or whoever has her—probably has it with her. The car was cleaned out."

A slight tug of relief found its way into her shattered mother's heart. She continued to pace and pray while Clay made his calls and Lance and Aaron discussed the incident.

Incident. Her daughter's kidnapping was an incident. The thought made her want to throw up. How could this have happened? She'd been so careful. Her thoughts continued to circle that loop until she couldn't get past it. "I did everything you said," she whispered. Lance and Aaron turned toward her. The pain in Aaron's eyes fueled her own. "How could this happen? How could Brian just take her away from Ginny? How could Ginny let his happen?" Her voice rose with each word and she couldn't seem to stop the sweeping anger mixed with hysteria and downright terror. "I. Did. *Everything.* You. Said!"

Aaron caught her by the forearms. She resisted for a brief moment then let him pull her against his chest. His heart thumped beneath her cheek as she saturated his shirt with her tears. He said nothing, just held her. With each sob, she mentally ordered herself to stop, to get control, but the thought of never seeing her child again set off more spasms of pain and grief. Finally, she drew in a deep breath and pulled away from the comfort of his embrace. He let her go, but led her into the den area. She noticed Clay and Lance had made themselves scarce. Aaron pressed a tissue into her hand and she dropped onto the couch.

"This probably isn't the best time to ask, but maybe

talking about something else will help." He lowered himself beside her.

She eyed him warily. "Okay."

"I've been thinking. You said something the other day that I've been meaning to ask you about and haven't gotten around to it."

Oh. That. She figured she knew what was coming.

"Will you tell me about the drug problem you mentioned?"

Yep, she was right. Oh, boy. She'd known he would address it at some point, but had hoped to avoid that conversation a bit longer. "Why do you want to know?"

He frowned. "Because if Brian is behind this—and it looks like he is—he could be working with someone. It already looks like Ginny's involved. Three men were hired to try and kidnap Sophia. We need to make sure no one else is in this loop. So can you think of anyone who has a past with drugs and might have found his or her way into your present for some kind of revenge? Someone who would be willing to take money to get rid of you?"

She pressed her fingertips to her burning eyes. "It was such a long time ago. I don't think this is related to that."

"It might not be, but Clay needs to address every possibility. And if you used to hang out with—" He paused and grimaced.

"Junkies?"

"Well, yes, but I was trying to find a better way to say it."

"There's not a better way. We were rich kids, but we were still addicts." She groaned and shook her head. "It was stupid. I was stupid. My dad went to prison when I was thirteen. Three years later he was home and wanting to make his marriage work. My mother would have none of it. She wanted him out of the house and he refused to go."

"So why didn't your mother leave?"

"She did eventually. But when everything started happening—when my father was finally released from prison and home—she had nowhere to go. She had no real friends. She was too ashamed to go to the church for help. But she finally had a friend say she could move in with her for a short time."

"She left you with your father?"

Zoe sighed. "Yes. And I get it now. My mother was depressed, desperate and very, very angry." She shrugged. "My dad finally consented to the divorce, but still refused to move out. The fighting was just—" she spread her hands and shuddered "—awful, to say the least. I was looking for an escape. I found that in painting. And then drugs. I knew I shouldn't have, but one night, the fighting was just too much. My father was bitter about his prison time. My mother was packing her suitcase and screaming at the top of her lungs about how it was a shame he didn't even have the decency to leave her and me in peace and go find a place of his own, he yelled back that he didn't have a job or any money so how was he supposed to make that happen..." She took a deep breath and brushed away a stray tear. "I went over to my boyfriend's house and he gave me what I'd been refusing for a while. I tried a little cocaine." She shrugged. "And it was...amazing. I was able to forget. Just for a bit, but it was such a *relief.* I didn't seem to have any ill effects from it so tried it again. And again. And soon it was all I thought about, all I craved. And before I realized what had happened, I was an addict." She gave a derisive laugh. "I kept telling myself I could handle it, that it wasn't any big deal and that I'd quit when things got better at home. But…"

"But you couldn't quit."

"No, I couldn't. By the time life had settled down a bit, I was well and truly hooked."

"How'd you get clean?"

"Rehab. My parents paid for me to go, but refused to let me come home after I was out." She shrugged. "They'd moved on while I was away. Sold the house at this point and gone their separate ways. Neither of them wanted me back home. I can't say I completely blame them. I was horrible. I stole from them. I was defiant, disrespectful, mean-spirited." She gave a choked laugh. "That was the one thing they could agree on through the whole thing. I couldn't come back home."

"You were angry, lashing out at them while they were so focused on themselves."

"Oh, very much so. I knew what I was doing was wrong, but I wanted to hurt them. My father was a bigwig in the community, albeit a fallen one. I wanted him and all of his bigwig friends to know that he had a junkie for a daughter and that it was all his fault."

"You didn't blame your mother?"

"Not so much. She was part of the issue, but she was just weak. She couldn't deal with my father's theft, the trial, the conviction, the jail time. She just kind of checked out. But my father, he was a different story. He was livid to say the least."

"What *did* he say?"

"He told me I was no longer his child." She rubbed her eyes again and he took her hand. The fact that he hadn't run from her said a lot for his character. It encouraged her to finish the story. "So I went to my youth pastor at the church we attended sporadically. He managed to get me into a program sponsored by the church. And while I knew I needed help, I wasn't sure I could kick the habit. But the program was a good one with good people and excellent counselors." She shrugged. "I also got into a Bible study with a woman who seemed very taken with me. She really encouraged me, supported me…loved me." She took a deep breath. "And prayed for me. I eventually got out, went to college and left the drugs in the past. But it wasn't easy."

"I'm sure it wasn't. So that's where you were when you dropped off the radar for a year?"

She frowned. "Maybe. Why?"

"Clay did some checking up on you and said he couldn't find anything on you for about a year. Amber went to her sources and came back and said she knew where you'd been but it wasn't any of our business and if you wanted us to know, you'd tell us."

"Oh." She wasn't sure how she felt about the fact that Clay and Amber both had investigated her background, but guessed she understood why. She gave a slow nod then a small shrug. "But that's why I don't think it's anyone from my past. The old boyfriend who provided the drugs is also clean and is living and working in Haiti with some charitable organization."

"I'll get Lance to check on him anyway."

She nodded and stood. "His name's Matthew Holder.

I'm going to my room. I need some time alone. Please come get me if you hear anything."

"Zoe—"

She held up a hand. "I just need some time, Aaron."

"Okay."

She could tell he didn't want her to leave, but she'd said enough and now she just wanted to be alone. To try and find her way out of the yawning black hole of pain and fear for her child. To process that Brian Cartee had been the one behind the attack on Joy and possibly had Sophia.

She shut the bedroom door behind her and sank onto the bed. Sophia's favorite stuffed animal had gotten caught between the pillow and the headboard. Zoe gripped it and clutched it to her chest. "Please, God, take care of my baby." She shed more tears into the soft fur and continued to pray.

Aaron felt helpless. He *was* helpless. And he hated the feeling. "We've got to find her, Lance. What are we missing? Zoe seems so sure it's not someone from her past."

Lance looked at his phone. "Well, Brian Cartee's dropped off the grid. We can't track him through his phone because he's not using it."

"Probably has a burner to communicate with whoever is behind this."

"Why do you think he's not the leader in this whole thing?" Lance asked.

"I don't really know. Call it just a gut feeling."

"Sometimes that's the best thing to go by."

"Yeah."

Lance glanced toward the back of the house. "Is she all right?"

Aaron blew out a sigh. "No, not really, but she will be. Eventually."

Clay stepped into the room, his face drawn, brows almost meeting at the bridge of his nose.

Aaron froze. "What is it? What else is wrong?"

"I just spoke to Amber."

"Amber?" Aaron raised a brow. "What's up with her?"

"Apparently she's got some pretty amazing contacts who owe her a ton of favors. Anyway, she just called to say that she did background checks on all of Zoe's family members. One person came back red-flagged."

"Wait a minute. You did background checks. Nothing showed up."

"Yes, I did one on Nina and Gregory when it looked like they had something to do with everything going on. The one person I didn't do was Alexander Collier."

"Zoe's father-in-law?"

"Yeah." Clay glanced at his phone again and shook his head.

"What showed up in Amber's search?"

"Collier's in debt up to his eyeballs, and his home is getting ready to be foreclosed on. He's been hanging on by his fingernails, but she said in about two more months, he's done."

"But it makes no sense for him to go after Sophia and Zoe because she doesn't have the money to bail him out."

"Obviously he knows something we don't," Clay said. "We have to tell her."

"Yeah."

"But how?"

The phone in her pocket buzzed, waking her from a restless doze. She blinked and rubbed her eyes then grabbed her phone praying the person on the other end had some news about Sophia. She glanced at the screen and winced. Her father-in-law. What was she going to tell him? That she'd failed? That she'd allowed his granddaughter to be taken? With another choked sob, she answered the call. "Hello?"

"I want you to listen to me very carefully."

Something in his tone made her sit up straight. "All right. What is it?"

"I want you to get out of the house without anyone seeing you."

She stilled. "What?"

"I know where Sophia is."

"What? Where? Is she okay? She has diabetes, Alexander, you know that. She needs her medicine. I need to get to her."

"She's safe and will stay that way for now as long as you follow my instructions."

Realization crashed over Zoe. "You," she whispered.

"Yes. Me."

Her whole body trembled. Her father-in-law had tried to kidnap his own grandchild and he'd hired men to kill Zoe. "Why?"

"Does it matter?"

"Of course it matters!"

"Shh. You don't want anyone to overhear you. Now look out of your window."

Zoe stood, her legs shaking and threatening to give way, but she locked her muscles and strode to the window. "Where's Ginny? Did you kill her?" She glanced out and found Alexander's tall form. He stood on the other side of the property fence, phone pressed to his ear, baseball cap pulled low over his eyes. No one would think anything about him being there. He looked like a neighbor hanging out in his backyard having a phone conversation with a friend. "I see you," she said.

"Good." He turned slightly and glanced in her direction. "And I see you. Ginny isn't important right now. What's important is that you follow my directions exactly."

"I will. Tell me."

"Don't hang up until I tell you that you can. Get your keys and get out of the house without anyone noticing, walk down the street and get into the white Cadillac parked three doors down. I'll be waiting."

Her keys? Her purse was on the table next to the front door. "What if I can't?" she whispered.

"You'll find a way. Now come on. The longer you take the shorter Sophia's life span gets."

Zoe flinched. "Would you really hurt your own granddaughter?"

He scoffed. "You've never known me at all, have you?"

"Apparently not."

"Understand this, Zoe." His deadly tone had her full attention. "I will do whatever it takes to accomplish my goals and if that means Sophia dies, then so be it."

Zoe's breath left her. She turned from the window, hesitating as she considered her options. Then realized she had no options. At least for now. She looked at the pen on the small desk in the corner, picked it up and searched frantically for a piece of paper.

"What are you doing Zoe? What's taking so long?"

"I'm trying to figure out how to get out of the house without anyone seeing me. It might take me a minute."

She scanned the desk again and looked back at the end table. If she crossed in front of the window, he would see her—and know she wasn't out of the room yet. She settled the pen against the wood of the desk and pressed. And the ink wouldn't flow. Stifling a sob of frustration, she pressed harder and gouged *Alexander has Sophia. White Cad—*

"Zoe..."

She didn't dare stay a moment longer. She dropped the pen, took a deep breath and left the bedroom and entered the hall. She could hear Alexander's breaths in her ear. He was nervous about this. And well he should be.

"Zoe?" The low warning in his voice made her shiver.

"I'm coming," she whispered.

She heard voices from the kitchen. Somehow she had to slip out the front door without them hearing or seeing. How? She drew closer and paused just outside the door as though planning to eavesdrop.

"...got Sophia," Clay said.

"Bottom line," Aaron said, "is that he wants Sophia alive and Zoe dead. Somehow it all comes back to money."

"So how are we going to break this to Zoe?" Aaron said.

She peered around the corner. Clay had his back to

her, but Aaron was leaning against the counter with his arms crossed against his chest.

Zoe took a deep breath and waited, heart pounding. If one of them decided to leave the kitchen, he'd see her. She risked another glance.

Aaron dropped his hands and turned to get his glass from the counter. No time to hesitate. She slipped past the opening and into the foyer, grabbed her purse from the small table near the door and tucked it under her arm.

"Where are you, Zoe?" She could hear the anger in Alexander's voice, but couldn't take a chance on responding. Not yet. She twisted the knob of the front door and pulled it open wide enough to slip through then shut it slowly, careful to not make any noise.

She turned and took a deep breath. "I'm outside."

"Very good." The sudden confidence in his voice made her want to vomit. Was she wrong? Should she have signaled to Aaron or Lance somehow? No, she couldn't risk Alexander finding out and hurting Sophia. She remembered his tone when he said he would do anything to accomplish his goals. She had no doubt he'd hurt Sophia.

She looked up and down the street and spotted Yvonne Mayfield sweeping the front porch of the bed-and-breakfast. Zoe turned her gaze away, praying the woman would spot her, but doing nothing that would cause Alexander to suspect she was trying to get the woman's attention. Yvonne never looked up. Zoe bit the inside of her cheek. "Keep walking," Alexander said. "Come down the steps and turn left. Walk to the car and get in. Now."

Zoe did as ordered.

"Zoe? Is that you, hon?"

Zoe nearly stumbled, but didn't look back as she continued toward the white Cadillac. So Yvonne had seen her. If Alexander had the windows up, maybe he wouldn't realize the woman had called out to her. She got to the car and opened the passenger door. Her gaze went to the backseat but of course Sophia wasn't there. She stared at her father-in-law. "Where is she?"

"She's safe."

"How do I know that?"

He held up his cell phone and she stared at the picture on the screen. Sophia was sitting at a kitchen table drinking a glass of milk. She knew that kitchen. Betrayal stabbed sharp and deep. "She's with Nina? Nina's behind this, too?"

"Get in and give me your cell phone."

Zoe resisted throwing a glance back toward her home and slid into the passenger seat. He snatched her phone from her fingers and powered it down. Her hands trembled and she clasped them together between her knees. Her child was safe for the moment, now it was up to her to figure out how to stay alive.

He pulled a roll of duct tape from beneath the seat and she cringed. "Alexander, please…"

His diamond-hard gaze cut into her. "Give me your hands."

She couldn't do it. "I'm not going to fight you," she said softly. "You have my child." She held his eyes, keeping hers steady. "As long as you have control of her, you have control of me."

He lifted a gun and pointed it at her head. "Give me your hands."

Her breath caught. Death stared her in the eye. She lifted her hands. He quickly taped them together, then shoved her back against the passenger door. Zoe felt the comforting weight of the small gun against her ankle. Unfortunately she had no way to get to it. "Why do you want me dead? Why send those men to kill me and kidnap Sophia?"

"I need money, Zoe. A lot of money."

She stared at him and he pulled away from the curb. Fear clawed at her but she controlled it. She had to. Sophia was counting on her. "But I don't have a lot of money, Alexander. You know that as well as I do. You were there for the reading of the will. All I have is the horse and a little bit of life insurance money from Trevor—and I'll sign the horse over to you today. You can sell him for a quarter of a million."

"Two hundred fifty thousand is simply a drop in the bucket. And you're worth more than you think you are. Trevor took out a two-million-dollar life insurance policy on you a year before he died."

Chapter 15

The knock on the door pulled Aaron from his thoughts on how to tell Zoe it looked like her father-in-law was behind the attempts on her life. Lance stood and followed him into the foyer. A peek out the window drained some of his tension. "It's Sabrina's grandmother." He opened the door. "Hi, Mrs. Mayfield."

"I just saw Zoe get into someone's car down the street. I called out to her, but she acted like she didn't hear me. With all the trouble she's been having I figured I'd better come see if everything was all right."

Aaron didn't answer. He bolted down the hall and found Zoe's bedroom door open. He glanced around the room and found it empty. Without bothering to investigate further, he spun on his heel. "Lance! She's not here." He raced back into the foyer.

Mrs. Mayfield shook her head. "Of course she's not here. I just told you she got in a car and left with that man."

"What man?"

"Well, I don't know his name, but I did think to write down the license plate. It's a white Cadillac." She pulled a scrap of paper from her pocket and handed it over to Lance. "I would have been here faster, but I had to go inside and find a piece of paper or I would have forgotten the number between my place and here."

Lance kissed her cheek and pulled out his phone. He glanced at Aaron. "Try calling her on her cell."

Aaron nodded, but had a sinking feeling in his stomach. He dialed her number and as he was afraid it would, it went straight to voice mail. He hung up and found Lance writing something down.

Mrs. Mayfield still stood in the foyer wringing her hands. "I'll be praying."

"Yes, please," Aaron said. "Pray hard."

"Got it," Lance said.

"Got what?"

"The car is a rental out of Knoxville."

"Whose name is it in?"

"Jedidiah Mason."

Aaron flinched. "Jed. One of the guys who held us all hostage at the ranch. He's the one who got away."

"No doubt hired by Alexander Collier. Fortunately, this company puts GPS trackers on all of their rentals." He pressed another button on his phone.

Aaron felt hope surge. Finally, it was time to bring this to an end. He just prayed they found Zoe before it was too late.

* * *

Zoe was stunned, rocked to her very core as his words echoed over and over in her mind. "Two-million-dollar life insurance policy?" Surely she'd heard wrong. "That's crazy."

"Yes. And I need that two million dollars. Yesterday."

"Why?" she whispered. "Trevor never said a word. I never found any paperwork." Alexander's jaw tightened and he stared straight ahead, his knuckles white on the wheel as he drove. Realization came like a burst of lightning. "You told him to do it, didn't you? You talked him into getting the life insurance policy."

Alexander shrugged. "I suggested it. I simply had to mention that once an addict always an addict. Pressed home the point that he couldn't know for sure that you wouldn't revert to your old ways, that you might overdose one day. It took some convincing, but he went along with it eventually. Just like everything I suggested." He cut his eyes to her. "Except when I told him not to marry you. His one defiance."

"He loved you. Practically worshipped you," Zoe said. Sickness curled in her belly. How did she not know about the policy? "When does the two-year contestability period end?"

"You know about that, huh?"

"Yes. When?"

"Today."

"That was you on the phone at the ranch," she whispered. "You called from Nina and Gregory's house when the men had Sophia and me at the Updike ranch. Didn't you? To tell them not to kill me because if they had—"

"Yes." He turned left and she frowned.

"Because if I died before today," she continued, "the insurance company has the right to take their time and investigate everything, delaying payment, but once the two-year contestability period is passed, they'll pay out within thirty days." She closed her eyes and leaned her head against the window. "You've been planning to kill me for two years." It wasn't a question.

"It's nothing personal. I've made some bad investments. Even got Gregory and Nina involved. Gregory was smart, but I was too stubborn to listen to him when he told me to sell. I kept thinking the stock would turn around."

"But it didn't."

"No, it didn't. I've been managing to keep my head above water, but just barely. And now it's all about to come crashing down around me. Unless I come up with some big money in the next couple of months, I'm ruined." He shot her another sideways glance.

She felt light-headed. He talked about killing her like it was just another item to check off his daily to-do list. "Where does Brian fit in all of this?"

He glanced at her. "What do you mean?"

"He was the one who tried to break in last night. Aaron chased him, tackled him and pulled his mask off. He was in Nina and Gregory's house earlier and recognized him in a photo."

Alexander's nostrils flared and his jaw tightened. "I didn't realize he'd messed up so bad." The man heaved a sigh. "Well, at least I don't have to worry about him talking. There's no way anyone can connect him to me."

She stared at Alexander, the sick feeling building at the base of her throat. "What do you mean?"

He slid her a glance. "Shut up."

Grief pierced her and she knew that Brian was dead. "You killed him."

"I said shut up!"

"Why him?" she insisted. "Why involve him?" In spite of the trouble the man had brought down on her, she didn't wish him dead.

His fingers flexed on the wheel. "He wanted that stupid horse. I told him you'd stolen Sophia away from me and I just wanted to talk to you but I couldn't even get close to you. I told him if he would simply bring you to me using whatever means necessary, I'd sign the horse over to him."

"But you don't have the right to do that. The papers are in my name."

"Brian didn't know that."

She ran her palms down her thighs as her brain whirled. The man was sick. "You planned to kill him all along."

He shrugged. "Once you turned up dead, I couldn't have Brian going to the police, could I?"

"Of course not."

He frowned at her sarcasm. She bit her tongue against the rest of the words she wanted to hurl at him, exercising extreme self-control to keep them from slipping from her lips. *Oh, God, please help me.*

"What were you doing at Nina and Gregory's the day the men attacked us?" she asked. "Are they in on this, too?"

"Of course not. Nina's pushy and likes things her way, but she doesn't have the stomach for something like this. And Gregory—" he snorted "—he's just a 'yes, ma'am' man when it comes to Nina. Whatever Nina says goes." He tapped the wheel and glanced in the rear-view mirror. "I'd forgotten they were out of town when I stopped by. Gregory's been selling some of my wife's antique pieces and I needed to get a check from him. While I was there Pete called me on my burner phone, but the battery was almost dead. I was getting ready to get in the car and leave, but could tell the situation demanded immediate attention when I heard the gun-shots. I went in the house to use the landline to call him back." His jaw flexed. "What are the odds that Pete's cell phone would fall into law enforcement hands and they'd trace the number back?"

"But they did. And they know someone was in touch with Pete the day everything happened at the ranch. Why do you think you can kill me now and—"

"Because I can," he snapped. "I have to." He shook his head. "Like I said, it's nothing personal. The money from your insurance policy goes to Sophia."

"And Sophia goes to Nina and Gregory as will the trust fund money," she said. "What are you going to do? Kill them, too?"

He snorted. "Nope. You're going to sign a codicil naming me as the beneficiary. I'll wait a month or so and miraculously find the paper and the money will be turned over to me. It's as simple as that. With you dead and Sophia in my custody, I'll have immediate access to her trust fund. And then your life insurance money will come in over the next few weeks and everything will fall into place."

"What about Sophia? What's going to happen to her?"

"Assuming you cooperate, Nina will get to keep Sophia. Nina was heartbroken you two refused to move in with her after Trevor died. She'll have no problem taking in her poor orphaned niece."

Cooperate. As in let him kill her. As in asking her to give her life so her child could live. She would. If she had to. But what would Sophia's life be like without Zoe? Raised by Nina and Gregory? "Wait a minute, if you didn't want me dead before today, why try to kill me all those times?"

"I wasn't trying to kill you, I was trying to get rid of all of the watchdogs. They were guarding you so tight I couldn't get to you. Those idiots at the ranch nearly ruined everything. I hired them to kidnap the two of you, not start this incredible mess." She blinked and thought back to all of the times they'd been chased or shot at. Every time she'd had someone with her. She shuddered.

When he pulled into the drive of the Updike ranch, she gasped. "I want to see Sophia. Why are we coming here?"

"Because this is where you're going to realize the futility of your situation and resort to your old drug habits. Unfortunately, you overdose."

Horrified, she stared at the syringe he'd produced from seemingly out of nowhere. "I won't," she whispered.

"You will," he growled, "or Sophia dies. Your choice."

Chapter 16

Aaron drummed his fingers on the door handle of the car as Clay drove and Lance gave him directions according to the GPS tracker. "Take a right here."

From the backseat, Aaron didn't have a good view of the electronic map system, but the route was familiar. He sat forward. "Wait a minute. That's taking us to the Updike farm. He's taking her out there. Why?"

"It's remote, no one's there," Lance said quietly.

Aaron sat back with a thump. "He's taking her there to kill her. Hurry up."

"Going as fast as I can," Clay said. "You know we're making a mighty big assumption that she's in that car."

"Mrs. Mayfield said she got in a white Cadillac," Aaron said. "The license plate matches the one we're following. I think it's a safe assumption she's in the car.

I don't know who has her—Jed or Brian or even Collier himself, but Zoe's in that car and I'm guessing she was forced to make the decision to either get in or risk something happening to Sophia. We need to get to her as fast as possible."

Clay glanced at Lance. "I agree. Call for backup. Every unit available needs to head to the Updike farm."

The tension in Aaron's belly curled tighter. "We're still fifteen minutes away. A lot can happen in fifteen minutes."

Clay barked orders into the radio while Aaron sent up prayers for Zoe and Sophia's safety. How had this happened? How had Alexander gotten her out of the house right under their very noses? Where was Sophia? Was she with Alexander and Zoe?

Traffic on the road to the farm was heavy enough to slow them down slightly in spite of the fact that Clay had the siren going. They still had to slow down as people pulled over and maneuver safely through intersections. "Come on, Clay."

"Going as fast as I can."

Aaron prayed it was fast enough.

Zoe's panic tripled when Alexander stopped the car. He got out and shut the door then started around toward her side. She leaned over and with her bound hands pulled the cuff of her jeans up enough to get to the strap holding the small pistol in the ankle holster. She slipped it off and glanced up to see him almost at her door.

She pulled her pant leg down just as he opened the door and grasped her upper arm. He hauled her out. "Alexander, please don't do this."

"It's not like I really want to, Zoe. It's just the way things have worked out."

"Where's Ginny? How did you convince her to go along with you?"

"How do you know I did?"

"Because Ginny said something about massive amounts of security on Sophia's school and the house when I was determined to keep Sophia home today. Ginny convinced me Sophia would be safe because of it and it was the only reason I let her go. But there was no extra security. She had to think on her feet and make that up so she could get Sophia away from me."

"You always were a smart girl."

"Well?"

"Ginny has a special-needs sister in Nashville who loves her very expensive private group home. Unfortunately Ginny's parents have fallen on hard times. I simply offered to pay the girl's fees for the next year if she would let me protect Sophia. It took some convincing, but once the money was in her account she agreed. As long as I promised not to hurt Sophia." He rolled his eyes and placed a hand over his heart and mocked, "She's my granddaughter, my dead son's child, I would never hurt her. I just want the best for her. Look at all the danger she's in. Zoe may be willing to trust her life into the hands of the local sheriff's office, and that's her decision, but I want my granddaughter to have more protection than that. Please, Ginny, I can't do this without your help. Zoe won't let me get near her. I have money, I can hire bodyguards, but I can't do all that if she's not with me. What will it take to convince you?" Zoe couldn't take her eyes from him. He deserved an Oscar. His sincerity, his pleading eyes nearly convinced even her.

She could see how Ginny fell for it. Was that why Ginny had questioned Zoe the night Brian had tried to break into the house? Had she been feeling Zoe out? Trying to determine how Zoe felt about her father-in-law? Zoe felt sick. Never in a million years would she have suspected him capable of this kind of thing. He pushed her toward the barn and she stumbled along the snow-covered grass. "Why did you try to kidnap Sophia when she was on her way home from school? What purpose would that serve?"

"I was going to be the hero. I was going to pay the ransom, return your daughter to you and then talk you into making me guardian should anything happen to you. After all, it's obvious how much I loved and wanted her."

Zoe wanted to weep. "I never would have agreed."

"Sure you would have. You would have owed me. It's just the way you're wired. Then once the papers were signed and all legal, you would have suffered a terrible car accident at some point in the near future."

"Sometime after today," she said. Her voice sounded dull. Resigned. She had to get away from him. Sophia was safe for now. She'd thought he was taking her to Knoxville, that she would have more time to think, to plan her escape. But if she didn't do something fast, she was dead.

"Definitely after today."

Zoe stopped walking. "But you tried to run me off the road shortly after Sophia's kidnapping attempt. You could have killed me."

"Could have, but I didn't think it would. The point was to scare you into running to me for help." He gave her a rough shove that almost sent her to her knees.

She kept her balance. "But of course I didn't."

"No, of course not. That little plan backfired and sent you running, period."

"And yet you still managed to find me?"

He laughed. "I knew where you were two days after you left. You forget that I have friends in high places. Police officer friends who were very sympathetic to the fact that my daughter-in-law had taken my grand-daughter and moved away without leaving her contact information. One had no trouble finding you and passing that information along to me."

Zoe's sinking feeling dipped lower. "Well, if you knew where I was the whole time, why wait a month to come after me?"

"It's all about the timing, Zoe. It takes time to plan these things. To research the people you associated with, to find the right people to hire to…find you."

"Time to plot my murder?"

"If you want to be crass about it." He stopped in front of the barn and held the gun steady on her. "But of course all that went down the drain because people are incompetent. I find that if I want things done right, I just have to do them myself." He gestured toward the door. "Now get inside. You'll be safe in the barn."

"Safe?"

"Wrong word." He narrowed his eyes. "Hidden if you prefer. Regardless of what you call it, this will be a good place for you to pass out from your overdose. One of the hands will find you day after tomorrow."

He twisted to open the barn door and for just a moment he was distracted. She lifted a foot and planted it against the back of his right knee in a swift hard kick. He hollered and went down.

Zoe spun and took off around the side of the barn.

Clay rolled onto the Updike property at a slow crawl. "What are you doing?"

"Don't want to tip him off that we're here," Clay said. "We need to use caution. The GPS say he's still on the property?" he asked Lance.

"Yes, the car is here."

Aaron wanted to bolt from the backseat and go find Zoe, but he curbed his impatience. He sure didn't want to make a bad situation worse by being impulsive. "So what are we waiting for?"

"Backup," Clay said.

"Zoe might not have time for backup," Aaron hissed. "We need to find her now." He looked at the snow-covered ground. "Those tire tracks are fresh. All we have to do is follow them."

"We can't go busting in trying to find her. We could set him off if he realizes we know he's here."

"Then let's do a subtle search. I don't care how we do it, we just need to do it now." Clay hesitated then glanced at Lance. "What would you do if it was Sabrina?" Aaron pressed.

"Fine," Clay conceded. "But you stay back. You're not a cop."

"I'll stay back, just start looking."

Clay started following the tire tracks. Lance kept glancing first one way then the other. Aaron knew he was looking for a sniper. He had to admit that spot between his shoulder blades itched, but he hoped if the man who had Zoe was working alone, he was occupied with her, not parked on a hill waiting for someone to show up.

The tracks led to the barn.

He took one step and heard a muffled cry.

Zoe let out another scream as Alexander hauled her to her feet. He'd tackled her before she'd gotten too far. Desperation clawed at her. She kicked out and caught him in the chin. His fist cracked against her cheek. She dropped to the ground. Pain rocketed through her and for a moment the world spun. He dropped beside her and his hand gripped her upper arm.

"Zoe!"

She froze. Alexander froze. Then cursed. He planted the weapon against her head. "Make one more sound and I'll kill you right here."

She trembled, but stayed quiet. Then she heard them. Voices moving toward the barn. Alexander's harsh breathing echoed in her ear. She had to get away from him. But how? Still on the hard, cold ground, she could feel him waiting, his tension level near the snapping point. She pulled her leg up toward her hands.

Thankfully, he didn't seem to notice her movement as he kept his attention focused on the voices. Slowly, so slowly, she pulled the leg of her jeans up revealing the weapon still strapped to her ankle.

The sound of feet moving closer had Alexander's muscles bunching tighter. As well as his grip on her bicep. Just an inch farther, and she could wrap her fingers around the butt of the gun. She shifted. "Be still," he snapped. She stilled. If he looked down her body, he'd see the gun in plain sight. But he didn't. As soon as she obeyed, he turned back to the approaching men. He moved the barrel of the weapon from the side of her head and aimed it at Aaron. Her breath caught.

"Tracks end here," she heard Clay say softly. "There's the white Cadillac."

Aaron spun, his eyes probing. Lance did the same.

And Alexander adjusted his aim.

"Watch out!"

At Zoe's cry the three men ducked behind the Cadillac, and Alexander gave a roar of fury even as he brought the weapon around to slam it against the side of her head. But she was already moving, bending at the waist to get the gun from the holster, and he caught her with only a glancing blow to her shoulder.

She had her bound hands wrapped around the gun. She pulled it from the holster as Alexander turned his weapon back toward the men. The crack of his gun made her ears ring, but she didn't stop. She rolled and placed her muzzle against Alexander's thigh and pulled the trigger.

He cried out and dropped his weapon. Zoe rolled to her knees and pushed herself to her feet even while Alexander was scrambling for the gun. She stepped forward and planted her weapon against his temple. "Move and it will be the last thing you do."

"Zoe!" Clay hollered.

"Over here! Behind the barn!" The shakes wanted to set in, but she held strong. Aaron would be here in just a moment then she would be able to break down.

Alexander glared up at her even while he clamped his hands around his wounded leg. Without a word to her, he reached into the pocket of his coat and pulled out the roll of duct tape.

"What are you doing?" she asked, breathless and trembling. "It's over," she said.

Instead of answering her, he pulled a long strip off the roll and started wrapping it around his leg and she realized he was making a tourniquet. Zoe backed up, the weapon still on him. With a grunt he ripped the rest of the strip and dropped the tape to the ground. He sat there, shoulders heaving, his features pale.

She continued her backward journey never taking her eyes from Alexander.

Clay and Lance rounded the corner of the barn, weapons raised. "Police! Freeze! Show your hands now!" Clay's harsh orders went ignored. Alexander didn't move.

A loud crack broke the air and dirt and snow spewed up from the ground beside Alexander. Zoe saw the flash come from the trees bordering the property. Who was there? Another officer?

She had no more time to wonder as Clay and Lance ducked back around the corner and Alexander surged to his feet and came after her. Zoe let out another cry and pulled the trigger. The bullet caught the man in the upper shoulder and he spun but didn't go down. He lunged around on his good leg and limped after her.

Zoe back-pedaled and turned to run, but her right foot came down on a large rock. Her ankle twisted and with a cry she tumbled to the ground unable to break her fall with her hands still taped together. Her weapon flew from her fingers, the air whooshed from her lungs.

In the distance a gunshot sounded and she jerked. Expected to feel a burst of pain, but nothing. Then a body slammed into her and she went to the ground one more time.

She felt a prick against her neck. "Now, if you move again," Alexander panted, "this heroin will make you one dead junkie, are we clear?"

She felt the warmth of the blood from his shoulder wound against her back. She almost nodded and thought better of it. "Yes," she whispered.

Aaron, Lance and Clay appeared once again. Lance and Clay held their weapons ready as they took in the scene. She saw Aaron's hope slide from his face and horror take up residence.

"Get up," Alexander demanded. Zoe climbed painfully to her feet as did her very pale-faced father-in-law. "Tell them to back off now."

"Don't come over here, Aaron! He's got a syringe full of heroin he's threatening to inject me with. Back up, please."

Aaron blanched then stayed still. Lance and Clay stopped, but held their guns aimed in Alexander's direction.

"Good," Alexander whispered. "Now all I want is to get out of here. I'm going to use you to do that, understand?"

"Yes."

"We're going to walk around the barn and toward the car."

She started in the direction he ordered, and he limped

along beside her, his breathing heavy against her ear. Once they rounded the side of the barn, she stopped and he stumbled against her. The needle pierced her neck, and she winced and pulled away. His grip on her arm tightened. She stared at the line of police cars and law enforcement officers parked in the yard. Aaron, Clay and Lance came into her line of sight from the other side of the barn. They were able to slip behind the cruiser to use it as protection in case other shots sounded. Zoe couldn't help but wonder who else was out there in the woods shooting. A sniper with the police department? Had the person meant to hit Alexander? Or had he been aiming for Zoe and just missed?

"Alexander, you're trapped," Clay called. "Let's end this now before anyone else gets hurt."

"The house," Alexander told her. "Go to the house."

Zoe didn't like the fact that he was completely ignoring Clay. He really thought he was going to find a way out of this. "Who shot you, Alexander?" she asked, her voice shaky and weak.

"A sniper, probably. A lousy shot if you ask me. Call your sniper off, Sheriff, or I'll make this a murder-suicide. You want that on your conscience?"

"It wasn't a sniper, Collier," Clay called. "We didn't have anyone up in the trees."

"Like I'm supposed to believe that?"

"It's true. If it were one of mine, you'd be on the ground dead, a bullet in your brain, not your shoulder."

Zoe cleared her throat and caught Aaron's eye and saw the intense worry in the lines of his face. Clay stood next to him as well as Lance. All three of them, as well as the other law enforcement officers, watched them. Zoe knew Alexander was either going to try and use her as a hostage to negotiate his way out. Failing that, she felt certain there would be a murder-suicide. With a sick certainty, she knew that if it came down to getting caught and going to prison or dying, he'd choose to die.

She was going to have to do something.

"You messed up, Zoe. Bad. Now Sophia is going to die," he told her.

She kept walking, her brain groping for any kind of way to get away from him. She knew he had enough of the drug in the syringe to kill her quickly. It would have an almost immediate effect. She'd feel sleepy, pass out and forget to breathe. And unless there was immediate medical attention, she'd die. But once she was in the house, she had almost no hope of surviving.

"Please, Alexander," she whispered. Begging him was futile, but she could hope for a distraction.

"Shut. Up." He leaned heavily against her. He turned her to face the deputies as he passed, shifting so he never had his back to them. Aaron took a step toward them. Clay pulled him back. Alexander stumbled. The needle went into the back of her neck. She cried out and tried to pull away from him.

"Zoe!" Aaron's cry spurred her. She spun into Alexander's grip, felt the syringe fall from her. Two shots rang out. Alexander fell at her feet.

She felt the effects of the drug and realized Alexander must have pressed the syringe. Dizziness hit her, she relaxed and fell to the ground and let the sensations sweep her even as darkness claimed her.

Chapter 17

Aaron paced outside Zoe's hospital room, his prayers for her never ceasing. Clay and Lance were also there working on paperwork even as they waited for Zoe to wake up. Clay stood at the nurse's station pounding on his laptop. Lance walked up and clapped Aaron on the shoulder. "She's going to be all right. She just fainted. The doc said there was very little trace of the drug in her system. Only slightly more than what was on the needle when Alexander pulled the liquid into the syringe."

"But there was some. He did manage to press the syringe before we stopped him."

"Yes, but not much."

"It might not matter," Aaron said. "It could still send her back into her addiction."

"I know," Lance said softly. "But she didn't pass out

because of the drug. The doctor said she passed out due to the stress of the situation, and she really only needs to sleep and heal. We'll be thankful she didn't suffer any worse than some cuts and bruises."

"True."

"And we'll just pray that she doesn't even notice the small amount of the drug." He cleared his throat. "The good thing is Nina and Gregory didn't have any idea of what Collier was doing. They've got their lake house on the market to sell and are determined to help Zoe in any way they can."

"Zoe will be glad. She and her in-laws weren't super close, but she'll be relieved to know they didn't want her dead."

"Sophia is with them. I talked to her a little bit and told her that her mother wanted to see her real soon. She sounded happy. I let Nina tell her about Zoe being in the hospital."

"Can you send someone to pick Sophia up? She'll be the first face Zoe wants to see when wakes up."

"I'm way ahead of you. Nina's driving her here herself."

Aaron nodded. "Great. Did you find the jockey?"

"Yes. He had a single gunshot wound to the back of his head. A hiker found him just outside of Knoxville in a wooded area. It's amazing he was found this fast. He was really off the beaten path."

Sadness filled Aaron. The man had brought about his death with his own greed, but Aaron thought the punishment didn't fit the crime. Cartee had wanted the horse, and Alexander had used that desire to fuel his greed. Definitely sad. "What about the shot that came from the trees and hit Alexander in the shoulder? That wasn't one of your guys?"

"Nope. Parker made his way up there after the shot and found the shooter. It was Jedediah Mason. Parker shot him before Jed could get off another shot. He's dead."

Aaron closed his eyes for a brief moment. So much death. And it was so senseless and unneeded. "What was he doing up there?"

"Trying to shoot Alexander apparently. Before he died he said something about no honor among thieves. Alexander had backed out on paying him."

"So he was going to kill Alexander."

"Yep."

"How's Ginny?"

"Hanging in there. She woke up and was able to tell Clay what happened."

Ginny had been found not too far from her wrecked vehicle with a bullet in her side. "She pretty much verified the evidence they gathered at the scene. And the school phone records traced back to her cell. She was the one who called the school and pretended to be Zoe."

Aaron winced. "Okay. Then what?"

"She'd arranged to meet Alexander and give him Sophia. He'd deposited ten grand in her account to pay for her sister to be able to stay in her home."

Aaron sucked in a breath. "Collier did his homework, didn't he?"

"He did. After he learned where Zoe was, he started investigating into the pasts of all of us on the police force to figure out which person might possibly be open to his schemes."

"And he discovered Ginny's weakness."

"Yep. She said he called her and told her he knew Zoe was in trouble and was worried about Sophia being caught in the middle. He asked her to help him at least get Sophia away from everything. When she hesitated, he told her he knew about her sister and was willing to help her if she would help him."

"So she met Collier and gave him Sophia. Why shoot her? The money was already in her account. It's not like he could get it back."

Lance shrugged. "I figured it was because he didn't want any witnesses. But she said she changed her mind and refused to hand Sophia over to him."

Aaron blinked. "You believe her?"

Lance nodded. "Yes, I do. She was weeping and begging my forgiveness."

"So he shot her."

"Shot her and left her for dead. He destroyed the cruiser's radio and took her cell phone. She said Brian Cartee was there, too."

Aaron sighed and pinched the bridge of his nose. "Man."

"Yeah. Ginny said she played dead until Alexander, Brian and Sophia drove off. She hated to just let them take Sophia, but figured if they knew she was alive, she wouldn't have the chance to let anyone know who Sophia was with. When they were gone, she managed to walk until she passed out. She rolled down into the ditch—the reason it took so long to find her."

A nurse stepped out of the room and smiled at Aaron. "Mrs. Collier is awake and asking for two people. Aaron and Sophia?"

"I'm Aaron. Sophia's on her way. May I see Zoe?"

"Of course."

She stepped aside, and Aaron slipped through the open door. The room was dark so he opened the blinds then turned toward the woman who'd come to mean more to him than breathing itself. "Hey." He stepped up to the bed and took her hand.

"Hey," she said. "Where's Sophia? Is she all right?"

Her fear nearly undid him. "She's fine. Nina's on the way right now bringing her to you."

Tears filled her eyes and dripped down her temples. Aaron grabbed a handful of tissues from the box on her end table and dried the wetness. "No need to cry. Really, she's just fine."

"Oh, thank you, God."

"Yes."

She sniffed. "I've been so angry with Him."

"Who?"

"God. First my baby was diagnosed with diabetes, then Trevor was killed and I felt so guilty."

He sat down beside her. "Why? Why guilty?"

"Because he didn't deserve me. He deserved someone so much better." She sighed and closed her eyes. "I loved him, but I loved him because he was…safe. Solid and secure. I've always felt guilty that I didn't love him…more. And then he was killed and I never had the chance."

"He was what you needed at the time."

"Oh, yes, he was definitely that."

"Was he happy?"

She smiled, a sad little curve of her lips. "Yes. I can

honestly say he was happy. We had a good life and he loved Sophia with his whole heart."

He gripped her fingers. "I don't think you give yourself enough credit. You're amazing."

She gave a half laugh, half sob. "Amazing? No, not really."

He leaned over and kissed her. When he pulled back she was staring at him. "Do you trust me?" he asked.

"Yes."

He smiled. "I like that there wasn't any hesitation there."

"How could I not trust you? You've put your own life ahead of mine."

"Just like you did with Sophia."

"Of course."

"So if you would do that for your child, then don't you think God would do that for you?"

She paused. Then nodded. "Yes, he would. He did. He sent his only son to die for me."

"Exactly. So don't bash yourself. You are made in His image, and He felt you were worth dying for. That makes you amazing."

She looked down at her hands. "I never thought about it like that," she whispered. "I've never thought I was worth much of anything. My parents didn't think I was worth fighting for. My brother didn't think I was worth hanging around for, and I guess I've always wondered why Trevor loved me like he did."

"Was Trevor a Christian?"

"Yes." She smiled. "He was."

"Then he saw what I see, what God sees. A beautiful woman, inside and out. A mother who loves her child enough to die for her. A woman who puts others above herself. Don't you see that?"

Red flooded her face, and Aaron hugged her. "No, not really. But I guess when you put it that way…" she mumbled against his shoulder. She leaned back. "I just felt so…betrayed by God. I'd struggled to get clean, to get my life on track and I know He was there with me every step of the way. And then I got mad at Him when Sophia developed diabetes, three years ago. Then Trevor died, and it's just been a hard year." She gave a small shrug. "And then I met you and knowing what your family has been through up to this point and seeing their faithfulness has been a real eye-opener. I want that kind of faith, as well."

"You have it."

"Well, I'm definitely working on it."

"We'll work on it together if you'll let me." He paused and took a deep breath. "I love you, Zoe." She gasped and stared up at him. He shrugged. "Call me crazy, but I do. I've known you were the one for me from the time we met at the diner." He tapped her chin and her mouth shut with a snap. "I can see I've shocked you. You don't have to say anything, but I wanted to tell you what's in my heart. I don't want you to leave, but if you feel you have to move back to Knoxville, I'll follow you. I can set up a practice anywhere, but I just don't want to lose you. Unless you want me to get lost." Uncertainty filled him, her stunned expression keeping him from being able to breathe.

She studied him then shook her head. "I don't know what to say."

"Do you want me to get lost?"

"No! No, not at all."

"Well, that's a relief." He smiled and she gave a low laugh. He turned serious again. "If you don't want me to get lost, just tell me what's in your heart."

She drew in a deep breath and let it out slowly then nodded. "I have to say, my heart's pretty full right now."

"Good to hear."

She plucked at the sheet with her free hand then looked him in the eye. "I had a good life back in Knoxville, some good friends I look forward to reconnecting with now that I wouldn't be putting any of them in danger. But I think I've come to realize that my life there is now a part of my past. When we arrived in Wrangler's Corner, it was a bit like coming home. And even during all the craziness, every time I thought about leaving, I would get this hollow ache in my stomach."

"So what are you saying?"

"I'm saying I want to stay here. Sophia loves it. She loves you."

He understood how she felt when she said her heart was full. Something else they had in common. "And what about her mother?"

Zoe swallowed and pulled in a deep breath. Butterflies settled in her stomach and she wondered if she could even get the words she wanted to say through the tightness in her throat. "Her mother loves you, too, Aaron." His hands tightened around hers. "I think I've loved you from the moment you carried Sophia across that river, protecting her as though she were your own."

"I want her to be."

And then she couldn't speak anymore. He leaned

over and kissed her as though the only way he could tell her he loved her was through the kiss. She wrapped her arms around his neck and pulled him closer.

"Does this mean you're getting married?"

Zoe yanked back with a gasp. "Sophia!" She held her arms open and Sophia ran across the small space to hop on the bed and snuggled down next to her. "I've missed you!"

"I missed you, too, but I had fun with Aunt Nina." She frowned and gently touched the bruises Alexander had left on Zoe's face. "Are you okay? I was scared when Aunt Nina said we had to come to the hospital to see you. Did the bad men come back and hurt you?"

Zoe's eyes met Nina's red-rimmed and puffy ones. "I'm fine, honey. Just a little accident, that's all. All the bad men are gone, and we're safe as we can be. My wounds will heal." *Thank you, God.*

A brilliant smile broke out on Sophia's face, and her eyes looked lighter than they had in weeks. Zoe's heart ached at the stress the past few weeks had brought into her child's life. But that was over now. Sophia hugged her again. "I'm glad. Is Ginny okay, too? Her car broke down, and Grandpop came along to help. Isn't that crazy?"

"Hmm. Yes. Crazy." How much had Sophia seen with the incident that had landed Ginny in the hospital with a gunshot wound?

Aaron came to kneel in front of Sophia. He took her hand in his. "What exactly happened with Ginny's car breaking down?"

Sophia shrugged. "I'm not really sure. Ginny said her car broke down so she called someone to come help us.

Brian and Grandpop showed up. Grandpop asked Ginny if he could help her and she said no, that was all right, she was waiting for someone else."

"She did?" Zoe asked.

"Yes. She said something about changing her mind, and Grandpop got really mad. He told Brian to take me to the car while he and Ginny talked. So I went with Brian, but the car was pretty far away and I couldn't tell if Grandpop got her car started again or not."

"What happened to Brian after you got in the car with Grandpop?" Just saying the man's name made her want to gag. She looked up to see tears streaming down Nina's face. Aaron passed the box of tissues over to Nina and she grabbed several.

"I don't know," Sophia said. "Grandpop drove me to Nina's, and then he and Brian went somewhere."

She shuddered as she thought of the end Brian had met. So Alexander had dropped Sophia off then killed Brian. At least Sophia had been spared seeing Ginny hurt. Which led her to believe Alexander had been serious about leaving Sophia with Nina and Gregory. He hadn't wanted her traumatized—or a witness—to his violence. Zoe sent up a prayer of thankfulness that her child had been spared that.

Aaron hugged Sophia. "I'm glad you're all right, kid."

Sophia leaned back, grasped his face between her hands and kissed his nose. "Thanks, Doctor Aaron. I'm fine." She glanced at her mother then back to Aaron. "So are you going to marry my mom?"

Aaron flushed, but Zoe loved that he didn't look away from Sophia. "If she'll have me."

"Oh, *we* will," Sophia said.

Zoe gave a choked laugh. "And that's that, huh?"

Sophia grinned at her. "Of course."

Nina sniffed and blew out a sigh. Her gaze danced between Zoe and Aaron. "It looks like you have some unfinished business here. Is it all right if Sophia stays with me at the hotel tonight?" At Zoe's hesitation, Nina lifted a hand. "It's fine, I understand why you might not want to."

Zoe glanced at Aaron then Sophia. "I just hate for you to have to stay at a hotel. You're welcome to stay at the house and use my room." Sophia's shoulders slumped and Zoe raised a brow. "But maybe if Sophia wants to stay at the hotel, it could be arranged." She ran a hand over her child's soft hair. "What do you want to do?"

Sophia slanted her eyes at her aunt. "They have an indoor pool, right?"

Nina laughed and swiped her nose with the tissue. "Yes, they do."

Sophia nodded and turned to Zoe. "I think I'd like to go with Aunt Nina if that's all right."

"But you don't have a swimsuit."

Sophia's cheeks turned red, and she dropped her gaze. She shuffled her feet then looked up at Zoe through her lashes. "Well, I *might* have overheard Aunt Nina and Uncle Gregory making plans about bringing me to see you and she *might* have mentioned staying at the Marriott just outside of Wrangler's Corner and everybody knows they have an indoor pool…" She lifted her hands—the picture of innocence.

"So you *might* have packed the bathing suit you usually keep at Nina's?"

"I *might* have."

"All right, you can go."

Sophia squealed and gave Zoe another hug, turned to Aaron and held up her arms. He picked her up, and she squeezed his neck. Then she scurried down and raced to her aunt's side to grasp the woman's hand.

They turned to go and Nina looked back over her shoulder. "Thank you," she whispered.

Zoe nodded. "Thank you. For everything."

When the door shut behind them Aaron moved back to his spot on the bed. "Now. Where were we?"

She felt the heat rise in her cheeks. "Um—"

"Oh, yes, I remember." He lowered his head once more and captured her lips for yet another tender kiss. When he pulled back, he studied her. She shifted and gave a small laugh. "What?"

"You don't seem to have any lingering side effects from the drug."

She let her smile fall away. "No. Not right now." She bit her lip. "Aaron, I want…" She stopped and twisted the sheet into a ball then smoothed it back over her legs.

He covered her fidgeting hands with his. "What? What do you want, Zoe?"

She met his gaze. "I want to explore what we have. I want it more than anything, but you have to understand what you're getting into if you decide you want to be with me. I've been clean for over ten years—discounting today."

"I don't count today."

His tenderness made her want to cry, but she had to make sure he understood. "There are still days I struggle, Aaron. Not as many after all this time, true, but there *are* days I want a hit."

"But you don't get one."

"No. I don't, but it can be very difficult for me—and those around me—until it passes."

He cupped her cheek. "I can handle it. What do you do when the craving hits?"

"I either eat chocolate or go running. Or both."

"Excellent."

She lifted a brow. "Why?"

"Those are two things I can do with you."

"Really?" A tear slipped out. She couldn't help it.

He swiped it away. "Really."

"If you're sure. Please be very, very sure."

He kissed her again then leaned his forehead against hers. "Look at me." She did. "I love you. Not one of us is perfect or without baggage, but together we can overcome that and build a great life together. Us and Sophia. The Three Musketeers, okay?"

She gave a relieved, watery laugh. "Okay, that sounds like a deal."

He kissed her again. "Definitely a deal."

She pulled back again. "I have a question."

"What's that?"

"Did Clay and Sabrina ever name their baby?"

Aaron blinked then a laugh burst from him. "Yes. They named her Hannah."

"Oh, that's a lovely name."

"We think so."

"Okay, that's all I wanted to know. You can kiss me again."

So he did.

Epilogue

Thanksgiving

Zoe stared at the huge family around the monster table. Mrs. Starke was in her element, and she beamed as she presided over the organized chaos. There were people everywhere, spilling in and out of every room, upstairs and down. Zoe had given up trying to remember names. Sophia played with two other little girls about her age and was giddy with excitement. She'd never had a holiday such as the one playing out now.

And neither had Zoe. Arms slipped around her waist from behind, and Zoe tilted her head to smile up at her fiancé. "Are you overwhelmed?" he asked.

"Completely, but it's lovely. Fascinating. This is how you grew up?"

"Every year at every holiday. Of course it's a lot bigger now, but yes, it was just as nuts back when I was a kid, too." He chuckled. "Dad had to clean out the barn and set up tables in front of all the stalls. He's got the heaters running, and the kids will eat out there with a few adult chaperones."

"All your cousins are here. Aunts, uncles." A familiar face stepped into the foyer. "And Lance, too."

"Lance has become part of the family. He doesn't have a lot of his own so we've sort of adopted him."

"You're good people, you Starkes," she said.

"Thanks." He looked up and froze.

Zoe slipped out of his arms and followed his gaze. "What is it?" Before he could answer, she saw the reason for his stillness. "Amber!" She waded through the mass of humanity and reached her longtime friend. Amber grinned and held out her arms. Zoe grabbed her in a big hug. "I'm so glad you're here. I can't tell you how grateful I am you sent me out here."

She shot a subtle glance at her brother. "I'd say Aaron owes me."

Zoe giggled. "Big time."

Amber gave another laugh, this one a bit more subdued. "I have a question for you, Zoe."

Zoe stilled. "What's that?"

"Will you step outside with me for a minute?"

"What's going on?" Aaron asked. He slid an arm across Zoe's shoulder and she leaned into him.

But curiosity had her eyeing Amber. "Sure, I'll step outside with you."

"I'm coming, too," Aaron said.

Amber nodded and the three of them slipped out the

front door onto the big wraparound porch. People still mingled in the chilly afternoon air, but at least it was quieter than the house. "What is it?"

"If I told you that I found your brother, would you want to see him?"

The words hung in the air while Zoe fought for breath. "Yes," she was finally able to gasp. "Yes, I'd love to see him."

Amber seemed to lose some of her tension. "Good." She looked at the far end of the porch. "See that guy sitting down there?"

Zoe turned to look and caught her breath when her eyes landed on the man Amber indicated. She'd know him anywhere. He was older, but it was him. "Toby?" He stood and faced her. Her older brother, her friend, and at one point in her life, her protector. She walked up and stood in front of him. Tears threatened, but she held them back. "I've missed you."

Tears gathered in his own eyes and he stepped forward to wrap her in his arms and bury his nose in her hair. "Oh, man, Zoe, I've missed you, too."

"Where have you been?"

"It's a long story."

"I've got time if you do."

"All I can say is I didn't mean to desert you. Abandon you all those years ago. But Dad was so awful, he told me that you hated me and never wanted to see me again."

Zoe gaped. "That's not true!"

"I know that now thanks to Amber, but at the time, after that fight, I believed him. You were so mad at me for leaving and going to college."

"I tried to tell you I was sorry, that I didn't mean it, but I couldn't find you," she whispered.

He closed his eyes. "It's not your fault. I did a little disappearing act. I joined the Marines about a month after I left. And then from there, I went to work for the government."

"In what capacity?"

He hesitated. "I can't tell you."

She blinked. "You have one of those jobs."

He gave a self-conscious smile. "Yes. I shouldn't have even told you that much, but I'm going to have to disappear again, and I don't want you feeling abandoned yet again."

"But I've just found you. I don't want you to leave." She sounded like a five-year-old and didn't care.

Toby hugged her then Amber. "I can stay for a day or so, then will have to take off." His lips turned down. "I'm sorry, it's all I've got."

Zoe nodded and swiped a few stray tears. "I'll take it."

"Great. Now you want to introduce me to the guy who's been watching you like a lovesick puppy?"

Zoe and Amber laughed and Aaron grinned. She made the introductions and then jumped when a bell sounded. Aaron grabbed her hand. "Dinner is ready."

Zoe tucked her hand in his. "Let's go eat."

They found their way to one of the large tables and Aaron pulled her seat out for her. He introduced her to those around her. Seth, Aaron's brother, had a baby boy tucked into the crook of his left arm. "Seth's riding in the National Finals Rodeo the first week in December. Again."

"Congratulations, that's huge."

Seth grinned at her. "Thanks, and it's nice to meet you. Didn't think anyone would lasso this brother of mine. You caught a good one."

Tonya, Seth's wife, smacked his arm—the one without the baby. "Really, Seth? Behave."

He ducked. "Sorry." Zoe didn't see any remorse in his bright blue eyes.

"Who's the little one?" she asked.

"That's Brady. He's three months old." Pride beamed from Seth's face. Sabrina came and swooped little Brady right out of his daddy's arm.

She grinned at Zoe. "Hi. My mom has Hannah so I'm going to just love on this little doll for a few minutes."

Zoe nodded. "I don't blame you a bit."

Aaron leaned over. "Do you think you can handle this crazy crew on a permanent basis?"

Butterflies swarmed in her stomach as his warm breath caressed her ear. She gripped his fingers. "I think I can handle anything with you at my side," she told him.

His eyes brightened and he bent down to steal a kiss in front of everyone. She knew her cheeks were as red as Sabrina's fire-engine top, but she didn't care a bit.

Sophia squealed and grabbed his arm to hug it to her chest. "I'm glad you're marrying my mom."

"I am, too, sweetheart."

Sophia tilted her head and stared up at him. "So…"

"Yes?" Aaron asked.

"Can I call you 'Daddy'?" The question was so faint Zoe almost didn't hear it.

But the craziness around them faded as she watched Aaron pick Sophia up into his strong, capable arms. He kissed her cheek and settled her on his lap. "I can't think of anything that I would like more." He paused and slid an arm around Zoe's shoulders to pull her next to him. She could hardly breathe through the emotions filling her. Sophia smiled, a shy, gap-toothed smile. Then she looked at Aaron's mother, Mrs. Starke, who'd walked around the table to stand next to them. Tears glistened in her eyes.

"Doctor Aaron's going to be my daddy and you're going to be my grandma."

The woman nodded. "That's the best news I've heard today."

Sophia slid off her future daddy's lap and back into her chair. "I'm hungry."

Aaron still had his arm around Zoe's shoulder. He kissed her ear. "And I'm blessed."

"Correction. We're blessed."

"Amen to that." He kissed her again. "Now, the kid's hungry. Let's eat."

* * * * *

Laura Scott is a nurse by day and an author by night. She has always loved romance and read faith-based books by Grace Livingston Hill in her teenage years. She's thrilled to have published over twenty-five books for Love Inspired Suspense. She has two adult children and lives in Milwaukee, Wisconsin, with her husband of over thirty years. Please visit Laura at laurascottbooks.com, as she loves to hear from her readers.

Books by Laura Scott

Love Inspired Suspense

Justice Seekers

Soldier's Christmas Secrets
Guarded by the Soldier

Callahan Confidential

Shielding His Christmas Witness
The Only Witness
Christmas Amnesia
Shattered Lullaby
Primary Suspect
Protecting His Secret Son

True Blue K-9 Unit: Brooklyn

Copycat Killer

Visit the Author Profile page at Harlequin.com for more titles.

UNDER THE LAWMAN'S PROTECTION

Laura Scott

He will cover you with his feathers,
and under his wings you will find refuge;
His faithfulness will be your shield and rampart.

—*Psalms* 91:4

This book is dedicated to my friend Olga Lita. Thanks, Olga, for the wonderful support you've provided over the years. Your friendship means more to me than you'll ever know.

Chapter 1

Swat team member Isaac Morrison paused outside the sheriff's-department headquarters and replayed the garbled voice-mail message for the third time.

Ice...cover blown...danger...help Leah and Ben...

The voice sounded like his buddy Shane "Hawk" Hawkins, and the use of his old nickname, Ice, gave credence to the fact that Hawk had left the message despite the unknown phone number. Was Hawk calling from a throwaway phone? Possibly. Isaac had tried to return the call twice, but it wouldn't go through.

Strange to be hearing from Hawk now, when they hadn't really been in touch for the past sixteen months, but the urgency in Hawk's static-filled message was impossible to ignore.

What in the world was going on? Isaac jogged to his

Jeep, located in the far corner of the parking lot beneath a street lamp, his brain whirling with possibilities. Leah was Hawk's sister, and if he remembered correctly, Ben was her young son. By now the boy would be about five or so, and the thought that they might be in danger spurred Isaac into action. He revved up his Jeep and headed toward the interstate, wincing a bit at the fact that the time was approaching eight o'clock at night.

Hawk had left the message well over an hour ago. Isaac had had his phone on silent during his most recent tactical situation. He'd been called in as a negotiator at a local bank, where a drug addict had held a woman hostage in order to get money to fund his habit. Thankfully, they'd managed to take down the man before he shot or injured any innocent bystanders.

A good day for the Milwaukee County SWAT team, but the brief moment of satisfaction quickly evaporated with this latest threat. What if Isaac was already too late to protect Leah and Ben? He stomped on the accelerator, pushing the speed limit. He knew that Hawk's sister was the only family his buddy had left in the world, and the two were extremely close. The situation had to be serious for Hawk to call for help.

Isaac had met Hawk twelve years ago at Saint Jermaine's Youth Center, which was basically a school for delinquent teens, and during their first month there Hawk had saved his life. They'd been friends ever since, but Hawk had never asked for anything from him.

Until now.

Isaac hoped that Leah was still living in the same small home he remembered, located just inside the city limits. If she'd moved since the last time he saw her, he was in trouble, because he couldn't even remember her married name. Nelson? Nichols? Even though her husband had died roughly four years ago, he was pretty sure she hadn't remarried. Otherwise why would Hawk call him? Surely he would have contacted her new husband if she had one.

Isaac drove through the dark, damp March night, wondering if Leah would even remember him. He'd met her only a few times, and the last occasion must have been at her husband's funeral. The only good thing now was that he was still wearing his uniform, so at least she would be able to recognize him as one of the good guys.

Ironic that he and Hawk had both turned their troubled lives around to go into law enforcement. Hawk had taken a job with the City of Milwaukee Police Department, while Isaac had gone the route of joining the Milwaukee County Sheriff's Department. As they were located in two completely different jurisdictions, their paths hadn't crossed in the line of duty.

Hawk had mentioned that his cover was blown, so he must have been investigating something serious while being undercover. But what? It would have helped to have some idea of the source of potential danger.

As he approached Leah and Ben's house, located at the bottom of a dead-end street, Isaac cut his headlights and slowed to a stop several yards away from the end of her driveway.

For a long moment he sat there, watching for any signs of life. But the windows were dark, and from the street he couldn't see any hint of light or movement inside. At eight-thirty on a Friday night, it was hard to believe Leah and Ben would be already asleep.

Either they weren't home yet or he was too late to save them.

Every nerve in his body rebelled at that thought, so he decided to investigate. He reached up to pull the bulb out of the dome light and then slipped out of his Jeep, hugging the shadows as he made his way closer to Leah's small house. In contrast, her yard was spacious and boasted several tall trees, one with a tire swing hanging from a thick branch. Seeing the swing reminded him of his dead son, and for a moment the pain of losing Jeremy nearly sent Isaac to his knees. He missed his son so much, but forced himself to concentrate on the task at hand. He tore his gaze from the swing, sweeping a wide glance across the yard to make sure that nothing was out of place.

No signs of a crime didn't mean one hadn't taken place. The warning itch along the back of his neck couldn't be ignored.

Moving slowly, he made his way around to the back of the house. There were still no lights anywhere and all was quiet. Leah didn't have anyone living to her left, but the neighbors to the right must be home, based on the blue glow of a television set in what appeared to be a living room. Surely if something had happened here, they would have been alerted.

He checked the back door to verify it was locked. He made a mental note to tell Leah she needed motion-sensor lights mounted in the backyard as well as out front above the garage. He was a little surprised that Hawk hadn't already taken care of that. Isaac rounded the corner of the house and abruptly stopped in his tracks, flattening himself against the siding when he saw a figure dressed from head to toe in black. The man had a ski mask covering his face, and he was stealthily making his way through Leah's front yard.

Hawk was right. Leah and Ben were in danger!

Isaac wished he'd asked a few of his SWAT teammates to come along, especially Caleb or Deck, but it was too late for that. Even if he called them, they were forty-five minutes away, and there wasn't a second to waste. He pulled his weapon and crouched low, trying to keep the intruder in his line of vision.

He considered calling 911 for backup, but feared the masked man would hear him. Using a cell phone, he'd have to give the dispatcher his location and even soft, muffled sounds carried loudly through the night. Right now, Isaac had the element of surprise on his side.

But he froze when the intruder hid alongside the large oak tree, the one with the tire swing hanging from it.

Clearly, the masked man was waiting for Leah and Ben.

Belatedly, Isaac noticed a pair of headlights approaching along the street, growing brighter and brighter as the car neared the house. The vehicle was an older-model sedan, but with the lights in his eyes, he couldn't tell for sure if the driver was male or female.

The possibility that Leah and Ben were coming home at this exact moment sent a shiver down his back. Had the masked man been following them? Or had his timing been pure luck?

Isaac didn't believe in coincidences. And he couldn't help wondering if the guy in black had a partner waiting somewhere nearby. He hadn't seen anyone, but that didn't mean someone wasn't still out there.

Isaac stayed at the corner of the house, his eyes trained on the oak tree. He had to assume the masked man would wait until the most opportune time to attack. The sedan pulled into the driveway and idled outside the garage. Isaac thought it was odd that the garage door didn't open, especially after several seconds passed.

Then he saw the driver's door open.

The events unraveled in slow motion. The masked intruder made his move, darting out from behind the tree and roughly grabbing the arm of the woman who'd gotten out of the car.

No! Isaac sprinted across the yard toward them. "Stop! Police!"

In a heartbeat, the man in black spun around, holding Leah in front of him as a hostage. Isaac froze when he saw he was pointing a gun at her temple. Her eyes were wide with terror and she kept glancing helplessly at the car, where her son was crying. Isaac couldn't afford to give him any reason to shoot.

"Look, no one has to get hurt here, okay?" He used his best negotiating tone and lifted his hands, pointing his weapon upward, indicating he wasn't going to shoot, either. If the masked man did have a partner, Isaac was dead meat, but there wasn't much he could do about it now. Maybe the people watching television next door would hear the commotion and call the cops? He could only hope.

Isaac forced himself to calm down enough to go through the techniques he'd perfected over the years. "Listen, I'm sure this is just a big misunderstanding. Why don't you let the woman go?"

The masked man glanced around frantically, either

looking for help or trying to figure out where Isaac had come from and if he had backup. The second thought gave him hope that the intruder didn't have a partner hidden out in the darkness. "Get out of here," the man said in a rough, muffled tone. "This isn't your business."

"I'm sorry, but I can't do that." Isaac tried to hold the man's gaze, but it wasn't easy in the darkness. The dome light of the sedan was the only illumination aside from the quarter moon hanging low in the sky. "I'm a cop and I can't let you hurt this woman. Why don't you tell me what you want? I'm sure we can work something out."

"Go away or I'll shoot."

Isaac knew the key to negotiating was to find some sort of common ground. Not easy to do when you knew nothing about the stranger holding a gun. But he sensed the guy didn't want to shoot Leah or would have done so already. That might be something to work with. "Please put the gun down. I have backup coming in less than five minutes. If you put the gun down, I promise no one will get hurt."

The masked man ignored him, glancing around as if trying to figure out his next move.

Isaac eased forward, still holding his hands up. Leah's pale face surrounded by a cloud of dark curls looked scared to death, and he blocked the image from his mind. If he allowed himself to worry about her, he'd mess this up. He had to remain focused on the intruder.

Unfortunately, Isaac had absolutely no clue what was going on, which had him at a distinct disadvantage. "Do you want money? Is that it? I'll give you my wallet if you'll let the woman go."

"Stop talking!" The masked man was losing control

of the situation, and Isaac knew he had to find a way to make that crack in the guy's plan work to his advantage.

Inside the car, Ben was crying out for his mommy, and the noise seemed to be grating on the gunman's nerves. Isaac risked a glance inside the vehicle, and suddenly the man made his move.

"Take her!" he shouted. With a herculean push, he threw Leah away from him and turned to run.

Isaac had little choice but to grab Leah, preventing her from hitting the ground. She clutched him tightly as he stared over her shoulder as the man in black disappeared in the darkness.

As much as he wanted to chase after him, Isaac stayed right where he was. He held Leah steady, knowing his priority needed to be protecting Hawk's sister and her son.

Leah Nichols closed her eyes for a moment, silently thanking God for keeping her safe. But she couldn't understand why the masked man had tried to kidnap her in the first place. What was going on? She had no idea, but couldn't shake the idea that whoever the guy with the gun was, he'd be back.

She had to get Ben out of here now! She needed to get someplace safe and to call her brother. Shane would protect her and her son.

Leah shoved away from the cop, trying to pull herself together. "Thank you," she murmured before turning back to the car, where Ben was still crying in the backseat. "Hey, Ben, I'm here. It's okay. We're fine."

"Leah, you and Ben should come with me."

She spun toward the cop, shaken by the fact that he

knew their names. "Who are you?" she demanded. "And why are you here, anyway?"

"Don't you remember me? Isaac Morrison? I'm friends with your brother, Hawk, er, Shane. He sent me here to look after you."

Leah narrowed her gaze and shook her head. She vaguely remembered Hawk's friend Ice, also known as Isaac, but hadn't seen him in years. Since her husband's funeral? Maybe. Yet could she really be sure this cop was who he said he was? She had only a vague memory of Shane's friend, but his height and his military-short, sandy-brown hair did seem familiar.

On the other hand, it seemed strange to her that Shane wouldn't come to help her himself. Or send one of his buddies, such as his partner from the force. This cop's uniform wasn't at all similar to the type that her brother used to wear. A fact that put her on edge.

"I appreciate your help, really, but I'll be fine on my own. Thanks anyway."

She slid back into her vehicle, intending to leave, but the cop grabbed her door before she could get it shut. "Leah, I don't know what's going on, but it's pretty clear you need protection. I swear I'm not going to hurt you or your son."

Leah battled a wave of helplessness. Should she really trust this guy?

"Here, listen to this message." The cop hunkered down next to her, playing with his phone. Abruptly, a brief static-filled message blared from the speaker.

Ice...cover blown...danger...help Leah and Ben...

The words sent a chill down her spine. She recognized Shane's voice, and the fact that her brother was clearly in trouble concerned her. "You need to help Shane," she blurted out. "I'll go to a hotel or something, but you need to help my brother."

But the cop was shaking his head. "No, I'm not leaving you and Ben alone. Don't you understand how much danger you're in? How long do you think it will take the bad guy to track your car? He was waiting here for you when you got home, and I'm sure he knows what type of vehicle you're driving. He probably even has the license-plate number."

Shiver after shiver racked her body and she knew with certainty the cop was right. Leah had taken Ben to a birthday party for one of his classmates at the Fun Zone. How had the masked man known what time to expect her? And why hadn't her garage door opened?

Belatedly, she realized that the light she'd left burning over the kitchen sink was also out. Had the gunman cut the power? She couldn't think of any other explanation.

"Leah, please." The cop reached out to gently cover her hand with his, and she forced herself to meet his intense gaze. "Do you want to see my ID to prove I'm Isaac Morrison? I know it's been a long time, but you have to believe I'm not going to hurt you."

She knew he was right and tried to calm her frayed nerves. "I'm sorry to be so paranoid," she murmured apologetically. "I'm just a bit rattled after everything that's happened."

Isaac smiled, and the expression softened his features, making her realize how handsome he was. Had he always been? Or had she just not noticed until now?

"You're entitled to be rattled," he assured her. "Let's get you and Ben someplace safe for tonight and then I'll see if I can get in touch with your brother. We'll discuss our next steps in the morning."

Tears pricked her eyes at his obvious concern. He'd saved her life tonight, and instead of saying thank you, she'd snapped at him. Of course they needed to leave, and right away. If the gunman knew what she was driving, she and Ben weren't safe.

She sniffed, blinked back her tears and nodded. "Sounds good. Thank you, Isaac. For everything."

"No problem." He rose to his feet. "Why don't you grab Ben and I'll take care of his booster seat?"

She slid out of the car and tucked her keys in her jacket pocket before heading around to the opposite side to get Ben. The cop followed and waited patiently until she had lifted her son in her arms before reaching for the car seat.

"Is that your Jeep parked on the road?" she asked.

"Yes. Wait for me, though." He tucked the booster seat under his arm and then lightly grasped her arm, escorting her down the street, sweeping his gaze over the area as if ready for anything.

The idea that the gunman might not have been alone made her stomach twist with fear. Although if he'd had help, wouldn't that person have come forward to even the odds?

Maybe, maybe not. Killing a cop was something most criminals tried to avoid, at least according to what Shane was always telling her. But then again, her brother often downplayed just how dangerous his job was, especially since he worked in a district that handled the highest rate of violent crime. Shane knew that she'd purposefully chosen a man who wasn't a cop for a husband because of the fact that their father had been killed in the line of duty. Not that marrying a lawyer had helped her any. Elliot had been killed by a drunk driver, despite his *safe* job.

She pushed aside a wave of despair over losing her husband, knowing this wasn't the time to think about the past. She needed to concentrate on keeping her son safe.

Where was Shane now? She couldn't bear the thought of something happening to her brother. He had to be all right, he just had to be. Her son had already lost a father he didn't even remember.

Surely God wouldn't take his uncle, too?

She stumbled and would have fallen if not for Isaac's hand beneath her arm.

"Leah?"

His low, gentle voice helped keep the panic at bay. She took a deep breath and let it out slowly. It had been a long time since she'd leaned on a man for support, and she couldn't deny appreciating the fact she wasn't alone. "I'm fine."

Isaac opened the Jeep door and quickly threaded the belt through Ben's booster seat. He stepped back, giving her room to get her son settled inside.

"I love you, Ben," she whispered, pressing a kiss to the top of his head.

"I love you, too, Mommy."

Tears threatened again, and since she wasn't the crying type, she had to assume that they were a delayed reaction from the horrific experience of being held at gunpoint. Her son was only five years old, but she was afraid he might have nightmares from seeing the gunman grab her. She brushed the dampness away as she climbed past her son so that she could sit in the back, next to him.

If Isaac was annoyed with her choice to stay in the rear rather than next to him, he didn't let on. He shut the door behind her and then jogged around to get into the driver's seat. He started the engine and glanced back at her. "Buckle up."

She reached for the seat belt a bit embarrassed that she hadn't remembered. As an E.R. nurse, she'd seen more than enough car-crash victims and normally the gesture was automatic. But nothing about this night was normal.

She rested her head back against the seat and closed her eyes. Almost instantly the memory of the masked man grabbing her from behind the wheel flashed in her brain, so she pried her eyelids open and stared out the window, willing the image away.

When Isaac slowed down to turn onto one of the main highways leading away from town, she frowned and leaned forward. "Where exactly are you taking us?" she asked.

"There's a hotel that isn't too far from our SWAT headquarters," he said, meeting her gaze in the rear-view mirror.

"Why do we have to go all the way across town?" she asked. "There are plenty of hotels closer to my house."

"Yes, but I don't think staying close to your house is a wise thing to do right now." He was using the same calm, reasonable tone that he'd used with the gunman, and for some reason that irked her. "The guy knew where you lived and what time you were coming home.

Trust me, the farther away we can get from your place, the better."

"I know, but what if Shane comes looking for me?" She couldn't understand why they had to go so far away.

"We'll let your brother know where we are," Isaac assured her. "Did that guy say anything to you before I arrived?"

She didn't really want to relive those moments, but understood that Isaac was only trying to get information. And she'd do whatever necessary to help her brother. She licked her dry lips. "He told me that if I screamed he'd shoot."

"I'm sorry you had to go through that."

The sincere note in her rescuer's voice made her eyes fill with tears, which she rapidly blinked away. She had to be strong, for Shane's sake as well as Ben's. She tried to recall every detail of her brief encounter. "The garage door wouldn't open and the light I left on above the kitchen sink was out, too. Do you think he cut the electricity?"

"Very possibly, but unfortunately, I didn't see him do anything like that. I only saw him hiding behind your big oak tree. Is it possible you were followed? I can't help wondering if he might have cut the power earlier."

The thought that she might have been followed to the birthday party at Fun Zone only put her more on edge. How could she not have noticed?

Although why would she even look for someone following her? Being an E.R. nurse was hardly dangerous. And suddenly Leah was overwhelmed by a wave of helplessness. She closed her eyes again and prayed.

Please, Lord, thank You for saving me and Ben from

the gunman. I ask that You keep Shane, Isaac, me and Ben safe in Your care. Amen.

Her emotions calmed down after her prayer, and for the first time since pulling into her driveway, she felt as if she was on the right path.

If her brother had sent Isaac to keep her and Ben safe, then Leah needed to trust his judgment. And to trust in God. She couldn't do this on her own.

"The place I'm taking you and Ben is called the Forty Winks Hotel." He captured her gaze in the rearview mirror. "It's a cute establishment. We've used it before. You and Ben will be safe there."

Safe. She liked the sound of that. Oddly enough, she was glad Isaac was here, protecting her and Ben.

But abruptly, the Jeep jerked sharply to the right, causing her to cry out in alarm. Isaac wrestled with the steering wheel in a vain attempt to stay on the road, but it was no use.

What was going on? Leah swallowed a scream and grabbed her son's hand, praying for God to watch over them and ignoring the way her seat belt bit sharply into her shoulder as the vehicle plunged into a ditch.

Chapter 2

"Leah? Ben?" Isaac fought to get free of his seat belt so he could make sure his passengers were safe. "Are you both all right?"

Ben was crying and Leah was trying to console him. "Shh, Ben, we're okay. Everything's fine. Don't cry, sweetie. Please don't cry."

Hearing Ben sob ripped at his heart. Yet there wasn't time to waste. "We need to get out of here."

"What? Why?"

He didn't want to scare Leah more than she already was, but he believed someone had taken a shot at them. "Try to keep your head down and don't get out of the car yet, okay? I don't think this was an accident." He quickly called the dispatch center, giving the code for officer needing assistance. "We're not far from Highway 22," he informed them.

"Ten-four."

He hung up and then called Caleb's number. Thankfully, his teammate answered on the second ring. "You interrupted our family time," Caleb mumbled. "This better be important."

"I'm sorry, but I need backup," Isaac said. "I'm fairly certain someone caused me to crash my Jeep."

"All right, I'll grab Deck, too." Caleb didn't hesitate to come to his aid, and Isaac knew he was lucky to have friends like them. "Where are you?"

Isaac gave his location and then disconnected from the call, feeling better knowing the two men he trusted the most would be there soon. Of course, the dispatcher would send someone out as well, but Isaac needed members of the SWAT team to help him figure out exactly what they were dealing with.

"So you think someone made us crash?" Leah asked fearfully.

He glanced back at her, trying to figure out how much to say in front of Ben. "It's just a hunch, but yeah. The tires on this Jeep are brand-new and I didn't see anything on the road that could have caused this. Just stay down. I'm going to go out and make sure there isn't someone out there."

"Wait!" she cried as he was about to open his car door. "Don't go. Stay here with us."

He was torn between two impossible choices. If someone had shot out the tires on purpose, he couldn't just wait for that person to come and finish them off. Nor did he want to leave Leah and Ben here alone.

So far he wasn't doing the greatest job of keeping Hawk's sister and her son safe. If he'd been wearing his bulletproof gear he would be in better shape to go out to investigate.

Isaac peered out the window, trying to see if anyone was out there. Sitting here was making him crazy, so he decided doing something was better than nothing.

"I'm armed, Leah, so don't worry about me. I promise I'll do whatever it takes to keep you and Ben safe."

He could tell she wanted to protest, but she bit her lip and nodded. She pulled her son out of his booster seat and tucked him next to her, so that he was protected on either side. Then she curled her body around him. The fact that she would risk herself to protect Ben gave Isaac a funny feeling in the center of his chest.

Leah's actions were humbling. He hadn't been attracted to a woman in a long time, not since his wife had left him for a guy who turned out to be mentally unstable. A man who'd shot Becky, Jeremy and then himself in a fit of depressed anger.

But this wasn't the time to ruminate over the past. Isaac's ex-wife and son were gone and nothing in the world would bring them back. So Isaac would do the next best thing—protect Leah and Ben with his life if necessary.

Isaac hadn't replaced the bulb in the dome light, so he wasn't too worried about broadcasting his movements. He pushed open the driver's-side door and used it as a shield as he swept his gaze around, searching for any sign of danger. The country road he'd taken was deserted, which wasn't at all reassuring. He had to assume that someone had hidden in the trees along the opposite side of the road, waiting for his Jeep to show up so they could take a shot at him. The last thing he wanted to do was sit here and wait for yet another gun-man to show up.

He was positive he hadn't been followed, which left only one option. The masked man must have known he was a sheriff's deputy, maybe by recognizing the uni-form, and he'd come this way hoping to ambush him, since this was the main road leading to the sheriff's-department headquarters.

How much time did they have before there was an-other attempt to take Leah and Ben? Probably not much.

Isaac had to decide right now if they'd be safer out-side or waiting in the Jeep. Normally he didn't have trouble making decisions.

But for some reason, he couldn't seem to get the image of the gunman holding Leah hostage out of his mind. The personal responsibility gnawed at him.

Outside the Jeep, he abruptly decided. For sure, they needed to get outside to hide, so they weren't sitting ducks.

He climbed back in and closed the door. "We're going to get out on the passenger side, okay? I'll go first and then you and Ben will follow."

Leah lifted her tearstained face and nodded. Her si-lent tears made him feel bad for her, but he forced him-self to concentrate. Awkwardly, he climbed over the gearshift and then pushed open the passenger door. Stay-ing behind the protection of the car, he opened the door to the back, taking the booster seat out first, to give Leah and Ben room to maneuver.

"Come on out," he said in a low voice.

Leah lifted Ben and handed him over. Isaac moved to the side, keeping the boy in front of him so that Ben was sandwiched between him and the car. Leah climbed out, too, and immediately reached for her son.

"Stay down," Isaac said, moving so that he was directly behind her.

"Where are we going?" she asked in a whisper.

Good question. There weren't streetlights, but the scant amount of lingering snow on the ground reflected the moonlight, making it brighter than he was comfortable with. "See that small cluster of trees?" He indicated an area directly behind him. "We're going to hide there."

Fear shimmered in her eyes, but she gave a jerky nod of agreement.

"You and Ben first. I'll protect you from behind. Ready? Let's go."

Leah clutched her son close and ran up the slippery embankment toward the trees, moving faster than he'd anticipated. Then again, adrenaline had a way of giving the body a boost when needed the most. He held his weapon ready and kept pace behind her.

When Leah and Ben were safe in the grove, Isaac gave a little sigh of relief. He was about to join them when his foot slipped on a patch of melting snow. He fell to his knees and felt something whiz past his head.

A bullet?

"Get down," he ordered hoarsely, practically throwing himself on top of Leah.

"What happened?" she asked in a muffled tone.

He didn't want to scare her, but he couldn't lie to her, either. "I'm pretty sure someone is shooting at us. Sit down at the base of this big tree and hold Ben in your lap. My backup will be here soon."

Leah did as he asked, sliding to the ground and hugging her boy close. Isaac could hear her murmuring something, and he leaned down, trying to hear what she was saying.

It was then he realized she was praying.

Dear Lord, keep us safe in Your care! Give Isaac the strength and the courage to defeat our enemy. We ask this in Christ the Lord. Amen.

Normally he wasn't the praying type, but right now, Isaac couldn't deny they needed all the help they could get. And if that meant praying, he was all for it.

Leah cuddled Ben close, whispering prayers as a way to keep them both calm. She felt terrible about how he had been crying on and off, clearly not understanding what was going on. To be fair, she didn't really understand, either.

Why would someone come after her and Ben? Not just once tonight, but twice? She was very grateful she was here with Isaac rather than being alone.

"There, do you hear that?" her brother's friend asked softly.

She couldn't hear anything beyond the thundering of her heart. She was about to shake her head when she heard the faint wail of a siren.

Help is on the way!

"Maybe you should call them and let them know where we are," she suggested.

"No, the light from my phone would be a beacon showing our location to the shooter. As it is, he already knows we're on the move. But from the angle of the bullet, he must still be up in the trees somewhere, which is good for us, as that means he isn't in the process of making his way over here on foot. Unless he has a partner."

"But why is he shooting at all? I don't understand."

Isaac scowled. "He was probably trying to take me out of the picture so that he had a clear path to get to you."

She swallowed hard, wishing she hadn't asked.

The radio on Isaac's lapel crackled and he quickly muffled the sound with his gloved hands. "ETA?" he whispered.

"Less than five."

"Shooter in the tree line on the south side of the street," he murmured. "Stay down."

"Ten-four."

Leah began reciting the Lord's Prayer. She could feel Isaac's gaze on her and she couldn't help wondering if he wasn't a Christian. Not that she should be surprised, because her brother went to church only when she forced the issue. And even then he mostly attended for Ben's sake.

"We're not beat yet," Isaac said when she'd finished her prayer. "We're going to be fine as soon as my teammates Caleb and Deck get here."

"I know. But praying keeps me calm. I take it you don't have the same experience?"

He gave a brief shake of his head and averted his gaze. "Nope. The only times I go to church are for weddings or funerals. And truth be told, in my line of work it's more of the latter."

She knew very well what he meant. Hadn't she learned that firsthand? Her father had died in the line of duty, as had one of his colleagues. And on top of that, she'd lost her husband to a drunk driver on his third DUI offense.

Too much loss for one person to handle.

Since the last thing she wanted to think about was the dangers associated with Shane's and Isaac's respective jobs, she twisted around so she could see the road.

"Red lights in the distance," Isaac murmured in his low, reassuring tone. "My team will be here soon."

"Thank You, Lord," she murmured.

"Amen," Ben said in a small voice. Her eyes welled up with tears at her son's sentiment. At that moment she was grateful she'd taken him to church every week.

"See, Ben? We're safe now."

"But, Mommy, I'm cold," he whined.

"I know, sweetie." She brushed her lips over Ben's forehead. "Mr. Isaac's friends will be here soon and then we'll be able to get into a warm car, okay?"

"We're hiding in a cluster of trees at your three o'clock," Isaac murmured into the radio.

"Ten-four."

"They're not going to search the trees across the street, are they?" Leah asked, trying not to be too blunt, for Ben's sake.

"No, getting you two to safety is our main priority."

Once again she was glad she wasn't out here alone. So far, Isaac had proved to be dedicated in his mission to protect her and Ben.

Maybe her brother had chosen wisely after all. Even though she never wanted to be married to a cop, especially seeing what her mother had gone through after losing her father, being helped by one who was determined to protect you wasn't all bad.

The red lights grew brighter and soon she saw two sheriff's-department vehicles park behind Isaac's ditched Jeep. First one dark figure climbed out of the car, dressed in full SWAT gear, and then a second figure joined him. Within minutes, they made their way over to their hiding spot amid the trees.

"Hey, Isaac, what's the deal? Haven't you had enough adventure for one day?" the shorter of the two asked in a low voice.

"Knock it off," he growled, not looking the least bit amused. "Listen, I need you and Caleb to create a wall of armor so that we can get Leah and Ben down to your vehicle. I'm fairly certain the shooter was on the other side of the road."

"No problem. We're ready."

"Okay, Leah, I want you to slowly stand up, while keeping your head down," Isaac instructed.

"Okay." Rising to her feet was easier said than done, since her legs had gone numb. Plus Isaac hadn't moved back very far, so there wasn't a lot of room to maneuver.

But then Caleb, or was it Declan, reached down and helped her up. Isaac stayed behind her, while the other officer took Ben. Clustered together as one, they slowly moved across the muddy terrain, heading in the direction of the vehicles. When they reached the nearest one, Leah set Ben on the rear seat and climbed in beside him. One of Isaac's friends brought over the booster seat and soon Ben was securely fastened inside.

"Stay here," Isaac said in a low voice. "The windows are bulletproof, so there's no reason to be afraid. We'll be out of here soon enough."

"Okay." She couldn't deny being relieved to know

the windows were reinforced. But that didn't stop her from searching the trees across the street, looking for any sign of the masked man.

Isaac spoke to the other two officers outside for a few minutes before he slid in behind the wheel. He cranked the key and blasted the heat. "We'll be leaving in a few minutes."

"W-what about y-your J-Jeep?" she asked, her teeth chattering as her entire body began to shake. Reaction from the night's events had finally hit her, and she couldn't seem to get her body under control.

"The guys will make sure it gets back to the station. We want the crime-scene techs to take a look at my rear tire. Not that there's much left to examine."

Leah gave a jerky nod, unable to trust her voice not to betray her. Isaac turned in his seat and pinned her with a direct gaze.

"I'm going to make sure you and Ben get someplace safe for the rest of the night," he said in a serious tone. "Okay?"

"S-sure." She could tell he was feeling bad about everything that had just happened, but none of this was his fault.

Of course, it wasn't exactly her fault, either.

She suppressed another shiver, wishing she knew where her brother was. And couldn't help wondering if she'd ever feel safe again.

Isaac inwardly winced when Leah wrapped her arms around her abdomen as if trying to keep herself from shaking.

He scrubbed his hands over his face, telling himself it

was not a good idea to scoot in beside her to offer comfort. He'd managed to keep his distance from any romantic entanglements over the past few years, and this was hardly the time or the place to change his mind. Especially with his friend's sister, no matter how beautiful she was.

Still, he wished there was a way to ease Leah's fears. To let her know that she was handling this better than anyone could expect.

He shook his head at his foolishness and peered through the windshield. Having Caleb and Declan outside, trying to put the puzzle pieces together for him, didn't sit well. He wanted to be out there in the middle of the action.

But Hawk was his friend and Leah was his responsibility, not theirs, though they'd both offered to help in any way they could.

As soon as he had his charges in a safe place, Isaac would need to find a way to get in touch with Hawk. Someone wanted Leah and Ben, and the only thing that made sense to him was that they needed some leverage to draw his friend out of hiding.

Hawk had mentioned that his cover was blown, and Leah and Ben were in danger. But from whom? What in the world was Hawk involved in?

"Isaac?" Caleb rapped on the window. "You need to come out here and see this."

He lifted his hand to show he'd heard. He turned back toward Leah. "I'll only be a minute, okay?"

She nodded, but didn't meet his gaze. She looked so weary, as if she might keel over at any moment.

Guilt weighed heavily on his shoulders as he turned

back and pushed open the driver's-side door. He followed Caleb over to his Jeep, where Deck was standing with a flashlight trained on the rear fender.

"What is it?" he asked.

"Check this out." Deck aimed his beam of light at the lower edge of the wheel well. "What do you think? Looks like a bullet hole to me."

Isaac stared in shock as the implication of the small round hole sank deep. "The shooter took two shots at the tire," he murmured slowly. "He must have missed the first time."

"Yeah, but not by much," Caleb pointed out. "And you both know how difficult it is to hit a tire on a moving vehicle. The average citizen could never pull this off. Our perp is a sharpshooter of some kind, maybe a sniper from the armed forces."

"Yeah," Isaac agreed grimly, turning to look up at his two closest friends. "Or maybe a cop, like us."

Caleb and Deck exchanged grim glances and then nodded. "You could be right," Caleb acknowledged. "It wouldn't be the first time we encountered a dirty cop on the force."

No, it wouldn't. Isaac stared at the small round hole in the fender. Keeping Leah and Ben safe wouldn't be nearly as easy if they had a cop or some other guy with military training on his tail.

But failure was not an option.

Chapter 3

Leah was relieved when Isaac returned to the sheriff's-deputy SUV after just a few short minutes. "C-can we leave now?" she asked.

"Yes," he responded shortly, as if he wasn't happy about something. He put the SUV in gear and pulled out onto the highway. The silence stretched between them as Isaac drove, taking a series of turns that made her wonder if he was making sure no one was following.

The warmth from the heater finally penetrated her chilled body and she relaxed against the seat, feeling safe at least for the moment.

She peeked over at her son. Ben's eyes had drifted closed, as he was no doubt exhausted after his crying jag. She was glad he was able to get some rest. "What did Caleb want to show you?" she asked in a low tone.

Isaac's eyes briefly met hers in the rearview mirror. "Evidence."

"Of what?"

There was another long silence. "A bullet hole located in the Jeep's fender."

She swallowed hard. Suspecting that the tire was shot on purpose and knowing beyond a shadow of a doubt were two different things. All because someone wanted to get to her and Ben? Why? What in the world had Shane gotten mixed up in? "We need to talk to my brother," she murmured.

"I know. I tried to call him earlier, but he didn't pick up, and there wasn't a voice-mail box set up on his phone, so I couldn't leave him a message. I'll try again later."

She was surprised to note it was only about ten-fifteen at night. For some reason, the hour felt much later. Or maybe it was just that so much had happened in such a short time. "Are we still going to the Forty Winks Hotel?"

Isaac shook his head. "No, I've decided to go to a different place Deck suggested. Both Caleb and he have used the Forty Winks before, and right now I'd rather go someplace with fewer ties to the SWAT team, just to be on the safe side. Deck has reserved two adjoining rooms for us."

Adjoining rooms? She hadn't thought much beyond getting to the hotel, but now realized she should have known that Isaac wouldn't just leave her and Ben there alone. Of course he'd want to stay close at hand, especially after this latest close call in the Jeep. Two attempts to shoot them in less than two hours must be some sort of record. She was glad she wasn't going to be totally alone. And having adjoining rooms would provide some modicum of privacy.

She watched the street signs, trying to familiarize herself with the area. Most of the Wisconsin-winter snow had melted, leaving a slushy, muddy mess in its wake. A quarter moon hung in the sky, but the stars were faint and difficult to see, no doubt because Isaac was driving them closer to the city.

Fifteen minutes later, he pulled into the parking lot of a place called the American Lodge. She thought the Forty Winks Hotel sounded better, but obviously she wasn't in a position to argue. The Lodge wasn't very big, but there were two stories. She leaned forward and tapped Isaac's shoulder. "I'd rather be on the ground floor if possible," she said. "Ben is at the age where he climbs everything, and I don't want to risk him going over the balcony."

"No problem," Isaac murmured. He drew up in front of the lobby. "Stay here and wait for me, okay?"

She nodded and rested against the seat cushion, wishing she had a change of clothes with her. Her jeans were splattered with mud from their mad dash to the trees. Hopefully, Isaac would ask for some basic toiletries at the front desk.

Ben was still asleep in his booster seat and she wished she didn't have to wake him up. After everything they'd been through, he deserved a little peace.

Isaac returned from the lobby with two key packets in his hand. He handed one to her and then drove around the side of the building. "We're in rooms 10 and 12, last two on the first floor."

"Okay." She turned, released the seat belt and eased Ben out of the booster seat.

"Do you want me to carry him inside?" Isaac offered.

She hesitated, but then nodded. The adrenaline rush had faded, leaving her feeling shaky and weak. Her muscles felt sore, as if she'd run some sort of marathon rather than a short sprint to a grove of trees. She climbed out her side of the vehicle while Isaac opened the other back door.

He gently lifted Ben out of his car seat and carried him toward their room. Leah pulled the plastic key card out and unlocked the door. After flipping on the light, she stood back so that Isaac could set Ben on one of the two double beds, choosing the one closest to the bathroom.

The room was clean, but smelled a bit musty, as if it hadn't been used in a few days. Still, she was grateful to be here.

"The clerk at the desk provided a few toiletries for us." Isaac fished the items out of his coat pocket and set toothbrushes, toothpaste and a comb on the dresser. Then he crossed over to the connecting door. "I need you to leave this unlocked, okay? I'll open my side, as well."

She nodded wearily. "I understand. Thanks again, for everything."

Isaac stared at her for a long moment, his dark eyes intense. The strange awareness between them unnerved her and she took a step backward, as if more distance would help. He looked as if he wanted to say something more, but then he turned and strode toward the door. "If you need anything at all, let me know."

"I will."

When the door closed behind him, she felt a momentary flash of panic. Ridiculous, since he was only going right next door. She crossed over and opened the connecting door, listening for sounds from the other room. It didn't take long for Isaac to unlock and open his door.

"Are you okay?" he asked when he saw her standing there, obviously waiting.

She forced a smile, hoping he wouldn't notice her blush. "Yes, of course. Good night."

"Good night."

She left a one-inch gap in the door before making her way over to Ben. Carefully, so as to not wake him up, she removed his winter coat, hat and shoes. She left his long-sleeved T-shirt and jeans on in lieu of pajamas. Setting the outer clothing aside, she bent over and pressed a kiss to the top of his head, thanking God once again for keeping her son safe.

Ben wiggled around, muttering something incomprehensible before burrowing into the pillow. She pulled the covers up over him and then made her way to the bathroom. She washed her hands and face, then dabbed at the mud splatters on her jeans with a soapy washcloth. She used the toothbrush and toothpaste, but didn't bother with the comb, since her naturally curly hair would be better served with a brush. She went back into the room and sat on the edge of her bed, cradling her head in her hands.

She needed to get some sleep, but couldn't make herself crawl in between the sheets. Instead, her mind whirled with questions. Where was Shane? What had he stumbled into? Was he hiding? Hurt? Or worse?

After a brief internal debate, she stood up and went

back over to the connecting doors, tapping lightly to get Isaac's attention.

"What's wrong?" He leaped to his feet, instantly on alert.

"Nothing," she quickly assured him. "I can't sleep."

Isaac nodded and sank back down on his seat. "I know. I tried calling Hawk again, but there's no answer."

"That doesn't sound good," she said with a frown.

"He knows how to reach me," Isaac pointed out. "I'm sure he'll get in touch soon."

She stared at him for a long moment, trying to gauge his mood. "I feel like we need to do something to help him. Something more than sitting here."

Isaac gestured to the chair across from him and then rubbed his hand across the shadow of his beard. "Do you have any idea what your brother is investigating?"

She sank into the chair, trying to remember anything Shane had said. "Not really. He doesn't talk about his job very much. I know he was assigned a new partner about four months ago, some guy by the name of Trey."

Isaac's eyes lit up. "Do you know his last name?"

She pressed her fingers against her temples, trying to remember. "Something like a tree," she murmured, thinking back to the conversation she'd had with Shane. "Birchwood. Trey Birchwood."

Isaac leaned forward. "What else did he say? Did he get along with Birchwood?"

"Shane mentioned Trey was from another district and that the guy was okay." She shrugged and grimaced. "You have to understand that Shane didn't ever say anything negative about his job. He kept all the dangerous details to himself."

"Understandable that he wouldn't want you to worry," Isaac said. "But surely he would have said something if he had real concerns about his new partner."

"Not necessarily," she argued. "Shane glosses over everything bad because he knows I really don't like the fact that he's in constant danger." Admitting her fears out loud wasn't easy, but if it helped her brother, the embarrassment was well worth it. "When he mentioned his new partner, his tone was rather offhand. I wish I knew if there was some sort of rift between them, but I don't because I never asked." She was angry with herself now, although she certainly hadn't known that she'd end up in danger.

Isaac held her gaze for a long minute and she tried not to squirm in her seat. "I take it you don't approve of your brother's career choice?"

She took a deep breath and let it out slowly. "Did Shane happen to mention that our dad died in the line of duty?"

Isaac nodded. "Yes, he told me back when we were at Saint Jermaine's."

"Well, then you know that Shane went a little crazy after our dad died. That's when he started getting into trouble. I'm pretty sure he got caught up in drugs for a bit, although he never admitted that to me. I know he was arrested, and thankfully, the judge sentenced him to Saint Jermaine's rather than sending him to jail."

"Yeah, I was grateful for the chance to go there, as well."

She was a little surprised to know that Isaac and Shane had both been at Saint Jermaine's, but then realized she shouldn't be. Shane was three years older than her and she had been only fourteen when he was sent to the boys' school. And much of that time, the year or two after her father's death, was nothing more than a blur, especially once their mother started hitting the bottle. Her mom had died while Leah was in college, and from that point on, she and Shane had depended on each other.

Glancing at Isaac, she was glad to know he'd been given the same opportunity to turn his life around as her brother had. And it was interesting that they both had chosen law enforcement.

She gave herself a mental shake. Why was she concerned about Isaac's life? She'd married Elliot right out of nursing school and lost him barely two years later. She had no intention of opening herself up to that kind of hurt again.

"Well, thanks, Leah," Isaac said, breaking into her thoughts. "I'll see what I can find out about your brother's new partner. Now, do me a favor and try to get some sleep."

He was right—there was nothing else she could do tonight. And he obviously wanted her to leave, so she rose to her feet and walked toward the connecting door. She glanced back at Isaac over her shoulder and was disconcerted to find him watching her intently. "Good night," she murmured before slipping through the opening to her own room.

As she crawled into bed, she told herself that she'd imagined the disappointment reflected on Isaac's face when she'd mentioned not liking her brother's career choice. And if she hadn't imagined it, she was still glad he understood exactly where she was coming from.

They might have been thrown together by circumstances outside their control, but she knew very well that as soon as they found her brother, they'd go their separate ways.

And truthfully, she couldn't help hoping that happened sooner than later. Because she wasn't ready to even consider getting romantically involved again.

Not now and maybe not ever.

Isaac watched Leah walk away, telling himself that it was a good thing there couldn't be anything more between them than friendship. So what if she was so beautiful it made his gut ache? It wasn't as if he intended to get married again, not after his first wife had left him, taking their son with her. And when his ex-wife's new boyfriend went crazy, killing her and then Jeremy and then himself, the hole in Isaac's heart had gotten wider and deeper.

Two years had passed but he still missed his son every single day. And deep down, he hadn't found a way to forgive himself for his wife's leaving him. He should have known she wasn't happy. She'd always told him he worked too many hours, but he hadn't listened.

And now it was too late to right the wrong.

Maybe his teammates Caleb and Declan had managed to find a way to make their relationships work, even with their crazy schedules, but Isaac had failed and wasn't interested in trying again.

So why was he disappointed to find out Leah wasn't interested in someone like him?

He shook off the bizarre feeling and made a call to the Fifth District asking for Trey Birchwood. He was told the cop was off duty for the weekend, so that wasn't much help. It was Friday night, so it could be that Trey was actually off work. Or it could be that he'd specifically requested time off for some unknown reason.

Talking to Trey might not offer any insight as to what Hawk was involved with, but Isaac needed to try. That was the only lead he had at the moment.

He prowled the room, glancing out the window to scan the parking lot, making sure no one was lurking around. The lot was mostly empty and he'd parked the SUV in front of his door, rather than closer to Leah's. And he'd backed it in, so they could drive off in a hurry if needed.

He reached for his phone to check in with Caleb and Deck, nearly dropping it when the cell vibrated in his hand. His pulse jumped as he recognized the number of Hawk's throwaway phone. "Hawk? Are you okay?"

"Are Leah and Ben safe?" His friend's voice was grave, and Isaac couldn't help but wonder if his buddy was injured.

"Yes, but there have already been two attempts to get them. A gunman showed up at their house and then someone else shot out the tire on my Jeep. What's going on?"

"My cover is blown." Static filled the line and Isaac strained to listen. "Don't trust anyone in my district, understand?"

"Not even Trey Birchwood?"

More static, but then Hawk's voice came through. "No. Not until I know more about what's going on."

Isaac couldn't tell if Hawk normally got along well with his new partner or not, but since he wasn't trusting any of the guys from his district, it was a moot point. "You have to give me something to go on. I want to help you."

"You are helping me by keeping Leah and Ben safe. These guys will do anything to find me, including using my family as bait."

Isaac knew his initial instincts were correct. The gunman wanted Leah and Ben alive, to draw Hawk out of hiding.

"Remember Saint Jermaine's?" Hawk asked, breaking into his thoughts.

Isaac frowned. "Yeah. What about it?"

"There were a couple of guys who bragged about running illegal guns."

"I remember." The tiny hairs on the back of Isaac's neck lifted in alarm. "Are you investigating some sort of illegal gun trade?"

"Yes. I was approached by an agent with the ATF, and it's bigger than I anticipated. I'm convinced there are dirty cops involved."

So he was right about the sharpshooter being an officer. Isaac knew there were rare occasions when cops turned bad, and investigating those situations was always tricky.

Still, knowing the Bureau of Alcohol, Tobacco and Firearms was involved made him feel a little better. At least Hawk wasn't hanging out there totally alone. "Talk to me. What can I do?"

"Keep my sister and her boy safe. I'll figure out the rest myself."

"What's the name of your ATF contact?" Isaac pressed.

There was a pause. "Cameron Walker, but don't

contact him. Not yet. I'll let you know if I need anything more."

"Where are you?"

"Hiding. Don't even try to find me. I'm constantly on the move."

Isaac wished there was something he could do for his friend. "Look, I have a couple of guys on my team that I'd trust with my life," he said quickly. "We can help you. You can't do this alone, buddy."

"I have to go." Hawk abruptly disconnected the call, leaving Isaac battling a wave of helplessness.

He didn't know much more than he had before Hawk phoned, other than to have his suspicions confirmed about why the gunman had gone after Leah and Ben. Still, hearing that Hawk was investigating illegal weapons under the supervision of the ATF was something. Most criminals on the streets knew exactly where to find guns that they wanted, since they were practically everywhere. Isaac couldn't even begin to think of where to start, especially considering Hawk's claim that he'd stumbled upon something big.

Isaac stretched out on the bed fully dressed, thinking about the little bit Hawk had revealed. He remembered his team had been called to a mall shooting about a week ago. He'd been the negotiator for the tactical situation, while Caleb had functioned as the sharpshooter. The weapon they'd recovered at the scene had been obviously illegal, with the serial numbers filed off.

Isaac sat up, knowing the gun was likely still in the evidence room. The possible connection was thin, but still worth investigating.

He picked up his phone, but then hesitated. It was

well after midnight and the gun wasn't going anywhere tonight. No sense in dragging Caleb or Deck out now.

It could wait until morning.

Isaac turned the television on low, scanning the various news channels. Unfortunately, no baseball spring-training games were on this late at night.

The sound of a car engine caught his attention. He rolled off the bed, grabbed his weapon and crossed over to the window. He peered through the slight opening in the curtains, trying to see what had caused the noise.

The parking lot appeared deserted, but then he saw the quick flash of taillights moving away.

Could be nothing, but after the troubling conversation with Hawk, Isaac didn't want to assume anything, especially if dirty cops were involved. He stared at the now-empty parking lot for a minute and then eased back, walking toward the connecting door, intending to get Leah and Ben up. They wouldn't like leaving again, but he'd rather play it safe than sorry.

He'd taken only two steps when the sound of breaking glass echoed through the night. He stumbled and glanced over his shoulder at the same time his eyes started to burn.

Tear gas!

He dived through the connecting door, slamming it shut behind him. He needed to get Leah and Ben out of here now!

Chapter 4

Leah woke up with a start when Isaac came barreling through the connecting door into their room. She gasped and stared in shock when he shut it behind him and then ripped the comforter off her bed and stuffed it along the bottom edge of the door.

"Grab Ben. We need to get out of here."

Leah didn't question Isaac's command as her eyes began to burn. She scrambled out of bed, grateful she'd slept in her clothes, and quickly roused her son. She tugged his winter clothes on despite his sleepy protest.

"Use these to cover your faces," Isaac said, handing her two wet towels. She threw one over her shoulder and drew Ben up against it, then draped another around her neck so that it was close to her mouth. It was the best she could do while carrying her son. "This way," Isaac said, urging her toward the bathroom.

It didn't take long for Isaac to break open the small window there. "I'm going out first so that I can help the two of you through, okay?"

She clutched Ben close and nodded. It wasn't easy for Isaac to get his broad-shouldered frame through the small opening, and she let out a sigh of relief when he finally made it.

"Okay, Ben, it's your turn." Isaac said.

"No, don't wanna go!" he wailed, grabbing her around the neck and hanging on tight.

It nearly broke her heart to pull him away. "We have to, Ben. Mr. Isaac is out there to catch you, and I'll hold you once we're outside, okay?"

"No-o-o," he cried, deep wrenching sobs that tore at her.

Leah forced herself to push him through the window into Isaac's waiting arms. She wiped her own tears away before attempting to climb after her son. She could hear Isaac whispering soothing words to Ben, and he stopped crying except for the occasional hiccuping sniffle.

Isaac's strong hand guided her through the opening and soon she was on solid ground. She took Ben and tossed the wet towels aside, gulping in deep breaths of fresh air.

"See those trees fifty feet from here?" Isaac asked in a low whisper, his breath tickling her ear. She swallowed hard and nodded. "I want you to run there, and I'll be right behind you."

After hiking Ben higher in her arms, she took off at a slow jog, mostly because she couldn't see more than a few feet in front of her face. She didn't realize she was holding her breath until her chest started to burn. She took a deep gulping breath and the tightness eased. After what seemed like forever, she reached the trees, darting behind them and sagging against a solid trunk.

Isaac joined her a few seconds later. "See anything?" she whispered.

He shook his head. "No, but we need to keep moving."

Of course they did. She sighed and pulled herself upright, shifting Ben to her other hip. Her arm muscles screamed in protest, but she forced herself to ignore the pain. Although maybe once this was all over, she'd have to start lifting weights so she wasn't so weak.

"I'd take him, but I need to cover your back," Isaac whispered, reading her thoughts.

"I'm fine." She made her way through the trees, grateful to see there was a clearing on the other side. She glanced up and noticed there was a church steeple not far away. "Isaac, can we go to that church up ahead?" she whispered.

"Sure, but keep to the shadows, in case they've figured out we've escaped."

Leah picked up her pace, despite her weary muscles. The church steeple was like a beacon, drawing her closer. She silently prayed as they made their way down the street, putting as much distance as possible between them and the American Lodge.

Leah wanted to cry with relief when the church loomed before her. Although as they approached the steps, it belatedly occurred to her that the doors were likely locked.

"Wait—I want you two to stay hidden over here," Isaac said, drawing her away from the front steps.

She didn't have the strength or the will to argue. She huddled down near the corner of the building with Ben on her lap, not even caring that her jeans were getting all muddy again.

Too afraid to close her eyes, she peered through the darkness, making sure there were no cars coming toward them. From this angle she couldn't see what Isaac was doing, but since she was fairly certain the church was locked up, it didn't matter. Maybe he was checking for a side entrance or something.

Cold from the ground seeped through her clothing, making her shiver. She thought she might be warmer if she stood back up, but struggling to her feet wasn't easy, especially with Ben's weight in her arms.

"Leah?" Isaac seemed to pop up out of nowhere. "Come on. Let's get inside."

Inside the church? She was surprised but grateful as Isaac supported her, his arm anchoring her waist. Once they were safely in, he closed the door behind them.

She sank into a pew and then carefully set Ben down beside her. Clasping her hands together, she bowed her head and prayed.

"Thank You for providing us shelter, Lord. And thank You for keeping us safe from harm. Please continue to guide us to safety. Amen."

Isaac listened to Leah's softly uttered prayer and couldn't help wondering if her faith really offered as much support as she claimed. She certainly seemed to pray a lot, although he couldn't blame her, since she'd also been in constant danger.

He scrubbed his hands over his face, mentally kicking himself for nearly getting them captured once again. They'd been found too easily.

But how?

He crossed over to where Leah sat and edged in beside her. "I'm sorry about this," he murmured. "I promise I'll do a better job of protecting you and Ben from here on."

Her attempt at a smile fell short, but he gave her points for trying. "It's not your fault, Isaac."

It was his fault, but there was no sense in hammering the issue any further. Looking backward wasn't going to help; they needed to move forward from here. "I talked to your brother earlier and he told me that he thinks there is a dirty cop involved in this mess."

Leah's face brightened. "You spoke to Shane? Is he okay?"

"He's hiding, but he's okay for now," Isaac confirmed.

"I'm so glad to hear that," she murmured. "I've been so worried about him."

"I know." Isaac put his arm around her shoulders and gave her a quick hug. "I have to think that whoever the shooter was at the side of the road somehow got the plate number for the police vehicle. The gunman likely didn't know that we had connecting rooms and simply tossed the gas canister into the one where the vehicle was parked." He was glad now that he hadn't left it in front of Leah and Ben's room.

"But how did they find us?" she asked.

"I wish I knew," Isaac admitted. "But it's obvious we need a vehicle with no ties to the SWAT team."

"Where on earth are we going to get another car?"

"Don't worry. Caleb and Deck will come through for us." Isaac hated to wake his buddies up again, especially at two in the morning, but what choice did he have? The church was a good sanctuary for now, but it was too close to the hotel for comfort. Once the person who'd thrown the tear gas realized they'd gotten away, they'd start to widen their search radius, and the church would become an obvious target.

At least, that was what he would do. And if a dirty cop was involved, he'd probably do the same thing.

Isaac pulled out his phone and called Deck. A few weeks ago, his buddy had been trying to sell his sister's old car. Maybe, just maybe, he hadn't sold it yet. The older-model vehicle would be perfect for them to use for a few days. And since Declan's sister had a different last name, it would be ideal.

Declan didn't answer right away, and when he finally did, he didn't sound too happy. "What?" he asked in a sleepy tone.

"I'm sorry, Deck, but we've been found. Someone threw a canister of tear gas into my hotel room. Do you still have your sister's old car?"

There was a long pause and Isaac hoped his buddy hadn't fallen back asleep. But when Deck spoke again, he sounded more awake. "Yeah, I still have it. Where are you and Leah now?"

"At the church located down the road from the hotel. If you could get here as soon as possible, we'd appreciate it."

"No problem. I'll have Bobby drive the spare car, since he's home on spring break."

"That works. If you could bring a computer, too, I'd appreciate it."

"A computer? Sure, I can loan you mine. What are you searching for?"

"Anything that explains what's going on," Isaac said, being purposefully vague. He didn't want to expose his friends to more danger. "Thanks, and I'm sorry to keep bothering you."

"You were there for me when I needed help, so it's no problem. We'll be there in fifteen to twenty minutes."

"We'll be waiting." Isaac disconnected the call, feeling better that they had a solid escape plan.

"Who's Bobby?" Leah asked.

She'd obviously heard the entire conversation—not a surprise, since she was sitting right next to him. So close he could smell the cinnamon scent that seemed to cling to her skin. "His brother-in-law."

"And you helped Declan out, the way he's helping you now?" she pressed.

He slowly nodded. "Yeah, about six months ago. We've always been there for each other no matter what."

"Mommy, I'm hungry," Ben said in a plaintive tone.

"I'm sorry, sweetie, but I don't have anything right now," Leah said, smoothing a hand over her son's hair. "Close your eyes and try to get some rest."

"We can stop and pick up something once we have a different set of wheels," Isaac offered.

"I think once he falls asleep, he'll be fine," Leah murmured.

"Yeah, well, all this running around is making me

hungry, too," Isaac said in a wry tone as he rose to his feet. "Stay here. I'm going to make sure we're still in the clear."

He didn't really think they'd been followed, but he needed to put some distance between them. Leah's cinnamon-and-spice scent was wreaking havoc with his concentration. She was so beautiful, even after everything they'd been through, with her naturally curly black hair and heart-shaped face. There couldn't be anything but friendship between them, so why was he suddenly thinking of her as a woman he was attracted to?

He needed to get that thought out of his head right now. After pushing open the church door a crack, he peered outside. He couldn't see far, but what he did see seemed quiet and deserted.

Leah hadn't asked him how he'd gotten inside the church, and he was glad he didn't have to explain how he'd picked the lock. He couldn't help but think the church pastor wouldn't be too thrilled to know how easy it was to break in. Then again, maybe he should let the pastor know so he could change the locks.

But that would have to wait until they'd gotten safely out of this mess.

Waiting for Deck and Bobby to show up was agonizing, each second passing with excruciating slowness. Isaac paced back and forth, peering outside every so often.

Finally his phone rang, and he was relieved to see Deck's number. "Hey, are you close?"

"Yeah, we're parked in the back behind the church," Deck informed him. "Didn't see anyone suspicious hanging around, either."

"Thanks, Deck. We'll be outside soon." Isaac clicked off, then locked the main doors of the church before heading over to Leah and Ben. "They're here with the car, Leah. Do you want me to carry Ben?"

She looked dead on her feet, but still shook her head. "I'm worried he'll cry."

Isaac understood her concern, since there hadn't exactly been time to bond with the boy. Although he needed to spend more time with Ben so the boy wouldn't be afraid of him.

He led the way through the church to the back door. Leah followed slowly, carrying Ben, who was once again half-asleep.

There were two cars in the lot, both with their engines running but their lights off. Isaac stayed right beside Leah, sweeping his gaze over the area to verify they hadn't been found by the shooter.

As they approached the vehicles, a young man climbed out from behind the wheel of the older sedan and stepped forward. Isaac recognized Bobby Collins and gratefully took the keys he handed over.

"There's a booster seat in the back for the kid," Bobby said. "Figured that would be one less thing to worry about."

"Where did you get it?" Isaac asked in surprise.

"Caleb donated it," Declan said, coming out to join them. He handed Isaac a computer case. "Apparently his daughter, Kaitlin, had two of them."

"Thank you," Leah said with a tremulous smile.

"No problem." Bobby ducked his head shyly and sauntered over to the other car. Declan slapped Isaac on the back and then went to join his brother-in-law.

Isaac waited for Leah to get Ben settled in the booster seat before he opened the front passenger door for her.

He didn't breathe easy until the church was far behind them. Isaac knew he needed to find another place to stay for what was left of the night, and this time he wasn't about to tell anyone, even his friends, where they were going.

Driving through the night, he finally came across a hotel that boasted two-bedroom suites. The concept offered the best of both worlds, so he pulled in and parked.

Leah had been dozing and came awake in a rush when the car stopped. "Where are we?" she asked, rubbing her eyes.

"Brookside Suites Hotel," Isaac said. "They offer two-bedroom suites, so you and Ben can share one room and I'll use the other."

"Looks expensive," Leah murmured.

Isaac didn't answer, because he'd already had the same thought. But they couldn't afford to be cheap when it came to making sure they were safe. As it was, he'd need to convince the clerk to take cash when they were ready to check out.

It didn't take long to secure a room, although the man insisted on having a credit-card number on file in case there was any damage. Apparently Isaac's badge helped lend credibility, as the clerk reluctantly agreed to take payment in cash.

This time, Isaac carried Ben inside the hotel. The boy had fallen back asleep and barely stirred as they rode the elevator to the third floor. They had an inside room, and Isaac figured that they'd be much harder to find in a place like this, even if somehow the shooter figured out what kind of car they were driving, a nearly impossible feat.

Surely they'd be safe here.

Isaac waited for Leah to unlock the door and flip on the lights. The place was nice, as it should be for the price he'd paid. There was a comfortable living area, complete with a small kitchenette, so they could cook their own meals if they were going to stay for a few days.

The first bedroom had two double beds, and he waited while Leah pulled down the covers so he could set Ben down in the one nearest the bathroom.

She quickly stripped the boy's coat, hat mittens and boots off before covering him with the sheet and blanket. For a moment she simply stood there, staring down at her sleeping child. Isaac eased toward the door, thinking that maybe she wanted some privacy.

But she surprised him by turning and following him out to the living area. "It's hard to believe we're finally safe," she murmured, running a hand through her hair.

Isaac had to stop himself from wrapping her in his arms and holding her close. He cleared his throat and nodded. "No one knows we're here, Leah. The car can't be traced to us, either. We are safe."

Her smile was a tad pathetic, but still made his heart race. "I finally believe that."

He cleared his throat again, hoping she couldn't tell how nervous he was. "I'm going to go back down to get the laptop, okay?"

"Sounds good."

He left the room, thinking for sure Leah would be tucked in bed by the time he returned. He wouldn't blame her one bit, since he doubted she'd gotten much sleep before the tear-gas incident.

Grabbing the computer case out of the backseat didn't take long, and within minutes he was back upstairs, using his key card to access the room. When he opened the door, he was surprised to find Leah curled in a corner of the sofa, waiting for him.

She glanced over when he walked in. "Did you want me to order something to eat? You mentioned you were hungry."

Isaac was touched by her offer. When was the last time anyone cared about whether he was tired or hungry?

"Thanks for the thought, but I doubt they'll provide room service this late." He set the computer case down on the small table in the kitchenette.

"Really?" Leah seemed surprised and then shrugged. "You're probably right. It's closer to breakfast, anyway."

"Get some sleep, Leah," he suggested in a low tone. "I'm sure you're exhausted."

She dropped her gaze and nodded. "I am, but truthfully, I'm afraid I'll have nightmares."

The urge to offer comfort was strong. "I'm sorry," he murmured helplessly.

"It's okay." She uncurled herself from the sofa and stood. To his surprise, she crossed over to him and put her hand on his arm. "Thanks for keeping us safe, Isaac." She stood on her tiptoes and brushed a kiss across his cheek before turning to head into her room.

It took every ounce of willpower he possessed to let her walk away, when all he really wanted to do was haul her close for a real kiss. He didn't let out his breath until she'd closed the door behind her, the cinnamon-and-spice scent lingering long after she'd gone.

He gave himself a stern talking-to as he headed into his room. He wasn't in the market for a relationship. And Hawk wouldn't appreciate knowing how much Isaac thought about kissing his sister.

From here on out, he needed to keep his distance from Leah. For both their sakes.

Chapter 5

Leah awoke with a start, to find bright sunlight streaming through the window. For a minute she couldn't figure out where she was, but then the events from the night before came rushing back to her.

The masked man, the Jeep sliding into a ditch, the canister of tear gas. She pushed her tangled hair away from her face, amazed that she'd slept so soundly after all that. When she glanced over at Ben's bed, her heart flew into her throat, because it was empty.

"Ben?" She leaped out of bed and dashed over to open the door. She needn't have worried, for Isaac had everything under control. He was seated beside Ben, the two of them enjoying a hearty meal of scrambled eggs and bacon.

"Good morning, Leah," Isaac said. "Are you hungry?

I didn't order anything for you yet, because I didn't want the food to get cold."

"I— Um, yes. I'm hungry." She was glad to see that Ben must be getting over his nervousness around Isaac. They looked quite cozy eating breakfast together.

"It will take a few minutes for them to deliver," Isaac said as he reached for the phone. "But I have coffee here if you want some."

"I'd love a cup." Leah crossed over and helped herself to a steaming mug. She doused it with cream and then carried it back to her room. If breakfast was going to be a while, she'd spend the time getting cleaned up.

She emerged from the bathroom twenty minutes later, feeling much better even though her mud-splattered jeans were beyond redemption. But she pulled them on anyway, because she didn't have anything else to wear.

Making a mental note to convince Isaac they needed to go shopping, she came out of the bedroom to the enticing aroma of bacon and eggs.

"Smells delicious," she said, pulling out a chair next to her son. At this moment it was almost as if none of the terrible things had happened last night.

"Trust me, it is." Isaac stood and moved his dirty dishes out of the way so she'd have more room.

"Mr. Isaac is a policeman just like Uncle Shane," Ben said, his eyes gleaming with excitement. "Isn't that cool?"

She forced a smile for Ben's sake. "You bet."

"Are we gonna see Uncle Shane soon?" he asked.

"I'm not sure. I think he's working," she hedged.

"He saves people, right, Mommy?" Ben persisted.

"Yes, he does. And so does Mr. Isaac."

"Ben, how about we let your mom eat her food before it gets cold?" Isaac suggested.

"Okay."

Leah gave Isaac a grateful smile and then bowed her head for a quick, silent prayer of thanks before digging into her breakfast. She had to admit the food was amazing, or maybe it was just that she was incredibly hungry.

Isaac went over to the sofa and began working on his computer.

"Can I watch cartoons, Mom?" Ben asked as he finished his eggs. "Please?"

"Sure," she said, glancing at Isaac. He smiled and picked up the remote, finding a children's channel without difficulty.

Ben abandoned his dirty dishes, running toward the sofa. Without a moment's hesitation, he climbed up and settled in beside Isaac.

For a moment Leah stared at the two of them sitting together, wishing for something she couldn't have. She gave herself a mental shake and concentrated on finishing her breakfast.

The sound of cartoons reminded her of Saturday mornings at home. Sometimes, if he happened to be off work, Shane would come and join them.

Thinking about her brother made her push her empty plate away with a heavy sigh. Here she was, enjoying a nice breakfast, while her brother was who knew where, fighting to stay alive. What was wrong with her?

Quickly, she cleared away the dirty dishes, stacking them on the tray and pushing it out into the hallway for the hotel staff to pick up.

"Isaac? Could you come over here for a minute?"

He looked surprised, but set his computer aside to stand.

"Please bring the laptop," she added.

Isaac's eyebrows rose, but he did as she requested, unplugging the cord and carrying everything over to the small table. "What's wrong?" he asked in a low voice.

"We have to do something to find Shane." She wasn't about to take no for an answer. "There must be something we can do to help him."

"I understand how difficult this must be for you," Isaac said. "But I offered to help your brother and all he asked was that I keep you and Ben safe."

"Yeah, but who's helping him?" she asked in an exasperated tone. "We can't just sit here twiddling our thumbs. Shane admitted he's in trouble, and we have to do something to help."

"Do you have any idea where to start?" Isaac asked.

Her shoulders slumped in defeat. She didn't have any clue where Shane might be. How could she? Her chest ached with the sick realization that it was her own fault. She'd allowed him to keep the dangerous aspects of his job a secret. In fact, she'd forced the issue, often changing the subject if he brought up something that reminded her of the way they'd lost their father.

Losing their dad had destroyed their family. Her mother had turned to alcohol, Shane had gotten into trouble and she'd buried herself in her studies, trying to block everything else out.

But no more hiding from reality. She drew in a ragged breath. "There has to be something we can do," she insisted. "What about Shane's partner? Trey Birchwood? Couldn't we try to find him and talk to him?"

"That might be a good place to start," Isaac agreed. "Hawk said not to trust him, but that doesn't mean we can't ask him a few questions. But first I have to find out what he looks like."

Leah sipped her coffee as Isaac punched the computer keys, pulling up Trey's driver's license. He spun the computer toward her so she could see the screen. "Does that look like him?"

She chewed her lower lip as she stared at the grainy photograph on the screen. "I only met him once, but I'm pretty sure that's him."

"All right, I'll take a drive past his place, see if he's around. When I called the Fifth District police station late last night, they said he was off work this weekend."

"Wait a minute. I want to go with you," she protested with a frown.

But Isaac was already shaking his head. "I can't put you and Ben in danger. I promised Hawk I'd keep you safe."

"I understand, and trust me, I want to keep Ben safe, too. But we also need to buy a few things, at least a change of clothes and something to help keep Ben entertained for a while, as I'm sure cartoons aren't going to hold his interest for long. Couldn't we go to one of those big-box stores? And maybe cruise past Trey Birchwood's house on the way?"

Isaac scowled, but glanced over at Ben, as if considering her idea. "I guess you're right," he admitted finally. "We should probably pick up a few things."

"I have some cash," she said, in case he was worried

about how much she planned to spend. "And I have my debit card, too."

"Cash only," he said in a stern tone. "We don't want to leave an electronic trail."

She pursed her lips, mentally calculating how much she had on hand. Luckily, she'd gotten in the habit of carrying a small, secret stash of cash for emergencies, and this was definitely an emergency. "All right, no cards. When can we leave?"

Isaac hesitated. "Soon, since it's almost checkout time." Her disappointment must have shown, because he added, "I'm not sure if staying here another night is the right thing to do. I feel like we should keep moving, just in case."

She glanced around the cozy suite, wishing they could stay another day, but knowing that it was far too expensive. And besides, moving around was probably the smart thing to do.

"All right, that gives us roughly thirty minutes or so. Is there anything else we can search for on the laptop?"

"Mom, cartoons are over," Ben shouted. "Can we go swimming? Or find a playground?"

Isaac shut down the computer. "We're going shopping first, okay?"

"Shopping, yuck," the boy muttered with a pout.

"I thought maybe you'd like to get the new handheld video game that's out," Leah offered. "But if you'd rather not…"

"I do! I want it!" Ben's mood instantly did a three-sixty, making her smile.

Isaac chuckled, too. "All right, let's get going."

Leah ducked into the bathroom to gather up the toiletries and stuff them into her purse. She was desperate to wash her hair, but needed to purchase a brush first or her curly hair would be nothing but a snarled mess.

Ben and Isaac were waiting by the door when she returned, and they left together to walk down to the parking lot. The sky was overcast, but it wasn't raining, at least not yet, but it was windy. Tree branches swayed wildly as Isaac led the way to their car, which was good, since she couldn't remember much after they'd left the church. She made a mental note of the sedan's color and tag number.

"Stay here. I'll be right back after I check out," Isaac instructed.

She nodded, glad the car's heater was turned on high. Maybe it was the howling wind that made her feel chilled. Certainly there was no reason to be afraid.

"Where's Mr. Isaac?" Ben asked after two minutes had passed. "We need to hurry up and buy my game."

"He's paying for the room, and don't worry. We'll get to the store soon enough." Leah didn't like having to buy a video game for Ben, but clearly, the poor kid needed something to do in the endless string of hotel rooms.

She made a mental note to make sure the next place they stayed was near some playground equipment. Granted, the weather wasn't great, but it would still be good for Ben to spend some time outdoors.

There was a loud thud that caused her heart to leap into her throat. It took a minute for her to realize that a tree branch had broken loose and hit the side of the building.

Isaac returned, sliding into the driver's seat. As he

glanced over at her, flashing a reassuring grin, she realized just how nice it was to have him beside her.

And she wondered if God had brought Isaac into her life for more than one reason. To keep her safe, yes, but maybe also to show him the way to faith and God?

If so, that was a mission she couldn't ignore.

Isaac wasn't fond of shopping, but he had to admit that poring over the various handheld video games with Ben was kind of fun. Isaac didn't know much about the various games, but it was clear the boy did.

Spending time like this was what he missed the most after losing Jeremy. Isaac treasured the memories he had and grieved for the ones he'd never have again.

While he and Ben spent time in the games department, Leah went off to find the clothing and toiletries she wanted. When she came back, he was surprised to find that she'd tossed in a few items for him, too.

"These might not be the correct size, so if you want to go try them on that's fine," she said, her cheeks pink with embarrassment.

He glanced at the tags and lifted a brow. "Good eye. These should fit fine."

She ducked her head and shrugged. "I simply bought the size that Shane wears," she murmured. "Did you find the video game you wanted?" she asked Ben.

"Yep. Me and Mr. Isaac picked this one," he said, waving it in front of her face. "But can I have the dinosaurs, too? Please?"

Isaac pulled the box of plastic dinosaurs off the shelf. "Sure you can," he said, placing it into the already-filled cart. He tried to figure out how much their bill would be and wondered if he should have hit Declan up for a loan.

Leah sent him an exasperated glance, but nodded. "Sure. Anything else? How about the toy cars?"

"Okay!" Ben's eyes were wide with excitement and Isaac couldn't help but grin in response. He barely remembered ever being as happy as Ben was, but then again, his home life hadn't been anything close to Ben's, either.

His dad had taken off when he was thirteen, and his mother had trailed a series of men through their apartment for the next few years. Isaac had often avoided going home, hanging out with his friends instead. Of course, that was exactly how he'd managed to get in trouble. And then arrested for selling drugs. It was a bad choice to make, doing something as drastic as selling drugs to get money for food, but at least he'd been given the chance to get back on track.

He shook off his thoughts, knowing this was hardly the time to take a stroll down memory lane. He wasn't the only kid with a rough upbringing, and he certainly wouldn't be the last. And every year he made an anonymous donation to the Saint Jermaine boys' school, so that other kids would have the same chance to turn their lives around that he and Hawk had had.

Leah headed for the checkout line, and he followed more slowly, pulling out his wallet and counting how much cash he had. They couldn't afford to use everything, since they'd need to save some for the hotel they'd need to find later that night.

"Wait—what are you doing?" he asked when Leah drew a stack of bills from the depths of her purse.

"Most of this is for me and Ben," she said, handing her money to the clerk.

"Don't spend all of it," Isaac protested. "Here, I'll pay for my stuff."

She reluctantly accepted his money, and he planned to call Deck for additional cash as soon as possible. Isaac had no idea how long they'd be on the run, but he knew it could easily be days, if not up to a week.

He grabbed the bags before she could and followed her and Ben back to the car. He stashed their purchases in the trunk, except for the video game, and then slid behind the wheel.

Leah opened the package and inserted the batteries before handing the game back to Ben. At least having it would give the poor kid something to do.

"Are we going to drive over to Trey's now?" she asked in a low voice.

"Yeah, we'll check things out," Isaac agreed. It was still early, just past one o'clock in the afternoon. Even if he wanted to get another hotel room, they wouldn't be able to check in for a couple of hours yet. Surely it couldn't hurt to drive over to Trey's apartment building and scope the place out?

He had the address plugged into the GPS on his phone, and Leah gave him directions.

"I think that's the place," she said excitedly after verifying with the GPS. "The middle white-and-black brick building."

He nodded. The four-family apartment building was nestled between two other similar ones. "We're looking for a dark blue Ford Taurus," he said as he pulled into the parking lot behind the place.

"I don't see it," Leah murmured.

He didn't, either, and the lot wasn't all that big, so he turned around and drove back out to the street, making another loop around the block.

"Now what?" Leah asked. "Should we wait here for a while?"

Isaac pulled over to the side of the road and drummed his fingers on the steering wheel. "I don't know," he said in a low voice. "We could be wasting our time. For all we know, Trey is out of town."

"I guess you're right," Leah murmured in a dejected tone. "But what else can we do to help Shane?"

Good question. Too bad he didn't have an equally good idea. They could sit here all day without seeing Trey at all. Was Trey helping Hawk? Or busy trying to set him up? Either way, Trey was really the only lead they had.

Isaac should have insisted that Hawk give him more to go on. He could try getting in touch with that ATF agent, Cameron Walker, but Hawk had specifically asked him not to do that.

Isaac was just about to pull away from the curb when he saw a dark blue car approaching. He straightened in his seat, peering through the windshield at the driver.

"Is that Trey?" Leah whispered.

"I think so." Sure enough, the car turned into the driveway of the apartment building. Isaac couldn't afford to let this opportunity to talk to Hawk's partner slide through his fingers, so he glanced at Leah. "Get behind the wheel and keep the car idling," he instructed. "I'm going to see if I can talk to Trey, but if anything happens, I want you to drive away, okay? Don't worry about me. Just make sure that you and Ben stay safe."

Her blue eyes were wide, but she nodded. "I understand."

He glanced up and down the street, making sure that no one was obviously watching him, before he slid out of the driver's-side door and ducked his head against the wind.

He'd parked down the street, hoping to blend in with some of the other cars that were parked there. He forced himself to adopt a leisurely pace as he headed toward the apartments. Isaac walked up the driveway, then paused by a large evergreen tree that towered next to the building.

Now that he was here, he tried to formulate in his mind exactly what he was going to say to Trey Birchwood. Hawk had told him not to trust anyone, but Isaac had to believe that Trey knew something about what his partner's undercover operation involved. He'd just have to play it by ear and hope Hawk's partner let something slip.

Not the best plan in the world, but good enough for now.

Isaac was about to make his way around the tree and down the driveway when a man came striding past, wearing a black leather jacket and a black ball cap pulled low over his face.

There was something familiar about the way the guy moved, and for a moment the image of the masked man lurking outside Leah and Ben's house flashed in Isaac's mind. He quickly lifted his phone and snapped a picture, even though he knew he wouldn't get a good view of the man's face. Isaac eased himself farther into the narrow space between the tree and the building, hoping he wouldn't be noticed hiding there.

But Isaac needn't have worried; the guy never looked back. Instead, he jumped into an SUV and drove away, thankfully in the opposite direction from where Leah and Ben were waiting.

Isaac had a bad feeling about what had just happened, and he quickly rounded the tree and jogged to the parking lot. He saw Trey's vehicle in the back corner, and for a moment he thought the car was empty.

But as he drew closer, he realized that a figure was slumped over the steering wheel.

Isaac's gut tightened as he quickened his pace. Within moments he reached the driver's-side window of the blue car and peered inside.

A bullet hole in Trey's temple confirmed his worst suspicions.

Hawk's partner was dead.

And Isaac was pretty sure the guy in the black leather jacket, the same guy who'd tried to kidnap Leah and Ben, had killed him.

Chapter 6

Leah gripped the steering wheel, craning her neck so that she could watch Isaac's progress as he crossed the street and then huddled behind the pine tree.

What on earth was he waiting for?

The tiny hairs on the nape of her neck lifted when she saw a man with a black leather jacket and cap stride down the driveway of the apartment building. She ducked her head, but he climbed into an SUV that was parked on the other side of the road.

As he drove away, she stared at his license plate, but caught only the first three letters, *CXF*. She repeated them over and over in her mind so that she wouldn't forget.

When she glanced at the pine tree, her stomach dropped when she realized Isaac wasn't there. She gripped the steering wheel harder, hoping nothing was wrong. Was she overreacting about seeing the man in the black jacket? Could it be that he lived in the building and for some reason hadn't bothered to park in the lot?

Behind her, Ben played his video game, oblivious to her racing thoughts. She toyed with the idea of driving off, the way Isaac had told her to. Except that nothing dangerous had happened, right?

So why did she feel this weird, impending sense of doom?

She craned her neck so that she had a good view of the driveway, but there was still no sign of Isaac. Leah gnawed her lower lip, worried about him. Surely he was safe in broad daylight?

It seemed like an hour later, but it was really only eight minutes before she caught a glimpse of him coming down the driveway. As he jogged toward the car, she pried her hands from the steering wheel and awkwardly crawled over the center console to the passenger seat.

He slid behind the wheel, his jaw set and his expression grim.

"What happened?" she asked as he put the car in gear and drove away. He didn't rush, but seemed to take his time as he made his way around the block.

Isaac glanced in the rearview mirror and she couldn't help swiveling in her seat to see for herself if someone was behind them. As far as she could tell, they weren't being followed.

"Did you get to talk to Trey?" she asked after several minutes had passed.

"No. Unfortunately, Trey Birchwood is dead."

"What?" Leah's jaw dropped in horror and she wondered if she'd heard him wrong. "But we saw him drive into the parking lot."

"The guy in the black jacket must have been waiting for him," Isaac murmured. "I should have flagged Trey down before he pulled in...."

"Wait a minute. That guy in the black leather jacket? The one who jumped into the SUV? That guy?"

Isaac glanced at her in surprise. "You saw him?"

She nodded. "Yeah, I saw him. I tried to get his license number, but only caught the first three letters, *CXF*. But I noticed what kind of car he was driving." She told him the brand.

Isaac raised his eyebrows and whistled. "Expensive car, but at least knowing that along with the first three letters of the plate number should help us track down the owner."

"Unless it's stolen," Leah said in a wry tone. "Then we're back to square one."

"Not exactly. I did find one other clue," Isaac said as he headed onto the interstate. She wanted to ask where they were going, but suspected he didn't have a specific destination in mind.

"Really?"

He nodded. "There was blood on the asphalt, likely seeping out from the driver's-side door, so I looked under the car and found a shell casing. It's not much, but it's better than nothing."

Leah frowned. "What can a shell casing tell us?"

For the first time since he'd come back to the car, Isaac smiled. "Believe me, a single shell casing can tell us more than you think. It can reflect the killer's signature, so to speak. Although having the bullet would be even better."

She'd take his word for it. "Shouldn't we call the police about Trey?"

"Yes, but we're not using our personal cell phones," Isaac said in a firm tone. "We can't risk anyone tracing us to the call. We'll find another of those big-box stores and buy a couple of prepaid cell phones, just in case."

Leah couldn't argue with his logic, and it wasn't as if a short delay would cause more harm to Trey. "Why do you think he was killed?"

Isaac let out a heavy sigh. "I wish I knew. Could be that Trey did set up your brother and had to be silenced because he was a loose end. Or it could be the exact opposite—that Trey was actually innocent and was killed because he wouldn't turn on his partner. Based on how they tried to get to you, I'm inclined to believe the latter."

Leah shivered and sent up a quick prayer for Trey Birchwood, just in case he was nothing more than an innocent bystander.

She didn't say anything more until Isaac pulled into the parking lot of another big store. "We can wait here," she offered.

He nodded. "I'll be right back."

She watched him stride into the entrance and then leaned her forehead on the passenger-side window. It was two o'clock in the afternoon and she was already exhausted. How did Isaac do this sort of thing on a regular basis?

She had no idea, but it was clear she wasn't cut out for it. She refused to open her heart, only to get hurt again.

This wasn't the life she wanted. Not for herself and certainly not for Ben.

Isaac quickly purchased the prepaid phones and then made his way back to the car. As much as he wanted to make the call to the Fifth District police station right away, he needed to power up the devices and activate them before he could use them.

He slid behind the wheel and handed the bag containing the phones to Leah.

"Where should we go now?" she asked.

"It's just past two-thirty, but we might be able to find a place that will let us check in early." At least, he hoped so. The sooner he could call in Trey's murder, the better.

"Okay. We should probably pick up something to eat, too, since I'm sure Ben will be hungry."

Isaac nodded, having the same thought. It had been a long time since he'd had to worry about keeping on a schedule for the sake of a child. He headed west on the interstate, keeping a keen eye out for a suitable hotel, not caring that he was going farther and farther out of town. As far as he was concerned, the farther away from Trey's dead body, the better.

When he came across another hotel that offered suites, he exited the freeway and pulled into the parking lot.

The clerk was nice enough to give them the room right away. Isaac hauled in their shopping bags and then quickly charged up the prepaid phones.

Leah and Ben took their time going through all the

purchases, and soon the boy had the dinosaurs spread out on the living room table. Isaac stared for a minute, remembering how much Jeremy had loved dinosaurs. The ache in his heart wasn't as bad as it used to be. He tore his gaze away with an effort and quickly activated the phones.

Thankfully, it didn't take long for the process to work, and he went out in the hallway to make his call to the police station.

It wasn't easy. The dispatcher pressed him for details, and eventually he simply hung up, knowing that while they might think he was some sort of crazy man, they'd still investigate the information he'd given them.

It bothered him that he'd taken the shell casing from the crime scene. Obviously, it was a key piece of evidence, one that the police would need to solve Trey Birchwood's murder. But if someone inside the Fifth District was dirty, Isaac couldn't afford to give up the only clue they had. At least not until he'd had a chance to put the information into their database.

He sat down in the stairwell for a moment, staring at the phone. Resolutely, he punched in Hawk's number, wishing he could talk to his friend about Trey's death. But he wasn't surprised to get a message saying the number was out of service.

That was the same message he'd gotten before, and eventually Hawk had called him back. Isaac stashed the disposable phone in his pocket and scrubbed his hands over his face. Trey's murder had brought an abrupt end to the only lead he had. So now what?

His priority was still to keep Leah and Ben safe, and being here in a different hotel in a different city was the first step in doing that. Just like Hawk, he knew they couldn't afford to stay in one place for long.

For a moment he felt as if the weight of the world was on his shoulders. What if he messed up? He was fortunate that the killer hadn't seen Leah and Ben in the vehicle outside Trey's apartment building, or things could have ended much differently.

Isaac couldn't bear the thought of letting them down, the same way he had Becky and Jeremy.

"Isaac?"

He jerked his head up to find Leah standing behind him, a worried expression on her face.

"Are you all right?" she asked, her eyes full of concern.

He managed to stop himself from shaking his head. "Yeah. I just got off the phone with the police station. I'm sure they think I'm some sort of goofball, but I did tell them about Trey."

She nodded, then came to sit beside him. "You're not in this alone," she said in a low tone. "God is always with us, showing us the way. He'll keep us safe."

Isaac wasn't so sure he shared her belief, yet at the same time, he found himself hoping she was right. Because right now, he wouldn't mind a little help.

Praying wasn't his thing, but he figured God was probably watching over Leah and Ben. So he lifted his eyes upward and silently prayed, *Please keep Leah and Ben safe!*

The dread around his heart lightened. "We'd better get back inside," he said, rising to his feet and holding out a hand to Leah. When she placed her small palm in his, an odd tingling sensation caught him off guard.

Was he losing his grip on reality? He sure hoped not.

"Ben found a children's movie on TV," Leah said as they walked back to the room. "But I think he's getting hungry."

"How about I order a pizza?" Isaac offered. "With everything that happened, we forgot to pick up something to go."

"Ben's favorite is pepperoni," she said with a smile. "If you want anything more adventurous, you better order half and half."

"What do you like on your pizza?" he asked. "I'd rather make sure you get what you like, too."

Her cheeks went pink again and she shrugged. "I love just about anything except anchovies."

A woman after his own heart. "I'm not fond of the little fishes, either, so how about I get a medium pizza with the works for us and a small pepperoni for Ben?"

"That's great, if you think we can afford it," she said as she used her key to open the door.

"I have plenty of money," he assured her. "I just need Declan to bring me more cash."

"I have money, too," she pointed out. "Just so we're clear."

He could tell she didn't want to be indebted to him, and for some reason that made him upset. She and Ben were innocent bystanders in all this. She shouldn't have to use her own money to keep herself safe.

But there would be plenty of time to argue about money later. Right now, his growling stomach propelled him to the hotel phone, where he quickly placed their pizza order.

After he finished, he crossed over to the kitchen

table, where Leah was sitting in front of the laptop. "What are you looking for?" he asked, dropping into the chair beside her.

"I was trying to find that website you used earlier, to see if I could plug in the first three letters of that license plate," she admitted.

"You won't have the same access I have." Isaac turned the computer so that he could access the secure website that allowed him to search license-plate numbers.

"What were those three letters again?" he asked.

"CXF," she answered, hovering near his shoulder, her nearness a definite distraction.

He tried to ignore his awareness of her as he typed in the partial plate and the make and model of the vehicle before hitting the search key. There were literally dozens of possibilities, but soon he was able to weed them down to three likely candidates.

"Write these names down," Isaac said. "I'll ask Caleb and Declan to run them through the system. Maybe we'll get a hit."

"All right," Leah agreed. "Although none of the names sound familiar."

"I know. I was hoping one would ring a bell with me, too. But don't forget your theory that the car could be stolen."

Leah grimaced. "I hope not."

He eased his chair away, wishing the pizza would hurry up and get there. Leah's scent was driving him crazy and he knew better than to get tangled up with a woman who made it clear she didn't date cops. Which was probably for the best, since he wasn't ready to get emotionally involved with a woman anyway.

As soon as they finished eating, he planned to ask Caleb or Declan to come out with more cash and to pick up the shell casing. Right now, that casing was the best clue they had, and he was anxious to get moving on it.

The phone rang and he leaped at the chance to put more distance between him and Leah. "Hello?"

"There's a pizza delivery here for room 2204."

"I'll be right down." He hung up the phone and glanced at Leah. "Our food is here. I'll be right back. Don't open the door for anyone but me."

She nodded and he left to go down to the lobby, feeling a little foolish for being so paranoid. But the image of Trey's dead body seemed to be permanently ingrained on his mind.

By the time he arrived back in the suite, Leah had cleared off the small table and somehow managed to pry Ben away from his movie. Isaac set the boxes down and opened the tops.

"Yummy! I'm starving," Ben said, obviously anxious to start eating.

"Wait—we have to pray first, remember?" Leah captured her son's hand before he could grab for a piece of pizza. "Besides, it's probably hot."

Isaac hid a smile as he settled into the empty chair on the other side of Ben, who put his tiny palms together and bowed his head.

Isaac followed the child's example, waiting for Leah to begin her prayer.

"Dear Lord, we thank You for providing this wonderful food for us and for keeping us safe for another day. We also ask You to guide Shane home, keeping him safe from harm. And lastly we ask You to have mercy on Trey Birchwood's soul. Amen."

"Amen," Ben echoed.

"Amen," Isaac added. He felt Leah's surprised gaze rest on him, but in a flash the poignant moment was gone as she served Ben a slice of pizza.

Sharing a meal with them was nice, even if it reminded him of what he'd lost. The memories of the past weren't strong enough to diminish the reality of the present, and for the first time in the two years since Jeremy had died, Isaac found a measure of peace in the idea that maybe, just maybe, his son's soul was safe in God's care, too.

"Are you all right?" Leah asked, dragging him from his thoughts.

"Yeah, fine." He forced a smile, not sure she'd appreciate the fact that he was thinking about how nice it must be to have a family. Of course, normally Hawk would be here, instead of him.

"Vroom, vroom," Ben said before taking a big bite out of his pizza.

"Ben, please stop playing with your food," she said in a stern voice.

"I'm not playing. My pizza is a real car," Ben pointed out with logic that only another five-year-old would understand. "Vroom."

Leah sighed and glanced at Isaac as if looking for support. "Ben, you heard your mother," he said. "Finish your pizza, or if you're already full, then go wash up."

For a moment Ben stared at him, as if debating whether or not to listen, but then he popped the last bit of pizza into his mouth and reached for a napkin. "All done," he announced, through a mouthful of food.

"Go wash up in the bathroom, Ben," Leah said. She stood and began cleaning up the mess.

"Let's save the leftovers for later," Isaac suggested, putting all the pizza onto one plate. "After all, we may as well put the fridge to good use."

"Sounds like a plan."

Once the kitchen table was cleared, Ben came scampering back, putting his arms around Leah's waist. "Will you play dinosaurs with me? Puleeze?"

"Sure." She took him over to where the dinosaurs were scattered, and soon they were both making growling animal noises. Had Becky ever done that with Jeremy? Not that Isaac could remember. Then again, he'd usually picked up all the overtime he was offered, to help pay for all the nice things Becky liked to buy.

Shaking his head, he booted up his computer. There was something familiar about the guy he'd seen leaving the parking lot of Trey's apartment building, so he thought he'd start with doing a search on some of the kids he remembered from Saint Jermaine's. It wasn't easy—not just because eleven years had passed, but because they'd all had nicknames back then. It took a while to remember their real names.

Isaac searched a few, but didn't hit anything significant until he typed in *Wade Sharkey*. Wade's nickname had been Shark back then, and he'd picked a fight with Isaac, right after Isaac had gotten there, waving the tiny knife in his face.

Wade had a lot of friends back then, and they'd all ganged up against Isaac until Hawk had shown up, de-

Laura Scott   309

fusing the situation. Wade had made a couple of other
attempts to get even with Isaac, punching him in the
kidney when no one was looking, and one night he'd
sneaked into Isaac's room and tried to suffocate him
with a pillow. Once again, Hawk had saved him and
tossed Wade out on his ear.

From that point on, there had been an uneasy truce
between them. Isaac couldn't deny that he'd watched
his back often, but about six months later, Wade had
been sent back home.

Isaac stared at the adult photograph of Wade Sharkey, a mug shot taken about three years ago. Clearly,
Wade hadn't turned his life around after leaving Saint
Jermaine's. Instead, he'd done a stint in jail for armed
robbery.

"Did you find something?" Leah asked, coming over
to sit beside him.

He gestured to the computer screen. "Not really. This
is just one of the kids your brother and I knew back at
Saint Jermaine's."

Leah sucked in a harsh breath and Isaac frowned.
"What is it? You recognize him?"

She slowly nodded. "He went to our high school. He
was three years older than me, in Shane's class."

Isaac scowled. "You're saying he was friends with
your brother?"

She shrugged. "They hung out together sometimes,
and he came to our house once. I remember, because I
gave him a black eye when he forcefully tried to kiss
me."

A flash of anger hit hard and Isaac had to take a
couple of deep breaths to fight it back. Ridiculous to

want to give Wade another black eye for something he'd done years ago.

"I bet Wade is part of the illegal arms dealing," he said in a low voice. "And that's why the ATF asked for your brother's help. Your brother was probably the best chance they had for getting close to Wade."

"Wade was a scary guy," Leah admitted in a low tone. "At least, back in high school, he scared me."

Isaac took her hand and gave it a reassuring squeeze. "I know, but don't worry. I'm not about to let him anywhere near you."

She tightened her fingers around his, and as he stared at their joined hands, he silently vowed to keep his promise.

Or die trying.

Chapter 7

Leah clung to Isaac's hand and did her best to tear her gaze away from the disturbing image of Wade Sharkey on the laptop screen. He'd tried to kiss her, but she'd managed to get away before he could do anything more.

"Do you think he's involved in whatever Shane was investigating?" she asked, meeting Isaac's troubled gaze. "I wouldn't put it past him to do something criminal."

"Yeah, I think he's involved," Isaac admitted. "But try not to worry about this, Leah. He's not going to lay a finger on you as long as I'm here."

His words warmed her heart, and once again she realized how nice it was to have Isaac here, protecting her and Ben. Elliot would have tried to protect them, too, but he hadn't had the training Isaac did. Was she really comparing her husband to Isaac? What was she thinking? She cleared her throat and nodded. "I know. And right now, I'm more concerned about my brother." She shook her head helplessly. "Wade isn't the type of guy you want as your enemy."

"I agree," Isaac muttered. "He tried to kill me back at Saint Jermaine's, and Hawk saved my life. I'm not sure what your brother did to win him over, but from that point on he never tried to hurt me again. And I never did find out why Shark had it out for me in the first place."

"Shark?" she echoed in confusion before she made the connection. Wade's last name was Sharkey. "Oh, is that another of those nicknames you guys used back then?"

Isaac nodded. "Yeah."

"Unfortunately, that one suits him." Leah took a deep breath and forced a smile. "I guess the good news is that we have another clue." She subtly tugged her hand from his and then immediately missed his warm, comforting touch.

Isaac scowled. "But this clue doesn't help me much. Wade isn't going to be an easy man to find."

Her stomach twisted with fear. "You're not going to try to do that, are you?"

"I have to do something to help your brother, but I won't leave you here alone. I'll get Declan or Caleb to come and stay with you and Ben."

She wanted to protest, because truthfully, she'd be far more comfortable with Isaac. Yet shouldn't one cop be similar to another? It wasn't as if Caleb and Declan were complete strangers; she'd met them before.

Yet she wanted to be with Isaac instead of his team-mates. Because he made her feel safe in a way no one else did.

Despite her best efforts to keep her distance, she realized she was beginning to get emotionally involved with Isaac Morrison. But she couldn't afford to let down her guard. That was a path that would only lead to emotional destruction.

Getting over Elliot's death had been hard enough. Especially since she'd had Ben, barely more than a baby at the time, to consider. She couldn't do it again. She couldn't afford to take the chance that she'd end up like her mother, broken and seeking solace in the bottom of a bottle.

Leah drew in a steadying breath. A relationship with any man, especially Isaac, was out of the question. For now they were forced to work together, because Shane needed help. So what if she was attracted to Isaac? She'd just have to get over it.

She forced herself to meet Isaac's gaze. "I'll be fine with Caleb or Declan," she agreed reluctantly. "But please be careful."

Isaac's smile was crooked. "I always am," he assured her.

Leah remembered her father saying the same thing, but in the end, all the caution in the world hadn't kept him safe.

But Elliot hadn't been safe, either.

She'd do her best to put Isaac's fate in the hands of God. And continue to pray for his safety.

That was as much as she'd allow herself to do.

* * *

Isaac could tell Leah was worried, and he wished there was a way he could assure her that everything would be fine.

He rose to his feet and pulled out his phone. Declan didn't answer, so he left a message. Thankfully, Caleb picked up.

"Hey, Caleb," Isaac greeted him. "I need a favor."

"Figured as much," his friend drawled. "What's up?"

"First of all, I need cash. You know I'm good for it."

"No problem," Caleb agreed easily. "How much?"

Isaac named an amount and was glad when his teammate didn't seem too shocked. Then again, both Caleb and Declan knew what it was like to stay hidden without leaving an electronic trail. Isaac had been there to help them, the same way they were assisting him now.

It was good to have friends who covered your back.

"Okay, what else?" Caleb asked.

This was the tricky part. "I need you to stay with Leah and Ben for a while so I can do some legwork."

"Do you need help with the legwork, too?" Caleb asked. "I'll track down Deck."

"I already left him a message, so he might not be available. I can handle it alone, no worries," Isaac assured him. "There's a number of things we need to follow up on, three license-plate numbers that could belong to the guy who tried to snatch Leah and Ben. I also have a shell casing from a crime scene that I'd like you to run through the lab."

"Quite the list of favors," Caleb said drily. "Anything else?"

"Yeah, I want to know everything there is to know about ex-con Wade Sharkey."

"Who?" Caleb's tone held confusion.

"Check him out. He did time for armed robbery and is likely involved in the attempt to get to Leah and Ben."

Isaac could hear the tapping of computer keys in the background and wasn't surprised when Caleb let out a low whistle. "Yeah, I found him, and I'll see what we can dig up about his more recent activities. When do you want me to come over to sit with Leah and Ben?"

Isaac glanced at the clock and winced. "We've eaten an early dinner, but I'm sure you want to have dinner with your family, so maybe as soon as you're finished?"

"I'll come right away. Kaitlin and Noelle can eat without me."

That gave Isaac an idea. "You could eat dinner with your family and then bring them along. There's a pool here if Kaitlin likes to swim. I'm sure Ben wouldn't mind having a playmate."

"Great idea," Caleb agreed. "Kaitlin would love that. Tell me where you are again?"

Isaac gave the address and then disconnected from the call. He glanced at Leah, realizing she'd been listening to his side of the conversation. "I guess I should have run those plans by you first, huh?"

She shrugged. "No, it's fine. There's a shopping mall across the street, and we can pick up some swimming gear there. Ben will be ecstatic."

Isaac was glad she wasn't upset, but he could tell something was still bothering her. "Let's walk over now, okay? I want to be ready to leave as soon as Caleb gets here."

Leah pulled on her coat and helped get Ben into his. She was unusually quiet as they walked over to the discount store to buy swimsuits. It didn't take long, and within twenty minutes they were back in the hotel room.

Isaac jotted down some notes on Wade's last known address before shutting off the computer.

It was located within the Fifth District, which only made him more convinced that Wade was part of the illegal gunrunning. The address also happened to be smack-dab in the middle of one of the highest crime areas of the county, a fact Isaac purposefully didn't mention to Leah.

No sense in making her even more worried than she already was.

Isaac understood that she couldn't help thinking about her father's death on the job. It was a fate every cop on the force faced, although thankfully, deaths weren't as common anymore. The force put more time and effort into training, and the newest version of body armor also helped.

But he couldn't deny the risk and logically understood Leah's reluctance to be in that kind of position again, especially since she had Ben to worry about. After all, hadn't Isaac's job ruined his first marriage?

It had.

Too bad he couldn't seem to pry Leah out of his mind.

Leah was happy to see that Caleb had brought his wife, Noelle, along with their daughter. Kaitlin was a year or so older than Ben, but they seemed to get along fine.

Leah sat in a deck chair beside Noelle while Caleb

joined the kids in the pool. She had to smile as the children splashed and tried to dunk him, which of course wasn't happening. Thankfully, Ben had taken swimming lessons, so she was comfortable watching from the side of the pool.

"Caleb certainly is great with kids," Leah said.

Noelle smiled and nodded, patting her slightly rounded stomach. "He's a wonderful father. And we're expecting another baby in about five months."

"Really? Congratulations!" Leah remembered how excited she and Elliot had been when she'd found out she was pregnant. "How is Kaitlin handling the news?"

"She's excited, too. I think she'll be a great big sister."

"I'm sure she will be," Leah agreed. She gave Noelle credit not just for being married to a cop—a member of the SWAT team, no less—but also having a family. "How do you handle it?" she asked. At the other woman's confused expression, she added, "You know, living with the stress of Caleb's job."

"It isn't easy," Noelle agreed. "But I don't sit by the radio like some of the cops' wives do. I teach preschool, so that tends to keep me busy."

"But don't you worry about him getting hurt?" Her expression turned serious.

"Sure, I worry about him. What cop's wife doesn't worry about her loved ones? But I have faith and pray every day that God will watch over Caleb."

Leah nodded, feeling a little ashamed that she'd even broached the subject. "Faith helps us get through all the difficult times, doesn't it?"

"Absolutely," Noelle agreed. "Look, you're in danger

right now, and I'm sure that isn't because of anything you did, right?"

Leah let out a small laugh. "I'm a nurse—not exactly a dangerous job."

"Exactly my point. There are no guarantees for any of us. But I am glad that Isaac has been able to be there for you and Ben. He's a great guy."

If Noelle was trying to set her up with Isaac, she was on the wrong path. "I feel bad that you had to come out here to babysit me," Leah said, changing the subject. "I'm sure you had better things to do on a Saturday night."

"Are you kidding? I was thrilled at the chance of getting out of the house to bring Kaitlin to an indoor pool. And I'm sure your son is glad to have a playmate for a while."

"He is." She fell silent, watching the way Ben blossomed beneath Caleb's attention. Shane had been trying to fill the role of father figure for her son, but no matter how hard her brother tried, he couldn't be there as often as Ben needed.

And what would happen if her brother found someone to share his life with? Oh, Shane wouldn't abandon Ben completely, but she couldn't fault him for spending time with his own family.

Avoiding relationships hadn't been a conscious decision in the beginning, not during the first year or so after Elliot's death. If not for Ben, Leah wasn't sure she'd have found a way to get past her grief. There was a part of her that wanted to give up the way her mother had. Thankfully, the other part of her was just as determined not to.

But in the past two years she'd had several men ask her out, a couple of doctors at work and a construction worker from her parish. She hadn't been interested in going out with them, despite their so-called safe careers.

So why was she so attracted to Isaac? A man who was absolutely wrong for her on so many levels?

Maybe she needed to have her head examined. This was likely nothing more than a silly infatuation that would surely go away once her life went back to normal.

And if it didn't, she had only herself to blame.

Isaac avoided the freeway, taking a winding route along several side streets to get to the general area of Wade's last known address.

He was glad he was driving Deck's old car, since anything nicer would have been way out of place among the graffiti-painted buildings with boarded-up windows. Several cars around him had music blaring from the speakers, loud enough to be heard several feet away.

It would have been nice if Deck had been able to come with him, but unfortunately, he'd been out working on a suspicious device left at a shopping mall. And Isaac needed Caleb to stay with Leah and Ben.

Isaac wasn't foolish; he wasn't about to recklessly confront Wade, especially if he was surrounded by his buddies. He needed to get Shark alone, using their connected past to see if Wade knew anything about Hawk.

Finding the address wasn't difficult, but the apartment building looked to be deserted. Based on its dilapidated appearance, he figured it might even be condemned. For all he knew, Wade had moved someplace else.

Isaac referred to his notes, but didn't see the black car that, according to the DMV, was registered to Wade. Then again, the plates hadn't been renewed for the past two years, so the guy could be driving anything.

Isaac let out a sigh of frustration. Driving down here might be nothing but a bust. What had made him think he'd actually run into Wade? Especially on a chilly March evening?

Despite the cool temperatures, there were a few people out and about, and one particular group caught his eye. Even from a distance he could tell a drug deal was going down. But he wasn't here to worry about that. He needed to find Wade.

He passed a liquor store and caught a glimpse of another small group of guys inside. One of them looked familiar. He decided to park his car and continue on foot, to get closer.

Thankfully, he'd changed into the dark clothing Leah had picked out for him, black jeans and a sweatshirt, so he blended easily into the night. Most of the streetlights were burned out or broken, and it took a minute for his eyes to adjust to the darkness. The wind was cold and he pulled the hood of his sweatshirt over his head before making his way back to the liquor store.

He had no intention of going inside, just needed to get close enough to the glass door to see what was going on.

Walking slowly, Isaac tried to blend in with the rough neighborhood as he glanced into the liquor store. He caught a glimpse of a gun and a roll of cash exchanging hands. Satisfaction surged as his hunch proved correct.

The liquor store was being used as a hub for the sale of illegal weapons.

At that moment, the guy taking the money glanced over and locked gazes with Isaac. Not Wade, but another guy he recognized from Saint Jermaine's, one of Wade's sidekicks.

Isaac tore his eyes away and hunched his shoulders as he headed on around the block, taking the long way back to where he'd left his car. Every instinct screamed to run, but he forced himself to take his time, just in case the guy from Saint Jermaine's hadn't recognized him. He tried not to look too guilty as he rounded the corner.

A wave of relief hit hard when he reached his vehicle. Isaac found himself silently praying as he revved up the engine and pulled away from the curb. He had little choice but to drive past the liquor store, since there wasn't a cross street and making a U-turn would only cause more unwanted attention.

His brief moment of relief faded when he saw the guy he'd locked gazes with standing in the street facing him. As he approached, the man lifted his gun and pointed it directly at him.

Isaac cranked the steering wheel and ducked to avoid being hit as the sound of gunfire echoed through the night. He stomped on the accelerator, nearly clipping a parked car as he avoided the gunman in a desperate attempt to get back to Leah and Ben.

Chapter 8

Leah couldn't seem to relax as the hours crept by. She put up a good front, laughing when Ben did a cannonball that managed to splash the adults sitting a good two feet from the edge of the pool and chatting with Noelle as if she didn't have a care in the world.

But she watched the clock, nerves stretched thin.

When Noelle declared it was time to get out of the water, Leah didn't protest. When Ben did another cannonball rather than getting out the way she'd told him to, she narrowed her gaze and glared at him.

"Now, Ben." She didn't have to use her stern tone often, but her son was clearly trying to show off for his new friend, Kaitlin.

But of course, Kaitlin wasn't even paying attention to him; she was huddled up in a large towel, being dried off by Noelle. Caleb had also gotten out of the water to grab a towel, and without anyone else in the pool, Ben didn't have a reason to stay.

He reluctantly climbed out and came toward Leah. She wrapped him in a towel and held him close. "I hope you had fun," she said as she helped dry him off.

He nodded vigorously. "Lotsa fun!"

"Good. I'm glad." She was happy that he'd been able to relax and play for a few hours. He was the innocent victim in all this.

She glanced at the clock again, to find it was only ten minutes past the last time she'd looked, and she tried not to worry. Whatever he was doing was taking Isaac a long time. Truthfully, she'd expected him back by now.

"Why don't we go back up to our suite so the kids can watch a movie?" she suggested, pasting a happy smile on her face. She felt bad that Caleb couldn't leave until Isaac returned.

"Which movie?" Kaitlin asked eagerly.

Leah racked her brain to come up with the title of the latest children's film that had recently been released on DVD. "You and Ben can pick," she said. "There are a couple of movies on demand that are available."

"Sounds good," Noelle agreed. "And I'll make some microwave popcorn."

Leah led the way up to the suite, using her key card to enter before holding the door for the others. She and Noelle insisted the kids change into dry clothes, which they did in record time. Within minutes the pair had picked a movie and were settled on the sofa with a bag of microwave popcorn. Leah was impressed that Noelle had come prepared with snacks.

Caleb had taken a seat at the table and was working on the laptop computer. Since Noelle seemed content to watch the movie, Leah crossed over to sit beside him.

"What are you looking for?" she asked.

"Isaac asked me to check into a couple of things," he said without looking up.

She leaned forward and saw that he was doing a search on Wade Sharkey. A chill snaked down her back and she hated the idea that Isaac was out there looking for him.

After about fifteen minutes, Caleb sat back with a sigh. "There isn't much out there on this guy. He sure knows how to fly under the radar."

That news was not reassuring. "We have names and addresses for owners of these three license plates," she said, holding out the notes. "One of them was possibly involved in the attempt to kidnap me."

"Hmm…" Caleb drew them closer and began entering the information into the computer. She didn't have access to police databases the way he did, and they had only the one computer, so there wasn't much she could do except watch.

Isaac's teammate frowned as he stared at the screen, and her stomach tightened. "What is it? Did you find something?"

"One of these cars belongs to a cop, but he reported it stolen," Caleb admitted. "Cop's name is Aaron Winslow."

Her pulse jumped at the news. "He must be the dirty cop that my brother mentioned."

Caleb grimaced and shook his head. "Hold on—we can't jump to conclusions, Leah. First of all, I've already checked, and Winslow isn't in the same district as your brother. And even then, if someone wanted to throw suspicion on a cop, the best thing to do is to steal their vehicle to use in a crime."

He had a good point. "Okay, but don't you think it's a bit of a coincidence that my brother thinks there's a dirty cop who blew his cover, and it just so happens that a cop's car is stolen to commit a crime? I'm not sure I buy that."

"Maybe, maybe not," Caleb murmured. "But if we could find something else to link this cop to the crime, then I'd be convinced."

Leah wasn't sure how on earth they'd manage to do that, but before she could ask anything more, she heard the door open. Isaac was back! She leaped from her seat, knocking it over backward in her haste.

"Whoa, take it easy," Caleb said with a smile, righting the chair as she crossed over to Isaac.

"Are you all right?" she asked, raking her gaze over him, searching for blood.

"I'm fine," he assured her, reaching out to give her a brief hug. The gesture was so quick she couldn't help but wonder if she'd imagined it.

"Well?" Caleb asked. "Did you find anything?"

Isaac stepped back and nodded. "I think I stumbled across a place where they're doing some of their gun deals," he admitted. "Do you have a minute, Caleb? I want to show you something."

"Sure," he said easily. He crossed over and planted a kiss on the top of his wife's head. "Be right back," he assured her.

Leah wasn't about to be left behind, so she followed them out the door.

"Uh, why don't you wait here?" Isaac stopped in the hall, clearly not wanting her to tag along. "We'll be back in a few minutes."

What was with the sudden secrecy? She suppressed a sting of hurt. She didn't like the way Isaac was trying to put her off and had no intention of sitting around and waiting for him. She squared her shoulders and tucked a stray curl behind her ear. "No way. I'm coming with you."

Isaac stared at her for a long moment, a flash of helplessness, or maybe it was frustration, darkening his features before he threw his hands in the air. "Fine, suit yourself."

"I will." She trailed behind the two men, her stomach twisting with every step. When they walked outside, she hugged herself as the wind whipped around them.

Caleb let out a low whistle and she shoved her hair out of her eyes, trying to figure out what was wrong. Had Isaac cracked up the car?

But then she saw it—a small hole in the center of the windshield. And she knew without being told that it had been made by a bullet.

Someone had taken a shot at Isaac.

And looking at the placement of the hole, she knew it was a minor miracle that he hadn't been injured or killed.

Isaac watched Leah go pale and wished she would have listened to him and stayed inside. He'd wanted to spare her the fear and horror that now shadowed her eyes.

"We'd better call a glass company in to get that repaired," Caleb said. "Driving around with a bullet hole in your windshield is a good way to get pulled over."

"Yeah, no kidding. But that wasn't why I asked you to come out here. There's a slug in the passenger seat. We need to pry it out and see if it matches any other crimes."

Isaac opened the passenger door and crawled inside. The bullet had struck the outer edge of the seat, closest to the driver's side. Six inches nearer and he would have been hit.

Swerving had saved his life, since he wasn't wearing body armor beneath his sweatshirt. Something he definitely should have considered, based on his plan to skulk around in the district with the highest crime rate.

He pushed the thought aside and used his penknife to widen the opening around the slug.

"It's jammed in there pretty good," he muttered.

"Do you need help?" Caleb asked.

"Nah, just give me a few minutes." He widened the hole until he could see all the way down to the wooden frame. Finally, he caught a glimpse of the slug embedded inside. He wasn't sure he'd be able to get it out using only his pocketknife, since the tweezers that came with it weren't superstrong.

He didn't want to add any marks to the bullet fragment, so he stopped and backed out of the car. "We're going to need a field kit to get that out," he said.

"I might have one in my car," Caleb stated, heading off to where he'd parked.

Isaac turned toward Leah, searching for something

to say, but she was already walking away, heading back inside the hotel.

Somehow, he didn't think she'd gone in just because she was cold.

He knew that seeing the hole in the windshield and knowing there was a bullet fragment in the seat cushion had only proved to her just how dangerous his job was.

A sense of loss hit hard and he tried not to rub the ache in his chest. Stupid to feel bad about this, since he'd known all along that a relationship between them was out of the question.

Besides, he wasn't ready to have another family. What if he messed up again? And even if he was interested, Leah would never date a cop.

Better for his brain to get the message sooner rather than later.

"Here, let me try," Caleb said after he'd returned with the kit. He nudged Isaac aside and climbed into the passenger seat. It didn't take long with the proper equipment, and soon Caleb had the bullet fragment tucked into a small evidence bag.

"Not sure we'll get much off this," he said doubtfully. "It's pretty smashed up."

"Yeah, the shot came from close range. I was hoping the seat cushion may have protected it some."

Caleb shrugged. "It's still worth a try. I'll get this and the shell casing in tomorrow morning."

Isaac forced a smile. "Thanks. I appreciate your help. Especially coming over here tonight to stay with Leah and Ben."

Caleb waved him off. "It's nothing. Trust me, Kaitlin had a great time, and Noelle didn't mind getting out

of the house for a while. But we'd better head home."
His buddy cocked his head to the side. "Are you going
to be all right here with Leah?"

"Why wouldn't I be? She's upset, but she'll get over
it eventually." He almost winced at his own offhand
comment. As if he didn't care about what Leah was
going through.

Caleb snorted and shook his head. "You can't fool
me, bro. I've been there and I know when a man is getting emotionally tangled with a woman. And you are
definitely getting twisted up with that one."

"I don't plan on getting married again. One failure
was enough for me. Besides, I get the feeling that Leah
doesn't date cops. So whatever you think you're seeing is nothing more than your overactive imagination."
Isaac slammed the car door with more force than was
necessary. "Let's go get the rest of your family. And if
you could call a glass company to come fix the hole,
I'd appreciate it. I'd phone them myself but they'd ask
for a credit card."

"I'll cover it, no problem."

Isaac led the way inside, surprised to find Leah chatting with Noelle as if she didn't have a care in the world.

Why he was bothered by that, he had no idea. He
pulled out his phone, intending to call Leah's brother,
when he remembered the photos he'd taken.

"Caleb, wait. Before you leave, take a look at these
pictures." Isaac plugged his phone into the computer and
downloaded the few he'd taken of the men standing on
the street corner. "What do you think? Do any of these
guys look familiar?"

His buddy squinted at the grainy pictures before shaking his head. "Not really."

"What about this one here?" Isaac had managed to get a decent profile shot of a guy standing inside the liquor store, the same one he'd recognized from Saint Jermaine's.

The one who'd shot at him without so much as blinking an eye.

"Sorry, man, he doesn't look familiar at all."

Isaac nodded. "Okay, just thought I'd check." He knew Hawk would remember him. Would likely even remember his name. This guy wasn't on the list he'd dredged up from his memory earlier.

But the shooter must be working with Wade. Isaac couldn't believe the tie back to Saint Jermaine's was nothing more than a coincidence.

"Okay. Thanks anyway." Isaac knew he needed to set up a meeting with Hawk. But that was easier said than done. His buddy didn't answer his phone or call very often.

"Movie's over," Leah announced. "Time to get ready for bed."

"No! I don't wanna go to bed." Ben thrust his lower lip out stubbornly. "Me and Kaitlin want to have a sleepover."

Isaac hid a smile as Leah stared at her son with exasperation.

"No sleepovers," Noelle said firmly. "Kaitlin, say thank you to Mrs. Nichols and Ben for inviting us to come and swim in the pool."

"Thank you, Mrs. Nichols and Ben," Kaitlin parroted. "I had lots of fun."

"Me, too," Ben declared, unwilling to be left out. "Mom, can Kaitlin come back tomorrow?"

"We'll see," Leah said, and he groaned, the same way Jeremy used to, knowing that "we'll see" really meant no. For a moment guilt over losing his son stabbed deep.

Leah gave Noelle a quick hug and smiled at Caleb as they gathered their things together. But as soon as the door was closed behind their guests, Leah avoided Isaac's gaze and hustled Ben into their room to get ready for bed.

Isaac scrubbed his hands over his face, wishing she'd come back out so they could talk, but after five minutes stretched to ten and then to fifteen, he knew it wasn't happening.

His heart squeezed, but he tried to shake it off. He pulled out the disposable phone and called Hawk. To his utter surprise, his buddy answered.

"Yeah?"

There was so much to tell him that Isaac took a minute to formulate his thoughts. "Your partner, Trey Birchwood, was murdered by the same guy who tried to grab Leah and Ben. I managed to take a shell casing from the scene of the crime and plan to run it through the system. While I was out looking for Wade Sharkey, I stumbled across Stan's Liquor Store, which appears to be a common place to do gun-sale business. I recognized one of the guys as going to Saint Jermaine's, but I can't think of his name, other than he went by the nickname Steel. He recognized me, too, and tried to kill me."

"You've been busy," Hawk said, in a tone so quiet Isaac could barely hear him. Hawk had to be hiding somewhere, and Isaac wished his friend would trust him enough to tell him where. "I thought I told you to stay out of this. Your only job is to watch over Leah and Ben."

Isaac reined in his temper with an effort. "Look, knock it off, okay? You can't do this alone. Besides, you don't know your sister very well if you think she's content with sitting here doing nothing while you're out there fighting for your life. I'm going to text you this photo, and I need you to tell me this guy's name."

"Okay, I'll call you back."

He disconnected from the line and Isaac blew out a heavy breath as he sent the photo of the guy who'd shot at him to Hawk's phone. It didn't take long for his friend to call him back.

"His name is Joey Stainwhite, but everyone called him Steel because he had nerves of iron when it came to doing anything dangerous. And he's definitely in this with Wade."

"That's what I thought. Okay, where are you? I think we'd be better off working as a team."

"Not yet. I'm...in the middle of something."

Hawk's evasiveness was really starting to make Isaac mad. "Don't you care about your sister at all? Don't you understand how worried sick she is about you? What could be more important than coming in to work with us?"

Hawk didn't answer right away, and Isaac hoped that he'd knocked some sense into his buddy's thick skull. "Soon, I promise," he finally said.

"What about your ATF contact? Have you tried him?"

"I have, but no answer yet."

"Okay, I'll give you until morning, and then we're coming to get you whether you like it or not."

"I hear you. Gotta go." And just that quickly the connection between them was broken.

Isaac ground his teeth in frustration and just barely managed not to throw the disposable phone across the room. He spun around, intending to head to the kitchen table, but stopped abruptly when he saw Leah hovering just outside the doorway to her room. From the shocked expression on her face, she'd obviously heard his side of the call with her brother.

He mentally kicked himself for being so stupid, but how was he to know she'd come out? Unless she'd overheard him and had come to find out what was going on? No, he didn't think he'd been talking that loudly.

Well, at least not until the end of the conversation. He knew he'd lost his temper then.

Leah was watching him, her dark hair curling around her shoulders, her eyes clinging to his, and he had to swallow hard to stop himself from going over there to pull her into his arms.

Bad idea, he reminded himself. Really, really bad idea.

"I'm sorry for losing my temper like that," he said helplessly, thinking he hadn't apologized this much since his wife had filed for divorce and left, taking Jeremy when she'd moved in with her new boyfriend. The one she'd had an affair with while he'd been working so many extra hours.

The one who'd eventually killed her and Isaac's son.

"None of this is your fault, Isaac," Leah said softly.

"You're in the middle of this mess because my brother dragged you into it."

She was mostly right, but he shook his head anyway. "This is what cops do, Leah. We fight the bad guys and try to put them behind bars. If I wasn't working on this case, I'd be working on something else."

A flash of pain darkened her eyes and he mentally kicked himself again, harder. Why in the world had he reminded her about his dangerous career?

"What did Shane say?" she asked, stepping closer.

Isaac curled his fingers into fists to keep from reaching for her. "He knew the name of the guy who shot at me, which is good news. Now I can put a warrant out for his arrest."

"I heard you trying to convince him to meet with us," she said, coming closer still. So close her cinnamon-and-spice scent teased his nostrils. "Thank you for doing that."

He shrugged, since his attempt had fallen on deaf ears. "I don't like him being out there alone."

"He's stubborn, isn't he?" Leah said with a wry smile. "Guess that's another trait he gets from our father."

Isaac lifted a brow. "A trait you share," he pointed out drily.

When she took another step toward him, he needed every ounce of willpower he had not to take a step back. Didn't she realize the effect she had on him?

Obviously not.

"Isaac…" Her voice trailed off as she reached out to touch his arm, the heat of her small hand burning through the fleece of his sweatshirt. "I'm so glad you weren't hurt," she whispered.

His thoughts scattered, but there was one thing he knew he needed to tell her. "I prayed and immediately felt calm. And I owe that to you."

A smile bloomed on her face and suddenly he couldn't help himself.

He pulled her into his arms and kissed her, ignoring the tiny voice in his head that warned he might be making a mistake.

Because having Leah in his arms felt exactly right.

Chapter 9

After a momentary shock of surprise, Leah melted against Isaac, savoring his kiss. It had been so long since she'd kissed a man, she'd completely forgotten how wonderful it was to share this intimacy. To be held protectively, as if she was something precious.

To be wanted.

And cared for.

She couldn't say how long the kiss lasted, but when Isaac lifted his head to breathe, she clung to his broad shoulders for a long, heartbreaking moment. He was so tall, so different from her husband.

Wait a minute. What was she doing? She'd vowed not to love another man after Elliot died. She shouldn't be doing this. Kissing Isaac was not smart.

Regretfully, she pulled away and stepped back, drawing a deep, cleansing breath even though she knew she wouldn't forget the impact of Isaac's kiss.

Ever.

"Leah," he began, but she quickly shook her head.

"Don't," she begged. "Don't apologize or say anything else, either. Let's just enjoy the moment we shared and move on."

Isaac's eyebrows levered up and then pulled together into a frown as he stared at her for a long moment, his mouth drawn into a thin, tense line. His dark eyes were difficult to read, and she told herself she didn't want to know what he was thinking, because she was already hanging on to her control by a thin thread.

"Good night, Isaac," she said, forcing herself to turn and head into the bedroom she shared with Ben.

As she was closing the door behind her, she heard his husky voice. "Good night, Leah."

She needed every ounce of willpower flowing through her bloodstream to close the door. Even then, she leaned weakly against it. No matter how much she was attracted to Isaac, entering into a relationship with him or with any man wasn't what she wanted. She couldn't imagine losing another husband. Maybe Noelle found a way to deal with Caleb's dangerous job, but then again, Noelle likely hadn't lost her father to the perils of being a cop.

And certainly Noelle hadn't watched her mother drink herself to death as a result of that loss.

Feeling stronger in her resolve, Leah washed her face and brushed her teeth in the bathroom, then crawled into bed. But sleep wouldn't come. She stared blindly up at the ceiling, rehashing everything that had just happened. She'd been so happy to hear that Isaac had prayed when he was in danger. There wasn't a greater honor than helping people find their way to the Lord.

And what she needed now was the power of prayer to deal with her own rioting emotions.

She closed her eyes and cleared her mind, opening her heart and her soul to God.

As Your willing servant, I ask You to show me the way, Lord. Provide me the wisdom I need to guide Isaac and the strength to face whatever the future holds. And please, Lord, keep my son and my brother safe in Your care. Amen.

Isaac dropped onto the edge of the sofa and cradled his head in his hands. *Nice move, kissing her senseless. What in the world were you thinking?*

Yeah, that was the problem, all right. Thinking hadn't really entered into the equation at all. And he was mad at himself for getting emotionally involved with Leah in the first place, especially since she'd made her position on not dating cops loud and clear.

Marriage and cops didn't go well together. He'd learned that when Becky had left him. So why was he even entertaining the idea of trying again?

For a moment he considered what he might do if he gave up being a cop. But the instant the idea entered his mind, he shoved it aside.

No way was he giving up his entire career for a woman. Besides, being an officer was who he was. His team meant a lot to him. Being a part of something good, putting the bad guys behind bars, was important to him, as well.

Anyone who truly cared about him wouldn't ask him to give it up.

So why didn't that make him feel any better?

Maybe the problem was really his. He couldn't give enough to a relationship because he gave everything to his career. It wouldn't be fair to drag any woman into marriage. And especially not Leah.

From now on, he needed to keep his distance from her.

He stood and crossed over to the window, which overlooked the back parking lot. He'd tucked his car beneath a tree, hoping to make the bullet hole in the windshield less obvious. The mud over the license plate was still intact, and he'd made sure he hadn't been followed.

But then he remembered the canister of tear gas breaking through the window of their first hotel room. That wouldn't happen here, since they were up on the second floor, but the fact that a dirty cop was involved bothered him.

Cops had way more resources available to them than the average layperson did.

He dropped the curtain and crossed over to the kitchen table, where the laptop was sitting. Hawk had given him the name Joey Stainwhite, so Isaac made the call to the department dispatcher to put a warrant out for Joey's arrest.

Once that task was completed, he tried to do a search on the guy, but of course he didn't find much. Other than the fact that Joey had a very similar police record as Wade.

Had they served time together? Isaac checked the records and wasn't surprised to find they had in fact done so. How had they gone from petty crime to dealing illegal weapons?

He stared at the computer screen, realizing that Wade and Joey had to be lower-level operatives. There had to be someone higher up who was the brains behind the operation.

And based on what Hawk had told him, the head honcho was very possibly a dirty cop.

A flashing red light coming through the crack in the curtains caught his eye. He scowled and leaped up to cross over to the window. When he looked outside, he could see a cop had someone pulled over.

Nothing to worry about—the officer likely was handing out a speeding ticket or DUI. But Isaac stayed by the window anyway, watching to make sure the policeman didn't stumble upon his car.

It seemed to take forever for the cop to finish, and even then he didn't leave right away. He had turned off the red flashing lights on the squad car, but what in the world was he doing out there?

Isaac was getting more and more nervous until finally the officer pulled away, making a wide U-turn before heading back out onto the highway.

For a moment Isaac debated waking Leah and Ben to head to a new hotel, chiding himself for not moving earlier.

No, he couldn't do it. There was no evidence of real danger, and after swimming all evening, Ben no doubt needed a good night's sleep.

But even though, logically, he knew they were safe, Isaac stretched out on the sofa rather than going into the bedroom. He planned to be ready, just in case.

Leah and Ben were his top priority. Anyone daring to come in would have to go through him to get to them.

Leah woke up the next morning to the sound of Ben's laughter coming from the living room. For a moment she was reminded of Saturday mornings when Elliot would get their son up so that she could sleep in.

The old, familiar pang of grief didn't follow on the heels of that thought, a fact that surprised her. There were times she had trouble remembering her husband's face, although she had pictures.

None with her now, though.

Leah had tried to keep Elliot's memory alive for Ben, but he'd been only a year old when his father died, far too young to retain any real memories.

And for some reason, that thought didn't make her sad this morning.

She leaped out of bed, more eager to see Isaac again than she should be. After hurrying through her shower and blow-drying her hair, she pulled on her jeans and sweater before following the enticing smell of breakfast.

"Good morning." Isaac greeted her cheerfully, despite looking rumpled and exhausted.

"Good morning," she responded lightly, unwilling to broach the subject of his sleepless night. After all, it had taken her far longer than it should have to fall asleep, thanks to his toe-curling kiss.

"Breakfast just arrived, so help yourself." Isaac gestured to the food waiting on the table. "And I found another place for us to stay tonight, one I'd like to run past you."

She frowned and took a seat at the kitchen table. "Another place? Why can't we stay here?"

Isaac shrugged and glanced at Ben. "I'll explain later. First, let's eat."

Leah waited for Isaac to sit down and was surprised when he folded his hands together, looking at her expectantly. She drew in a deep breath and bowed her head. "Dear Lord, we thank You for this wonderful food You've provided for us. We also thank You for keeping all of us safe from harm. We ask for Your grace and mercy as we begin our day. Amen."

"Amen," both Isaac and Ben echoed.

The food was delicious. She glanced around the suite, wishing they didn't have to leave. Had something happened last night? Something that had caused Isaac a restless night?

Ridiculous to assume he'd been kept awake by their kiss.

She really needed to get a grip already. They were dependent on each other for now, but as soon as Shane met up with them, they wouldn't need Isaac's help anymore. They'd go their separate ways.

She stared at her scrambled eggs, refusing to be depressed by the thought of Isaac leaving. Based on the hero worship in her son's eyes, she wasn't the only one who would miss him.

Her stomach twisted painfully and her previously ravenous appetite evaporated away. She pushed her food around for a few minutes before giving up the pretense.

"That was delicious. Thank you," she said, sliding away her half-eaten breakfast.

"You're welcome," Isaac said, frowning when he

saw the amount of food she hadn't eaten. Thankfully, he didn't say anything more as she busied herself with cleaning up.

As soon as Ben and he were finished eating, she turned toward Isaac. "Today is Sunday, right? I'd really like to attend church services."

He looked surprised at her request, but then slowly nodded. "All right, we can go back to that church from the other night if you'd like."

"Great—thanks." That was one issue solved. "I also need to call in to work. I had the weekend off but I'm scheduled to work tomorrow morning. I need to give them time to find my replacement."

"Uh, sure. No problem. I've already taken a few personal days myself, but you might want to take the whole week off, since we have no idea when this will be over."

"I can't call in sick for a whole week," she said, horrified that he'd even suggest such a thing.

"I understand, but I don't want anyone at work to know where you are or what's going on. We wouldn't want to inadvertently put anyone at the hospital in danger."

She nodded and took the disposable phone into the bedroom to make the call. What could she say that wouldn't be an outright lie? With a grimace she told the charge nurse on duty that she had some personal problems and couldn't come in to work. And when the woman tried to pry more information out of her, Leah quickly disconnected the call.

Good thing they were attending church, because she desperately needed the spiritual support right now.

She gathered their clothing and personal items together, packing everything into the duffel bag they'd purchased yesterday, which seemed like weeks ago. Then she hauled the duffel out to the living area.

"Here, I'd like to show you what I found," Isaac said, motioning her over. She dropped the bag on the floor near the door and crossed to the computer. "Check this place out. They have small two-bedroom cabins for rent, fairly cheap, since it's the off-season. And there's a playground for Ben, which I thought would be nice."

"Looks good," she agreed. "But it's pretty far away, isn't it?"

Isaac nodded. "Yeah, but I can't help thinking that being farther outside of town is better for us."

"What happened last night?" she asked.

"Nothing really, just a cop hanging out after he pulled someone over. Made me nervous, that's all." Isaac shut down the computer. "Are you ready to go?"

She nodded, and it didn't take long to check out of the hotel. What was surprising was that the bullet hole in the windshield was already repaired. "How did you get that done so fast?"

"Caleb made the call for first thing this morning. There's a company that drives out to where your car is located to fix broken or cracked windshields."

"Amazing," she muttered as Isaac stored their things in the trunk.

The ride to the church didn't take long, and just seeing the brick building with its stained-glass windows and steeple gave Leah a sense of coming home.

She wasn't sure what Isaac thought about attending church, since this wasn't a wedding or a funeral, but she was touched that he'd agreed regardless. With Ben sitting between them, she couldn't shake the idea that everyone around them likely thought they were a family.

She tried to concentrate on the service and the pastor's theme of forgiveness, but it wasn't easy. She kept glancing over at Isaac, amazed that he seemed to be intently following the sermon.

Did he need to forgive someone for something? And if so, why did she care?

It had taken time for her to fully forgive the drunk driver who'd hit Elliot head-on in a crash that cost her husband his life. Since it was the man's third DUI offense, he'd gotten sentenced to seven years in prison for vehicular homicide. She prayed he'd see the error of his ways and would turn his life around once he was released from jail.

She silently prayed for Isaac to find peace in forgiveness. And when he took her hand in his during the Lord's Prayer, she couldn't prevent the tiny thrill of awareness that shimmered through her.

The service was over much too quickly, but she was glad for the opportunity to attend. They made their way outside into the bright sunlight. The spring temperatures were finally warming up, and she couldn't help smiling when Ben let out a whoop and ran up and down the rows of cars.

"Over here, Ben," Isaac called, gesturing at their vehicle.

Her son had a lot of pent-up energy, because he continued running around with his arms spread wide, pretending to be an airplane.

Isaac took off after him, and she stood by the car, watching the two of them together. Isaac didn't yell at the boy, but lifted him up and flew him around and around like a plane.

"Do it again, Mr. Isaac, do it again," he begged.

"Once more and then we have to leave, all right?" Isaac waited until he nodded before swinging him in a circle again.

Ben was giggling madly as they finally returned to the car. Leah wanted to thank Isaac for being so kind to her son, but her throat felt too tight and she found herself blinking back the sting of tears.

"All set?" Isaac asked, glancing over at her.

"Yes," she managed to answer, avoiding his gaze by buckling her seat belt.

The drive along the country highway was nice and quiet on a Sunday afternoon. Isaac seemed to know where he was going, so she tried to sit back and enjoy the fact that they weren't running for their lives for once.

"We're almost there," Isaac said before Ben could ask for the fifth time. "The road leading to the log-cabin rentals is just up ahead."

The area around the cabins looked sparsely populated, and Leah couldn't help wondering if that was part of the reason Isaac had chosen the place. She smiled when Ben let out a whoop as he caught sight of the playground.

"Can I go play, Mom? Can I?" he asked anxiously.

She glanced over at Isaac and nodded. "Yes, but you have to wait until we get checked in, okay?"

Her son didn't appreciate the wait, but soon Isaac returned with the keys to their cabin. He handed one to her. "We're in number seven. I'll haul our stuff inside if you want to take Ben to the playground."

"Sure, that would be great." She slid out of the passenger seat and then opened the back door to help Ben out. He'd already unlatched the booster-seat strap by himself.

He ran ahead, teeming with exuberance. She followed more slowly, enjoying watching him. She was so fortunate to have him as a part of her life.

Despite the sun, the wind still held a chill, so after about forty-five minutes, she called him over. "It's time to go in."

"Okay." Her son had her dark hair and fair skin, and his cheeks were rosy from the cold. They walked down the path, finding cabin seven without difficulty.

Isaac was on the phone when they arrived, so she tried to keep Ben quiet so they wouldn't disturb him. She took off Ben's coat and glanced around their latest home away from home. The cabin was a tad smaller than the suite had been, but the two bedrooms flanking the living area were almost the same. Leah hung up their coats on a wooden rack behind the door and went to stand next to the blaze that Isaac had going in the fireplace.

He was scribbling notes on the stationery he must have taken from their previous hotel. "What else?" he asked when he'd finished.

There was another long pause as he listened to whoever was talking on the other end of the line, probably Caleb or Declan.

"Okay, call me as soon as you find something else," he said before disconnecting from the call.

"What's going on?" she asked.

Isaac glanced at Ben and then shrugged. "New details from the crime-scene techs."

She appreciated that he didn't want to say too much in front of her son, but she had a stake in this investigation, too. "Ben, why don't you get your cars out so you can play for a while?"

"Okay," he agreed.

"The room closest to the fireplace is yours," Isaac said when Ben headed in the wrong direction. "Be careful—it's hot."

Leah waited until her son was well out of earshot. "Tell me what they found."

"The shell casing is the same type found at the scene of an unsolved murder," he admitted. "Young man by the name of Enrique Morales."

She stared at Isaac blankly, thinking there had to be more to the story than this. "So, what does that mean?"

"Enrique also spent time at Saint Jermaine's school for delinquent teens," Isaac admitted. "And he was murdered exactly one week ago today."

She shivered, not liking the strong link to the place. "You think he was part of this whole illegal gun scheme?"

"Can't say for sure, but I do think it's possible. And if that is the case, then I can't help but wonder how many more people will die before we figure out who the top guy is," Isaac said grimly.

Leah swallowed hard, thinking about Shane. It was creepy the way everything seemed to revolve around Saint Jermaine's, a place where both Isaac and Shane had been sentenced to over twelve years ago. It wasn't as if they'd spent years there, either; the time frame was better measured in months. But clearly, whatever criminal activity had started back then had resurrected in the here and now.

Two deaths associated with this mess so far: Trey Birchwood and now Enrique Morales.

She had to convince her brother to meet with Isaac and her soon. Before he became the next victim.

Chapter 10

Isaac pushed away from the table feeling restless. The puzzle pieces were beginning to fall into place, but there were still way too many missing holes. And worse, he wasn't sure what steps he could take next to fill in the blanks.

"I want to talk to Shane," Leah said abruptly. "He has to let us come and pick him up."

Isaac nodded, agreeing with her concern. "I told him the same thing last night. So far he hasn't been willing to accept our help." He didn't add that the main reason Hawk was keeping his distance was because he didn't want to put Leah and Ben in any danger.

Hawk would rather die in the line of duty than risk the innocent lives of the people he loved.

And frankly, Isaac couldn't blame him. He'd do the same thing if the situation was reversed.

"Give me his number," Leah insisted. "Maybe I can convince him."

Isaac hesitated, but reached for his phone. Why not have Leah talk to him? Maybe hearing from his sister would help change Hawk's mind about coming in. "Here, use mine—he might not recognize your number." He watched Leah make the call, thinking he'd been more than ready to pick up Hawk last night. In fact, he'd pushed him as hard as he could, but to no avail.

Of course, Hawk didn't answer. Isaac knew by the brevity of the call that his buddy must have his phone off.

Leah let out a heavy sigh of frustration. "He's ignoring us," she muttered.

"Or he's in a place where he can't talk," Isaac pointed out.

"So now what?" she asked, throwing up her hands. "We can't just sit here and wait. We need to do something."

He didn't want to remind her about what had happened the last time he'd tried to *do* something. The bullet hole in his windshield had been repaired, but the seat cushion where he'd dug out the bullet was still a mess.

"Here, program the number into your phone, so that you have it, just in case."

She did as he suggested. "I still don't like the fact that there is nothing we can do to help him."

"I know," Isaac admitted. "Listen, why don't you and Ben enjoy some downtime?"

Leah rolled her eyes but didn't say anything more.

He understood she was chafing at being holed up in a small log cabin as much as he was. But he didn't have another option for her.

Belatedly, he remembered the gun they'd recovered from the mall shooting incident. So much had happened that he hadn't had time to ask someone to check for the weapon in the evidence room. "There might be one thing I can do," he said slowly. He called Declan's number, but his friend didn't answer. The thought of calling Caleb after his buddy had gone above and beyond to help him out last evening didn't sit well with him, either. Isaac didn't want to keep dragging his buddies away from their families.

The newest member of their team, Jenna Reed, had been with him during that mall incident. Maybe she'd be willing to check out the evidence room and see if there had been any headway on the ballistics evidence, as well.

Despite being blonde and petite, Jenna had surprised them all with her incredible sharpshooting skills. She might have placed second behind Caleb, but not by much. Yes, she had a bit of a chip on her shoulder, always determined to carry her own weight, sometimes to the point of being ridiculous. But she tolerated the general ribbing from the rest of the guys without getting too bent out of shape.

He called the dispatch center for her number, and once he phoned her, she surprised him by picking up on the second ring. "Reed," she said curtly.

"Hey, Jenna, it's Isaac. I need a favor if you have a few minutes."

"Sure. What's up?" There was a hint of surprise

in her tone, as if she hadn't expected him to call her for help.

He quickly explained what he wanted and she readily agreed. "I'll check out the evidence room and search on the ballistics report. Is this the number you want me to use to call you back when I have something?"

"Yeah. And, Jenna? Thanks."

"No problem."

He disconnected, once again thinking how great it was to have a team of people he trusted. Too bad Hawk didn't have the same level of teamwork within his district.

"Jenna?" Leah echoed. "Is she one of the dispatchers?"

Was Leah jealous of Jenna? No, had to be his imagination. "She's a sharpshooter for the SWAT team."

A tiny frown puckered Leah's brow. "And you trust her? The same way you trust Caleb and Declan?"

"Caleb and Declan are my best friends, so no, I don't trust Jenna in the exact same way. But she's a good cop and I've been in a few tactical situations with her. She can hold her own."

Leah flashed a lopsided smile. "Sorry to be on edge. I just don't want to risk anything happening to my brother. I know I'm driving you crazy, but I just can't imagine what Shane must be going through."

"I care about your brother, too, Leah," he reminded her. "I don't want to see anything happen to him, either."

She nodded, her expression thoughtful. "He and I have always been close, but even more so in the past few years since our parents died. Shane helped support me through nursing school, after Mom passed away. I'm not sure if I would have finished without him."

Isaac nodded. "He's super proud of everything you've accomplished."

"Goes both ways," she assured him. "I'm proud of him and you, too. Especially after the way you and Shane both turned your life around after being at Saint Jermaine's. I wonder why Wade didn't make the same decision?"

"I think Wade's lawyer must have pulled some strings to get him sentenced to the school rather than sent to jail," Isaac said with a frown. "He had several run-ins with the law prior to the time he was sentenced to Saint Jermaine's. The rest of us didn't. As first-time offenders, we were given the opportunity for a second chance."

"I know that Shane's public defender made a big deal out of the way we lost our father," Leah said softly. "I think he used it as a way to garner sympathy for the self-destructive choices that Shane made."

Isaac nodded, knowing his own attorney had done something similar. Not that he was anxious to share the details of his personal life with Leah. She and Shane had suffered a blow when their father died, but at least they'd had a dad. He'd tried to find his dad when he was eighteen, but his father had refused to see or talk to him. Isaac had moved on, but always wondered why his dad refused to have anything to do with him.

"What about you?" Leah asked, leaning forward and pinning him with her clear blue eyes. "How was it that your lawyer managed to convince a judge to let you go to the school?"

He hesitated, wondering just how much he should

tell her. "My mom… Well, let's just say she had problems. There were a lot of different men in her life, none of which seemed to hang around very long. She worked in a hair and nail salon, but we were constantly struggling to make ends meet." He shrugged and averted his gaze, not wanting to see the sympathy reflected in Leah's. "I was arrested for selling drugs because we didn't have any food at home. I think my story and the fact that it was a first drug-possession offense helped him plead my case."

"You had it rough, didn't you?" Leah asked softly.

He waved it off. "I'm nothing special. Lots of kids have it rough." He walked over to the fire and put another log on, wishing Leah would change the subject.

"Mommy, come look!" Ben said in an excited whisper.

Isaac followed Leah into the bedroom, hanging in the doorway as she and Ben stared through the window. Ben pointed at a spot in the glass. "Deers," he whispered in awe.

Sure enough, two white-tailed deer, likely a mother and her baby, were standing about fifty yards away, peeling bark off one of the trees. If they were aware of the humans watching from the window, they didn't show it.

"They're beautiful, aren't they?" Leah whispered, putting her arm around Ben's shoulders.

"We have to talk quiet so we don't scare them, right?" he asked.

"That's right," she agreed.

Isaac moved back to the living room, feeling a pang in his chest. Leah was a great mother to Ben, and watching them together reminded him of how much he'd missed with Becky and Jeremy.

His fault for not cutting back on his overtime hours. His fault for letting his career mean more to him than his family.

His fault for not loving Becky enough.

He dropped onto the edge of the sofa and ran his hand over his hair. He and Becky had gotten married too young and had Jeremy just a year later, but he hadn't loved her the way Caleb and Deck loved their wives. He could admit now what a mess he'd made of his life.

Leah was right to stay far away from him. He was a cop and a guy who didn't know how to find the right balance between his career and his personal life.

It was easier to focus on the former and ignore the latter.

When his disposable cell phone rang, he reached for it gratefully. He recognized Jenna's number. "Hey, Jenna, did you find something?"

"Yes, and I think you've been holding out on me," she accused without heat. "The ballistics from the gun we recovered at the mall shooting is the same type and caliber found in two recent murders."

Two murders? He gripped the phone tightly. "Enrique Morales was one of them, right?"

"Bingo. And the second is a dead cop by the name of Trey Birchwood," Jenna said.

Isaac's gut tightened at the news, even though this was exactly what he'd suspected.

"Birchwood and Morales weren't murdered with the exact same weapon as the one used in the mall shooting, but it's the same make, model and caliber of bullet. So tell me, how did you know?" Jenna demanded.

"Educated guess," he hedged.

"Don't give me that line," she snapped. "If you don't want to tell, fine, but don't pretend you're not in the middle of some sort of investigation. And you know I need to let Griff Vaughn know what you've found, since it's connected to the mall shooting."

"Look, Jenna, I'm helping out a friend who just happens to be working undercover, okay?" Isaac couldn't stop her from going to their boss, but he wanted to make sure she understood the gravity of the situation. "Things are happening pretty fast, and hopefully, I'll know more by tomorrow. If you really feel the need to tell Griff what you know, that's fine. But trust me, I'm working on it and hope to know more soon."

There was a long pause on the other end as Jenna considered his words. "Okay, fine. I'll hold off for now. But if you need help, call me. We're supposed to be part of a team, remember?"

He couldn't help but grin at her annoyed tone. "Yeah, I remember. And I will call you if I need help."

She snorted. "Yeah, right. Later, Morrison." She clicked off before he could say anything more.

Isaac realized that Jenna was all too aware of how close he was to Declan and Caleb, and why shouldn't he be? They were his best friends. But maybe Jenna felt left out by their closeness.

Nothing he could do about that now, but he made a mental note to mention the issue to his pals once this was over.

Right now, he had bigger concerns to think about.

Wade and his cohorts in crime were part of an underground ring selling illegal guns to criminals. And now three crime scenes were linked to the same type of gun.

Were there other crimes, too? He had to assume so, since he knew Wade had to be doing this for a while.

But if they put out an arrest warrant on Wade Sharkey right now, the top guy might get away. What if he left town, only to set up shop somewhere else, in another city or state?

No, they needed to figure out who was the mastermind of the gunrunning ring and take him down as soon as possible.

While keeping Leah and Ben safe at the same time.

A monumental task, at best.

Leah encouraged Ben to play a card game with her in an effort to keep him entertained. After several rounds of Go Fish, he lost interest and decided he wanted to play his video game. Left alone, she pulled out the Bible she'd found in a drawer and turned to her favorite Psalm, 23:4.

"Even though I walk through the darkest valley, I will fear no evil. For You are with me; Your rod and Your staff, they comfort me."

The words soothed her soul and helped to keep her calm. She could hear Isaac in the other room, tapping on the laptop, and even though she continued to read the rest of the psalm, she found herself wondering what Isaac was working on.

After a few minutes, she gave up and set the Bible aside. Ben was still focused on his game, so she crossed into the living room to look over Isaac's shoulder.

His expression was intense as he remained focused

on the screen, and for a moment she admired his square jaw, his sandy-brown hair and deep brown eyes. She caught a whiff of shaving cream and noticed that he'd nicked himself earlier that morning along the lower edge of his jaw. For a moment she was tempted to place a tiny kiss there.

Idiot, she chided herself. She cleared her throat and forced herself to take a step back. "Find anything new?"

"Not yet," he muttered. He pushed away from the computer and glanced up at her. "Are you hungry? We can think about what you and Ben would like for dinner."

"I'm okay for now, although didn't we pass a diner on the way in? Might be nice to have something different."

"We can get something to eat at the diner, no problem," Isaac agreed.

She noticed he'd made a list of notes as he worked on the computer. "What is all this?" she asked, running her index finger down the page. "A list of crimes in the Milwaukee area?"

"Yes, as a matter of fact, they are." Isaac didn't say anything more, so she sat down and began reading through the list.

It took a minute for her to see the pattern. "These are all crimes involving guns. You think these are all linked to the illegal sales?"

Isaac glanced at her and nodded. "Yes. I didn't realize that armed robberies and other gun-related crimes have doubled in the past three months." He rubbed the back of his neck and then tapped the computer screen. "I found an article from a few weeks ago, describing a recent press conference by the chief of police regarding the city's plan to create a task force to address the spike in crime."

Realization dawned. "Shane was sent undercover as part of the task force."

"You got it. Plus it's an election year for the mayor, so I'm sure he's not thrilled about having these stats released mere weeks before the good citizens get to vote on whether or not he gets to keep his job."

"Okay, I can see why this is important, but we already knew Shane was working undercover. How does any of this help us find him?"

"I don't know. I'm just trying to get a sense of the bigger picture here," Isaac admitted. "Every little bit helps."

"I think it's tedious," she muttered with a sigh.

Surprisingly, Isaac grinned. "That's because you think cops spend all their time shooting bad guys. There are a lot of tedious aspects to the job. And you're used to constant action, working on trauma patients that come rolling through the E.R."

"True." Ironic how much she missed her job now that she was forced to call off work for a few days. All the hustle and bustle of taking care of sick patients, never knowing what was coming through the doors next, made it a job that was never, ever boring.

Similar to Isaac's job in many ways, without the inherent danger, of course.

She purposefully shied away from thinking about Isaac being in danger. Although at the same time, watching him perform the investigational aspect of his job was oddly reassuring.

Why couldn't she seem to get Isaac out of her mind? She'd been blessed to have found love with her husband.

There was no reason to go down that path again. She believed what her pastor told her as far as Elliot being in a much better place, but that didn't mean she didn't miss him. That Ben didn't miss having a father.

Some people went their whole life without finding someone to love. She should be glad for the short time she'd had with Elliot, even if their marriage hadn't been perfect. What marriage was?

She didn't need to find someone else to take his place.

Isaac's musky scent was messing with her ability to concentrate, so she stood and crossed over to the fireplace. The glowing logs were still radiating heat, making the cabin warm and cozy.

When the sound of a cell phone broke the silence, she glanced over at Isaac, figuring it was Jenna or one of the other SWAT members calling him.

"It's your brother," Isaac said. "Do you want to talk to him?"

"Absolutely." She took the phone and tried to calm her racing heart. "Hello?" she said breathlessly. "Shane, is that you?"

"Yes, it's me." Her brother's familiar voice sent a wave of relief washing over her. Even if he was speaking so quietly she could barely hear him. "Why are you answering Ice's phone?"

"Because I wanted to talk to you. Are you okay?" she asked. "I've been so worried."

"You're not alone, are you?" Shane asked abruptly. "Ice is still there with you, right?"

She glanced over her shoulder at Isaac, who was watching her and listening intently. "Yes, he's here, keeping me and Ben safe. But I want to see you, Shane. Tell us where you are and we'll come and get you."

"Not yet," her brother hedged. "I'm getting close to finding some answers."

Her patience with his constant evasiveness was wearing thin. Leah was just about to give him a piece of her mind when she heard a loud noise, followed by her brother letting out a strangled cry of pain.

She tightened her grip on the phone. "Shane? What happened? Are you okay?"

But he didn't answer. There was nothing but an eerie silence on the other end of the line.

Her fingers shook with fear as she quickly called him back. But still no answer.

Tears blurred her vision and a sob rose in her throat. Her brother was hurt or worse, but she didn't even know how to find him.

What if he died before help arrived?

She couldn't bear the thought of losing her brother. Shane was her rock of support, as well as being a father figure for her son.

Please, Lord, keep Shane safe in Your care!

Chapter 11

Isaac watched the blood drain out of Leah's face and knew right away that something was wrong. He stood and crossed over to her, reaching for her hand. "What happened?"

The dazed expression in her blue eyes wrenched his heart. "There was a loud noise and Shane cried out as if he was hurt, and then he disconnected from the call." She shook her head helplessly. "We have to find him, Isaac. We have to find him!"

He wished it were that easy. Hawk hadn't been very forthright about any aspect of this case, which left Isaac stumbling around in the dark. He wanted to knock some sense into her brother, but right now, Leah was his bigger concern.

Her devastation was impossible to ignore, and she

needed support. He slipped his phone into his pocket and then pulled her close, wrapping his arms around her in a reassuring hug.

For a moment Leah held herself stiff, but then with a strangled sob she burrowed against him, clinging to him as if she wouldn't ever let go.

Isaac let her cry, wishing he could think of something reassuring to say.

But words failed him. Because he knew Hawk was in big trouble. For all they knew, his buddy could be dead.

As much as he wanted to protect Leah from the truth, she knew full well what her brother faced. Isaac kissed the top of her head, wishing there was more he could do for her.

Leah didn't cry for long. After a few minutes she sniffled loudly and lifted her head so that she could look up at him. "Isaac, will you pray with me?"

He gazed down into her watery blue eyes, knowing he could not refuse her request. "Of course I will."

Her tremulous smile made any embarrassment he might have felt inconsequential. He led her over to the sofa and sat down at an angle so he could partially face her.

Leah sat beside him and clasped both his hands in hers. She bowed her head and he followed her lead, bowing his, as well.

She was silent for a moment, so he took a deep breath and began to speak, hoping he would know the correct words to say. "Dear Lord, we ask You to watch over Shane, keeping him safe in Your care."

"And we ask that You guide him home to us," Leah added.

How was it that he hadn't realized how easy it was to pray? Isaac continued, "Lord, we also ask that You keep the three of us safe in Your care."

"And we ask that You guide us on Your chosen path. Amen."

"Amen," he echoed. He couldn't deny the sense of peace that washed over him and realized, not for the first time, just how powerful leaning on God's strength could be. And how important it was to have faith to guide you through the difficult times.

"Thank you, Isaac," Leah murmured, still holding on to his hands. "I'm thrilled that you believe in God and have begun to trust in His goodness and strength."

He surprised himself by wanting to share more with her. "You know, both Caleb and Declan have discovered faith in the past year, and I resisted following in their footsteps," he admitted. "Now I can't figure out why I did that. Why didn't I trust my closest friends enough to believe?"

Leah tilted her head to the side, an ebony curl brushing against her cheek. His fingers itched to smooth it away. "Giving up your old beliefs can be scary," she said. "But once you let go and open your heart to God, you realize that believing in Him isn't hard or scary at all."

"You're right—it's not one bit difficult." Isaac stared at their joined hands for a long moment. The choices he'd made in the past still haunted him. Mistakes that had cost him his wife and son.

"What's wrong, Isaac?" Leah asked. "You look troubled."

For the first time since losing his son, he found himself wanting to talk about what had happened. "I wish I would have found God sooner," he admitted. "I can't help thinking that if I had, my son might still be alive today."

"I didn't realize you had a son," Leah murmured, her eyes full of sadness. "Tell me about him."

"Jeremy was a great kid. He was always happy. He loved dump trucks and front-end loaders—he spent hours in the sandbox pretending to be a construction worker." The memory didn't bring the same level of sorrow that it had in the past.

"He sounds amazing," Leah said.

"He was." Isaac felt his chest tighten as he forced out the rest. "And it's my fault he's dead."

"I don't believe that," she scoffed gently. "You would never hurt your son."

The band around Isaac's chest was so tight it hurt to breathe. "You're right—I wouldn't hurt him intentionally, but my actions caused my wife to leave me, taking our three-year-old with her. Geoff, her new boyfriend, was charming when he wanted to be, but had a nasty temper when crossed."

Leah shifted on the sofa, putting her arm around Isaac's shoulders. "What did he do?"

He tensed for a moment. He hadn't told anyone the details of what had happened that night. The news had sensationalized the story to the point that he'd always avoided talking about it. "Becky had an affair with him, because I worked too many hours, putting my career before my family. She filed for divorce, left me and took Jeremy with her. I fought for joint custody and won. I went over to pick up my son at their house…" For a moment he couldn't continue.

Leah didn't say anything. She simply hugged him and waited for him to gather himself together.

"I heard shouting as I pulled up. I hurried up to the house and banged on the front door, demanding to be let in. I heard a gunshot and went crazy. I kicked open the door and saw Geoff holding a gun to Jeremy's head. I begged him not to shoot, but he killed my son and then turned the gun on himself."

"Oh, Isaac, I can't imagine how horrible that must have been for you," Leah murmured. "I'm so sorry you had to go through that."

"I probably could have saved him from shooting himself," he continued, wanting Leah to hear everything. "But I didn't move. Didn't do anything to stop him from taking his own life. I learned later from Becky's friend that she was going to leave him and come back to me. That's why Geoff killed her, killed my son and then himself. And I should have stopped him. I should have made him go to prison for what he did."

"You were in shock from losing your wife and son. I can't imagine anything more terrible. But that man's choices are not your fault," Leah said. "He chose to hurt your ex-wife and your son. He chose to take his own life. You're not responsible for his actions."

"Maybe not," Isaac agreed. He forced himself to meet Leah's gaze. "But I'm responsible for my actions, and I neglected my family. Neglected my marriage and my son. If I hadn't, Becky wouldn't have left me in the first place." He swallowed hard and forced himself to meet Leah's gaze. "And that is a choice I have to live with for the rest of my life."

Leah rested her head on Isaac's shoulder, inwardly reeling from what he'd been through. The very idea of losing Ben the way he'd lost his son, Jeremy, made her feel sick to her stomach. How terrible to have your child's life taken by someone else. She couldn't even imagine the terror Isaac had lived with.

But she needed to help him understand that God forgave all sins. Isaac wouldn't ever be able to move on if he didn't learn how to forgive Geoff and Becky.

And himself.

"I know a little about what you're going through," she said in a low tone. "Losing my husband when he was killed by a drunk driver—and Ben was barely a year old—was a terrible ordeal. I wouldn't have gotten through any of those days after the funeral if it wasn't for my faith. I went to church daily, leaned on our pastor for support. Even with my faith and the help of Shane and our pastor, there were many dark days."

Isaac turned and pulled her more fully into his arms. His masculine scent was soothing and she inhaled deeply, wishing she could stay here like this with him forever. "I'm sorry you had to go through that," he murmured. "I know your brother made sure that guy who hit him went to jail for a long time."

"Yes, he did. But there's more to the story," she admitted. "Something that I didn't even tell my brother about."

"What happened?" Isaac asked in a curt tone. "Did Elliot hurt you?"

"Not physically," she hastened to assure him. "But I learned later he wasn't coming home from work, the way everyone thought. He was coming from his colleague's condo. His female colleague's condo."

There was a heavy moment of silence. "I'm sure your husband had a good reason to be there," Isaac said slowly. "Don't automatically think the worst."

She pressed her lips together and shook her head. "Not according to the colleague. Victoria claimed they were in love and that Elliot was making plans to leave me."

"I don't believe it," Isaac protested hotly. "You can't trust her story. For all you know, she made the whole thing up as a way to hurt you."

He wasn't telling her anything she hadn't told herself. "Maybe," Leah allowed. "I've gone over every conversation Elliot and I had over the months prior to his death. He never gave me any indication that he wasn't happy. Never so much as hinted at being bored or feeling tied down. But he also seemed distracted—I assumed, by his work. I've tried to tell myself to ignore what Victoria said, but there's always been just the tiniest sliver of a doubt lingering in the back of my mind. He did spend a lot of hours working. Working with her."

"Where is Victoria now?" Isaac demanded. "I think I should pay her a visit. I'm sure I could get her to admit she made up the entire story."

Despite the seriousness of their conversation, a laugh bubbled up through Leah's throat at the thought of Isaac storming Victoria's condo and demanding the truth, her knight in shining armor. "Don't be ridiculous. Besides, she moved to a larger law firm in Chicago. I guess Milwaukee just wasn't big-time enough for her."

Isaac eased back, pinning Leah with his serious dark brown eyes. She had the crazy thought that she'd never get tired of looking up at him. "Don't give that woman the power to make you doubt your husband's love for a moment. Anyone who would say something like that to a grieving widow is meaner and lower than a snake. I have a feeling she lashed out at you because Elliot rebuffed her advances."

Leah couldn't help but smile. "Thank you, Isaac. I know you're probably right, and I shouldn't keep thinking about it. Especially since I need to forgive and forget in order to move on. Something you should try to do, too," she added. "One thing I've learned is that life is too short to hold grudges. God has forgiven us for our sins and we need to do the same—forgive those who've sinned against us."

Isaac grimaced a little but nodded. "I understand what you're saying, and I promise to try. It's not going to be easy, but I'll try."

"That's all we can ask of ourselves," she agreed.

"Mommy, I'm starving," Ben said, running out from the bedroom where he'd been playing his video game.

"I'm hungry, too," she said, subtly pulling away from Isaac's embrace, hoping her son hadn't noticed just how close they had been. "Isaac, didn't you mention going to a diner?"

"Yes, I did. Come on—let's go." He reached out and squeezed her hand as she rose to her feet.

As they made their way out to the car, she realized

that Isaac had lost his son as a result of someone else's actions, similar to the way she'd lost Elliot.

And neither one of those losses had anything to do with having a dangerous career.

Still, she couldn't seem to shake the idea that being in a relationship with Isaac would only cause more heartache. For her and possibly for Ben. What if things didn't work out? Her son would be crushed.

No, best thing for her would be to keep her distance from Isaac.

No matter how much she longed to stay in his arms, surrounded by his masculine scent and his strength.

Isaac couldn't deny feeling oddly content as he drove to the diner, a mile from their cabin, with Leah and Ben. This time, he led the before-meal prayer without feeling too self-conscious. "Dear Lord, thank You for providing this food we are about to eat and for watching over us as we seek the truth. We ask for You to forgive our sins and to guide us on Your chosen path. Amen."

"Amen," Leah and Ben echoed.

Leah's smile warmed Isaac's heart and he knew he was in danger of getting too emotionally involved, but couldn't seem to find the strength of will to pull back. Not after everything he and Leah had just shared.

She knew the worst about him, yet she hadn't pulled away in disgust. Hadn't condemned him for being a terrible husband and father. She'd accepted him despite his faults and had also confided in him. He was honored that she'd chosen to share her secrets.

After they'd placed their order, Ben announced he

wanted to draw a picture, using the crayons and paper the family-friendly diner provided.

"What are you going to draw?" Leah asked, sipping her water.

"A picture for Mr. Isaac," Ben said, without looking up.

A lump formed in his throat, but he nodded and forced himself to respond. "That would be great, Ben."

It struck him at that moment just how much Hawk's death would affect the little boy. Isaac knew from what Leah had said that Ben looked up to his uncle, seeing him as a surrogate father. He'd been too young to have any real memories of his dad.

"Hmm… What's that?" Leah asked, pointing to something indistinguishable on the paper.

"That's Mr. Isaac's gun," Ben answered enthusiastically. "He saved you from the bad man, remember?"

For a moment fear darkened Leah's eyes, but then she smiled and nodded. "Of course I remember," she said, running her hand down her son's back. "We're very lucky to have Mr. Isaac protecting us, aren't we?"

Ben nodded, but continued to concentrate on his picture. The stick figure holding a gun might not be a strong resemblance to him, but it was close enough to make Isaac smile.

And to harden his resolve. He needed to find Hawk and soon. His buddy hadn't wanted him to contact his ATF agent, Cameron Walker, but with Hawk potentially injured or worse, Isaac didn't really have much of a choice.

"Excuse me for a minute," he said, tossing his napkin aside and sliding out of the booth. Leah looked surprised, but no doubt assumed he needed to use the restroom.

Instead, he ducked outside and pulled out his disposable cell phone. There was no easy way to call directly to the Bureau of Alcohol, Tobacco and Firearms, but he knew that Nate Freemont, their SWAT technical guru, had connections.

He dialed Nate's number and waited impatiently for his teammate to answer. "Yeah?" Nate's tone was less than welcoming.

It took a minute for him to remember that Nate didn't recognize his number. "Hey, Nate, it's me, Isaac Morrison. Sorry about the unknown number, but I'm trying to stay off the grid."

"Hey, Isaac, what's up? Why the need to stay anonymous?"

The suspicion in Nate's tone wasn't reassuring. "I'm keeping a woman and her son safe as a favor for a friend of mine," he admitted, figuring that Nate would need something in order to help him out. "My friend is working undercover and needs help."

"What do you need from me?" Nate asked, the suspicion fading from his voice.

"Do you know anyone inside the ATF?" he asked. "I need to get in touch with an agent by the name of Cameron Walker."

"Yeah, I have connections there," Nate admitted. "It's Sunday evening, but let me see what I can do. Is this the number I should use to call you back?"

"Yeah, this number is good. Thanks, Nate. I owe you one."

"And don't think I won't find a way to cash in on that favor, either," he joked. "I'll let you know as soon as I have something."

"Great—thanks." Isaac disconnected the call, feeling certain Nate would come through for him.

Which was a good thing, since the sooner he spoke to Cam Walker, the better.

He headed back inside to join Leah and Ben. She glanced at him questioningly, but he simply smiled without saying anything. There would be plenty of time to talk to her later, once Walker called him back.

"Here's your picture, Mr. Isaac," Ben said.

He took the drawing and grinned. "This is great, Ben. Looks just like me!"

The boy nodded, digging into his chicken tenders with gusto. Isaac's burger and Leah's chicken sandwich had arrived as well, and no one said much as they ate.

When they finished, Isaac paid the bill. As they walked outside, his cell phone rang. Recognizing Nate's number, he quickly answered. "Do you have something?" he asked.

"Yeah, my contact agreed to get a message to Cameron Walker. I gave him this number to use—hope that's okay."

"It's perfect. Thanks a lot."

"Listen, Isaac, if you need help, let me know, okay?"

He appreciated Nate's willingness to help. It was the same offer Jenna had given him. "I will, Nate. Thanks again."

He clicked off his cell and glanced over at Leah.

She'd already helped Ben into his booster seat and was waiting by the car.

"I'm trying to get in touch with your brother's ATF contact," Isaac explained. "This guy should be able to help us find Shane."

"That's wonderful," Leah said, her eyes lighting up with hope. "Maybe our prayers will be answered."

"I'm with you," he agreed. He slid in behind the wheel at the same time Leah climbed in from her side. The trip back to the cabin didn't take long, but from the way Leah kept tapping her feet, he knew she was anxious for Walker to call him.

He was, too, for that matter.

But it wasn't until Leah had given Ben a bath and put him to bed that Isaac's cell phone rang. He noticed the number had a Madison area code, and since that was the capital, it made sense that Walker would live there.

"Hello?"

"Deputy Morrison?" the low voice on the other end of the call asked curtly.

"Yes, this is Deputy Isaac Morrison," he acknowledged. "Is this Cameron Walker?"

"Who gave you my name?" he demanded harshly.

Isaac frowned. This call wasn't going at all the way he'd expected. He decided to get right to the point. "Shane Hawkins gave me your name, and he's in trouble. I need you to help me find him."

There was a long pause. "I'll call you back," Walker said gruffly. And promptly disconnected.

Isaac stared at the phone in shock. What in the world was going on? Why wouldn't Walker talk to him?

Dozens of possible scenarios filtered through his

mind—none of them good. He tried to call Walker back, but the call went straight through to voice mail.

Leaving him exactly where he'd started, without a single lead to follow and no way of finding Leah's brother.

Chapter 12

Leah didn't sleep well that night. She dreamed about finding Shane dead and woke up with her heart pounding and her cheeks wet with tears. She dragged herself out of bed, glad to see that Isaac had picked up breakfast and already fed Ben.

After they finished eating, the hours dragged by slowly. There were only so many ways to entertain her son. And Isaac was like a caged animal, pacing the small cabin, checking his phone at least a dozen times every hour. She knew he was waiting to hear from Cameron Walker, the ATF agent working with Shane, but had no idea why it was taking so long for him to call back.

By early afternoon, she couldn't stand the tension for another minute. "How about we take Ben to the playground? It would be good to get out of here for a while."

Isaac looked as if he wanted to refuse, but he surprised her by nodding. "Okay, that sounds good."

Ben was ecstatic, jumping up and down between them. She grasped his hand and was taken off guard when Isaac took Ben's other hand. Ben gleefully lifted his feet off the ground, hanging on and swinging back and forth.

Once again, she was struck by the knowledge that anyone watching the three of them making their way down the path to the playground would assume they were a happy family. Leah was stunned to realize the thought didn't fill her with panic the way it might have a few days ago.

She glanced at Isaac from beneath her lashes, thinking once again how handsome he looked. She gave herself a mental shake. Why was she even considering a relationship with him? He could have his pick of any woman on the planet, so there was no reason for him to be interested in a widow with a son. Even if she was ready to try again, which she definitely wasn't.

As soon as the playground was within sight, Ben let go of their hands and ran forward with a whoop.

"Thank goodness it's not raining," she said, tucking a stray curl behind her ear. "That boy needs to burn off some energy."

Isaac smiled, but then frowned as he glanced up at the cloudy sky. "I wouldn't be surprised if we get rain later tonight," he said soberly. "Which could pose a problem when I head out to look for Hawk."

"You mean when *we* go and look for my brother," she corrected.

Isaac simply lifted a brow. "You need to stay here to keep an eye on Ben."

She followed her son's progress as he climbed the monkey bars. Of course she didn't want to place Ben in danger, but if Shane was hurt, her nursing skills might come in handy. "I was thinking about that," she said in a low voice. "What if we asked Caleb and Noelle to watch Ben for a while? He'd be safe with them and would also get a kick out of spending time with Kaitlin. They really bonded in the swimming pool."

Isaac's lips firmed in a thin line. "A better idea is for you to go with Ben to stay with Caleb and Noelle."

"What if Shane is hurt?" she pressed. "I want to help him, the way he helped me after Elliot died."

Isaac shook his head, but then shrugged. "We'll see what happens once I hear from Walker. And I'm getting worried, since he hasn't phoned or returned any of my calls. I don't like it."

She didn't like it, either.

And even though she tried not to think about the worst-case scenario, the images kept flitting through her mind. All she could do was put her faith in God.

Isaac scrubbed his hands over his face, the sick feeling in his gut getting worse with every minute that passed. Okay, maybe it made sense for Cam Walker to do a little digging into his background before trusting him, but certainly it wouldn't take this long. Not with the resources the ATF had at their disposal.

Once they returned to the cabin, he stoked the fire to get rid of the chill in the air. When his phone rang, he dropped the poker and hurried to pick up the call, fearing Walker wouldn't give him much time. "Yeah?"

"I'm not happy Hawk gave you my name," Cam said in lieu of a greeting. "He wasn't supposed to tell anyone about this op."

Isaac didn't like the guy's attitude. "Yeah, well, he's in trouble, so I don't really care."

There was a long pause. "How do you know he's in trouble?"

"Because you know as well as I do that his cover is blown," Isaac said curtly. "And there are dirty cops involved, aren't there?"

"Yeah, that's what we believe, although we don't have any proof," Walker admitted.

"You must have someone at the top of the suspect list?" Isaac pressed.

Another pause. "Two names—Trey Birchwood and Aaron Winslow."

Isaac frowned, not quite understanding why Hawk hadn't informed Cameron about Trey's murder. But he wasn't going to say anything if his buddy hadn't. And Aaron Winslow was the same suspect Hawk had identified as well, the guy who'd *claimed* his car was stolen.

Unfortunately, poking into Winslow's background hadn't turned up anything suspicious.

"Good to know," Isaac said.

"When's the last time you heard from Hawk?" Cameron asked.

"Yesterday early afternoon," he admitted. "Do you have any idea where we can find him?"

"He's been moving around a lot, but I think he's been

hiding in an abandoned shed located in a small town called Hanover, outside the city."

"Have you been there to meet with him?" Isaac demanded. He couldn't understand why the ATF agent wasn't doing more to help Hawk.

"I'm heading there now, but I'm a good hour away," Cameron responded. "Why don't you meet me there? Maybe between the two of us we'll be able to figure out where he might have gone."

"I will. Give me the closest cross street." He quickly jotted down the information Walker gave him. "I'll meet you there in an hour."

Isaac quickly called Caleb. "I need to drop off Leah and Ben for a couple of hours, if that's okay."

"Sure. We're having movie night and I know Kaitlin will be happy to spend time with Ben."

He could feel Leah's gaze boring into his chest, but he wasn't in the mood to argue. "Thanks. Be there shortly."

Leah was already dressed in jeans and a dark sweatshirt, and she was putting Ben's coat on before Isaac even finished the call. But once they were settled in the car, she glared at him. "I'm going with you," she said. "Don't bother wasting your breath to try and stop me."

He scowled and tried to think of a way to make her see reason. "I'll be able to move faster on my own," he pointed out.

She crossed her arms over her chest and he sighed when he recognized the stubborn look on her face. "Why haven't you called Declan to go along?"

"Deck hasn't gotten back to me, so I'm assuming he's busy with something else. And I don't need anyone else with me. I'll be working with the ATF agent."

"Fine. You and the ATF agent can do all the work. I'll just be there to provide any medical help Shane needs."

Isaac couldn't deny that having her nursing skills available might come in handy. But on the other hand, if Hawk was dead, he'd end up placing Leah in danger for no good reason.

Glancing over at her, he knew he couldn't point out that part. Better for her to have hope, at least until they knew the truth.

When he pulled up in front of Caleb's house, she didn't move to get out of the vehicle. No way was he going to convince her to stay, short of using a sandblaster to pry her out of the car.

"Okay, fine. You can come along, but you're going to do everything I say, agreed?"

"Agreed."

Caleb strode out to meet them, and Isaac climbed out and helped Ben get down from his booster seat. "'Bye, Mom," he yelled before running off to meet up with Kaitlin.

"Thanks, Caleb," Isaac said in a low tone. "I'll be in touch as soon as possible."

"No worries, we'll be fine," his teammate assured him before turning to walk back inside.

Isaac didn't waste any time getting to the intersection Walker had given him. Dusk had fallen early, thanks to the dark clouds looming overhead.

"We're looking for a dirt road," he said to Leah.

"Is that it?" she said, gesturing to a space between some trees. The road started out okay, but up ahead he could see two deep ruts in the mud.

No way was the car going to handle that. He drove

forward, glad to see there was a small clearing off to the right, just large enough to park the car. He pulled forward, the low-hanging tree branches scraping the top of the car. When they fell over the back window, offering a bit of coverage, he stopped and turned off the engine.

"I want you to stay here," he said, handing Leah the car keys. "And if anything goes wrong, you get out of here and head back to Caleb's house."

She opened her mouth to argue, but then closed it again without saying a word. He was glad she planned to adhere to her side of the bargain.

He opened his door, but then turned back to give her a quick kiss. The stunned expression on her face made him smile as he ducked outside, softly closing the door behind him.

But as he moved through the trees, avoiding the muddy drive, he kept his gun close at hand, ready for anything.

He wasn't sure exactly where this abandoned shed was located, so he tried to follow the general direction indicated by the muddy ruts. But when he noticed a dark shape looming to the right, he turned in that direction.

The dilapidated building looked like an abandoned shed. He crouched near a large tree, looking for any sign of life. Of course there was nothing.

He didn't want to believe that was because Hawk was already dead. Pushing the dire thought away, Isaac debated what to do. He didn't see any sign of the ATF agent. Granted, he was a little early, so maybe Walker had run into traffic on the way here.

After waiting a minute, Isaac decided to make his move. At the very least he needed to make sure that

Hawk wasn't lying on the floor inside, injured or worse. Staying low, he ran over to the corner closest to the door, which was hanging half-open on one rusty hinge.

He quickly slid inside the shed, nearly choking on the rank, musty smell that filled the place. He waited for his eyes to adjust to the darkness, but when he still couldn't see well enough, he pulled out his phone and cupped his hand over the screen to provide a sliver of light.

The shed was empty. But as he swept his gaze about, he could see there were scuff marks on the floor, as if someone might have been hiding there. Stepping farther into the building, he discovered there was an old army blanket stuffed in a corner.

And a dark, rusty smear on the edge of a wooden plank that might have been blood.

Isaac stood and made his way back toward the half-open shed door. Hawk had definitely been hiding out here at one time.

But where was he now?

Leah huddled in the corner of the passenger seat, trying to keep warm. No sense in complaining, since it was her own fault that she'd come along.

The area around her appeared to be deserted. She eased the passenger door open and climbed out so she could walk around to get her blood moving.

Besides, she should sit in the driver's seat in case she had to leave in a hurry.

The air outside the car was cool and breezy, but having room to move around helped. She did a series of high steps as silently as possible, feeling much warmer afterward.

Anxious to know what was going on, she crept through the brush with painstaking slowness, trying not to make any noise. She caught a glimpse of the abandoned shed and hunkered down to watch.

Not that it was easy to see much in the darkness. Out here there were no street lamps for miles. The dark clouds obliterated any potential light from the stars and moon.

There was a sudden flash of light beyond the shed, in the clearing behind it. Her pulse leaped at the possibility that the light had something to do with her brother. Was he trying to signal for help?

She stayed where she was, even though every cell in her body wanted nothing more than to rush over to see if that light was connected to Shane. But the potential that she might be wrong kept her rooted in place.

Her legs eventually ached from the uncomfortable position, but she did her best to ignore it. She remembered the first night she'd met Isaac, when the Jeep tire had been blown out. So much had happened since then, yet amazingly enough, the time could be measured in days.

A few days, yet it seemed like a lifetime ago.

She saw the flash of light again and caught a glimpse of a man before darkness surrounded him once more. She'd seen the guy's face for only barest of seconds, but knew he seemed familiar. She followed the dark figure as he moved through the area, hoping and praying he'd flash his light again.

The next time he did, the man's features clicked in her memory. He looked like Kirk Nash, Shane's boss, from the Fifth District.

She frowned. Why would Lieutenant Nash be out here in the darkness? What was he searching for? She didn't understand, but somehow knew that something wasn't right.

A movement near the shed caught her attention and she sucked in a harsh breath when she recognized Isaac creeping along the side of the building. He must have noticed the flickering light, too, and she wished there was a way to warn him about Nash. But calling his cell would only put him in danger.

Plus he'd be upset if he knew she was so close, so she eased back, retracing her steps to hide farther back in the woods, since she couldn't bring herself to go all the way to the car.

She needed to trust that Isaac knew what he was doing. He wasn't part of the SWAT team for nothing. If there was a way for him to find Shane and bring him back, he would.

So Leah silently prayed for strength and patience.

Isaac peered around the corner of the shed, waiting for the flash of light to return. He'd noticed it when he happened to glance at the right moment through the open window.

There it was again! It was so quick he might have missed it if he'd blinked.

But there was no doubt about it—someone was out there. Hawk? Or Cameron Walker?

It occurred to Isaac that he didn't know what Cam Walker looked like. What if the guy out there wasn't Walker at all? What if the dirty cops had been tipped off about the location of the shed? They could right now be out there waiting to ambush him.

He took a deep breath to calm his racing pulse. There was no way to know if the person out there with the light was friend or foe. And he didn't plan to show himself until he knew for sure one way or the other.

It was hard to imagine why Cameron would have lured him here. Maybe they thought that if they captured him, they'd have leverage with Hawk? But that would mean Cameron Walker was dirty, and Isaac wasn't quite ready to go there yet.

The next flash was closer, and he caught enough of a glimpse to realize the guy was looking down in the brush. Was he searching for a blood trail?

The tiny hairs on the back of Isaac's neck lifted in alarm. Something about this whole scenario didn't seem right. If the guy out there was Cameron Walker, why didn't he say something?

Whoever he was, he was making his way closer to the shed. Maybe he was Cameron Walker and maybe he wasn't, but somehow Isaac didn't think he should stick around long enough to find out.

Especially since there was no sign of Hawk.

Isaac went in the opposite direction, keeping the shed between himself and the other man. He needed to get back to the car and take off before this guy realized he'd ever been here.

Moving silently through the woods wasn't easy. He didn't dare go too fast, though everything in his body urged him to get back to Leah as soon as possible.

He neared the area where he thought he'd left the car, but didn't see it. Had he gone too far?

After making another sweep of the area, he spotted it, closer to the main road than he remembered. As he approached, he didn't see Leah inside and his chest squeezed with fear. Had someone taken her?

The sound of a twig snapping to his left had him swiveling around, his gun drawn. Every ounce of tension drained from his body when he recognized Leah.

"Isaac," she whispered, stumbling toward him. "Did you see him?"

"Let's get in the car," he whispered back, unwilling to have this conversation out where the man in the woods could still find them.

She nodded and pressed the keys into his hand. Opening and closing the car door seemed unusually loud, and once they were both safe inside, he jammed the key into the ignition, started the engine and took off.

There wasn't a moment to waste. He wanted to put as much distance between them and the guy back there as possible.

Leah must have sensed the seriousness of the situation because she didn't say a word until a good ten minutes had passed.

"Do you think he's following us?" she asked, craning around in her seat to peer out the back window.

"Not yet," he answered grimly. "I almost had a heart attack when I saw you hiding in the trees. Why didn't you stay in the car like I asked?"

"Don't yell at me, okay? I know I shouldn't have gone out there, but I'm glad I did. Did you see that guy searching the clearing around the shed with his light?"

"Yeah, I saw him. I'm sure it was the ATF agent, Cameron Walker."

"No, it wasn't," she corrected. "I managed to get a glimpse of his face and I recognized him. He's Lieutenant Kirk Nash, Shane's boss."

"Are you sure?" Isaac demanded.

"I'm sure. I've met him before." Leah sounded positive and he had no reason to doubt her.

Before he could ask more questions, there was a low groan from the rear of the sedan. The sound was so unexpected, he jerked the steering wheel sharply, nearly running them off the road.

Someone was back there!

Chapter 13

Leah's heart leaped into her throat as she swiveled to peer into the backseat.

"Get down," Isaac said harshly. He pulled over to the side of the road and abruptly stopped the car.

Leah ignored him, using her phone as a flashlight so she could see better. "Shane?" she asked incredulously. "How did you get in here?"

"I crawled," he said before letting out another low groan. "Good thing I saw you."

"What's wrong? What happened? Are you hurt?" Leah could hardly believe her brother was here, after all this time. And from what she could tell, not a moment too soon. Shane looked awful.

"Wait a minute! Hawk? Is that really you?" Isaac had

opened the back door and was standing there, holding his gun ready.

"Yeah. Took a hit—in my shoulder."

"Let me see." Leah quickly got out of the car and came around to where Isaac was standing, clearly dumbfounded. "I need to take a look at his wound."

"Not now," Shane protested in a low voice. "Keep driving. Need to get away."

Leah ignored him, although it wasn't easy to climb into the backseat with her brother sprawled half on and half off the cushions.

"He's right, Leah," Isaac said. "We need to get out of here."

No way was she leaving her brother's side. "I'm staying back here."

Isaac sighed and muttered, "Fine" before he closed the door after her and slid back behind the wheel. Within seconds he had the car on the road again.

Leah couldn't see much in the darkness, but just being near her brother brought a level of comfort. Ever since she'd heard him cry out in pain on the other end of the phone, she'd secretly feared the worst.

"Where's your wound?" she asked, bracing herself on the seat. "We need to apply pressure to minimize the blood loss."

"Left shoulder," he said with a grunt. "Bleeding seems to have slowed down."

She felt along his left side, following his arm up to his shoulder. When she felt beneath his jacket, she found the fabric of his shirt hardened with dried blood. She noticed he was shaking and understood that he was in shock, either from blood loss, infection or both.

"Isaac, will you crank the heat?" she asked, shrugging out of her sweatshirt. She was glad it was dark as she quickly stripped off the T-shirt she was wearing underneath before putting her sweatshirt back on.

"Sure. How is he?"

"Hanging in there," she responded, pressing her balled-up shirt against her brother's shoulder. Gunshot wounds were nothing to play around with. "We need to get him to a hospital as soon as possible."

"No hospital," Shane said, reaching out to grasp her arm with a strength that surprised her. "I mean it, Leah—no hospital."

"Look, I know gunshot wounds have to be reported to the police," she said. "But I promise I won't leave you alone."

"Doesn't matter," he mumbled. He was beginning to slur his words and she hated seeing him like this. "They'll try to pin this all on me."

"Shane, if you don't get medical help soon, you could die," she said. "You need antibiotics, fluids, maybe even a blood transfusion. I can't provide all that for you."

"Even more people could die if I don't stop the person in charge of this mess," Shane said. "Please, Leah, you have to trust me. No hospital."

"Let's get back to the cabin first," Isaac said, clearly trying to play the peacemaker. "Once you can see the full extent of Hawk's injuries, we'll decide our next steps."

Leah grimaced and nodded, feeling helpless. They could try going to a hospital that wasn't located in Milwaukee, but she knew that the doctors there would only transfer Shane to the closest level-one trauma center, which happened to be smack in the middle of the Milwaukee Police Department district. The only other one was over two hours away, and even they might transfer him regardless.

The only other option was to bring a physician to her brother. A physician and supplies.

As she turned the idea around in her mind, Leah thought of just the person who might be willing to do her a favor.

"Isaac, I need to make a call." She grasped the back of Isaac's seat as he took a sharp right. "Will you hand me my phone?"

"Depends. Who are you calling?" he demanded. "I don't think we should ignore your brother's concern about going to the hospital."

"I know, but I want to call a trauma-doctor friend of mine. I'm pretty sure she'll help us."

Isaac captured Leah's gaze in the rearview mirror. "Being friends is one thing. Breaking the law is something entirely different. I highly doubt this doctor will be willing to come remove a bullet without notifying the police."

"You don't know Dr. Gabriella Fielding," she responded. "I think she'll come, because last month I helped her out when we had a meth addict go crazy in the middle of the trauma bay."

"What do you mean?" Isaac demanded. "How exactly did you help her?"

Leah nibbled her lower lip, remembering that night all too well. "Our patient leaped off the trauma table, grabbed a scalpel and charged toward her. I shoved a bedside tray in front of him and then stomped on his hand to get the scalpel. He tossed me on my backside, but thankfully, the security guards took over from there, managing to hold him still enough that we could sedate him."

"You never told me that," Shane said. The light from the moon was barely enough to see his troubled gaze.

Leah winced and nodded. "I know. I didn't want you to worry. Honestly, it all happened so fast, I don't even remember making a conscious decision to do anything."

"And you think my job is dangerous," Isaac muttered. He shook his head. "The cabin is only a few miles away, in any case. Why don't you wait to see what you're dealing with before you call her?"

He had a point, especially since they were so close to the cabin. Leah felt certain Gabby would help, if she wasn't working.

And if she was, then Leah would just have to do her best to treat Shane until Gabby could get there.

Isaac was relieved to make it back to the cabin without a problem. He'd purposefully taken a long, winding route just to be sure they hadn't been followed. The entire fiasco at the shed still didn't sit well with him and he hoped Hawk would stay conscious until help arrived.

Getting Hawk into the cabin was no small feat. "You take his injured side. I'll take the other," he instructed Leah.

"Okay," she agreed.

Hawk was weak, and even with Leah's help, Isaac had to practically drag him inside. Since the sofa was closer than a bedroom, he headed in that direction, getting him there just as his friend's legs collapsed beneath him. He groaned as he landed with a thud.

"Sorry, man," Isaac exclaimed.

"Shane, are you all right?" Leah was leaning over him, her serious expression betraying the depth of her concern.

"Call your doctor friend," Isaac told her. "I'll help get him undressed enough so you can look at his wound."

Leah pressed her lips together as if she was near tears, but nodded and stepped away to make the call. He knelt on the floor beside Hawk and tugged at his jacket.

"What happened out there tonight, Hawk?" he asked in a low tone as he worked.

For a moment he thought his buddy was too far gone to answer, but then he opened his eyes. "The shed was my hiding spot, but they found me. So I took off and hid in the woods."

Isaac noticed Hawk winced when he tried to slip his injured arm out of the sleeve. He was trying to be gentle, but the blood-soaked clothing didn't give way easily. "You were shot yesterday, though, right?"

"Yeah, but I wasn't at the shed then. I was about ten miles down the road."

"Ten miles?" Isaac was shocked to hear that. "How did you manage to go ten miles without a vehicle?"

"It wasn't easy." Hawk closed his eyes and groaned again. "Took me forever, since I had to stay hidden the whole time."

"So how did they find you at the shed?" Isaac asked, trying to understand the chain of events.

"I knew I needed to keep going, but I must have passed out for a bit. When I came to, it was getting dark and I knew that they might find me. So I contacted Cam Walker. Told him where I was hiding and that I needed help."

That made sense, considering the timing of the ATF agent's phone call. "I was supposed to meet Walker there an hour after we talked," Isaac stated grimly. "Sounds like he contacted me as soon as he heard from you."

"He called you?" Confusion darkened Hawk's eyes, which were the same shade of blue as Leah's. "I don't understand. He never showed up."

A sick feeling lodged in Isaac's gut. "So that wasn't Walker looking for you in the woods?" he asked carefully. "Because Leah thought the guy out there was your boss, Lieutenant Nash."

"She's right," Hawk said grimly. "The minute I saw him, I knew I had to get out of there."

"You think he's involved?" Isaac asked.

His friend hesitated and then shook his head. "I honestly don't know. Either he's in on the whole illegal gun-running deal or someone else is feeding him wrong information. The guy I thought was involved was Aaron Winslow."

Made sense, since the stolen car belonged to Winslow, and Cameron had believed Winslow was guilty, too. Although maybe Cam had only heard that from Hawk?

Isaac's instincts were to believe the worst. He knew from what Caleb had been through last year that even the top brass could wallow in the mud, getting their badges dirty. Being the rank of lieutenant didn't mean squat if enough money was involved.

"Isaac, is it okay if I give Gabby directions to the cabin?" Leah asked.

"Yeah, it's fine." What choice did they have? Now that he had Hawk's shirt off, he saw that the bullet wound in his shoulder was far worse than he'd anticipated. And there wasn't an exit wound, which meant the slug was still embedded in his shoulder.

The doctor might be able to help stabilize Hawk temporarily, but Isaac didn't see how they would manage to avoid sending him to the hospital, sooner or later.

He could only hope that they'd break the case open before they had to take that chance.

Leah was relieved that Gabriella wasn't working and had agreed to come help take care of Shane. The trauma surgeon was bringing a bunch of supplies as well, including IV antibiotics.

Isaac had gotten Shane's jacket and shirt off, but his shoulder was a mess, so she headed into the kitchen to fill a bowl with hot water.

"What do you want to do about Ben?" Isaac asked from the fireplace, where he was building a roaring blaze.

"He's safe with Caleb for now, isn't he? I think we need to make sure Shane gets the help he needs before we go pick him up."

"All right," Isaac agreed. "I'll let Caleb know to keep Ben there overnight. I'm sure he won't mind."

"Thanks." She carried the water to the sofa and then brought over the stack of towels she'd taken from the bathroom. Shane's eyes were closed, but as much as she hated to bother him, she needed to clean his wound.

"Sorry, this might hurt a bit," she said as she gently pressed the warm washcloth over the area.

Shane flinched but didn't open his eyes, and she hoped he was simply sleeping and hadn't fallen unconscious.

The water turned a dark rusty-brown by the time she finished her task. And the skin around the opening looked red and puffy, a sure sign it was infected.

Leah rocked back on her heels, second-guessing her decision to go along with Shane's wishes. Maybe she should have insisted on taking her brother to the hospital.

If she hadn't caught that glimpse of Shane's boss out there in the clearing by the shed, she wouldn't have been as worried. But she had, and now she didn't have the faintest idea of whom they could trust.

She found a small package of gauze in the bathroom cabinet, no doubt left by a previous renter, and she placed it over the wound and then layered blankets over her brother to keep him warm.

While they waited for Gabby to arrive, Leah tried to get her brother to drink some broth she'd found in the cupboard, likely from the previous occupants. He took only a few sips before turning away.

Finally, she heard the sound of a car engine pulling up out front. Leah darted toward the door, but Isaac beat her to it, holding his weapon ready as he peered outside.

"Dr. Fielding?" Isaac asked in a low voice.

"Yes, it's me. Is Leah there?"

There was a hint of fear in her friend's tone, so Leah pushed Isaac aside to open the door. "I'm here, Gabby, and this is Deputy Isaac Morrison. Thank you so much for coming."

"Not a problem, since my social life is nonexistent. Besides, I owe you a favor," Gabby said with a wry smile. "Sorry it took me so long, but this place wasn't easy to find even with your directions."

"Here, let me help you with that," Isaac said, taking the large backpack she had slung over her shoulder.

"Thanks. Where's my patient?"

"Over here on the sofa. I cleaned his wound as best I could," Leah said. "But it still looks pretty bad. And I tried to get some fluids into him, too, but didn't have much luck."

"Hmm…" Gabby knelt beside Shane's prone figure. "You mentioned the bullet has been embedded inside his shoulder for over twenty-four hours?"

"At least—maybe a little longer," she confirmed.

"Not good. Is there any way to get him into one of the bedrooms? It's going to be too difficult to work on him here."

Isaac grimaced, but nodded. "I'll do my best."

"Shane? Can you help us by getting up?" Leah asked, giving her brother a small shake. "Come on. We need you to stretch out on one of the beds."

His eyelids fluttered open, and for a moment he looked confused, but then his expression cleared. "I'll try."

It took the three of them working together to haul Shane into the closest bedroom.

"Okay, first we need to start the IV fluids and antibiotics," Gabby said, digging through her backpack. "You said he doesn't have any known allergies, right?"

Leah nodded. "None that I know of."

"Okay, good. Once we have that done, I'll need to remove the bullet from the wound or it will fester and make the infection worse."

Leah nodded again. Gabriella's plan was exactly what she'd expected. "What can I do to help?"

"Why don't you start the IV while I get things set up. I'm going to need better lighting, too."

"I'll bring both lamps from the living room," Isaac said, obviously anxious to assist.

"Thanks." Gabby barely spared him a glance, her attention focused solely on her patient.

Leah's fingers were shaking as she started the IV in her brother's arm. She tried to tell herself this was just like being in the trauma room.

But it wasn't.

Once the fluids and antibiotics were infusing, Gabby gave Shane a non-narcotic painkiller. Leah didn't ask why she hadn't brought along narcotics. There was a limit to what Gabby would do, Leah knew, and taking narcotics without accounting for them wasn't one of them, since discrepancies had to be reported to the DEA. Quite honestly, she didn't blame Gabby one bit.

"Ready?" her friend asked, meeting her gaze.

Leah nodded. They both had sterile gloves on, even though the cabin was hardly a pristine environment. Still, Gabby had brought more supplies than Leah had expected, including sterile drapes and several surgical instruments. Leah picked up the two small retractors and gently held the edges of the wound open.

Shane flinched and gritted his teeth, but didn't protest as Gabby probed the wound as gently as possible with a forceps. Retrieving the bullet actually didn't take long at all, but she spent a lot of time flushing out the wound with an antibiotic solution before packing it with sterile gauze.

Finally the surgeon straightened, putting a hand against her lower back as she stretched her sore muscles. "That's all I can do for now," she said in a weary tone. "We can only hope it's enough."

Leah nodded and finished dressing the wound. "I hope so, too. Thanks so much for coming out here and bringing all the supplies."

"No problem." Gabby glanced down at Shane. "I don't suppose you want to tell me why you didn't take him to the hospital?"

Leah grimaced. Her friend deserved to know something after what she'd just done to save his life. "My brother is a cop and his boss might have been the one to blow his cover, causing him to be shot. Seemed safer to do it this way until we know more."

"I understand," Gabby said. "But how, exactly, are you going to find out the truth about his boss?"

Good question. Too bad Leah didn't have an equally good answer. She hadn't thought past getting Shane the medical treatment he needed. But now that he'd been taken care of, she realized that they were right back where they'd started from.

They still didn't know whom to trust.

Chapter 14

Isaac listened to the women's conversation with a sense of helplessness. Gabby wasn't a cop but she'd easily identified the main issue facing them. Hawk was safe, but they still needed to figure out whom to trust and where to go from here. Not that Isaac's friend would be going anywhere anytime soon. Clearly, he needed some rest and nourishment after being on the run for so long.

Dr. Gabby gathered her things together and left them alone. Leah swayed on her feet, looking wiped out.

"Why don't you get some rest?" Isaac suggested. "I'll keep an eye on your brother."

"Not yet," Leah protested. "I need to make sure that he gets his next dose of IV antibiotics in roughly…" she squinted at her watch "…four hours. At three in the morning."

"I'll wake you up then," Isaac said sternly. "You won't be any good to him if you fall apart from lack of sleep."

She let out a sigh and nodded. "All right, but not until I get him to drink more broth."

The stubborn glint was back in her eye, reminding Isaac of the way Hawk used to get when he was convinced he was right and everyone else was wrong. Arguing was useless, so he turned away and grabbed his phone to send Caleb a text message. The time was just after eleven, too late for a phone call, but he sent a message hoping his teammate would look at his phone first thing in the morning.

Then Isaac dropped down in front of the computer, trying to rub the exhaustion from his eyes. The broth Leah heated up for her brother smelled good, and he decided to make a cup for himself, too.

He sipped the warm liquid, pondering the computer screen. The answer had to be connected with Wade Sharkey and Joey Stainwhite. In fact, he'd hoped to have Stainwhite in custody by now. Setting his mug aside, Isaac tapped on the keys to pull up their respective mug shots. He stared at the two men thoughtfully. They were selling illegal weapons, guns that couldn't be traced by the serial number, obviously for profit. Perfect type of weapon to use for committing a crime, like the mall shooting incident, as it made the gun much more difficult to trace. And either Stan's Liquor Store or some similar place was where they handled their so-called business transactions.

It made sense, if you were into that sort of thing. And

he could see how the two guys had earned themselves reputations as a source for untraceable guns.

But he had to think bigger. Why would Sharkey and Stainwhite need contacts within the police department? Was it because one of the cops, maybe Aaron Winslow, had stumbled across their scheme and wanted a piece of the pie for himself? And if so, how was Lieutenant Nash involved, if at all? Or was there something more going on?

Abruptly, Isaac straightened as a thought popped into his head. What if the police department itself was a source for illegal guns? He knew firsthand how dozens of weapons were confiscated from crime scenes every week. They were saved as evidence for trial, but once a perp pleaded out, they were simply stored in boxes. Who would notice if a few went missing? Especially once the serial numbers were removed?

Isaac's pulse leaped with excitement. The Fifth District was in the middle of the city, an area with the highest crime rate. The cops who worked there must confiscate hundreds of weapons a month.

As he turned the idea over in his mind, he knew he was onto something. Every instinct in his body screamed that he was on the right track, but obviously he needed proof. Going to Griff Vaughn with his idea wasn't an option at this point. He'd asked Jenna to follow up with the ballistics on the gun from the mall shooting, but maybe they hadn't gone back far enough. If they could prove that the gun had been used in another crime located within the Fifth District of Milwaukee, then he'd have more of a connection to investigate. A connection that could potentially lead to the proof he desperately needed.

He was tempted to call Jenna right now, but it was late enough that he decided to go with a simple text message. Call me when you have time, Isaac.

Drumming his fingers on the table, his previous exhaustion having vanished, he tried to think of another angle to work. Finding out if Hawk's contact within the ATF, Cam Walker, had the same theory would help, but he wasn't willing to call the guy, not after the way things had gone down at the abandoned shed.

Would Hawk know what Cam's theory was? Maybe. Isaac pushed away from the computer and headed into the bedroom he'd given up for Hawk. He stopped in the doorway when he saw Leah sitting in a chair beside her brother's bed, her head cradled in her arms, apparently sound asleep. Hawk looked to be sleeping, too, and for a moment Isaac considered waking him up to discuss his theory. But his buddy's pale skin and the fresh bandage on his shoulder convinced him to wait until morning.

But he couldn't bear to leave Leah sitting there in such an awkward position. She'd wake up with a backache for sure. He crossed over and gently squeezed her shoulder. "Leah," he whispered. "Come on. You need to get some sleep."

"What?" She blinked groggily at him and then sat up with a wince. "What time is it?"

"Almost one in the morning," he whispered. "Get to bed. I'll wake you up in a few hours so you can administer the antibiotic."

"Okay." It was a testament to how tired she was that she didn't argue. He supported her with a hand under her arm as she staggered to her feet. She leaned heavily against him as they made their way into the second bedroom, the one she shared with Ben.

"Isaac?" She stood there, clutching his arm, and all he could remember was how sweet she'd tasted when he'd kissed her. How much he wanted to kiss her again.

Not now, Morrison, he told himself sternly.

"What? Do you need something?" he asked.

"I— Nothing. Thank you, for everything."

He sensed that wasn't really what she had been about to say, but since her eyes were half-closed, he didn't push it.

"You're welcome. Get some sleep." He helped her sit on the edge of the mattress, moving back to give her room.

"G'night," she mumbled as she crawled into bed fully dressed. She closed her eyes and didn't move, so he backed out of the room and softly closed the door behind him.

He blew out a heavy breath, wishing he'd asked her how to give the IV antibiotic so he wouldn't have to wake her at all, but it was too late now. He didn't want to make things worse by trying to figure it out on his own.

Isaac headed back to the kitchen table and tried to think of a good way to pass the next two hours. Unfortunately, he was limited as to what he could do from here.

Just as his eyes started to drift closed, his cell phone rang. He jerked awake. "Morrison," he said, covering up a wide yawn.

"I just got your text message. What's up?" Jenna asked.

He was surprised she'd called him so late, but he was

glad to have something concrete to do. "Remember that gun from the mall shooting?"

"Yeah. What about it?"

"How far back did you go as far as testing the ballistics reports?"

"Just a couple of months—why? What's going on?" She sounded eager to help, which eased his guilt for contacting her so late.

"I have a hunch but need proof. I'd like you to go back further, say a year or maybe even two. I think this gun has been used in another crime." He didn't want to give her too much information, because he wanted to see what she came up with. If he told her to just look in the Fifth District, she might miss something important.

For all he knew, other districts could be involved.

"All right, but you'd better fill me in and soon," Jenna said, sounding testy. "I'm capable of doing more than your menial labor."

"I know you are, and trust me, this isn't menial labor." He didn't know why Jenna was always determined to prove herself, but right now he was too tired to care. "Look, I would do the check from here if I could. I need your help, Jenna. If you want me to call someone else, I will."

"I'll do it," she muttered. "I'll let you know when I have something."

"Thanks. I appreciate it." Isaac disconnected from the call and sighed.

Ninety minutes and he could wake up Leah to administer the antibiotic, and then he'd get some sleep.

He had a feeling that by the morning he'd have a lot

more information to work with. And maybe he could talk to Hawk, too, come up with some sort of plan.

Because Leah and Ben weren't safe yet. Not by a long shot. And they wouldn't be safe until he found and arrested the dirty cop responsible for murdering Trey Birchwood and attempting to murder Hawk.

Isaac knew Leah was relieved to have found her brother, and so was he. But right now, the moment of peace felt too much like the calm before the storm.

And he was determined that Leah and Ben would survive, unscathed.

Leah woke up the next morning and bolted upright in bed. Had she overslept? Shane needed another dose of antibiotic at nine o'clock.

She dragged a hand through her hair, attempting to restore some order to her unruly curls, and climbed out of bed, mortified to realize she'd slept in her clothes. As much as she desperately wanted to shower and change, she went to check on Shane.

Following the enticing aroma of coffee, she headed to the main room. She was surprised to see Isaac was up, since he'd gone to bed well after she had. She only vaguely remembered him waking her to give Shane his three o'clock medication.

"Hey, how are you feeling?" Isaac asked when he saw her.

"Good. I'm just going to check on Shane."

"He's doing okay," Isaac said, rising to his feet and crossing to meet her by Shane's doorway. "I gave him more soup about thirty minutes ago."

"Really? How much did he drink?"

"All of it," Isaac said with a grin. "He's been asking for more than broth, but I told him we had to check with you first."

"I'm sure he can have something more," she agreed.

She entered Shane's bedroom, relieved to note that her brother looked much better. She placed a hand on his forehead, satisfied when he didn't feel too warm.

Thankfully, the fluids and antibiotics were doing their job.

"I hear you're hungry," she said.

"I am. I honestly can't tell you the last time I've eaten," Shane confessed. "At least two days ago."

Her heart squeezed in her chest, but she kept a smile on her face. "Okay, how about some scrambled eggs and toast?" She glanced at Isaac. "Maybe we could get a take-out order from the diner?"

"Good plan," he agreed. "Tell me what you want, too, and I'll get enough for all of us."

"How about four servings of scrambled eggs, toast, bacon and juice?" she suggested. "Leftovers wouldn't be the worst thing in the world. And Ben might be hungry when he gets here."

"Caleb promised to drop him off in about an hour, and I'm pretty sure he'll feed Ben breakfast beforehand," Isaac said. "But I'll get more than enough, just in case."

She nodded and turned back to Shane. "I'm so glad you're doing better," she said in a low tone. "You have no idea how worried I've been."

"Hey, I've been worried about you, too," he said, grimacing when he shifted in the bed. "I'm glad Ice has been here to look after you."

"It's almost time for your next dose of antibiotic,

but after that we can see about letting you get cleaned up a bit. No shower, though. We can't let your shoulder wound get wet."

Shane frowned but didn't argue. She actually couldn't blame him for wanting a shower.

"How much has Ice told you?" he inquired, changing the subject as she prepared the antibiotic infusion.

"What do you mean?" she asked, perplexed. "I know everything that's been going on."

"Really?" Her brother looked surprised.

"Why wouldn't I know? Isaac has been with me ever since the masked man tried to kidnap me and Ben."

"I guess I assumed you wouldn't want to know any of the details," Shane admitted. "You never wanted to know anything about the dangerous aspects of my job before."

Since he was right, she couldn't very well argue. She concentrated on hanging the IV medication and then turned to sit beside his bed.

"I'm sorry about that," she said in a low tone. "I realize now how foolish I've been. Refusing to listen to the details of your job certainly didn't make it less dangerous. And as a trauma nurse I see gunshot and stab victims being brought in all the time. I guess it was a stupid way to try and cope."

"Not stupid," he corrected, reaching out to take her hand. "I understand how hard it must be for you to know that I'm out on the streets doing the same job our father did."

She gripped his hand tightly and nodded. "It was hard, but that doesn't mean I don't owe you a huge apology. It was selfish of me to think only about myself. I should have realized how much support you needed, too. I'm embarrassed to admit that it took hearing you got hurt to make me realize what I was doing."

"Hey, you don't have to apologize to me," Shane protested. "I hated knowing how afraid you were for me. But this is the job I'm meant to do, Leah. I thought about changing careers for you, but I couldn't do it. Well," he amended, "I could, but I wouldn't be happy."

It struck her at that moment how much Isaac was the same way. He was obviously a great cop and valued being a part of the SWAT team. How could she ever expect him to do anything else?

Very simply, she couldn't. And he shouldn't have to change who he was or what he did for anyone.

Least of all for her.

Truthfully, she didn't want to change who he was. Over these past few days she'd needed him to keep her and Ben safe, which included taking advantage of all his cop skills.

And why was she even thinking about being with Isaac once this was all done? Other than that amazing kiss, he'd never given her any indication that he wanted to see her on a personal level.

So why couldn't she get the idea out of her mind?

"Mommy!" Ben came rushing into the bedroom and she turned and scooped him up in a huge hug.

"Oh, I missed you," she murmured against his neck. He smelled like baby shampoo, and she was so glad that he'd missed last night's events.

"Uncle Shane! You're here!" Ben wiggled to indicate he wanted to get down.

"Easy now—Uncle Shane has a big ouchie in his shoulder," she cautioned as she set her son on his feet.

"What happened?" Ben nimbly climbed onto the bed and crawled up beside Shane. "Did someone stab you?"

Oh, boy, since when did Ben get so bloodthirsty? "No, he wasn't stabbed," she corrected. "But his ouchie is infected, so we have to be very careful."

"I missed you," Ben said, resting his head against Shane's right side.

Her brother hugged him close and smiled. "I know, buddy. I missed you, too."

Leah had to look away, blinking the tears from her eyes. She should be happy. The outcome could have been so much worse.

"Hey, Ben, why don't you show your mom your new toy?" Isaac suggested from the doorway. "I need to talk to Uncle Shane for a few minutes."

"Okay. Come on, Mom—look at what Mr. Caleb bought for me." Ben scrambled off the bed as fast as he'd climbed on and dashed into the other room.

Leah hovered in the doorway. "Why do I feel like you're trying to get rid of me?"

Isaac ducked his head for a moment and then nodded. "You're right. I want to talk about our next steps with your brother. But you don't have to worry about anything, because no matter what, I'm going to make sure you and Ben are safe."

She crossed her arms over her chest. "I know you will, but I'd still like to hear the plan."

Isaac exchanged a long look with Shane, who merely shrugged. "You might as well let her stay."

"Okay, fine. But keep in mind this isn't a democracy

here. You don't get a vote on whether we go ahead with the plan or not."

She bit her lower lip and nodded. "Okay, but you have to admit that it was a good thing I was there last night, otherwise you might not have known that Lieutenant Nash was there instead of Cameron Walker."

Isaac inclined his head. "You're right about that. I just know how much you don't like hearing about the dangerous aspects of a cop's job."

"I'm over that," she said with a wave of her hand. "After everything we've been through, I think I understand what we're facing better than most."

"All right, then." Isaac stepped farther into the room and took the chair she'd used earlier. "I think we have to get in touch with Walker again," he said bluntly. "We need to set up another meeting, this time in the bright light of day."

"What if he's part of this?" Shane asked.

"We'll use a place that allows us to make sure he comes alone," Isaac said grimly. "I heard from my teammate Jenna, and she's confirmed that the gun used in the mall shooting a few weeks ago is the same one that was used to kill a gang member eighteen months ago. A gang shooting that was right in the middle of the Fifth District."

Shane grimaced. "Yeah, I've suspected that someone inside the police department is stealing guns from the evidence room and giving them to Shark and his gang to sell on the streets. For a cut of the profits, of course."

This was the first Leah had heard of it, but then again, she'd been too busy last night working with Gabriella to save Shane's life to keep up-to-date on the investigation.

"Did Cam know your theory, too?" Isaac asked.

"Yeah, and so did my boss."

Leah shivered, remembering how she'd recognized Lieutenant Nash out in the woods looking for Shane.

And she wished she knew if he was a friend or foe.

Chapter 15

Isaac glanced curiously at Leah. She was taking all this in far better than he'd anticipated. And what exactly did "I'm over that" mean? That she'd accepted the dangers of Shane's job?

Of his job?

Or just that she'd given up trying to shield herself from the truth? He suspected the way she'd avoided talking to her brother about his job had just been a coping mechanism, especially since she worked in the trauma room. All this time, she'd known exactly what Hawk had faced. But maybe she figured it was easier to ignore the gory details if she didn't talk about them.

The real problem was that she'd already lost someone she loved and wasn't ready to open herself up to that kind of hurt again. And frankly, Isaac didn't blame her. After all, he understood exactly what she was going through. He hadn't loved Becky enough, hadn't made time to nurture his marriage, and those careless actions had cost him his son. Sure, he could blame Becky's new boyfriend, but deep down, he knew it was still his fault.

He could almost hear Leah's voice in the back of his mind, urging him to forgive himself, the way God taught them to. And he was trying.

Sitting so close to her that he could smell the cinnamon-and-spice scent that clung to her skin, he wished they had time to be alone, to talk about the growing feelings he had for her. But they didn't.

He forced himself to tear his gaze away from her and concentrate on the matter at hand. "So I'll call Cameron Walker and request a meeting. But I want a good place to meet, somewhere I can have plenty of protection and backup."

Shane grimaced and nodded. "The shed wasn't a bad place for a meeting, but I doubt he'll want to go there again."

"Maybe, maybe not." Isaac turned the idea over in his mind. Could he make it work? He was familiar with the layout, and it would be easy to see in the daylight.

Of course, daylight made it harder to hide backup, especially since it was March and the trees were still mostly bare from the lingering winter.

"Do you really think Cam Walker will agree to meet?" Leah asked doubtfully. "I still don't understand why he didn't show up last night. Why would he have sent Lieutenant Nash instead?"

"I've been thinking about that," Shane murmured.

"Maybe Cam confided in the lieutenant about the proposed meeting and my boss decided to tag along. It's possible Walker was there but you didn't see him."

Isaac shook his head. "Between Leah and myself, I don't know how we could have missed him. I was inside the shed, saw the blanket you'd used and the blood from your wound. Your boss was outside, looking around the area, presumably for any sign of you. Where would Walker have been?"

Hawk shrugged and then winced and put a hand up to his injured shoulder. "Maybe he was deeper in the woods, looking for me. Did you see a vehicle of some sort?"

"No, but I didn't get a chance to do a full sweep of the area." Isaac wished he knew more, but there was no time to waste. He rubbed his hands on his jeans and stood. "I think I'll head back over to the shed now. See if I can figure out what really happened last night."

"Let me know if you find my weapon," Shane muttered.

"Wait—you can't go alone," Leah protested. "You need to take someone with you."

"I know. And I'll find someone." He hadn't heard from Deck since the night his buddy had been called out about a suspicious package, and he'd already bothered Caleb more than enough. He should probably give Jenna a call, since she knew the most about what was going on. And at least she'd know that he needed something more than menial labor.

She answered right away when he phoned her. "Hey, I was just about to call you," she said.

"You were?" he asked in surprise. "Why? What's going on?"

"Guess who we have in custody?" she asked.

His pulse jumped. "Joey Stainwhite?"

"You got it. Griff wants you to come in, since our pal Joey had a gun on him, one with the serial numbers filed off, the same make and model as the one used at the mall shooting. You never told me exactly why you wanted me to do the ballistics match for you, and I didn't push for information. But it's clear now that whatever case you're working on has just intersected with ours."

"Good news," Isaac said, glancing toward Hawk's bedroom. He didn't want to leave Leah, Ben and Hawk here alone, but at the same time, he hated to call Caleb back again after he'd just left. "I'll come in to talk to Stainwhite, but I need someone to come out here to keep my friend's sister and her son safe."

"Maybe give Declan a call?" she suggested.

"I can try. Tell Griff I'll be there soon." Isaac disconnected, thrilled to know that they finally had a break in the case.

He quickly dialed Deck's phone and was frustrated when his buddy didn't answer. There must be something going on, since Isaac hadn't heard from him in a few days, but he left a terse message asking for a return call anyway. Then he turned and headed back toward Hawk's bedroom.

Maybe if he gave his buddy his weapon to use, he could protect Leah and Ben for the short time Isaac was gone. Hawk was right-handed and the injury was to his left shoulder. And it wasn't as if anyone knew they were even here. This cabin had proved to be safe over the past twenty-four hours, so staying here awhile longer shouldn't matter.

Besides, grilling Joey Stainwhite wouldn't take too long. Isaac could be there and back in a couple of hours.

He went in and proposed his plan. Leah didn't look thrilled at the idea of his going in to talk to Joey Stainwhite, but she didn't protest.

Hawk gladly took the gun and Isaac understood that his buddy no doubt felt unsettled without his own weapon, which he'd lost somewhere outside the shed. "Don't worry. We'll be fine. Just see if you can get that guy to spill his guts, okay?"

"I'll do my best," Isaac promised.

Leah smiled weakly as she followed him out of Hawk's room. "I know it's silly, but be safe, okay?"

"I'm going to our headquarters," he reminded her. "There's nothing unsafe about it."

"I know that logically." She tapped her temple. "But I can't seem to shake the bad feeling in my gut."

"Oh, Leah," he said with a sigh. He reached out, pulled her into his arms and was glad when she wrapped hers tightly around his waist. "I promise you, I'll always be careful. I have too much to live for." It hadn't always been true. In those early days following Jeremy's death, Isaac had been a little too reckless, figuring nothing could hurt him as much as losing his son.

But now Leah, Ben and even Hawk were counting on him.

And he'd discovered that life was very much worth living.

"I'll pray for you," Leah said, her voice muffled against his shirt.

"I appreciate that," he said and meant it. "I've learned a lot about faith since meeting you, but I'm sure there's more to know."

Leah tipped her head back and gazed up at him. "I'd like to teach you once this is all over," she said.

"I'll take you up on that offer." He lowered his head and kissed her, hoping to show her with actions rather than words how he felt.

"Mommy, are you kissing Mr. Isaac?" Ben asked.

Leah quickly broke off the kiss, color flagging her cheeks. "Um, yes. He's leaving, so I'm kissing him goodbye."

Isaac coughed to hide a laugh. "That's right," he said, striving for a serious tone.

Ben looked perplexed. "But that's not the way you kiss Uncle Shane," he said with childlike logic.

Isaac glanced at Leah, who was studiously ignoring him. "Yes, well, that's because Isaac and I are friends and Uncle Shane is family. I think you should draw your uncle Shane a picture," she said, changing the subject. "Just like you did for Mr. Isaac."

"Okay." Leah's diversion worked and Ben ran over to get his paper and crayons.

Leah still looked embarrassed and Isaac decided not to push the issue, since he needed to leave. "I'll be back soon," he promised.

"I know." She smiled and then turned to follow her son. It was difficult to let her go without another kiss.

But they'd have time later to talk. Right now, it was time to get to work.

* * *

The drive back to Milwaukee seemed to take forever, but it was only twenty-five minutes later when he pulled into the lot and parked his borrowed vehicle next to the police-issued ones.

Griff and Jenna were waiting for him when he strode inside.

"You better fill me in on what's going on," Griff said with a scowl.

"I know." Isaac quickly described how Hawk's undercover stint had gone bad and how he'd been shot. "I can give you more details later, but right now I need to know where Stainwhite was picked up," he said to Griff.

His boss nodded and shrugged. "Actually, we got lucky. Someone called in an anonymous tip saying that Stainwhite would be at Stan's Liquor Store, so we sent a couple of deputies, and sure enough, there he was."

"A tip, huh?" Seemed odd that they'd get a call like that, although sometimes districts offered minor rewards for information, so maybe someone was desperate for a little cash. "Okay, let's see what he has to say."

"He's in room 1 with his public defender. Take Reed with you."

"Sure thing." Protocol was always to have two deputies present during an interview, so he followed Jenna as they headed over to where Stainwhite and his lawyer were waiting.

"Hey, Steel, how's it going?" Isaac said cheerfully.

Joey's scowl deepened. "Only my friends call me Steel," he said.

"Yeah, well, my friends call me Ice. Maybe you remember me better by that name."

Recognition dawned in Joey's sunken eyes. "You're a cop now?" he asked incredulously.

"Yep, and I'm the guy who's going to put you behind bars for attempted murder of a police officer."

"No way will you be able to claim attempted murder," the attorney declared.

"Yeah, I never tried to shoot no cop," Joey protested. "You got the wrong guy."

"See, that's where you're wrong, Steel. Because I saw you inside Stan's Liquor Store and watched you exchange a gun for a thick wad of cash. You saw me, came outside and stood in the middle of the road, firing directly at me in my car. I'm thinking the slug I pulled out of the seat is going to match that gun you had on you when you were arrested. I've got you cold, Steel. Who do you think the jury is going to believe? Me, a trusted cop, or a loser like you?"

All Joey's bravado vanished as he realized there was no chance to escape the charges. The lawyer didn't look too happy, either.

"Maybe we can do something for you," Jenna said, leaning forward to brace her elbows on the table. "But we'll need you to cooperate with us. Maybe tell us who all is involved in your little gun scheme?"

"Will you take attempted murder of a police officer off the table if he does?" the attorney asked.

"No way. I'm not going to snitch for you," Joey said abruptly, ignoring his lawyer. "He'll kill me if I do."

"Who will kill you? Shark?" Isaac pressed.

There was a flicker of recognition in Joey's eyes a moment before he shook his head. "Don't know anyone by that name," he said, crossing his arms. "You may as well take me back to my cell, 'cause I'm not talking."

Isaac exchanged a knowing glance with Jenna as Stainwhite's attorney tried to talk some sense into his client.

But in the end, they didn't get anything from him.

"I really thought he'd talk," Jenna said with a heavy sigh.

"I know. I thought so, too." Isaac glanced at his watch. "I gotta get back to Leah and Ben, but let me know if the ballistics match the slug I pulled out of my car, okay?"

"Will do," his teammate agreed.

Isaac strode outside to his car, anxious to get back to the log cabin. He hadn't gotten much from Stainwhite, but at least he knew the guy was off the streets for a while.

And there was always the chance that Steel might change his mind about spilling his guts after spending a few days behind bars.

Leah couldn't believe she'd allowed herself to get carried away in Isaac's kiss. She was mortified that Ben had caught them. Her son had never seen her with a man other than his father.

Never seen her with a man, period.

She told herself to get a grip, that there was no reason to believe she'd scarred Ben for life or anything.

But she did worry about her son getting too attached to Isaac. Maybe now that Shane was here, Ben wouldn't vie for Isaac's attention as much.

"Leah? Do you have a minute?" her brother called.

She hurried over. "Sure. What's up?"

"My phone battery is dead. Do you think you could charge it up with your adapters?"

"If it fits," she said, taking his cell and peering at the connection. "You're in luck. Looks to be the same kind that Isaac bought."

She went into the kitchen to get the charger, then took it to Shane's room. She plugged in the phone and handed it back to him. "You're not thinking of contacting that ATF guy, are you?"

"Yeah, I am." Shane stared at the cell for a minute. "I feel like I need to do something. We can't just sit here and wait for something to happen."

"Wait until Isaac gets here," she suggested. "Maybe he'll know something more that will help."

"All right," Shane conceded. "But the more I think about it, the more I believe you guys missed seeing Cameron Walker last night. He must have been there."

Leah lifted her hands helplessly. "He could have been," she agreed. "But I panicked when I saw your boss."

"Understandable." Shane yawned and blinked. "I don't know why I'm so tired."

"Your body is fighting off that nasty infection," she murmured drily. "Take a nap. Your next dose isn't due for another couple of hours."

Shane pried his eyelids open. "Not until Isaac returns."

At that moment she heard the sound of a car engine. "I think he might be back," she said.

"Stay here," Shane commanded as he swung his legs

over the side of the bed. "I'll check it out to make sure it's him."

Leah refrained from rolling her eyes, considering he'd just leaned heavily on her when he'd gotten up to use the bathroom. "Don't be silly—stay here. I'll peek through the window to make sure."

Without waiting for him to respond, she walked over and parted the curtains with her fingertip, relieved to see Isaac driving the old familiar sedan up to the cabin.

He hadn't been gone all that long, but the place had seemed empty without him.

Or maybe she'd just missed having him around.

"Don't worry. It's Isaac," she said to Shane.

"Good. I hope he managed to get some new information."

Isaac came in a few minutes later and headed straight for Shane's room. "Hey, how's it going?" he asked.

"You tell me," Leah's brother countered. "Tell me you got something to go on."

"Unfortunately, I didn't," he responded. "Steel wouldn't talk, despite his lawyer trying his best to convince him. He's scared to death of Shark."

"Figures," Shane muttered. "So now what?"

"I guess that's up to you," Isaac said. "Do you think we can trust Cam Walker and your boss?"

"Can't Griff help us?" Leah spoke up. "You said yourself that Shane's case is intertwined with yours now."

"Different jurisdictions," her brother said with a grimace. "I'm not sure how well that will go over."

"Griff has to be careful not to step on the Milwaukee P.D.'s toes," Isaac said. "But he might be willing to offer some help."

"I would hope so," she said with exasperation.

"Mommy, there's a man outside," Ben said from the other room.

"What?" Her heart leaped into her throat and she rushed over to where her son was sitting on the bed surrounded by his toy cars. "Are you sure?" she whispered.

Ben nodded. "I was looking for the deers but saw a man instead."

"I'm going to head outside to take a look," Isaac said. "Get Ben and take him into Shane's room."

She didn't need to be told twice. She scooped her son into her arms, allowing him to grab a couple of his toy cars to bring along, before following Isaac into the other room.

"I need my gun, just in case," Isaac said, reaching over Shane's lap for the weapon. "Stay down until I call all clear."

"Will do."

Leah swallowed hard and held Ben close. In the time they'd been here, they hadn't seen any other occupants, but surely they weren't the only ones around. It was highly likely that Ben had seen someone harmless, since it was broad daylight.

She desperately wanted to believe that the man Ben had seen didn't intend to harm them, but deep down, she feared the worst.

That whoever had shot Shane had managed to find them.

Chapter 16

Isaac moved silently through the wooded area around their cabin, his weapon held down at his side. Maybe he was overreacting to what Ben had seen, but he'd feel better once he knew for sure who was out there.

At first he didn't see anyone at all, but then he caught a glimpse of a man wearing a knit cap, standing behind a tree. Isaac's gut tightened in warning. Anyone innocent wouldn't be hiding like that.

Whoever this guy might be, he was clearly up to no good.

Isaac stayed in the shadows, moving so that he could get a better angle to see the man's face. He debated going back inside the cabin, but at that moment the guy moved out from behind the tree. He crouched low and ran across to a different set of trees, farther away.

Isaac frowned when he realized the man had gone to an area directly across from their cabin. From this new position he could watch the doorway.

A slow burn of anger had Isaac gripping his weapon tightly. He needed to take this guy out of the picture, but he would have to take a wide route in order to come up from behind and catch him unaware.

Hopefully, he'd be too busy watching the cabin to realize Isaac was behind him.

He hoped and prayed Leah and Ben would stay hidden beside Shane and keep away from the front door.

Moving slowly, Isaac melted into the trees and made his way round to get behind him. The trek took longer than he'd anticipated, and he still couldn't get a clear glimpse of the man's face.

When he finally had the guy in his line of vision, just a few feet ahead, he stealthily crept up behind him.

Isaac let out a soundless breath and then made his move, jumping forward and shoving against the man's back so that he was pinned against the tree. He pressed his gun against the guy's temple. "Don't move or I'll shoot. Drop your weapon—slow and easy so I don't flinch and accidentally kill you."

The man's body went tense, but he did as Isaac commanded, holding his gun out from his right side and dropping it to the ground. "Listen, my name is Lieutenant Nash and I'm with the Fifth District Police," he said. "You don't know what you're in the middle of, but you need to let me go so I can do my job. Innocent lives are at stake."

"Yeah, I'm well aware of the illegal gunrunning scam that is being partially funded with confiscated weapons from your precinct," Isaac said in a low tone. "And I don't trust you, so put your hands behind your head."

"You're making a big mistake," Lieutenant Nash said as he once again complied with Isaac's directive. "I'm not the leak inside the department. Trey Birchwood was the one leaking information. You have the wrong man."

"Maybe, maybe not, but we're not going to have this conversation right here." Isaac frantically considered what he could use to tie him up with, since he hadn't thought to bring rope or duct tape. He tugged on the string from his sweatshirt hood, thinking it was better than nothing.

And he'd have to trust that Nash didn't have a death wish and wouldn't try to run.

Just then Isaac noticed another man approaching the cabin from the other direction, wearing an ATF jacket. Cameron Walker? Most likely.

He took Nash's right wrist and twisted his arm behind his back, holding the gun at his side. He needed two hands to tie him up and didn't want to drop his weapon even for a second.

"Hey, good work," the ATF agent said as Isaac prodded Nash to walk toward the clearing. "You caught our dirty cop."

Isaac nodded, unable to deny that it certainly seemed that way. "Hold a gun on him while I tie him up," he said to Walker. "Nash, get down on the ground with your hands behind your back."

The lieutenant did as he was told, dropping to his knees and putting his arms behind his back. Isaac slipped his gun in the waistband of his jeans and wrapped the sweatshirt string tightly around Nash's wrists. But instead of helping him, Cam Walker dashed toward the cabin, kicked the door open and darted inside.

"What in the world?" Isaac quickly finished tying the knot and then let go of Nash, leaping to his feet. In that second he realized he'd made a grave mistake.

Walker had to be the guy who'd blown Hawk's cover, not Nash. Isaac had trusted the wrong guy!

He followed Cameron Walker inside and then froze when he realized Walker was already in Hawk's room, holding a gun on Leah, who was clutching Ben. For a moment Isaac couldn't breathe, flashing back to when Becky's new boyfriend had held a gun on Jeremy mere seconds before he'd pulled the trigger.

Please, Lord, please spare Leah and Ben!

"Stay where you are and drop the gun," Walker said harshly. "I have nothing to lose and I plan to kill you all anyway, so it doesn't matter to me if the woman and kid go first."

The last thing Isaac wanted to do was drop his weapon, but he slowly did as he'd been ordered, crouching as he did so.

"Kick it toward me," Walker commanded.

He kicked it under Hawk's bed instead so that it couldn't be used against them. Leah cried out in pain as Walker yanked her head back by her hair and pressed the gun more firmly against her temple. Ben started crying and Isaac could tell that the sound was bugging the gunman. The way the guy shifted his stance and glared at Ben reminded him of that first night, when a gunman had held Leah hostage.

Isaac believed this had to be the same man who'd

tried to kidnap Leah and Ben and killed Trey Birchwood.

But why had he killed Trey? That didn't make any
sense, based on what Nash had told him.

"You do anything like that again and I'll blow her
away," Walker said in a furious tone. "Understand?"

Isaac swallowed hard, feeling sick to his stomach,
and nodded. He needed to remember every bit of his
hostage-negotiator training. "Understood. Tell you what,
Walker—let the woman and the boy go and I'll be your
hostage instead."

"No way," Walker said with a leering grin. "In fact,
you're going to help me set this crime scene up to look
like you did it."

The sick feeling in his gut intensified. There had to
be a way to get through to this guy, but how?

"You're not the real Cam Walker, are you?" Hawk
said from his perch on the bed. Isaac noticed now that
Shane was sitting upright on the edge, directly across
from where Walker held Leah and Ben.

"Sure I am," the ATF agent said.

"No, I can tell your voice is different," Hawk said
with certainty. "I spoke to the real Cameron Walker
many times and I know you're not him. So who are you?
I bet you killed Walker and stole his identity."

"So what?" the impostor said offhandedly. "You'll
never know who I really am, so don't even bother asking."

"How did you find us?" Isaac asked. He knew he had
to find a way to keep the fake ATF agent talking and
hoped stroking his ego might work. All he needed was
enough time for Nash to get free. Since he'd rushed at

the end, he figured the lieutenant just might be able to work his way loose from the sweatshirt string and come in to help them. Or at least call for backup.

Unless he really was working with the fake Walker?

No, somehow it didn't seem like it. But even if so, there was nothing Isaac could do about it right now.

"Let me guess," he continued when the ATF agent didn't say anything. "You had someone call in the anonymous tip about Steel and then somehow tracked my car here, right?"

"Yeah, that's right," the ATF impostor sneered. "I knew your cop buddy was getting help from someone within the sheriff's department, and when you put the APB out on Stainwhite, I figured you were the key. It was pathetically easy to put a tracking device on your car and to follow you here."

Isaac wanted to kick himself for not figuring it out sooner, but it was no use worrying about that now. "And how does Nash fit in?" he asked.

A momentary flash of confusion washed over the guy's face and Isaac knew that the fake ATF agent didn't have a clue as to who was tied up outside. What did that mean? That the cop really was trying to help them?

"Where's Sharkey?" Hawk asked, changing the subject. "I'm surprised he's not here with you."

"He's not the leader of this arrangement," the fake Walker said smoothly. "And enough talking. We're going to set this up so that Hawkins takes the fall."

Isaac could barely stand to see the look of fear etched on Leah's face, and Ben's sobs tore at his heart. He racked his brain for another way to stall. And where was Nash? Shouldn't he have figured out a way to get free of his bonds by now?

"Looks like the sheriff's deputy has to be the first one to die," the fake ATF agent mused. "And then the woman and the kid, with the undercover cop the last, by his own hand, of course."

Isaac glanced at Hawk and saw his muscles tense. In that moment he understood what his buddy intended to do.

Without any other warning, Hawk launched himself at the impostor, who reacted by swinging the gun away from Leah toward the new threat. Hawk hit his arm a split second before the gun went off, sending a bullet whistling above his head. Isaac dived toward the fake agent as well, while Leah and Ben scrambled out of the way. From the corner of his eye, Isaac noted that she pushed her son into the farthest corner of the room, placing herself directly in front of him.

Isaac admired her courage. In fact, he admired a lot about her, and hopefully, he would have time to tell her.

With Hawk's help, he managed to get the Walker impostor subdued. Isaac held the man's hands behind his back, while Hawk tied him up with a string he tore off the miniblinds.

Nash finally barreled into the cabin, holding his gun, which he must have gone back to find in the woods, where Isaac had made him drop it. Nash crossed over, glaring at the impostor.

"Aaron Winslow, you're under arrest for murder, selling illegal guns and anything else we can pin on you," Lieutenant Nash said harshly.

Isaac sighed, relieved to know it was finally over. He

glanced over at Leah and Ben, wanting nothing more than to get them out of here.

"Look out!" Hawk shouted.

Isaac whirled around, horrified to see that Nash was aiming his weapon at him, rather than at Winslow. What was going on? Was Nash involved after all? Had he only pretended to arrest Winslow to gain access to the cabin?

Ben broke away from Leah and ran directly toward him, so he launched himself in front of the boy as two gunshots echoed through the cabin.

A deep, fiery pain slashed at his left side and he dropped to his knees, desperately glancing around to make sure that Ben was all right. The little boy was sobbing as Leah held him, but thankfully, there was no sign of blood. Isaac caught a glimpse of Shane holding Walker's gun toward Nash before darkness claimed him.

His last conscious thought was to thank God that Leah and Ben were finally safe.

"Leah, are you and Ben all right?" Shane asked, stumbling toward her.

"Y-yes," she managed to gasp, her mind still reeling from the events. Lieutenant Nash was lying on the floor, his chest soaked with blood where her brother had shot him. She forced herself to cross over to be sure he was dead before turning her attention to Isaac.

"Call 911," she told Shane. She grabbed the IV supplies and what was left of the gauze dressings from the bedside table and knelt beside Isaac.

Her heart squeezed when she saw the amount of blood soaking through his sweatshirt. She lifted the hem and pushed the fabric out of the way in order to assess the extent of the damage.

There was an entry wound that didn't look too terrible, but she felt along the back for the exit wound, knowing from experience that it would be far worse. The only good news was that the wound was on the edge of his side and the bullet wasn't still inside his body.

Her fingers shook as she opened gauze and pressed it over the front wound. Taking care of someone she knew and cared for was very different from treating strangers in the E.R. But she forced herself to think and act like a nurse. "Shane, I need your help. We have to roll him over and hold pressure on the exit wound."

Her brother was holding Ben with his good arm, but came over and set his nephew down on the floor. "All right, easy now." Together they managed to shift Isaac's weight so that he was lying on his right side. Maintaining pressure wouldn't be easy to accomplish from this angle, but it was worth a shot.

"Here, hold this," she said, putting a larger pad of gauze over the exit wound.

"Mommy, I'm scared," Ben said, trying to crawl into her lap. She wanted to hug and hold her son, but she needed to keep working to keep Isaac alive.

"Come on, Ben—why don't you come over here," Shane said. He tucked Ben close while still pressing on Isaac's wound.

"Okay," the boy said, sniffling loudly. He stayed close and then reached over to put his small hands on top of Shane's as if he wanted to help. She was worried about how Ben was handling all this, but at least he'd stopped crying.

"I love you, Ben," she said with a reassuring smile. She rolled up Isaac's sleeve to start an IV. His veins hadn't totally collapsed, which was a good sign that he hadn't lost too much blood.

Leah quickly inserted an IV in Isaac's forearm and hung a bag of fluids. She had only one left, so she hoped the ambulance would get here soon.

"How did you know Nash was involved?" she asked as she regulated the IV fluids. She'd never been so scared as when she'd watched Isaac leap in front of Ben.

He'd risked his life to save her son's.

"Winslow was from District Three, so the only way Nash could have known Winslow was involved was if he was in on it, too." Shane lifted his gaze to hers. "Trey told me he thought he saw Winslow and Nash together, but I wasn't sure if I could believe him. Now I wish I had, because I'm pretty sure Trey died as a result of seeing them together."

Leah closed her eyes for a moment, wishing that so many people hadn't had to die before they'd discovered the truth. She had a better appreciation for why Shane and Isaac chose to work in law enforcement. Criminals shouldn't be allowed to get away with murder.

"Will Mr. Isaac wake up?" Ben asked, his lower lip quivering.

"I'm certain he will," she assured him, even though she couldn't tell how much damage had been done internally. With the wound so close to the edge, he had a good chance. She leaned forward and smoothed her hand down the side of his face. "Isaac, can you hear me? You're going to be okay. Just hang on for the ambulance to arrive. Please, hang on."

"We should pray for him," Ben suggested.

A lump filled her throat, but she nodded. "Yes," she croaked. "We should."

"God, please make Mr. Isaac better," Ben said.

"Amen," Leah murmured, tears swimming in her eyes.

"Amen," Shane echoed. She noticed he kept glancing over to make sure the Walker impersonator was still trussed up.

A thumping noise caught her attention and she lifted her head in alarm. "Shane, do you hear that?"

"Take over here and I'll check it out," he said, rising to his feet.

She pressed on Isaac's injuries, using as much strength as she could, while hoping and praying that the sound wasn't an indication of more bad news.

But as the noise grew louder she recognized it as a helicopter. Could it be the Flight For Life aircraft coming for Isaac?

Shane poked his head through the bedroom door. "Help is here," he announced. "Police and the hospital chopper. Too many trees to land here, so they're putting it down on the road and will carry him out via stretcher."

"Thank goodness," Leah murmured.

Shane crossed over to where the fake Walker was lying facedown on the floor. "The cops have a lot of questions for you," he said, dragging him to his feet. He pressed the gun against his side and marched him past Leah, Ben and Isaac. "Starting with what happened to Cameron Walker."

Leah watched them leave, feeling a little sorry for the man who'd chosen the wrong path.

"Where's the injured cop?" someone shouted from the doorway.

"In here," Leah called. She forced herself to back away as two paramedics hurried into the room. "He has a through-and-through gunshot wound on the left side, and I've hung a liter of fluid and put on a pressure dressing."

"Nice. You've made our job that much easier," the first paramedic said in an admiring tone. "We're going to get him hooked up to our portable monitor and then transport him to the chopper."

"Are you taking him to Trinity Medical Center?" she asked. She wasn't sure which level-one trauma center was closest and hoped Isaac would be taken to the hospital she worked at.

"Yep. You can meet us there," he told her.

Nodding in agreement, she pulled Ben close as the paramedics made quick work of getting Isaac on the stretcher and wheeling him out of the cabin.

"Did you hear that, Ben? Our prayers have been answered."

"I'm glad, Mommy."

"Me, too," she whispered.

Now she needed to make sure that Isaac pulled through without any problem.

Because suddenly, she couldn't imagine her life without him.

Chapter 17

Isaac awoke to a throbbing pain along his left side, a fuzzy head and a serious case of cotton mouth. He squinted in the bright sunlight streaming through the window, trying to figure out where he was. The sight of an IV pump next to the bed reminded him of Hawk.

And Leah.

Concern pushed him further awake and he glanced around, noticing with a frown that he was in a hospital room. Alone. Where was everyone? There was a cup of water on a table beside him, so he reached out and took a tentative sip.

So far, so good. Now if only he could find someone with a few answers.

As if on cue, a tall man wearing a white lab coat entered the room, accompanied by a young woman wearing scrubs.

"Good morning, Mr. Morrison," the man said in greeting. "I'm Dr. Lansing, the surgeon who patched you up yesterday afternoon."

Yesterday afternoon? Alarm shot through him. "I've been out for twenty-four hours?"

"Well, technically, a little over sixteen, since you didn't get out of surgery until after 5:00 p.m. last night, and it's about 9:15 in the morning," the woman said with a smile. "I'm Claire, your nurse for the day."

Sixteen hours still sounded far too long, but right now he needed answers. "Okay, Doc, how bad is it?" Isaac asked, preferring to know the true extent of his injuries.

"Not as bad as I expected," Dr. Lansing admitted. "The trauma nurse who cared for you on the scene pretty much saved your life. By the time you arrived here you were relatively stable, and other than a spleen laceration and some muscle damage, you're doing great. You'll need to take it easy for a while, though, so that you don't cause that laceration to start bleeding again."

Leah had saved his life. He'd spent days trying to protect her and Ben, but in the end, she'd saved him.

He owed her a huge debt of gratitude.

"How long will I need to be off duty?" he asked, sensing the doc wasn't going to stick around for long.

"He's a sheriff's deputy," Claire interjected helpfully.

"Ten to twelve weeks," Dr. Lansing said. "Although I'm sure they can assign you some desk work after the first six weeks or so. Now, let's take a look at your wounds."

He grimaced and nodded. "Sure."

Claire helped him turn onto his right side so that they could look at his front and back wounds. While they changed his dressing, he gritted his teeth against the pain, not willing to complain and risk fuzzy-head syndrome from taking narcotics. He wondered if he should call his boss or wait for Griff to come to him.

"Everything looks good," Dr. Lansing pronounced, stripping off his gloves and heading over to the sink to wash his hands. The nurse finished taping his dressings in place before doing the same.

"Thanks for everything," Isaac said. Despite Leah's concerns about police work being a dangerous job, he'd actually never been shot in the line of duty before. Minor injuries, sure, but never anything serious.

Nothing requiring surgery.

Truth be told, he'd had more injuries when he'd run wild on the streets, before being sent to Saint Jermaine's.

"No problem. We're going to watch you for one more day before springing you out of here," Dr. Lansing added. "You'll need IV antibiotics for twenty-four hours, and we like to make sure your lab work remains stable before sending you home."

"Sounds good."

"You're lucky that bullet wasn't a half inch to the right," the doc added as the nurse made several notations in a computer system located in the corner of his room. "You would have lost several inches of your large intestine and possibly your left kidney."

"I understand. Thanks again." The close call wasn't lost on him. Isaac suspected Leah would say that God was watching over him, and after everything that had happened, he'd agree.

But where was she now? Had Hawk taken Leah and Ben home?

The fact that they weren't here seemed to send a glaring message. Not that he could really blame her, considering how close she'd come to losing her son. That moment Ben had rushed out in the line of fire was deeply etched in Isaac's mind. Which made him wonder if Leah had decided to move on with putting her life back together.

Without him.

Leah was glad to be able to sleep in her own bed. She knew Ben was also glad to be home, although that didn't stop him from having nightmares. After getting up twice to see to him, she'd let Ben crawl in with her. Thankfully, they'd both slept better after that.

Now that she was up, though, she desperately wanted to get back to the hospital to see how Isaac was doing.

Last evening, she'd told Isaac's boss, Griff Vaughn, everything she knew about what had happened, even as she worried about how Isaac was doing in surgery. Thankfully, the nursing staff knew her very well and popped out to give her updates.

Griff had spoken extensively with Shane, as well. From what she'd overheard, it sounded as if they'd used fingerprints to prove that the man who'd pretended to be Cameron Walker was in fact Aaron Winslow, as Lieutenant Nash had said. And thankfully, Winslow had agreed to cooperate for the chance of a lighter sentence. He had provided details on the illegal gun deals, admitting to taking weapons from the evidence room. Shane had seemed shocked to discover that a couple of districts were involved, which meant a huge Internal Affairs investigation was under way. And of course, they put out a warrant for Wade Sharkey's arrest.

It was hard to believe the danger was finally over. Or at least it would be once Ben stopped having nightmares and things got back into a normal routine. Leah had spoken with her own boss and explained everything. Her boss had been sympathetic and had given Leah the rest of the week off.

Since Ben was still sleeping, she decided to take a quick shower. Wearing clean clothes was a nice change, even though she debated far too long about which sweater to wear, as if Isaac would even notice. She shook her head at her own idiocy.

After she'd finished changing her clothes for the last time, Ben woke up and rubbed his eyes sleepily. "Mom, can we have pancakes for breakfast?"

"Um, sure." She was anxious to get to the hospital, but cooking pancakes wouldn't take that long. Truthfully, she should have gotten Ben up to go to school, but after his rough night, she'd figured it would be better to keep him home one more day. He was a bright kid and would be able to catch up quickly from the few days he'd missed.

Besides, she knew he needed to see for himself that Isaac was okay. Several times during his nightmares he'd cried out Isaac's name. She knew what he was going through, since the same image of Isaac leaping in front of Ben played over and over in her mind, too.

Isaac had risked his life for her son and she owed him more than she could ever repay.

Ben seemed to cheer up after finishing his favorite

breakfast. She hoped that once he saw Isaac was okay, he'd get over having bad dreams.

Leah hadn't let herself think beyond making sure Isaac was doing all right, but as she drove to the hospital, too many questions began to filter through her mind.

Would he want to see her again once he was released from the hospital? Or would they both go their separate ways? Did Ben remind him too much of his young son, Jeremy? Or was he ready to move on?

Was she ready to move on?

She tried to push away the never-ending thoughts ruminating in her head, but it wasn't easy. She felt more confused now than she had before. Being back home, thinking about the mundane aspects of her life, she couldn't imagine what she and Isaac even had in common.

No doubt she was making a big deal out of nothing. Isaac had never so much as hinted at a future between them. She was reading far too much into a simple kiss.

Well, a not-so-simple kiss.

She parked in the employee structure and walked inside with Ben. She knew where Isaac's room was located, as she'd stayed with him for a couple of hours after surgery. She'd wanted to remain until he'd woken up, but Ben had yawned so widely his jaw had popped, and she'd realized she needed to get home for her son's sake.

Shane hadn't gone home. He'd been admitted to a hospital room on the same floor as Isaac, just as a safety measure to make sure he was recovering well enough from his own gunshot wound.

Leah debated whom to visit first and told herself that

Ben's need to make sure Isaac was okay was more important than seeing her brother.

Even if she knew deep down that her need to see Isaac was more important, too.

As she approached his room, her steps slowed when she heard voices coming from the partially open doorway. At first she thought maybe the doctor was in there, but soon realized that wasn't the case.

"I can't believe you didn't bring me into this from the very beginning," a deep voice that sounded like Griff Vaughn's said. "And that you risked your life while not being officially on the job."

"I'm not going to apologize for risking my life for a child," Isaac said sternly. "I understand you're upset, and I'm sorry I didn't include you earlier. But I didn't have a speck of proof and it was my responsibility to keep Leah and Ben safe."

"Your responsibility is to me and the rest of your team," Griff responded harshly. "And you need to know the sheriff isn't at all happy about this."

Leah stepped away from Isaac's doorway, going down the hall until she couldn't hear them speaking. She shouldn't have been eavesdropping in the first place, but she'd been curious as to what Dr. Lansing had to say.

Unfortunately, she'd heard too much. The idea that Isaac might lose his job over her made her feel sick to her stomach. Ironic, since at one time she'd wished for exactly that.

"Mommy, where's Mr. Isaac?" Ben asked.

She glanced down at him. "Um, I think he's busy right now. Maybe we'll go visit Uncle Shane first, okay?"

Before she finished speaking, Griff Vaughn strode out of Isaac's room, his face darker than a thundercloud. His gaze locked on hers for a long heartbeat before he gave her a brief nod and strode toward the elevator.

This probably wasn't a good time to visit Isaac.

But Ben's lower lip trembled and she remembered his nightmares. "But I wanna see Mr. Isaac," he protested. "You said we could. You said he was better!"

She sighed and gave in. "Okay, but we can't stay too long," she cautioned, hoping that Isaac wouldn't mind.

They approached the doorway and she gave a tentative knock.

A deep raspy voice called, "Come in."

She pushed the door open and stepped over the threshold, holding Ben's hand. "Hi, how are you doing?"

A tired smile bloomed on Isaac's face. "Good. Better, now that you're here."

"Mr. Isaac," Ben cried, rushing over to the bed. "You're awake!"

Isaac's curious gaze met Leah's, but he addressed her son. "Yep, I'm awake. No need to worry. I'm doing great."

"We prayed and prayed for you," Ben said solemnly.

"Thank you, Ben," Isaac murmured. "I prayed for you and your mom, too. I was hoping you were both doing all right."

"I had bad dreams," the little boy said. He clasped the side rail and tried to climb up onto the bed.

"Whoa, there, what are you doing?" Leah rushed over to lift her son away. "You'll make Mr. Isaac's wound worse if you climb in with him."

"Nah, I'll be fine," Isaac protested.

She threw him an exasperated glance. "Don't be silly. What did the doctor have to say?"

Isaac shrugged. "Something about a laceration in my spleen and muscle damage. I'm off work for at least six to eight weeks, and then I can have desk duty."

She wasn't surprised and had a hunch that desk duty wasn't high on Isaac's list of fun things to do. "I need to thank you for saving Ben's life," she said in a low tone.

But he was already shaking his head. "According to the doc, you saved my life, too, so I think we're even."

She knew that wasn't true. He wouldn't have died from a lack of IV tubing, although maybe putting pressure on his wounds had helped. She longed to cross over and give him a hug, but couldn't seem to force herself to move from the spot.

"Well, we're glad to see you're doing fine," she said with forced cheerfulness. "We have to head over to see Shane, too. I don't know if you realize that they kept him here overnight."

Isaac scowled and struggled to push himself upright. "I didn't know. But hang on—I want to go with you."

"Don't you think you should wait for your nurse?"

"She told me I should get up and walk, so that's what I'm going to do." Isaac tugged a robe over his hospital gown and then swung his legs over the side of the bed. He swayed precariously and Leah went to steady him.

"Hang on. We need to make sure you don't pull out that IV." She waited a moment for him to get his bearings before leaving his side to head over to the other side of the room. After unplugging the IV pole, she wheeled it around the bed so that they could take it with them.

"Ready?" she asked.

Isaac gave a determined nod and stood. He grimaced and grasped the pole for support.

"Do you want something for pain?" she asked.

"Nope," he replied. "Where is your brother's room?"

"At the other end of the hall. This is the trauma-surgery floor. Most trauma postoperative patients come here."

"Handy," Isaac muttered as he moved awkwardly behind the IV pole.

"Isn't it, though," she agreed, keeping a sharp eye on him in case he stumbled and fell.

Ben skipped along beside them, clearly happy after seeing Isaac. Shane's room was at the very end of the corridor, farthest from the nurses' station and near the stairwell leading down to the lobby level.

"I'll get the door," Leah said, going around Isaac to push Shane's door open. She held Ben back, giving Isaac plenty of room to maneuver his way inside.

But when she followed Isaac into her brother's room, she stopped abruptly when she realized Shane wasn't alone.

Wade Sharkey was standing there, holding a gun. And when he flashed his evil smile, she swallowed a wave of nausea and pushed Ben behind her.

It was broad daylight, in a busy hospital, but apparently the danger wasn't over.

And somehow, she got the sense that Sharkey didn't care about his own life as much as he cared about seeking revenge.

* * *

Isaac couldn't believe that he'd brought Leah and Ben into the line of fire once again.

Why hadn't he considered Sharkey brazen enough to come into the hospital to finish them off? And Isaac was standing there in a hospital gown without a weapon in sight.

"Close the door," Sharkey said harshly.

Leah was closest to it and Isaac wished she'd make a run for it, but of course she didn't. Instead she reached out and pushed the door shut behind her.

"Well, well, if it isn't Hawk's pretty sister and Ice." Sharkey's gun didn't waver one inch. "This is perfect. I can take you all out at once."

"And risk getting arrested?" Hawk drawled. "I don't think so."

Sharkey laughed, the evil sound sending a chill down Isaac's spine. He knew full well what Shark was capable of. What he didn't know was if the guy was unbalanced enough to give up his own life for his cause. "You think I'm afraid of a couple of hospital security guards? They're not armed. I'll be out of here and down the staircase before anyone can catch me."

The certainty in Sharkey's voice worried him. Had he cased out the hospital somehow, finding the perfect escape route? The guy was clearly a cold-blooded killer and would stop at nothing to make sure his tracks were covered.

Isaac tried to think past the pain. There had to be a way out of this mess. His gaze landed on the bedside table, and he remembered how Leah had used it to help bring down a meth addict.

Maybe he could do something similar. He didn't have a gun, but he had an IV pole.

And there was no time to waste.

"There are cops downstairs right now," Hawk said flatly. "My captain told me he'd be here by eleven o'clock and it's two minutes to. You'd better get out while you can."

The attempt at a diversion worked. The minute Sharkey glanced up at the clock, Isaac made his move, shoving the bedside table into him as hard as he could and then grabbing the IV pole and swinging it at Sharkey's head.

Leah screamed from behind him and he hoped she and Ben were making a run for it. Hawk leaped out of the bed and somehow managed to grab Sharkey's gun.

Isaac managed to get Shark on the floor and held the IV pole across his upper chest, pressing down with every ounce of strength he possessed. He felt the sutures in his side pop open and warm fluid gush down his side, but he ignored it.

"You can let him up now," Hawk said, holding the gun steady.

"Not until help arrives," Isaac muttered. After yesterday's fiasco, he wasn't going to risk tying Sharkey up with anything short of metal handcuffs.

Within five minutes the police that Hawk had said were on their way arrived. They handcuffed Sharkey and dragged him out of the room, while dozens of hospital staff looked on.

A third cop interrogated Hawk while Isaac righted his IV pole. Leah cuddled Ben close for several minutes before straightening up to look at Isaac.

"You're bleeding," she said. She brought a towel and pressed it over the widening patch of blood on his gown.

"Yeah, well, it was worth it." He gazed down at her blue eyes and knew in that moment he would do anything in his power to make her happy. "You and Ben should have run out of the room. There's no way he would have followed you," he chided softly.

"I couldn't bear the thought that he might have shot you or Shane in retaliation," Leah said in a husky tone. "I'm so glad you're all right, Isaac."

"I'm sorry for putting you in danger," he murmured, brushing a dark curl from her cheek. "And I wouldn't blame you if you turned and walked away from me. But I hope you don't. I want a chance to tell you how much I care about you."

"Oh, Isaac, I care about you, too. Very much."

He thought he might be dreaming, but the shimmering emotion in her eyes gave him hope. He bent his head toward her, stealing a kiss.

"Are you kissing again?" Ben asked.

Isaac regretfully lifted his head, knowing this wasn't the best time and place for this. "Yeah. Sorry. Are you okay, Ben?" When the boy nodded, he was relieved. "How about we head back to my room?" he suggested.

"Sure, but don't the police have to talk to you, too?" Leah asked, glancing over her shoulder as they left.

"They can come and find me."

Back in his room, he sat down on the edge of the bed with relief. The throbbing pain in his side had only gotten worse since he'd taken down Sharkey, but he wasn't about to complain. He'd have risked far more to put that scum away for the rest of his life.

For a few minutes there was a bevy of activity as his nurse brought his antibiotic and then called Dr. Lansing to come and look at his wound. The surgeon wasn't pleased with his handiwork being ripped open, and Leah took Ben outside the room while they quickly sutured him back together.

When mother and son returned, Hawk was with them. "I've been discharged," he announced. "And Sharkey is going to jail for a long time."

"Thank goodness," Leah murmured.

"I thought I'd take Ben down for a snack at the vending machines," Hawk continued. "How about it, buddy? You want a treat?"

"Yeah!" He jumped up and down excitedly.

Isaac suspected that Hawk was taking Ben out of there on purpose to give him and Leah some time alone. Hawk must have noticed their kiss, too, and maybe wasn't upset about him dating his sister. Isaac was grateful for his support, but the minute they left he felt tongue-tied.

"I heard your boss yelling at you earlier," Leah said, twisting the edge of her sweater with nervous fingers. "I'm sorry if I caused problems for you at work. And I hope he's not going to do anything rash."

Isaac shrugged. "Griff has always been a fair boss. I'm sure he'll do the right thing. But it doesn't matter, really, because I would do it all again if it meant keeping you and Ben safe."

"Really?" She took a tentative step toward him.

"Really." He smiled and held out his hand, relieved when she took it and came to sit beside him. "Leah, I know life has been crazy since we met again, but I care about you so much. I don't want things to end between us now that the danger is truly over."

"I don't want that, either," she confessed. "I'd like to spend more time with you."

His heart soared with a mixture of joy and relief. "I love you, Leah." The words came surprisingly easy now. "I know it might be too soon for you, but I want you to know that I'll wait for as long as it takes for you to get over losing your husband."

"You won't have to wait long," she assured him with a tremulous smile. "Because I love you, too."

"Even though I'm a cop?" he pressed.

"Yes, because I wouldn't change anything about you, Isaac. You're strong, smart, protective and great with Ben. I love you exactly the way you are."

He was almost afraid to believe her. "I promise I won't sacrifice my relationship with you and Ben for the job," he vowed. "I'll put you both first."

"Isaac, you're not the only one responsible for the disintegration of your marriage," she said with a sad smile. "Your wife owns a piece, too. Maybe you made mistakes, but her having an affair wasn't the answer."

"I know," he agreed. "And it's taken almost dying for me to realize that you were right all along about forgiveness. If God can forgive my sins, then I have no choice but to forgive the man who took Jeremy's life. And to forgive myself. For the first time in years, I'm at peace."

"We'll be your family now," Leah said, resting her head on his shoulder. "I was so afraid to open myself up to love again, but somehow loving you makes me feel stronger instead of scared. You've taught me to be strong, Isaac."

"You were always stronger than you gave yourself credit for," he pointed out. "And you won't be sorry," he added solemnly. "I've learned from my mistakes. I'm so blessed to have you and Ben in my life."

"That goes double for me and Ben," she murmured.

Isaac turned to pull her more firmly into his arms.

And sealed their agreement with a kiss.

Epilogue

"Hi, Ben. How was school today?" Isaac asked as the boy raced into Leah's house.

"Supercool! One of the girls in my class got sick and threw up all over, so we didn't have to do any math!"

Isaac coughed to hide a laugh. "It's not cool that the girl was sick, Ben," he corrected.

"I know, but still, no math!"

Isaac shook his head with a wry grin and glanced at the clock. They had only a couple of hours until Leah got home from work. He'd been spending his days here, helping her with Ben, since Isaac was still on medical leave from work. Griff hadn't fired him, especially after Sharkey turned up at the hospital. And after his arrest they managed to close several open cases that were all related to the illegal gun scheme.

"Ben, listen, I want to talk to you for a minute, man-to-man," Isaac said.

"Okay." The boy followed him into the living room.

"Ben, I love your mom," Isaac began.

"Me, too," Ben said.

Isaac suppressed another chuckle. "Ah, that's good. I love your mom and I want to ask her to marry me, but I need to know if you're okay with that."

Ben scrunched up his face. "Are you going to keep kissing her?" he complained.

"Yes, I'd like to." He wasn't about to compromise that much. "But if I married your mom, I'd also be your dad." Isaac couldn't believe his future rested in the hands of an almost six-year-old.

"A real dad?" Ben asked, his eyes widening. "You'd live here with us and stay here forever and ever?"

Relief bloomed in Isaac's chest. "Yes, I'd live here with you and your mom forever and ever."

"Yay!" Ben jumped up from the sofa and rushed over to hug him.

Isaac held him tight and knew that he'd passed the first hurdle. Now he only needed to convince Leah.

"What if she says no?" Ben asked, pulling away with a frown.

"Then I'll keep asking until she says yes," Isaac assured him. "Now listen, here's the plan, okay?"

Ben giggled once he'd heard it. "Okay!"

Leah came home from work, exhausted but happy, because they'd saved a life in the trauma bay. They couldn't save them all, of course, but there was no better feeling than when they did.

"Isaac? Ben? I'm home," she announced as she stepped inside.

There were candles and three place settings of her best china on the dining room table. A bouquet of flowers sat between the candles, featuring orange blossoms, her favorite.

"What's the occasion?" she asked, making her way into the kitchen, where Isaac was stirring something tomato based on the stove. "Did you get cleared to go back to work on desk duty?"

"Next week," he confirmed. He drew her into his arms for a warm kiss. "Welcome home."

Leah blushed and pulled away from him, glancing around for Ben. "I hope you're not letting him play video games," she warned.

"No, he's cleaning his room. Ben, come and say hello to your mom," Isaac called. "Dinner will be ready in a few minutes."

She could get used to coming home to a man cooking her dinner and could admit to herself that she missed Isaac when he left every night to return home. She was grateful to have him throughout each day, but as soon as he went back to work, the pampering would end and they'd see even less of each other. "Smells delicious," she commented.

"Ben said your favorite meal was spaghetti."

She laughed. "Yes, and it just so happens to be Ben's favorite, too."

"Sit down at the table. I'll bring everything in," Isaac said.

"All right." She brushed another kiss across his lips

and then headed into the dining room. She sat down and smiled as Ben came into the room.

"Hi, Mom." He greeted her with a hug.

"Hi, yourself," she teased, kissing the top of his head before letting him wiggle free.

"We have a surprise for you," Ben announced as Isaac brought in a bowl of pasta.

"Wait a minute, Ben," Isaac warned. "I don't have everything ready yet."

"Hurry up," he said impatiently, hopping from one foot to the other.

Leah frowned, wondering what was going on. The two men in her life had cooked up some sort of surprise, but what? It wasn't her birthday, or Ben's, although his was less than a month away. But was it Isaac's? She was horrified that she didn't know and made a mental note to ask.

"Here's the spaghetti sauce and the garlic bread," Isaac announced as he set the items on the table. "Now, Ben."

Her son came over to her left side, while Isaac knelt beside her chair on the right. When she saw the small velvet ring box in Isaac's hand, her heart tripped and stumbled in her chest.

"Mom, will you marry Isaac? Please?"

Isaac audibly sighed. "Ben, you were supposed to let me ask her first," he pointed out gently.

"Oops. Sorry."

"Leah, will you please marry me?"

"Yes, Isaac, I'd love to marry you." She blinked away tears as he slid the diamond ring onto her finger.

"Yay, now I have a real dad!" Ben exclaimed.

Leah smiled and allowed Isaac to draw her to her feet and pull her close.

"And I'll have an amazing family," Isaac murmured before he lowered his head and claimed her mouth with his.

She kissed him back, thankful that God had given them both a second chance at love.

* * * * *

'Why do you think he—the Sunrise killer—leaves his
victims in the desert to await the sun coming up?"

"Why do you?" Duke countered.

The other man's neck reddened, and he cleared his
throat. "I'm not the FBI. But maybe—if all his victims
are artists—there's something artistically related to the
sunrise."

Insightful. Maybe too insightful?

If the killer was prowling art classes, that might be how
he was selecting his prey, but Duke didn't want to give
too much of his thoughts away. David was late forties,
and Duke wasn't ruling him out as a suspect at this point.
David had a clear avenue to the victims. Even if he wasn't
instructing classes, who was to say he wasn't attending?

Duke would see if he could get an analyst at the BAU to
do some behind-the-scenes digging on David Hyatt. This
could be a lead.

They finished their meals and paid the bill, then Duke
and Brigitte exited the café into the blazing sun. The storm
had done nothing but bring in more heat.

"You think the killer is targeting painters of sunrise don't you?" Brigitte fastened her seat belt and set her purs on the floorboard by her feet.

"I think it's possible. Other than gray eyes, nothing els fits. We have women in their twenties, thirties and fortie as victims. Three out of five lived in Los Artes, one in Gra Valle and one in El Paso, but they were all left in variou places in the desert near Gran Valle. So we can't be sur how or where he targeted them, but Los Artes is known a a hub for artists. Either way, artistry might be a good plac to help us narrow down the hunting ground."

He turned the ignition, but the engine didn't roll over Nothing but a click.

"Alternator? Battery?" Brigitte asked and fanned he face.

"No," Duke said, his stomach forming a knot. It didn' sound like either. The click was different. Like somethin had been locked into place. "Brigitte, get out of the car Now!"

At the same time, they opened their doors, and a Duke's foot hit the pavement, a deafening boom and wave of intense heat seared his back as his feet lifted of the ground.

Did Brigitte make it out of the car?

Don't miss
Cold Case Killer Profile *by Jessica R. Patch,*
available wherever Love Inspired Suspense
books and ebooks are sold.

LoveInspired.com

Love Harlequin romance?

DISCOVER.

Be the first to find out about promotions, news and exclusive content!

Facebook.com/HarlequinBooks

Twitter.com/HarlequinBooks

Instagram.com/HarlequinBooks

Pinterest.com/HarlequinBooks

YouTube.com/HarlequinBooks

ReaderService.com

EXPLORE.

Sign up for the Harlequin e-newsletter and download a free book from any series at **TryHarlequin.com**

CONNECT.

Join our Harlequin community to share your thoughts and connect with other romance readers!
Facebook.com/groups/HarlequinConnection

HARLEQUIN

Heartfelt or thrilling, passionate or uplifting—Harlequin is more than just happily-ever-after.

With twelve different series to choose from and new books available every month, you are sure to find stories that will move you, uplift you, inspire and delight you.

HNEWS2021